PARANOID

Center Point
Large Print

Also by Lisa Jackson and available from
Center Point Large Print:

Wicked Ways
Expecting to Die
You Will Pay
Ominous
One Last Breath
Liar, Liar
Willing to Die

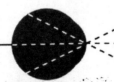

**This Large Print Book carries the
Seal of Approval of N.A.V.H.**

PARANOID

LISA JACKSON

CENTER POINT LARGE PRINT
THORNDIKE, MAINE

This Center Point Large Print edition
is published in the year 2019 by arrangement with
Kensington Publishing Corp.

Copyright © 2019 by Lisa Jackson LLC.

All rights reserved.

ISBN: 978-1-64358-282-5

Library of Congress Cataloging-in-Publication Data

Names: Jackson, Lisa, author.
Title: Paranoid / Lisa Jackson.
Description: Large print edition. | Thorndike, Maine :
    Center Point Large Print, [2019]
Identifiers: LCCN 2019021196 | ISBN 9781643582825 (large print :
    hardcover : acid-free paper)
Subjects: LCSH: Large type books. | GSAFD: Mystery fiction. |
    Suspense fiction.
Classification: LCC PS3560.A223 P37 2019b | DDC 813/.54—dc23
LC record available at https://lccn.loc.gov/2019021196

Now

Patient: "I see him. I see Luke. He's . . . he's alive and he's smiling. He says— oh, God—he says, 'I forgive you.' "

Therapist: "Where is he?"

Patient: "In the warehouse, I mean fish cannery . . . the abandoned one on the waterfront, built on piers over the river."

Therapist: "I know the one you mean. You've told me about it before."

Patient: "But it's been condemned. For a long time."

Therapist: "I know. Is anyone else there?"

Patient: "Yes. Oh yes. We are all there. The ones who were there on the night . . . on the night Luke died."

Therapist: "The night you were playing the game?"

Patient, frowning, voice a whisper: "Yes . . . it was supposed to be a game. We had those pretend guns. Trying to shoot each other."

Therapist: "Your friends?"

Patient, a deeper frown as the patient's head moves side to side: "No. Not all friends. Others were there."

Therapist: "You saw them?"

Patient: "It was too dark. But they were there."

Therapist: "And now? They're back?"

Patient, swallowing hard: "I don't know. But I think so. It's so dark."

Therapist: "But you're certain you're in the cannery."

Patient: "Yes. Yes! I hear the river running beneath the floor—smell it—and I hear voices of the other kids but not what they're saying. It's too noisy. All those clicking guns and pounding footsteps."

Therapist: "But you see Luke?"

Patient: "Yes!" The patient's lips twist into a fleeting smile. "Oh my God! He's . . . he's alive!"

Therapist: "You're talking to him?"

Patient: "Yes. I told you." The patient pauses. The smile fades. "But it's hard to hear him. Other kids are talking, and laughing; some of the guns are going off and echoing. The building is so big. So dark. So . . ."

Therapist: "So, what?"

Patient, becoming sober, almost frightened, hesitating before whispering: "Evil. It's like . . . it's like there's something else in that old building. Something hiding in the darkness."

The patient's voice begins to tremble. "Something . . . malicious." Then the panic sets in. As it always does. "Oh, God." The patient's tone is suddenly frantic. "I—we—have to get out. We have to leave. Now! We have to get out. We have to!"

Therapist, calmly: "It's time. You're rising. Getting out of the cannery. Leaving the building and the evil far behind you."

Patient: "But Luke! No! I can't abandon him. Oh my God. He's been shot! He's bleeding! I have to save him!"

Therapist: "You are becoming more aware."

Patient: "No! No! No! I can't leave him. I have to help!" The patient is in a full-blown panic. "Someone! Help!"

Therapist: "You must surface now. Leave this place for the time being. You are leaving the building. You must save yourself." The therapist is insistent, in control. "On my count."

Patient, frantic: "Yes! Okay. But . . . but I have to hurry! And bring Luke—"

Therapist: "Three. And you're leaving the Sea View cannery and the past behind."

Patient: "If I leave Luke, he'll die. All over again. I can't—"

Therapist, firmly: "Two. And you're nearly awake."

Patient: "I—I need to talk to him. To explain." But the patient is acquiescing.

Therapist: "One."

The patient's eyes open to the small, dimly lit room that smells faintly of jasmine. As the patient lies in the recliner staring at the ceiling, the patient's breathing returns to normal. Calm restored, the patient meets the therapist's eyes.

Smiling benignly, the therapist says softly, "And you're back."

PROLOGUE

20 years ago
Midnight
Edgewater, Oregon

*A*re *you out of your frickin' mind?*
The nagging voice in Rachel's brain chased after her as she ran through the dry weeds that had sprouted through decades-old asphalt. The night was dark, just a sliver of the moon visible, its pale light a dim glow that came and went in the undulating clouds overhead. Soon the clouds would settle and sprawl over the river, fog oozing and crawling through the forgotten piers and pilings to encase this abandoned building and move inland to cover the town. Through the thin mist, only one dim security light offered any sort of illumination, and she tripped twice before reaching the mesh fence surrounding the abandoned fish cannery.

You can't do this, Rachel. Really. Think about it. Your dad's a cop. A damned detective. Stop!

She didn't. Instead she slipped through a hole in the fence, her backpack catching on a jagged piece of wiring and ripping as she pressed forward, following her friend. Well, at least her once-upon-a-time friend. Now Rachel wasn't so sure. Petite, vibrant Lila was more interested in Rachel's older brother, Luke, than she was in Rachel.

"Hurry up!" Lila called over her shoulder from twenty yards ahead. Her blond hair reflected the weak light as she ran along the bridge, a narrow, crumbling roadway built on piers over the water.

Rachel sped up, following.

As she had forever, it seemed. Lila always came up with the plans and Rachel went along.

"I don't know why you do it," Luke had said about six months ago while driving home from school, Rachel riding shotgun. "It's like you're some kind of lap dog, y'know, a puppy following her around." He'd slid a glance her way, his blue eyes knowing.

"I am not," she'd argued, glancing out the window at the gray Oregon day, rain drizzling down the glass, but she'd felt the little sting of it, the truth to it. Luke had been right, though she'd hated to admit it.

Now, the tables had turned as he and Lila had become a "thing." Which was probably worse.

"Rach! Come on!" Lila now called over her shoulder. "We're already late!"

"Yeah, to our own funeral."

"Wha–oh, shut up!" Lila waved off Rachel's reticence and kept moving. According to Rachel's mother, Lila was a good girl gone bad, one who went through boyfriends faster than most people used up a roll of paper towels. "She's too smart and pretty for her own good. Always looking for trouble, that one," Melinda Gaston had warned on more than one occasion. "She's the kind of girl who sees what she wants and goes for it, no matter who she steps on in the process."

Most likely true. No, absolutely true.

"Come *on!*"

Rachel sped up, following the faint light of the reflective strips on the back of Lila's running shoes. Following. Ever following. A problem. She'd work on that, but not tonight.

The brackish smell of the river was thick as Rachel caught up with her friend at the largest of the buildings, a hulking barn-like structure built on now-rotting pilings. It rose dark and daunting, a huge, decrepit edifice that had been condemned years before.

"Great." Lila's tone was one of disgust. "Everyone else is already here."

"How do you know?" Rachel spoke in hushed tones, afraid that someone might hear her. She glanced around the empty pock-marked lot surrounding the long-vacant buildings, but saw no one. Still the back of her neck prickled in apprehension.

"I just do, okay?" A pause. "Listen. . . . Hear that?"

Sounds emanated through the ancient wooden walls. Muted voices, running footsteps, even a staccato *Pop! Pop! Pop!* Not like real gunfire. Just loud clicks.

Air guns.

Safe.

Still. It made her nervous. Rachel's stomach was in knots.

Another burst from an automatic.

Heart pounding, Rachel watched as Lila unzipped her own pack and pulled out a pistol, one that glinted in the bluish glare from the thin light of the single security lamp.

Rachel swallowed hard. Though she knew Lila's gun was just a replica that shot pellets, not bullets, it looked real. As did her own.

"I don't know—"

"What? You're going to wuss out now?" Lila said, unable to hide her disapproval. "After all your talk about wanting to do something 'outside the box,' something that would shock your mom and dad?"

"No, but—"

"Sure." Lila wasn't buying it. "Fine. Do what you want. You always do anyway. But I need to talk to Luke."

"Here?"

"Wherever."

Bang! Bang! Bang! Bang! Bang!

"What the hell is that?" Rachel demanded at the loud, quick-fire reports. "A real gun?"

"No. I don't think so."

"Then what?"

"Shit. It could be Moretti. Nate said he and Max were going to bring firecrackers to, you know, make the game more 'real.' Like it's not scary enough."

"What?"

"I know. Crazy, right?" Lila seemed undeterred. "Nate's such a dweeb! Never knows when to dial it back. He even has one of those things that make the gun sound louder and spark, y'know."

This was sounding worse by the minute. She knew Nate. The son of a doctor, he was Luke's best friend even though they had been in different classes in high school. "I think we should forget this—"

"I can't. I have to see Luke." Before Rachel could come up with any further arguments, Lila slipped through the narrow gap where the huge barn door hung open. Stomach churning, Rachel followed after.

Inside, the cavernous building was even eerier. Maybe it was her own mind playing tricks on her, but Rachel thought she smelled the remains of ancient fish guts and scales that had been stripped from the catch and dropped through open chutes in the floor to splash into the water below, where waiting harbor seals, sea lions, seagulls, and other scavengers snatched the bloody carcasses.

All in your mind. Remember that. This place has been abandoned for years.

That thought didn't calm her jangling nerves.

Just inside, Rachel paused at the door, getting her bearings. What no one else knew, not even Lila, was that she'd been here earlier, in the fading summer daylight, scoping out the interior to give herself a bit of an advantage. She had tried to embed in her mind a map of the hazards, the treacherous holes in the floor, the stacks of rusted barrels, the ladders and pulleys. Though she couldn't see anyone, she heard the others. Whispered conversation, footsteps scurrying along the ancient floor. The thud of feet climbing a metal ladder or shuffling across a catwalk overhead. The noises were barely audible over the wild beating of her heart.

These were her friends, she reminded herself, some kids she went to school with, others recent grads. Nothing to worry about—

Click! Click! Click, click, click!

A pellet gun went off behind her, firing rapidly. Missiles flying past her.

She flinched. Whipped around. Her hair flew over her eyes as she raised her pistol to aim at . . . nothing. Son of a bitch! Squinting, heart hammering, she thought she saw a shadow moving near the partially open door. Maybe . . . Her throat tightened and she aimed. But then again . . . maybe not. Her finger paused over the trigger. A bead of sweat ran down her face.

Could she really do it? Shoot the pistol at a

person? After all the warnings and admonitions from her parents? Heart clamoring, sweat oozing out of her pores, she swallowed against a desert dry throat. This was crazy. Nuts!

Rachel lowered her gun. "Lila, I don't think—" she started, her voice barely audible over scurrying feet and other whispers. But Lila had disappeared. Of course. Running after Luke.

She inched around the wall, remembering the central staircase, the catwalks overhead, the high rafters near a ceiling that rose cathedral-like above the remaining conveyor belts. Beneath the belts were a series of huge holes in the floor where the chutes, once covered, were now open.

Another automatic burst of pellets and Rachel automatically ducked, running to a spot under the open stairs, peering through the metal steps.

Bam, bam, bam! Someone clambered up the stairs at a dead run.

Rachel backed up quickly, nearly tripped and banged her head on a bit of fallen railing.

"Crap," she whispered under her breath as she heard, following the sharp series of shots, a flurry of footsteps, several people running, scrambling away, some laughing, others whispering. Her heart was pounding, her head throbbing, and though she told herself over and over again that there was nothing to worry about, she couldn't calm down. She was certain her folks would discover that she and Lila had lied, each telling their parents they were staying over at the other girl's home. Lila's mother might cover for them, but Rachel's parents, despite their upcoming divorce, would unite against their daughter's disobedience and lies. And if they were caught, trespassing in a condemned building . . . no, she should never have come.

Pop! Pop! Pop!

A series of shots rang through the building.

"Ow! Jesus!" a male voice shouted angrily. "Shit! Not in the face! Shit! You're a dead man, Hollander!" Nate Moretti. Furious as hell.

More shots. Louder. Or firecrackers? Kids were running. Frantic footsteps behind her. "Get out!" someone yelled.

"Reva? Where are you?" A girl . . . Geez, maybe Violet. "Reva! Mercedes!" The girl sounded frantic.

"Vi?" Rachel whispered. "Is that you?" She was holding up her gun and it shook in her hand.

Someone flew up the stairs, boots ringing.

More shots . . . with a flurry of flashes.

Everything about this was wrong!

"Rachel!" Violet again. Closer. *Crack!* "Oh! Shit! Aaaggghh! Frick! Damn it."

"What?"

"I ran into something. God, it hurts! My leg. My shin. Oh, I think . . . I think I'm bleeding. Oooh." Her voice was trembling, wet sounding. "It's so dark in here!"

16

Suddenly she was beside Rachel, hiding behind the metal staircase.

"I can't see anything." She was sniffling now, close enough to be heard over the constant pounding of footsteps and the sputtering shots and yelps of victims. "I should've worn my glasses."

"You didn't?" Rachel was squinting into the darkness between the rungs of the stairs. That didn't make sense. Not only was Violet blind as a bat without corrective lenses, a lot of the kids wore safety glasses.

"No. Didn't want them scratched."

That was probably a lie. Violet was self-conscious about her glasses, but now wasn't the time to call her on it.

Blam! Definitely *not* an air gun.

"Let's get out of here," Rachel said, and didn't wait for a response. She wasn't going to wait for Lila or risk getting hurt. Rounding the staircase, she started for the main door. If she had to she'd walk back to her house, alone in the dark. Another spray of pellets. Sparks flying, firecrackers sounding like real shots.

"I'm coming," Violet said. "Oh, man, my leg— ow! Shit! Ow! Stop it!"

This was crazy. With her free hand, Rachel grabbed Violet's arm. "Hurry," she said, but all of a sudden they were under attack, guns going off, rounds fired, sparks flaming, strings of lit

17

firecrackers booming and leaving smoke behind. "Move it!" she yelled to Violet as another burst of pellets screamed past, one pellet grazing her shoulder, another hitting her cheek and stinging. "Damn it."

Another barrage.

She didn't think twice, just shot back, moving toward the door.

Blam! Blam! Blam!

The firecrackers and gunshots echoed through the building.

"Aaaagh!" A male voice cried out. "What the hell? Oh, Jesus! I—I've been hit!"

Luke?

She froze. Something in his tone.

Violet screamed, a shrill, horrified sound.

Rachel turned to see her brother in the gloom. His face ashen, his eyes wide, blood staining the front of his shirt.

His knees gave out.

He fell to the floor and Violet's screams tore through the building.

Rachel dropped the gun.

CHAPTER 1

Edgewater, Oregon
Now

"Why not?" Violet Sperry poured herself another glass of wine and sank back into the thick pillows on the bed. She posed the question to her small dog, Honey, a silky Cavalier King Charles spaniel who was watching her from her doggy bed as Violet finished off the bottle. As if the dog could understand. But it was better than talking to yourself. At least she thought so. Or was it just as crazy to talk to the dog? She'd left one window open a crack, and a soft spring breeze was lifting the curtains as it swept into the room and brought with it the scent of honeysuckle, which blended with the heady aroma of the Merlot.

She swirled the glass and smiled at the glorious purple liquid before taking a satisfying sip of the oh-so-smooth wine. This would be her last glass. No matter what. She would not head downstairs and open another bottle. No, no, no. She set the empty one behind the lamp on her bedside table. She'd get rid of it—the "evidence"—tomorrow before Leonard returned.

Leonard.

Her husband of over fifteen years.

Once a slim athlete with a quick smile and thick brown hair, Leonard had been a man with a future when she'd met him, a man who was going to take on the world. He'd swept her off her feet and, really, he'd been the reason she'd moved past the trauma of the night of Luke Hollander's death. She'd been there twenty years ago. She'd seen him die. God, it was awful. She should never have gone to that damned cannery. She'd snuck out that night just to score points with Luke Hollander. Had she really intended to tell him that she was in love with him? He would have laughed her right out of that horrid old building. She hadn't been the only one with a major crush on Rachel Gaston's brother, or half brother or whatever he'd been.

Water under the bridge. Or maybe under the pier where that awful dilapidated building had been built.

Thankfully, it was all a long, long time ago.

And in the interim, she'd met Leonard, the man with all of his dreams.

None of which had panned out.

Yeah, they'd moved to Seattle, where he'd been intent on becoming an artist and had even bought into an art gallery, but that endeavor with its lofty ideals, pardon the pun, had been temporary. Of course. As had her stab at being a singer for a garage band that had never made it out of back alley pubs.

It hadn't worked out. For either of them.

After a couple of years Leonard had readily, no, almost *eagerly,* tossed away his dreams and moved back here to their hometown of Edgewater, where he'd taken a job with his father at the furniture store. There had been talk of him being a partner in the business, and eventually taking over Sperry's Fine Furnishings, but so far that hadn't panned out. His father was still in the store every day, looking over Leonard's shoulder as he tried his best to sell end tables, lamps, and side chairs to the stingy losers who still lived here.

Another swallow of wine to dispel any hint of dissatisfaction as she settled into the pillows of her bed, the best you could buy with a "breathable" but firm mattress and a contraption to make the head or foot rise with the mere push of a button.

One of the perks of being married to Leonard Sperry, furniture salesman extraordinaire.

Shit.

She glanced at her phone, where the message from Lila was on display. Squinting, she read again: Don't forget. Meeting for the reunion. My house. Tomorrow @ 7:30. Go Eagles!

As if.

No way was Violet attending the stupid twenty-year reunion, let alone joining the planning committee. And to talk about the high school

21

team? Twenty years after graduation? *Ugh!* She took a long swallow from her glass, then deleted the message. She'd never liked Lila back then, when she was a classmate, and she liked her even less now as some kind of Edgewater social climber and community leader. As if being married to an old man of an attorney and running around doing good deeds for this tiny nothing community were important. Besides, the man she married was old as dirt, and the father of a fellow classmate. "How sick is that?" she said into her glass.

And now Lila wanted her to be a part of the reunion meeting. Which was only part of her irritation. That stupid Mercedes Jennings . . . no, her name had changed . . . She was married to Tom Pope now. Well, anyway, that stupid Mercedes *Pope* was a damned reporter and wanted to interview her about Luke Hollander's death.

After twenty years. Some kind of retro piece for the local paper.

No way.

Make that no friggin' way.

High school and all the drama, tears, and tragedy were long over, thank God, and now she was married to Leonard and had three beautiful, wonderful fur babies and . . . She glanced out the window at the dark night. God, how had her life turned into such a mess?

Honey had padded across the room and was whining at the bedside.

"Oh, you," Violet said, her mood lifting at the sight of her happy dog. "Can't sleep? Well, get on up here." She patted the duvet and Honey didn't hesitate, just hopped up quickly as if expecting Violet to change her mind. Not likely. Leonard was the one who drew the line at pets in the bed. "There you go." She petted the dog's coppery coat.

As Honey settled against her on the thick pillows, her small body curled against Violet, she clicked through the channels to catch a late show. Much as she hated to admit it, she didn't sleep well when Leonard was out of town. It was stupid really, that she felt safer with him snoring beside her. Yeah, he was thirty pounds overweight and his once-lush hair had thinned to the point that he clipped what remained close to his skull. He disapproved of her affinity for wine—like, *really* disapproved—but Len put up with her quirks. When she told him she wasn't interested in having children, he'd gone along with it.

Hence the dogs. Her babies. Three purebred Cavalier King Charles spaniels. Honey on the bed with her and the other two curled up in matching beds near the armoire in the corner. She tried to set her glass on the bedside table and it slipped, sloshing wine onto the bed and into the partially open drawer in her nightstand.

"No!" She freaked for a second, then decided she'd deal with the mess in the morning. It was only a couple of spots on the duvet; she'd flip it over. She'd clean up the splash in the drawer when she got up tomorrow before her husband returned. Leonard would never suspect.

She was a bit buzzy, well, make that more than a bit, but what did it matter since Leonard was out of town until tomorrow? And her bones seemed to be melting in such a lovely fashion. Closing her eyes, she was barely aware that the late show host's monologue was over and he was interviewing his first guest, an actress with a new movie out and . . .

Honey shifted, a low growl coming from her throat.

"Shhh," Violet rasped thickly. She was drifting off.

A sharp bark.

Violet opened an eye and glanced to the beds where her other two dogs had been sleeping. Without her glasses she had to squint. The male, black and tan coat gleaming, was staring at the door. "Che, enough!" Geez, what was wrong with him? But he wasn't alone. From her bed, the third dog, Trix, a usually shy tricolor, was snarling, her gaze fixed on the entrance to the bedroom.

For a second, Violet felt a frisson of worry slide through her insides. What if Leonard had come back early? Crap! How could she hide her glass and the bottle and the . . . ?

Wait a sec! If Leonard was returning, the dogs wouldn't be growling. . . . No, more likely they would be yipping excitedly, ready to leap up and greet him. And she hadn't heard the rumble of the garage door as it rolled open.

She glanced at the clock. The glowing letters were a little blurry, but she could still make out the time.

12:47.

No, her husband wouldn't show up this late without calling. She fumbled on the bed table for her phone and glanced at the messages. Nothing from Leonard.

Clunk.

Her heart froze.

Had she heard something?

A noise from the hallway?

But all of the dogs were in here with her.

She swallowed and muted the television. On the screen the host and his guest were laughing uproariously though the TV was silent.

Violet strained to listen over the beating of her heart.

She heard nothing.

Not a sound.

But she *felt* as if something were wrong. Very, very wrong.

Don't let your nerves get the better of you.

Not a sound.

Beside her, Honey was stiff, her big eyes focused on the door.

Jesus, the damned dogs were freaking her out.

Che growled.

Trix snarled again.

This was no good. No damned good.

But probably nothing.

Had to be nothing.

Licking her lips, she tamped down her fear. The house was locked tight. She was sure of it. She'd checked the doors and windows herself. Hadn't she? No one could get in . . . well, unless they slipped through the doggy door in the kitchen or . . . oh, crap! The outside door to the garage. It was usually bolted shut but Leonard sometimes forgot to secure it when he took out the garbage and, of course, the inside door between the house and garage was always kept unlocked.

Her pulse inched up a notch, but she fought the anxiety whispering through her.

No reason to panic.

Yet.

Licking her lips again, she slowly opened the drawer to her nightstand, found her glasses, and slipped them on, despite the fact that they were blurry from the wine. Then, she silently retrieved her pistol. For a second, she flashed back to the first time she'd held a gun. That night. Two decades earlier. But then she'd held a pellet pistol in her palm. This heavier gun was the real thing, a Smith & Wesson 9mm Shield, a semiautomatic that could do real damage. She flipped off the safety, her fingers curling over the somewhat sticky grip.

Oh. God.

Swallowing hard, trying to clear her fuzzy mind, she slipped out of the sheets. When Honey started to follow she ordered, "Stay," under her breath, then turned her gaze onto the other two dogs, who were now standing in their beds, and hissed, "Stay!"

It's nothing. They most likely heard the neighbors . . . or maybe a mouse . . . or something, just not an intruder. Please, God, not an intruder.

She pressed her bare feet into her slippers and started for the door, nearly stumbling and dropping the damned pistol.

Get it together.

Another bark from Che.

"Shhh!"

Scraaape.

From the other side of the door.

She should call the police.

Who cared if they found her tipsy—no, drunk—and holding a firearm? It didn't matter that she could be imagining the whole scenario of someone breaking in.

But the dogs.

All at attention, watching the damned door.

It's nothing. It's nothing.

She reached for the door with her left hand, the gun in her right. Letting out her breath she twisted the knob, then swung the door inward and peered into the hallway, where a night-light gave off a weak glow, barely illuminating the stairwell.

She blinked and squinted.

Nothing.

No shadows moving.

No one lurking.

All in your mind.

Wait a second.

The door to the second bedroom seemed ajar. Surely it hadn't been that way when she'd passed it on the way to her room.

Or had it?

The hairs on the back of her neck lifted and she slipped to the door, pushed it open slowly, heard the slight creak of the old hinges.

She took one step into the room, saw the shades half down, light from the street lamp filtering onto the guest bed. She reached for the light switch.

Bam!

The door crashed into her.

Pain exploded in her face.

The cartilage in her nose cracked.

Her glasses crunched and fell to the floor.

Blood spurted everywhere.

"Ooow!" she screamed and raised her gun.

Strong fingers grabbed her wrist and twisted.

Agony tore up her arm and her elbow felt as if it would tear apart.

She forced her fingers to squeeze.

Blam!

The pistol blasted, the sound deafening. She flinched as whoever was in the room yanked the gun from her hand and wrenched her arm so hard she was certain it was breaking. She cried out in shrill pain and struggled to get away, but her attacker forced her backward. Her feet slipped. The dogs—her babies—were barking crazily now, scratching at the bedroom door.

She was being forced backward, bare feet sliding on the carpet, her eyes a blur with the blood. "No!" she cried as her back cracked against the railing. She blinked, tried to focus, just as something was forced over her eyes. A blindfold? Oh, Jesus, was this monster going to try to take her somewhere and didn't want her to see the area or who was attacking her?

Fear curdled in her guts. This maniac was going to rape or mutilate her and surely kill her.

She fought harder. Frantically she scraped at her face, trying to remove the mask, but it was fixed solidly. Glued to her skin.

Oh, God.

Panicked, completely blinded, she flailed at her attacker, trying to scratch, to gain some kind of purchase, but it was for naught. Still drunk, her movements imprecise, her head pounding in pain, she swung wildly and missed, turning around just as she felt her body being hoisted with an effort.

No!

A raspy voice demanded, "How does it feel to really be blind?"

What?

And then she was flying through the air, and dropping, a hand brushing the chain on the chandelier, the crystals tinkling. She knew in that split second that the marble floor of the foyer was rushing up at her.

She screamed at the top of her lungs but was silenced by the smack of the stone floor.

Bam!

She hit hard, her body slamming against the floor.

Every bone jarred, her skull cracking on impact. Her breath swooping out in a hissing rush, her teeth broken and rattling. She let out a low moan that sounded wet and tasted of the blood filling her mouth.

Oh, God.

She tried to move.

Couldn't.

Thankfully she remained conscious only long enough to be certain almost every bone in her body had shattered.

CHAPTER 2

B ang! Bang! Bang!
Gunshots echo through the Sea View cannery.

Rachel flattens against the wall. It sounds so real. Not like the click of the soft-pellet guns. But the report of a real pistol. Here, in this cavernous, decaying building that smells of rotten fish and sweat.

Bang! Bang!

Someone screams.

She looks down, sees the gun in her hand.

Oh, Jesus!

Heart hammering, she tosses the damned weapon aside. It skids across the floor only to slide into the open chute and tumble to the raging river below.

"Rachel?" Luke's voice comes to her and she sees him, pale faced and staggering, hand clutched to his chest, blood staining his splayed fingers. "Why?" He is perplexed as he falls. "Why did you—?"

Oh. God. No!

This time the scream is her own as he stumbles backward, his face disintegrating into a fleshy pulp being devoured by worms.

No! No! No!

• • •

Rachel's eyes flew open and she found herself staring at the ceiling of her own bedroom, the only light coming from the blue glow of her digital clock.

Five thirty-seven in the damned morning.

Calm down. It was just a dream. A nightmare. The same one that destroys your sleep two or three times a week.

Dear Lord. She let out a long, shaky breath and pushed the hair from her eyes. The house was quiet. Still. Only the rumble of the furnace creating any noise, but she did hear the muted pop of the newspaper deliveryman's old crate of a car, backfiring a street or two over.

If only she could stop this!

At least she hadn't woken her kids, nor, it seemed, her dog. A tawny, long-haired mutt whose square face suggested boxer while the wispy hair on his legs hinted at some kind of shepherd hidden somewhere in his lineage, Reno had been a family member since the day Cade had walked out the door. Rachel had rescued the gangly pup and he'd been the glue that had held the family together during those first painful weeks and months of the family shattering. From the first night, he'd claimed the foot of the bed as his resting spot and Rachel had never found the energy to force him into his kennel downstairs. Also, there was the simple fact that she felt safer with the dog in the room with her now that Cade was gone. She no longer even entertained the idea of making Reno sleep downstairs, and besides, she figured she had more important issues to deal with, or "bigger fish to fry," as her father had always said. He might still, but she couldn't be certain because she didn't talk to her dad too much these days.

Another issue to deal with.

As if she didn't have enough. She pulled the duvet over her head and burrowed deeper into her pillow. She still could get a few more minutes of shut-eye, if she could find a way to nod off again, preferably catching up with sleep that was devoid of nightmares. If she was going to dream, why not about something happy? A vacation in the Bahamas? Christmas with her grandparents? Or hot sex with some leading man? She could think of a few she wouldn't mind fantasizing about. . . .

But real life butted into her attempts at sleep and after a few fitful minutes, she reached for her phone on the bedside table, knocking over half a glass of water in the process. "Crap!" Great way to start the morning. She glanced at the phone and saw the date. No wonder the nightmare had been so real. "Crap, crap, crap!"

Twenty years to the day.

It was on this very date two decades ago when she'd lied to her parents about spending the night

33

with Lila, then, instead, had sneaked off to the old cannery.

Biggest mistake of her life.

"Deal with it," she said and stared up at the ceiling in the dark as she had so often. Too often. There was no going back to sleep now.

Yawning, she snapped on the bedside lamp. Warm light flooded the small room, with its sloped ceilings, the bedroom she'd once shared with Cade. Her heart tugged a bit, which infuriated her. No one could piss her off like her ex.

Don't think about him!

So what if you bought this cottage together or that your kids were born here, before the remodeling of this room, which had once been an attic? It's over. And it has been for a long time.

"Idiot," she said aloud, then forced her thoughts back to the coming day and its significance.

If this—what would you call it? Anniversary? God, that sounded bad—but if this day wasn't bad enough as it was, Lila had scheduled the final meeting of the high school reunion committee for this very night.

How sick was that?

When Rachel had pointed out the significance of the date and suggested they find another time, Lila's pretty face had shadowed for a second. "I know," she'd said, worry lines etching her forehead. "But it's the only night that works and it's the last weekend I've got available before the reunion. It's weird, but"—she'd offered Rachel a shaky smile and a shrug—"what're ya gonna do? It's been a long time, Rach." Lila had glanced away.

They'd been standing on the wide front porch of Lila's hillside home, shadows lengthening as the sun settled in the west. Lila had swept her gaze away from Rachel and over the rooftops of the town to the cold gray waters of the Columbia River where several fishing boats were visible. "It's hard for me, too, you know," she'd admitted, letting her usual cheery facade slip a little.

Rachel did know. Lila, it seemed, had never gotten over Luke, and the reason had become clear later that year when she'd borne Luke's son just before Christmas.

"But we have to move on, Rach," Lila had said, turning back to face her friend, her blond hair catching the fading sunlight. "And if I can, then anyone can. Right?" She'd tilted her head. "Including you."

Rachel hadn't argued. And how could she? Lila not only had moved on, she'd moved in with and eventually married Cade's father, a man over twice her age. All this despite bearing Luke a son, a boy he'd never had the chance to meet.

Because of you.

Because you killed your brother.

"No," she said out loud.

In less than a month the damned reunion would be over and maybe then—oh, God, please—she could get on with her life. Today was just another day. Just. One. More. And she'd go to the meeting tonight, even if it killed her. She couldn't let that one horrid mistake haunt her forever.

Two decades was long enough.

She glanced at the digital clock, glowing blue on the bedside stand.

Still not quite six.

She woke up about the same time every damned morning. A few minutes before her alarm was set to her favorite radio station so that she could rouse to music. Which was all a joke. Ever since she'd bought the clock, about two years earlier, the day after Cade had moved out, she'd never been awoken by the music, news or traffic reports, or even advertisements. Nope. All too often her damned nightmare brought her right to the surface and instantly awake, with or without the added audio of a car backfiring in the dawn.

She slapped off the alarm by habit, just to make sure it didn't start playing some hit from the eighties or a news report or whatever before she got back from her run. Then she rolled out of bed and nearly stepped on Reno on her way to the window, where she peeked through the curtains to the backyard below.

Fenced.

Secure.

And all of the doors were locked and the windows latched. She knew that. She'd gone through her nightly routine before going to bed last night. She'd counted the dead bolts. Four. Front door, back door, slider, and stairwell. And the windows as well. Sixteen in all, counting the ones in the basement, which she did. Each had been fastened securely.

In the predawn stillness, the yard was dark. She scanned the perimeter, squinting through the glass, assuring herself no one was lurking outside in the bushes and trees rimming the patchy grass.

She saw no one peeking through the branches of the oversized fir, no person flattened against the side of the carport.

Get a grip.

But this was part of her morning routine.

"All clear," she told herself with a sense of relief, then to the dog, who was already on his feet and stretching, "Ready to rock and roll?" She padded into the bathroom, where she splashed water on her face.

Glancing at the mirror, she saw her hair was its usual mess, wild reddish brown curls restrained by a band and pulled to the top of her head, but mussed to the point that several strands had escaped during her restless night. She tightened the band and frowned at her reflection.

A sudden memory slipped unbidden into her consciousness. In her mind's eye, she traveled back a few years and she remembered standing just so in only her bra and panties in front of the wide mirror over the double sinks. A warm mist filled the bathroom and Cade, fresh from the shower, had come up behind her. Still naked he'd slipped his arms around her waist, his fingers sliding beneath the elastic of her thong, dipping low as he nuzzled her neck from behind.

"Are you serious?" she had asked on a laugh.

"What do you think?" A black eyebrow had arched—she'd seen it in the fogging mirror. Taller than she by nearly a head, his skin a darker hue than hers, his muscles defined, his features sharp beneath a beard shadow, he'd looked at her, thin lips twitching in amusement, his hazel eyes dark with passion.

Oh. Dear. God.

Now, remembering, she tingled at the thought of it.

Sex.

She missed it.

That bothered her.

Worse yet, she missed him.

Which really pissed her off and she was loath to admit it. Wouldn't. Couldn't allow herself to be that pathetic as to want him back. She picked up her toothbrush, squeezed paste over the bristles, and brushed her teeth with a fervor that might have scraped the enamel right off her incisors if she hadn't caught herself. What was she doing, thinking about Cade?

"Loser," Rachel said, her mouth frothing with toothpaste. "Cheater." She rinsed her teeth by dipping her head under the faucet, swirling the cold water, then spitting into the sink. Standing, she looked in the mirror again and saw only her own image. Cade's chiseled features and the memory had thankfully faded. "Good. Stay away." Her eyebrows pulled together and she realized she was talking to her ex. Again. "Stupid!" Now, she was speaking to herself. Geez, was that any better? No wonder she still saw a shrink and had since Cade had walked out.

Or you pushed him out.

Anxiety reared its ugly head and she opened the mirrored cabinet, found her vial of Xanax on the top shelf, and twisted off the cap. She tossed a tablet into her open palm, leaving a few in the bottle, then stopped herself and counted the remaining pills. A total of five. Hadn't there been more? Hadn't the prescription been nearly full when she'd stopped taking them? She bit her lip. Couldn't remember. Yes, according to the label there had been thirty prescribed and she'd taken them daily for a while, then stopped . . . but she could've sworn there had been at least half of the month's prescription in the vial—more like fifteen.

Or had she been mistaken?

The last few weeks had been stressful and she'd taken one once in a while, so she must've gone through more than she'd thought.

Right?

No one would come up to her bathroom and steal the pills, leaving some. A thief would have taken the whole damned bottle.

Unless Harper or Dylan . . . no, no, no! Her kids would never steal meds from her. Nor would their friends. She thought of her children and their friends, all teenagers. "No."

But she didn't really know, did she?

There are six tablets remaining. Remember that.

She replaced the pill and recapped the plastic container, then closed the medicine cabinet and again saw her reflection, caught the worry in her eyes. The truth was that her kids were becoming strangers to her, keeping their own secrets, no longer dependent, no longer blurting out the truth when pressed.

All normal teenaged stuff.

But some of the Xanax is gone. You know it.

Unsure, she changed from the oversized T-shirt she wore as pajamas and pulled on her running gear: jog bra, long-sleeved T-shirt, and tights. Then, in stockinged feet, she hurried downstairs and paused at Harper's bedroom door.

All was quiet.

She peeked inside. Recently painted in shades

of gray, her room possessed some order if you didn't count the controlled mess of a makeup table covered in bottles, brushes, and tubes. Her daughter lay sleeping on top of her duvet, one arm flung over the edge of her bed, her blond hair falling over her face. Earbuds in place, of course, Harper was dead to the world.

Rachel pulled the door shut, then crossed the hall to her son's bedroom. Ignoring a DO NOT ENTER sign and a ridiculous swath of crime scene tape stretched across his door, she turned the handle and peered inside. Dylan was wound in a wrinkled pile of bedding, the top of his head all that was visible. The floor was littered with soda and vitamin water bottles, crumpled junk food wrappers, and game controllers, his space age desk covered with a variety of computers and video game equipment, all catching dust under the window.

She'd need a backhoe to clean the room if she ever decided to really clean it.

No, make that *he* would need the heavy equipment to do the job; it was his mess.

But Dylan was right; his room did look like a crime scene. Enough of a disaster to hide several dead bodies.

Time to change that.

She shut his door quietly, then, with Reno at her heels, double-checked to see that her flashlight and pepper spray were in her pocket, made certain the dead bolt on the front door had been thrown, then made her way through the kitchen and out the back door to the screened-in porch. She let Reno outside. While the dog nosed around the dewy yard, Rachel found her running shoes, slipped them on, and stretched. Finally, she snagged her jacket and the dog's leash from a peg and was out the door, locking it firmly behind her and wishing the ancient security system was still working. After snapping on the dog's leash, Rachel eyed the yard once more, noted that the gate was latched, then took off. She broke into a quick jog, Reno loping easily beside her.

The air was thick with the promise of rain, the streets were damp, and the sky was still showing a few stars in the coming dawn. But she was alone and very aware of others in the predawn light: dog walkers, paper deliverers, other joggers, people out and about. She ran through the neighborhood of post–World War II houses, homes built when the logging, saw-milling, and fishing industries were at their height. Some had been added onto over the years, some not. Unfortunately, the booming postwar economy had petered out over the ensuing years, and now Edgewater was no longer bustling and thriving but had become little more than a bedroom community for Astoria, positioned over ten miles west at the mouth of the Columbia.

Rachel's family had been here for generations

and maybe that was the reason she stayed. Now, with her current lack-of-job situation, that might change, she thought as she ducked under a low-hanging fir branch and kept her eyes on the cracked and buckled sidewalk, her peripheral vision taking in her surroundings.

At the highway that ran parallel to the river, traffic was light, so she and the dog cut across, against the light and through the back lot of a boat dealership to the bike path that ran along the Columbia's banks. A tanker was moving upriver, its massive shape barely visible in the mist that lay on the water's surface. Farther north, on the opposite shore, a few lights winked.

This was her favorite time of day, in those few hushed moments just before dawn, when the demons of the night shriveled out of her consciousness.

God, she was a freak.

No wonder Cade had taken up with another woman.

Cade again. "Stop it."

Setting her jaw, she pushed herself, increasing her pace. Beside her, Reno loped along, tongue lolling, ears flapping.

Despite the cool temperature she was beginning to sweat. She stepped up her speed, the dog adjusting his pace. Within minutes she rounded a sweeping bend in the path that ran behind Abe's all-night diner and caught sight of the Sea View cannery, or what remained of it, a moldering behemoth propped on rotting piers surrounded by a rusted and sagging fence, the same mesh barrier she'd slipped through so many years before. Her jaw tightened.

Twenty years.

And still it haunted her.

Still she ran out here to stare at it every morning, as if one day she would either have answers to the questions that had besieged her for half of her life, or more likely, she would finally give up and never run by the riverfront property again.

She replayed the scene in her mind.

"I just need to talk to Luke," Lila had insisted as they'd walked from her house to the cannery that night. "It's really, really important, and I need you with me."

"I could stay outside."

"Sure. I guess. But I don't know how long I'll be. I have to find him first and it's so dark. No flashlights allowed. And besides, you've already got your gun. Luke gave it to you."

"Yeah, I know." Rachel had felt the pellet gun's weight in her backpack.

"You don't have to play the game. Just . . . I need you tonight. I don't want to go alone." Lila had been biting her lower lip, worrying it, as if afraid Rachel would deny her.

"Fine. Okay, I'll come," Rachel had said as the scent of the river reached her nostrils.

44

And it had been the biggest mistake of her life.

Now, the aging waterfront complex seemed to grow larger and more sinister as she ran closer to the site that had been sold and resold but due to zoning restrictions and legal difficulties had never been developed. Now that was supposed to finally change, as evidenced by the bold SOLD banner taped over the faded FOR SALE sign where Lila Ryder's picture and phone number had faded. Odd, that she'd ended up with the listing, Rachel thought, that she had been integral in selling the very spot where her life, well, all their lives, had changed forever. But she'd done it. As Rachel understood it, in the last year a consortium of investors had filed for permits to develop the cannery pier into office space, restaurants, and shops, with condominiums going up at the water's edge. Good. It was time for the old monster of a building to die. Maybe with its passing the pain and guilt would finally fade away. Maybe that was all part of Lila's plan.

"Bring on the wrecking ball," she said as she slowed and jogged in place while staring at the building in which Luke had died.

Her back teeth gnashed as she gazed at the looming, dilapidated structure. Revulsion crawled up the back of her throat, as it always did when she thought back to that night. Still, she forced herself to run this path every damned day, until she could see the weathered walls of the Sea

View cannery with its now illegible, rusted sign dangling near the sagging barn door. This was her penance. Personally imposed. For taking the life of her brother.

Sadness and guilt tightened her throat.

"Come on," she whispered to the dog as she stared at the dilapidated building one last second.

Reno knew the drill and was already turning off the asphalt path to head along a dirt trail when she spied the man dressed in black, standing on the path behind her. Not moving. As if he, too, had stopped to view the cannery.

She told herself it was nothing, lots of people used the path, but she took off, putting her jog into high gear again. They raced through an empty lot where weeds collected dew and the dirt path was slick from the recent rain. The sun was just cresting the mountains to the east, soft light spangling the water, the landscape coming into clearer focus, the streetlights starting to fade away as she reached the edge of town again, then cut through two back alleys to the main street.

The man in black didn't follow.

Of course.

She turned a final corner and slowed to a walk, smiling as she saw the familiar neon sign. Tucked between an insurance office and a pizza parlor in an old hotel that had been converted into storefronts was her favorite coffee shop. The lighted sign, a large glowing coffee cup with a wisp of white steam curling over the rim, sat high over the awning and a sign that read: THE DAILY GRIND.

A beacon to the locals looking for an early morning cup of joe.

"Be right back," she said to the dog as she always did when she snapped Reno's leash to the leg of a bench. She caught the lifted eyebrows and shared glances from a few men who were seated outside and already sipping from their cups.

Tough.

It wasn't as if she wasn't used to stares cast her way or whispered asides. Once, several years earlier, she'd just slid under the awning of the barbershop where she was shepherding Dylan to get his hair trimmed when she'd gotten an earful from two women who had been coming out of a store in the same strip mall.

"She's the one . . . remember, I told you about her?"

Rachel had glanced over her shoulder and found the taller of the women actually pointing at her.

"Hey!" Rachel had said, but the woman was undeterred. In her midfifties, her expression hard, she had walked to the driver's side of an ancient and dented station wagon.

"She killed her brother down at that crappy old cannery, the one just west of town?"

"Her?" The younger woman, round and

squinting behind red glasses, had looked straight at Rachel.

"Yep. Literally got away with murder, if you ask me. Claimed it was an accident. Other kids who were there, playing some kind of sick game, they backed her up. And her old man, he was a cop at the time. A detective. He's the one who found her." Unlocking the car, she had clucked her tongue. "A damned shame." Her friend had slid inside the interior of the old Chevy, but the driver had remained beside the open door, glaring at Rachel over the sun-bleached roof and silently daring her to start something.

"How can she live with herself?" her friend had asked and pulled the passenger door shut.

"Lord knows."

"Mom?" Dylan had said, tugging her arm.

Rather than make a scene in front of her son, Rachel had shepherded him into the shop, where the barber was waiting. But she'd been furious and had watched through the wide window as the car had pulled out of the parking spot and slowly moved down the street. Even now, five or so years later, she felt the back of her neck heat at the memory.

She hadn't known either woman.

Had seen the older one only one other time, driving that same old gold wagon through town.

But everyone in this small town knew about Rachel. About that night.

And no one seemed to forget.

She cleared her throat and pushed the memory aside as she shoved open the screen door and the warm scents of hot coffee and baked goods drifted outside. An espresso machine gurgled and hissed. Near the back of the establishment, four regulars had camped out with iPhones and newspapers scattered over a round table.

Brit Watkins, one of Rachel's high school classmates, was working the counter. Tall and slim, she wore her blond hair pulled back into a tight bun. Large gold hoops dangling from her ears, a baby bump visible beneath her apron, she glanced up from filling a cup. "Hey, Rach," Brit said and slid the cup over to the man in line in front of Rachel, a guy in his seventies with a silvery beard-shadow. He paid for his purchase with exact change, then left another quarter in the tip jar and moved aside to doctor his cup with cream and some kind of sugar substitute.

"What'll it be?" Brit asked.

"How about a sixteen-ounce coffee."

"You got it." Brit's smile didn't quite touch her eyes, but then it never had. Not since that night. Maybe not before. Brit was one of the kids who'd been in the factory that night, and like most of the people who'd been at the scene of the tragedy, she was a little reserved around the woman who'd been charged with killing her half brother.

Rachel nodded. "And a maple bar and chocolate donut with sprinkles."

Brit arched an eyebrow.

"For the kids." She smiled. "But don't judge me."

"Breakfast of champions," Brit said, one side of her mouth lifting as she poured the coffee, then bagged the pastries.

"They've had a rough week. No—that's not really true. Their lives are pure bliss. *I've* had a rough week."

Brit actually chuckled. A rarity. "I get it. Teenagers. I've got four on the payroll, if you count Mickey, who never seems to show up for his shift. So . . . here ya go." She handed over a white sack and Rachel's change.

Rachel dropped the coins into the open tip jar out of habit. "You're going to Lila's tonight, right? For the meeting."

"What? Wait. No." Brit glanced at a calendar hanging over a bookcase laden with ceramic cups. "Oh, darn. Really? Is that tonight?"

"Uh-huh."

"Shoot! I should never have let Lila rope me into it," she said, her forehead puckering in consternation. "I guess Pete will have to handle the kids tonight." She blew out a long sigh. "It's just I'm so tired, all the time. I get in here before five in the morning five days a week, and with this one"—she tapped her protruding belly— "I'm *always* tired." Another sigh as the front door opened and a woman dressed in heels, a slim skirt, and a leather jacket entered.

"Are you coming?" Rachel asked.

"Not much choice. I said I'd cater the event and I will. Pete had a fit that I volunteered, but once I'd agreed, I really couldn't back out. It was last year and now"—she glanced down at her protruding belly—"an 'oops.'"

Rachel knew all about Brit's surprise pregnancy. Her husband, Pete, was thrilled, in search of that ever-elusive son after three girls. Brit? Not so much.

"I can't believe Lila talked me into catering the thing. Geez, why did I agree to it?" Brit wiped the steam wand of the espresso machine with a vengeance. "I should have my head examined."

"She can be very persuasive."

"And then some," Brit said with a snort.

Lila. Forever the enigma. Once Rachel's best friend. Mother of Luke's son. And now married to Cade's father. Which made her Rachel's ex–stepmother-in-law and created a situation that was beyond weird or "sick," as her son said. In Rachel's estimation, Dylan wasn't all that far off the mark. Six years after graduation Lila had eloped with Charles Ryder, a widower who was twenty-five years older than she. Somehow, the marriage had lasted, even as Rachel and Cade's had foundered.

She didn't want to think about that. Ever.

CHAPTER 3

Cade threw out an arm, fingers scrabbling on the sheets as he searched for Rachel and came up empty. Half asleep, he opened a bleary eye just as the reality of his life surfaced. He was alone. In his bed. In his condo. "Crap."

How long would it be for it to really sink in that he was divorced, that his ex-wife had moved on, and that he had better get the hell over her? He'd screwed up and he was paying for it. Every damned day.

"Son of a . . ." He rolled off the bed, a twenty-year-old double he'd shared with Rachel before they'd bought the newer queen sized. That one he'd left at the house with his wife when she'd kicked him out. This saggy one he'd scrounged from the garage.

It was time to do something about that, too.

A new mattress, a new life.

Yeah, right.

Stretching and hearing his spine pop, he walked through his condo and noted the open laptop in the living room, where he'd left on a light. His TV was still tuned to a twenty-four-hour news station, the volume barely audible. Scattered around his recliner were three days' worth of newspapers, and on the table, several case files he'd been reading. Then his gaze landed on the half-full bottle of scotch and the empty glass sitting next to it.

No wonder his head pounded.

"Stupid," he told himself as he picked up the bottle and smelled the heady scent of the liquor before recapping the bottle and hauling it into his small kitchen, where he jammed it into the cupboard over the refrigerator. He should pour it out. Take away the temptation, but he didn't. Just as he hadn't for the past couple of years. At first, after the breakup, he'd drunk to forget, or to rebel or to dull the senses. Something he'd never wanted to analyze too closely. Lately, though, it had become more than that. Not just a drink he savored in the evening after a long day's work, but more like three or four or more. At every physical he only copped to having one or two a week, but he figured the docs saw through that.

Who was he kidding?

His jaw tightened and he told himself that he had a handle on his alcohol consumption, that he didn't have a problem, that he wasn't like his father-in-law . . . whoa, make that his *ex*–father-in-law, Ned Gaston, whose reputation for his love of the bottle preceded his forced retirement from the department. Ned? Rachel's father? *That* guy had a problem. Along with a temper that was legendary.

So don't go down that path, Ryder. Be smart.

He downed two ibuprofen with a glass of water, then spent the next half hour doing push-ups and pull-ups on a bar he'd screwed into the closet doorway before moving to the rowing machine. He pushed himself hard and was covered in sweat by the time he'd stepped off. Then a quick shower and shave. He dressed by rote and his hangover, if that's what it was, had dissipated by the time he'd gathered his case files and laptop and headed out the door to the beat-up pickup he'd bought from his older brother just after the divorce. A ten-year-old Chevy Silverado crew cab wasn't exactly what he'd thought he'd needed, but, being as the truck was paid for, maybe he'd been wrong.

It wasn't the first time.

He grabbed a cup of coffee and a scone at a drive-through kiosk, then drove to the station, a small brick building in the older part of town, the city jail attached. Inside, he sat at his desk, the same space Rachel's father, Ned, had occupied, back in the day. As he'd already drained his first cup, he headed to the break room, which was little more than an alcove off the hallway leading to the jail. Comprising two tables, a scattering of chairs, a coffee station, and refrigerator, the area was often empty. This morning, though, two officers were seated at the round table, the local paper spread out between them. Mendoza was reading the sports page, while Nowak was working on the daily jumble.

"What the hell is that word?" Nowak muttered to himself, clicking his pen. "N-A-X-L—"

Cade glanced down at the letters. "Larynx."

"What?"

"Like your throat."

"I *know* that, but . . . oh, hell." Nowak was a beefy, fiftyish deputy with red hair clipped in a buzz, a fleshy face, and small features set close together. He'd been with the department for as long as Cade could remember, a "lifer." One of three or four locals who'd gone to high school and maybe some college but ended up here.

Mendoza didn't bother swallowing a smile and glanced up, dark eyes glinting. "Maybe he's just smarter than you, Ed," he said as Donna Jean Porter, the secretary for the department, swept in.

"Be nice, boys," she warned with a knowing smile. In her late forties and divorced, Donna was short, blond, and always fighting her weight with the latest fad diet. She'd been with the department longer than Cade and had gone through boyfriends as fast as she did diet plans. She set a container of what looked like cottage cheese into the refrigerator.

"We're always nice," Mendoza said.

"Yeah, right." A phone rang in the front of the department, and she was out of the lunchroom, her heels clicking on the hallway as she made her way to the front desk.

"And just for the record," Nowak called after

her, "Ryder's not smarter than me. Just better at these goddamned things." Nowak took a sip of his coffee and wrote the letters in the appropriate squares as Cade's gaze landed on the front page. He heard Donna in the reception area, trying to calm down someone on the phone. "I'm sure he'll turn up, but yes, we'll be on the lookout for him. You've talked to the local shelter and vet, yes, yes, I know . . . what breed again . . . ?" But the conversation faded as he stared down at the newspaper and the headline leapt out at him:

TWENTY-YEAR-OLD MYSTERY STILL HAUNTS TOWN

and in smaller letters:

WHO KILLED LUKE HOLLANDER?

Cade froze. Stared at the headline, his gut tightening as he read the first paragraph:

Twenty years ago on this date, Luke Hollander died from a gunshot wound at the abandoned Sea View cannery located a mile west of Edgewater. A group of teenagers had been playing what turned out to be a deadly game near midnight when tragedy occurred. One of the game's organizers, Luke Hollander, was shot at the cannery and though taken to the local hospital, he was pronounced dead on arrival. His half sister, Rachel Gaston, was taken into custody and accused of the crime, though she was later acquitted. The victim's stepfather, Detective Ned Gaston, was the first officer on the scene. . . .

"Oh, Jesus," Cade whispered as he read the rest of the column, the first in a four-part series, in which several people were quoted. Two photographs accompanied the piece. The first was a head shot: Luke's senior picture. He smiled at the camera, blue eyes sparkling, blond hair falling over his forehead. Not even twenty and already he'd had the chiseled, strong features of a man. The second photograph was less distinct, but Cade recognized it as the grainy shot of Ned Gaston helping his own daughter into the back of a patrol car on the night of the tragedy, when everyone, Rachel included, believed she'd shot her half brother. At that point Luke was still alive, being rushed to the local hospital, only to be pronounced DOA, despite the desperate measures taken by the EMTs in the ambulance.

"What?" Nowak asked, bringing Cade back to the present.

"Nothing." A lie. But Nowak didn't call him out.

This wasn't good.

Dredging up the horror of the past would only cause more trouble.

And Rachel would be devastated. She already had anxiety issues and, well, maybe even more than that. *Fuck,* he thought. *Fuck. Fuck. Fuck!* The byline indicated that Mercedes Pope, one of Rachel's former classmates, had written the article. In it both Nathan Moretti and Lila Ryder had been quoted, two more "friends." Nathan had been Luke's friend and fellow athlete while Lila, well, she had dated Luke, ended up having his kid. She'd also gone to the Sea View cannery with Rachel that night. Now, of course, in a bizarre twist of fate, Lila was his damned stepmother.

This town was just too damned small.

"Somethin' wrong?" Mendoza asked, looking up from the baseball scores, but Cade didn't bother answering, just strode out of the lunch-room and headed back to his desk. He hadn't noted the significance of the date this morning, but he was sure as hell that Rachel had.

He wondered if she had known about the article.

Maybe.

But probably not.

And she wasn't quoted in the piece.

Mercedes Pope had been at the cannery that night as well. Now she owned part of the newspaper her grandfather had founded some fifty years earlier. And, it seemed, had decided to dredge up the ice-cold case now.

"Great," Cade said aloud. "Just . . . great."

Rachel had never gotten over the trauma of Luke's death. "Damn it all to hell."

His phone buzzed as he made his way back to his desk. He glanced at the screen.

Kayleigh's number came into view.

Shit, no.

His jaw tightened and he clicked the message off before reading it.

Not now.

The day had already started off on the wrong foot.

But the good news?

It wasn't yet eight in the morning.

There was a damned good chance things would only get worse.

Rachel kicked off her shoes on the back porch, then stepped inside the kitchen and dropped the bakery sack on the counter. A fresh pot of coffee was already brewing, thanks to autoperk. She tapped on each kid's door, calling through the panels, "Time to get up. C'mon, 'rise and shine,'" using the same time-worn phrase her mother had a quarter of a century earlier to motivate Rachel and Luke from their beds. It worked about as well today as it had then. "Move it! We don't want to be late."

A groan from Harper's room.

Nothing emanating from Dylan's.

No surprise there.

Upstairs, she showered and changed, pushed her hair into a high ponytail and dabbed on lipstick and mascara before hesitating at the bathroom mirror and eyeing her reflection. She should bring up the missing drugs with the kids. Actually she had to, she thought, and opened the cabinet to retrieve the bottle before slipping it into her pocket. Then she trundled down to the first floor, where she discovered Harper, eyes at half-mast, standing at the kitchen counter.

"Doughnut in the bag," Rachel said, pointing to the white sack. "Juice in the fridge."

"Just coffee."

"You drink coffee?" Dumbfounded, Rachel eyed her daughter. "Since when?"

"I dunno. A while."

This was news to Rachel.

Harper yawned. "Three more days of it and then a cleanse."

"A cleanse? Like a diet?" Rachel skewered her daughter with a glare as she found two coffee cups in the cupboard. She eyed Harper's slim frame and said, "You don't need to diet," as she poured from the glass carafe.

"It's not to lose weight, Mom."

Was there just the hint of a know-it-all sneer in her daughter's voice?

Great.

"It's healthy." Harper reached across the counter and into the cupboard for the sugar bowl, found a teaspoon in the drawer, then shoveled three spoonfuls into her cup. In the refrigerator she found a carton of hazelnut creamer, then added a thick stream into her cup and searched the refrigerator again. "Don't we have any syrup? Oh, wait, here it is." She extracted a brown plastic bottle and squirted two thick blobs of chocolate into her concoction.

Rachel's stomach turned over. "So . . . what's in this cleanse?"

"Lots of good stuff." Harper looked around the kitchen countertop, found her phone on the counter, then added, "Like, y'know, lots of juices . . . Tea maybe, fresh stuff, no sugar . . . y'know to detox your body."

Rachel frowned at her daughter's cup, now filled with enough sugar to cause a diabetic coma. "Now you've got toxins?"

Harper made a sound of disgust. As if her mother were the most stupid woman in the world. "Everybody does," she said and took a sip of her coffee, scowled, and found the sugar bowl again. Another heaping teaspoonful went into her cup.

"You could always take up sports again." Harper had been a track star just a year earlier, one of the fastest runners at Edgewater High, but as her interest in boys had increased, her dedication to the team had waned and this year she hadn't bothered with track. No amount of talking had convinced her otherwise.

Rachel said, "If you don't want the doughnut, we've got granola and yogurt or eggs or just the whites or fruit or multigrain bread for toast."

Harper scowled, giving Rachel a look that said more clearly than words: *You just don't get it, Mom.*

Probably not.

"I think since I'm starting Monday this would be okay." She opened the bag with Reno looking on, hoping that Harper would drop a crumb or two.

"Your brother up?"

"Dunno." Harper shrugged.

"Dylan!" Rachel glanced at the clock, saw that they were going to be late. Carrying her own cup, she made her way down the hall and rapped on the door. Ignoring all the dire warnings glued to the panels, she pushed the door open. "Hey, bud," she called, annoyed when she saw him in the same position he'd been in an hour earlier. He was breathing steadily, his lips parted, his thick eyelashes sweeping his cheek. His head was propped on the wound-up corner of his duvet, his pillow having slid to the floor to settle onto a paper plate that showed the leftover crust of a take-out pizza. "Time to get up."

He moved, pulling the covers over his head.

"School."

A groan as he threw back the coverlet and squinted open one eye. For a second he looked so much like his father, Rachel blinked. He wasn't Cade's doppelganger by any means, but the Ryder genes were evident in her son. Cade and his brothers had been blessed with strong jaws; heads of thick, dark hair; sharp features; and intense hazel eyes that seemed to vary in color with the light. Dylan was no exception.

If only he'd been blessed with some of his father's work ethic.

"I think I'll pass," Dylan said.

"On school? Nope." Leaning a shoulder against the doorjamb, she took a swallow from her cup. "Get up, bud."

"It's almost the end of the year."

"All the more reason to finish with a bang."

"Ugh." Again he yanked a blanket over his head.

"It's Friday. You know what that means. I've been to the bakery."

He grumbled, "Don't care."

"If you say so."

Rachel left then, returning to the kitchen and hearing the thud of bare feet hitting the floor behind her, then uneven footsteps as Dylan stumbled out of his room to the bathroom. She could always count on his empty stomach and full bladder to force him from his lair filled with video game consoles, computer monitors, and bobbleheads of sports figures. His bed was secondary to his equipment.

Now, thankfully, he was up. Step one.

In the kitchen, Harper sat at the table, her "coffee" forgotten, the doughnut half eaten as she texted rapidly, her fingers flying over the screen of her phone.

Rachel heard the groan of old pipes and the rush of water as Dylan turned on the shower. Less than five minutes later, his hair wet, Dylan showed up in a hoodie and ripped jeans. He made a beeline for the white bag and ate the maple bar in three bites. "You gonna finish that?" he asked Harper, eyeing her half-eaten doughnut as he opened the refrigerator door to find the carton of orange juice.

"You can have it."

"Good." Before she could change her mind, he swept the uneaten half doughnut from the table and into his mouth in one swift motion. Afterward, he washed down the donut with juice he drank straight from the carton.

"Oh, gross! Jesus, Dylan, you're a frickin' Neanderthal. Don't you know about backwash?"

"Don't care."

"Obviously." She gave a mock shudder and cast her mother a disgusted glare. "Can't you do something about him? He's like this . . . this . . . mega embarrassment."

Rachel said, "Hey, Dylan, you know better."

He made a disgusted huff. "I just don't know what's the big deal." He returned the carton with a minuscule amount of OJ to the refrigerator.

"You don't know?" Harper repeated. She slipped her phone into her pocket. "You're beyond disgusting. More like disturbing."

"Ah, ah, ah. No insults," Rachel cut in, then pulled out the pill bottle that had been burning a hole in her pocket. Without saying a word she placed it on the counter.

The kids exchanged glances.

Not a good sign.

"What's that?" Dylan finally asked.

"My Xanax, or what's left of the prescription."

He frowned, his eyebrows slamming together while Harper had gone chalk white.

"So?" Dylan asked.

"So, I think some pills are missing," she said and waited for a reaction.

"What do you mean?" Her son again.

Harper sent her brother a how-can-you-be-so-dense look. "She means she thinks we took them."

"Us?" Dylan said, and his face fell. As if he were shocked.

Real emotion?

Or a well-practiced act?

At fifteen, Dylan was almost impossible to read. As a younger kid, her son had been an open book. Now? Not so much.

The same could be said of his sister.

"We didn't steal your damned drugs," Harper said, recovering. "What do you think we'd do with them? Like what? Sell them at school?"

"What?" Dylan said, apparently shocked.

Rachel shook her head. "Geez, I hope not."

"Mom. Really?" Harper was pissed.

Fabulous. So far the morning was on a roll.

"I'm just letting you know."

"And accusing us." Harper let out a sigh. "I can't believe it."

"Neither can I," Rachel said, refusing to be baited. She hadn't accused them, not really. She'd just let her kids know what was happening. "Okay." She pocketed the bottle once more. "Come on. Get your backpacks and let's all get into the car."

"So now we just forget about it?" Harper raised a dubious eyebrow and pursed her lips in disgust.

"No way. Never forget about it. Xanax can be dangerous. You know that." She was serious.

"Yeah, I do. So does he." Harper hooked a thumb at her brother. "Oh, God, forget it. Okay? We've heard this all before. From, like, everyone. Teachers, and Dad, now you. We get it."

So . . . that was that. Rachel decided she'd made her point and didn't want to push it. So she changed the subject and said to the dog, waiting expectantly at the door, "You want to go for a ride?" Reno's tail swept the floor frantically.

"See, he's ready," she said to Dylan as she opened the back door and Reno shot through.

Harper rolled her eyes. "God, Mom, he's a *dog*. He's ready to go anywhere."

"Take a lesson."

"Yeah, right." She shoved her phone into her backpack and stormed out, letting the screen door slam behind her. "I'm driving."

"Not this morning. We're late."

Dylan, tiny earbuds already in his ears, camo backpack slung across one shoulder, walked past the refrigerator without grabbing anything for lunch. His head bouncing to some silent beat, he ignored his jacket hanging on a rack near the back door and strode outside.

"Not your problem," Rachel told herself as she headed for the detached garage and her ten-year-old Ford Explorer. If he got cold enough or hungry enough, he'd learn. Both kids knew the rules. Once they were in high school, they had to take some responsibility. Still she had to bite her tongue and refrain from announcing that the temperature wasn't going to get out of the fifties this morning.

Surely he'd learn. Surely.

They piled into the SUV, Harper stung that she wasn't allowed to take control of the wheel, riding shotgun, the dog and Dylan claiming the back seat.

The morning, as usual, was off to a fantastic start.

CHAPTER 4

Kayleigh called.

Not a text, but an actual phone call.

This time Cade picked up. It was stupid to keep avoiding her.

"So what? Now you don't respond to texts?" she asked, and he imagined her green eyes sparking with a mixture of amusement and irritation. She'd always had a keen sense of humor; that had been part of the attraction. That and long nights when they'd been forced together during stakeouts. They'd both been detectives with the sheriff's department. That, like so many other things, had changed. Unconsciously, he rubbed at the scar on his neck, a reminder that he'd nearly lost his life.

"Busy," he said, which wasn't really a lie. "Just trying to get settled in at my desk "

"Well, don't." She was all business. "We've got something going down here and I think you'll want to check it out."

"What? And down where?"

"Homicide. At least it looks like that. In Hillside Acres, on Bonaventure Boulevard, at the end of the cul-de-sac."

Hillside Acres was a development that had never been annexed to the city.

Kayleigh told him the address and added, "I know it's not your jurisdiction, but I thought you'd want in." He was already out of his chair and reaching for his jacket.

"The victim is a woman. Violet Sperry. Husband was out of town, came home early and found her in the foyer. ME's already here and they'll be packing her up soon, so you'd better get over here."

"Jesus. I know her."

"Knew," Kayleigh corrected.

"Yeah. Right. Knew. She went to school with Rachel."

"And everyone else in town, I gather."

"Yeah. I'm on my way." He clicked off and headed down the short hallway and through the tiny break area to the back door. It was starting to rain, the wind kicking up, and as he drove out of town he caught a glimpse of the river, white caps roiling as if it were November instead of May.

Someone had killed Violet Sperry? Why? He didn't know much about her, other than she'd been in Rachel's loose group of high school friends and had testified during the trial. She and Rach weren't close, as far as he knew, even though Violet, like so many others, had settled in Edgewater. He drove past the high school on his way out of town, thought about his kids for a second and his own misspent youth for

69

another couple of beats before passing the old cannery where Luke Hollander, another victim of homicide, had died. Cade, a couple of years older and in college at the time, hadn't been involved in the tragedy that night, but both his younger brother, Court, and, of course, Rachel, had been there. Rachel had even been charged with her slain brother's murder.

Even she believed it.

At least they'd reduced the charge to negligent manslaughter, but even that crime had been washed from her record, the judge citing her age, disorientation, and conflicting testimony of everyone who had been there.

Had she done it?

Made a mistake and killed the half brother she'd looked up to?

Cade wasn't certain, but as the sprawling, ramshackle building disappeared in his rearview he wondered if some of the rumors had been true, the most damning being that Rachel's father, a detective who'd been the first responder, had hidden evidence or at the very least had been negligent at the scene in an effort to save his daughter.

A mystery, to be sure.

And one never completely solved.

He thought of the article in the paper, written by a woman who had been at the crime scene that night. Why would she dredge it all up again? Was it just a case of bringing a sensational crime back into the spotlight?

A sensational, unsolved crime.

That wasn't exactly true, he thought, flipping his wipers to a higher speed as the storm increased. Though the case hadn't been officially closed, it wasn't exactly open, either. Maybe *cold* was the right way to describe it. Ice cold.

On the way to school, Rachel brought up the reunion meeting.

Surprisingly her son actually heard her. "Wait . . . we have to go?" he asked from the back seat. For the first time he showed some interest in the conversation and pulled one earbud from his ear.

"Yeah. It's at Lila's house." Even after all these years she could not refer to Lila as her kids' grandmother. It just felt wrong.

"Stepgrandmama," Harper said, needling her mother. Then, "Will Lucas be there?" Harper was gazing out the passenger-side window, running her finger along the glass.

"I don't know. Probably." Lucas had yet to move out of the historic house on the hill owned by his stepfather, the home where Cade and his brothers had grown up. The place where their mother had died.

"Good." Lately Harper had taken more of an interest in her older cousin. They'd been closer as younger kids, drifted apart during Harper's time in junior high, but now, with Lucas attending the local community college, and Harper in high school, they had connected again, which Rachel saw as a good thing. Harper, starting at the end of her sophomore year, had started drifting. Her grades had slipped, but just a little, and her circle of friends had changed. Lately it seemed as if she'd been harboring secrets and that was a worry. As for Dylan . . . who knew? He'd become a mystery to Rachel.

As she'd become to her own parents at that age.

"I thought we were goin' to Dad's," Harper said, cutting into her thoughts as Dylan plugged in again, out of the conversation once more.

Rachel explained, "You are, but he'll be home late."

"Can't he pick us up?"

"Look, this is just easier. For me. So go with it. I'll drop you off after the meeting. Okay?"

No response.

Rachel added, "So when you get home from school, pack whatever you want to take to his place."

"You won't be there?"

"Maybe not." She didn't elaborate.

Harper let out a sound of disgust. "Great."

"That a problem?"

"I, um, I have plans tonight."

"With whom?"

"Does it matter? If I have to go to Dad's?" She

pulled a face that looked as if she'd just sucked on a lemon.

"Take it up with him," Rachel said, though it kind of killed her, giving up control of the kids. Just didn't seem right. And Harper, at seventeen, was on the cusp of danger, just as Rachel had been at that very age. Harper was "old" for her class, just missing the cutoff because of an October birth date. At the time Rachel thought it would be a blessing and allow her daughter to be the most mature in her class. Now she wasn't so sure. Harper seemed bored with school and interested in God only knew what.

"He never lets me do anything," her daughter grumbled. Radiating disappointment, she leaned her head against the passenger window.

Not true, Rachel thought. At least not all the time. Despite the fact that Cade was a cop, he could be a lot less strict than she was. It all depended on the situation. He seemed to trust the kids' instincts more, allowed them to make mistakes on their own while she'd spent most of her adult life ensuring their safety, making certain they didn't get hurt, probably, she admitted grudgingly to herself, to the point that she did clip their wings or make them less confident.

One more thing to work on. Great.

"You know, Harper, it wouldn't kill you to lighten up."

"How would you know?"

That hit home.

"At least I try."

"Do you?" her daughter asked and rolled her eyes before turning her gaze past the window to the sidewalks of the small town, where pedestrians, shoppers, dog walkers, and skateboarders milled in front of storefronts.

The rain had started again, and Rachel flipped on her wipers as she stopped at the one light between her home and the high school, the same brick-and-mortar two-storied building she'd attended twenty years earlier. A new gym and science wing had been added about five years ago, and there had been work to earthquake-proof it retroactively, but otherwise the building, constructed between the two world wars, hadn't changed much.

Just like the rest of the town that had been booming after the Second World War. Logging camps, sawmills, and the fish cannery had been working around the clock, she'd heard from her grandparents. And then in the late seventies things had begun slowing down, the bustling town no longer growing, but stagnant.

As they approached the school, Dylan said, "I think I'll pass on going to Lucas's with you. I'll just stay home and then you can pick me up and take me to Dad's."

"Not an option." Dylan spent too much time alone as it was. It seemed he spent more time hooked into the Internet, where he connected with other gamers, rather than with real, flesh-and-blood friends. And then there were the missing antianxiety pills. If any more went missing . . .

"Ah, man," Dylan complained. "I hate going over there."

"You'll survive."

Rachel made the final turn onto the street where the high school stood. "Besides, the meeting shouldn't last too long."

Dylan was craning his neck to peer around the front seat where his sister was still moping as she stared through the rain-splattered windshield. "This is good," he announced, meaning he wanted to be dropped off a block from the school rather than suffer the indignity of being driven into the drop-off area near the front doors. "Right here."

Fine. Rather than argue, Rachel slid her Ford into an empty spot near the gymnasium. Her kids piled out of the Explorer, Harper flipping up the hood of her jacket, Dylan bareheaded, earbuds still in place, as he dashed across the wet lawn to a side door.

When had her children grown up? How had the years passed so quickly since they were blond toddlers whose squabbles had been about toys and pretzels, toddlers who had looked at her with adoring, trusting eyes? Wasn't that just a few years ago? Before they'd both become secretive?

They'd been happy then, she thought with more than a bit of nostalgia. A young family of four—

A horn blasted behind her and she realized she was actually taking up two spots on the street, the blinker of her SUV still flashing as she'd daydreamed. She held up an apologetic hand and eased onto the street while the driver nosed into the spot, nearly hitting her. In her rearview, Rachel saw five kids clamber out of the silver sedan. The driver, a pretty blond girl, quickly tossed a cigarette onto the wet pavement and stubbed it out before running to catch up with the rest of her friends just as the first bell sounded.

And so it was. Her kids ditching her as she'd ditched her own mother. How many times had she told Melinda to park two blocks away from the school?

What was the old saying?

What goes around, comes around?

Well, amen to that.

CHAPTER 5

Cade turned off the main highway and wound through a development of cookie-cutter houses that had been built in the midnineties, all two-story, all with double-car garages out front, all with landscaping that had matured.

At one end of a cul-de-sac was the Sperry home. Like the other houses, it had a small bit of yard pressed up to the front walkway with a few bushes and flowers that were starting to bloom. A honeysuckle vine ran up a trellis, but the grass was patchy and yellowed from animals using it as a toilet.

Two cruisers with lights flashing blocked the drive, and crime scene tape stretched across the sidewalk, while uniformed officers kept a group of neighbors at bay. The crime scene techs had arrived, their van visible, and a rescue unit had been deployed. Cade parked down the street, jogged through the rain, and flashed his badge at one of the officers.

On the porch he signed into the scene and slipped on shoe coverings, then walked inside.

The body of Violet Sperry was sprawled across the marble tiles of the foyer. Wearing pajamas, she was splayed at an awkward angle, one leg bending backward at the knee, a bone protruding near one elbow, blood congealing around her.

His stomach turned over.

He recognized her despite a broken and bloodied nose, bruised face, and eyes covered by a thick piece of blue tape.

Dear God.

He'd seen his share of dead bodies in his work and during a tour of duty in Afghanistan, but this . . . His back teeth clenched hard.

Photographers were taking digital pictures and a videographer was filming while other techs dusted for finger- or footprints and still others searched and vacuumed for trace evidence.

Across the room he spotted Kayleigh in black pants and a short black rain jacket, her red hair tucked back beneath a baseball cap. She eased down the stairs around a tech dusting for fingerprints and headed toward him. Slim and fit, a dusting of freckles across her nose, her eyes wide and intelligent, she offered him a fleeting smile.

"Homicide?" he asked. "You're sure?"

"Oh, yeah." She was leaning down, staring at the body, nodding. Emotionless. "Unless she was into some kind of kinky stuff that included taping your eyes shut."

"You never know." But his attempt at dark humor didn't hit home. In fact, it backfired as she glanced at him, eyebrows inching upward, in silent question about his own proclivities.

He ignored the tightening in his gut. "So what have you got?"

"She was supposed to be alone last night," Kayleigh said, straightening. "The husband was out of town, and they don't have kids. From what we can tell, she was already in bed. Watching TV—it was still on. Her phone, TV remote, and iPad were in the bedclothes, like she'd just tossed them aside. There was a wineglass and bottle on the nightstand."

From another room he heard the distinct bark of dogs.

"Hers," Kayleigh said, glancing to the hallway off the foyer. "Three prized little . . . spaniels of some kind." She fluttered her fingers in an I-don't-know gesture. "Not cockers, I don't think, but close. King something or other . . ."

"King Charles. But the Cavalier comes first," the tech who had been dusting the railing supplied. Thin and balding, wearing gloves and safety glasses, he added, "Cavalier King Charles. Cute dogs. Locked in crates in the laundry room."

"Whatever," she said. "Big name for little dogs."

Cade said, "They—the dogs—were . . . where? With her?"

"So it appears. It looks like she got out of bed and left them locked in the bedroom, where they scratched the hell out of the door, according to the husband, Leonard Sperry. His story is that he got back from a fishing trip to Bend. Came home earlier than expected, walked in from the garage"—Kayleigh pointed to a door off the main hallway—"and found her, here. Nearly tripped over her."

"God."

"Yeah, I know. We're checking his alibi, but at first glance it looks solid . . . and he's pretty messed up. He claims he called nine-one-one immediately but knew she was dead." She met the questions in Cade's eyes so intently he almost went back to a forbidden memory, but he didn't. If she sensed it, she hid it well and added, "I believe him. So far. Once we check on his whereabouts and their finances and all, then we'll see."

"Forced entry?" Cade asked.

She shook her head. "No evidence. But the garage door to the backyard is open and a gate, too. The husband says they never unlatched the gate because of the dogs, and he's beating himself up for possibly not locking that door the last time he took the trash to the bins outside." She frowned. "If he did it, he's a damned good actor."

"He could have worked with someone."

"A paid assassin?"

"Yeah. Killer for hire."

"Could be, I guess. We're already checking

all his accounts and the will and life insurance policies."

"And his social life? He could have been involved with someone, having an affair."

He noticed the back of her neck stiffen. "Always possible, isn't it?" If she was referring to anything other than the case, she hid it. "We'll find out, but from his reaction, I think not. We've got officers checking for footprints and we'll start interviewing the neighbors to find out if anyone saw something out of the ordinary."

Cade glanced around to the living room, running off the staircase in one direction, and the family room, tucked farther back. "Where is he?"

"The husband? With Drummond." She pointed toward the front door. "Outside in a cruiser."

"Mind if I talk to him?"

"Be my guest."

"Let's look around first."

"You got it."

They walked through a home that was neat, everything in its place, dog beds in the living room and family room as well as in the master bedroom. In the sleeping area, a king-sized bed was mussed, one side obviously having been recently occupied, the cream-colored duvet thrown back, an impression on the pillows. An empty wine bottle and glass sat on a bedside table while a large flat-screen flickered silently on the opposite wall.

"As I said, TV was on, muted when we got here. Just like it is now. The only thing changed was Sperry taking the dogs down to the laundry room, where he crated them. He said he didn't disturb anything else."

"After he called in the emergency?"

"Yeah." They walked from the bedroom to the landing overlooking the foyer. "And though the victim wasn't shot, there's a bullet hole in the ceiling." Kayleigh indicated a spot overhead and the hole in the drywall. "We've already got the bullet."

"No bullet wound on the victim?" Cade stood next to the railing, eyeing the death scene below, where the ME was bending over the body.

"Not that we could see. The lab will confirm."

"Then why use the gun? That hole in the plaster is new, right?"

"The husband said it wasn't there when he left."

"So either the killer threatened or tried to shoot her and failed in a struggle, then lost control of the weapon . . ."

". . . or she shot," Kayleigh said. "Protecting herself. She had a gun. A nine-millimeter Smith & Wesson. It's missing. According to the husband, Violet always kept it in the nightstand near her bed. But we've searched. Gone."

"So the attacker stole it or she got rid of it."

"Sperry is pretty sure it was in the drawer the

night before he left for his trip. He was searching for the remote to the TV the night before and saw it. And a clip. Missing as well."

"Huh."

"So," Kayleigh went on as she eyed the scene, "I say she heard a noise, grabbed the gun, got up and locked the dogs in the room, then went into the hallway to see what was going on." As she was laying out her theory to him, Kayleigh was moving toward the open door, then through.

"Somehow, our killer jumped her, or had a weapon of his own and they struggled, and a gun went off. Maybe he panicked, pitched her over the railing." She was on the landing now, near one of the scuffed rails.

"After slapping tape over her eyes."

Kayleigh nodded. "Right."

"Maybe." Cade wasn't sure. "You said, 'he.' You think the assailant is male?"

"Don't know for certain. But someone with enough strength to hoist her over the rail."

"Wouldn't take much . . . just a push and gravity would take over." Cade studied the smooth wood of the railing, the two spindles that had broken, then peered over the top, to the floor below, where Violet's body was still sprawled.

"So, she was a friend of Rachel's?" Kayleigh asked.

"At one time."

He started down the stairs. "They hung out in high school some, I think, graduated from high school in the same class. Violet gave testimony at the trial."

"Where Rachel was charged with Luke Hollander's death."

"Yeah."

"And you?"

"I met her once. Ran into her and her husband at an antique car show at Musial Park, oh, maybe seven or eight years ago. We'd taken the kids."

"She and Rachel weren't tight, not friends any longer?" Kayleigh asked, a bit of an edge to her voice as they reached the first floor.

"No. Not really friends anymore." The truth was that Rachel wasn't close to anyone since high school, but he saw no reason to bring it up as it had nothing to do with the case.

The ME was finished and EMTs were getting ready to bag the body. His guts twisted as he took a final look at Violet, her face almost unrecognizable, her body bloodied, her broken limbs at impossible angles, her eyes covered with that thick mask.

Who the hell had done this?

Who wanted her dead?

And why?

"Let's go talk with the husband." With Kayleigh following, he walked out to the front yard, where the ground smelled damp and earthy, but the rain had stopped. For the moment, the storm had abated.

It was weird not to have to go into work. Rachel had held some kind of a job since she'd been in high school, first working as a waitress, then later as a clerk at the bank, and then, even though pregnant with Harper, she'd discovered she had a proclivity for technology and had ridden the tech wave, learning through classes at the community college and online study. Her most recent employment had been as the bookkeeper/computer specialist for a local hardware store that had been bought out by a national chain with their own computer system and accounting department and she was let go.

So she should be able to find another job quickly, she hoped, or find a way to make her side business more lucrative. She'd also flirted with the idea of moving away, maybe to Portland or Seattle, but wouldn't consider it until the kids were out of high school. Three more years. Harper would be a senior next year, Dylan a sophomore. And she did consult as a technical advisor, a fledgling operation with half a dozen clients that she might have to bolster. She had some savings, but that would go quickly once Harper started college.

Don't even go there; she's got to get through high school first.

She poured herself another cup of coffee and sat down at the kitchen table, opening up her iPad and sweeping through her e-mail. No job offers. Then, she saw the tab for news and opened to the local paper.

She was raising her cup to her lips when she read the headline:

TWENTY-YEAR-OLD-MYSTERY STILL HAUNTS TOWN

WHO KILLED LUKE HOLLANDER?

By Mercedes Pope

"What?" Rachel's heart nearly stopped; she set the cup down with trembling hands and coffee sloshed onto the mail scattered over the tabletop. She didn't care, barely noticed. She focused on the two photographs accompanying the text. The head shot was one of Luke's senior pictures, many of which still graced her mother's mantel. The second was a damning image snapped by a photographer that night that showed Ned helping Rachel into the back of a cruiser. Her face was turned, in profile, horror evident on her features, while her father was solemn beside her, holding the door open, both of them oddly illuminated by the lights from the police vehicles.

"Oh, God. No." She shook her head as she

scanned the article and her thoughts raced. Why would Mercedes do this? Why hadn't she called, given Rachel a heads-up?

But she did call. And text. Remember? You assumed it was about the reunion and elected not to reply.

Her stomach did a nosedive. She read the story three times even though she knew all the salient facts; she'd lived them: Stupid kids playing a dangerous game at the old warehouse. Someone noticing and calling the police to report trespassers. The cops arriving and finding one of the boys near death, struck by the bullet of a real gun supposedly fired by his half sister. That girl being arrested. That girl being her.

Rachel couldn't stop tears from filling her eyes, couldn't stop the guilt that burrowed deep in her heart. Nor could she tamp down the anger that she felt creeping in, a dark fury that someone she'd thought of as a friend would do this. To her. To her parents. To her children. But then Mercedes, who'd gone by Mercy then, had never been one to pull punches, had she? And she'd never liked Luke. She'd been one of the few of Rachel's friends who had seen through Luke's smile and bravado.

She looked away and cleared her throat.

Even if Mercedes had called to warn her, the article felt like a betrayal. For God's sake, Mercedes had been at the cannery that night, a willing participant, like so many classmates and recent graduates.

Twenty years had passed and it seemed like yesterday.

She clicked off the newspaper app. Told herself she just had to get through the rest of the day and the damned meeting tonight, and things could go back to normal. Or as normal as they had been.

Wait a second.

She clicked onto the article again and noticed a note at the bottom.

Part 1 of a 4-part series.

"What? No. No . . . no." Then, as if her *friend* were in the room with her, she whispered, "God, Mercedes, why?"

Because she's not your friend. Face it, Rachel, she never has been.

Mercy had to have known how dredging up Luke's death would impact Rachel and her family. How everything had changed that night. Everything. Rachel's fractured family had completely shattered, and her friends, the kids she'd hung out with at school, had all avoided her during the last few weeks before graduation. And who could blame them? She'd been shell-shocked, convinced she'd murdered her brother. Charged with the crime.

She wondered how her mother was dealing with this article, and her dad, what did he think? Neither had been quoted in the paper. Only

Nate Moretti and Lila Ryder. Nate had said, "It's still hard, you know. Luke was my best friend, and yeah, I was there but I don't know how it happened." Lila's quote was a little more dramatic: "I miss him every day. Luke's the father of my son, Lucas, who is Luke's namesake, but it's been hard on me, and hard on my boy, of course, never knowing his real dad."

Tears burned the back of Rachel's eyes but she fought them back. What was it her mother had always said? "No use crying over spilled milk." But in this case buckets of tears had been spilled. In the days after Luke's death, they'd all cried.

Mom.

Had she read this? Oh. God.

It will never be over, she thought as she slid her phone from her pocket and poked her mother's number from her list of favorites.

Melinda picked up on the second ring. "Hi," she said, obviously knowing Rachel was calling. But her voice had no life.

Damn it.

"Hey, Mom."

"I saw it. That's what you're calling about. Right? The article in the paper or the fact that it's the . . ." She let her voice fade, but they both knew she was mentioning the date.

"Yeah. I wanted to know that you're okay."

A beat. Then, "Well . . ."

What to say? "It's tough."

"Yes. That it is. That it is . . . for all of us. For you, too," she said. "And, I suppose, your father."

"Yes," Rachel agreed and noted, once again, her mother never spoke of Ned Gaston by his name. That would probably never change. They tolerated each other . . . barely—standing together at Rachel's wedding not speaking, avoiding each other at the reception, and, over the years, when they were forced to be in the same room, avoiding conversation, pretending the other didn't exist.

They acted like polite strangers.

Ridiculous.

"Are you . . . are you going to the cemetery?" Rachel asked.

A pause. "Yes."

Stupid question. "Want company?"

"You're going?"

No, I hadn't thought I was, but . . . "Yeah." She glanced at the clock and mentally calculated her day, what she needed to get done before she picked up the kids from school. "I'd guess before noon."

"Maybe I'll see you then. I'm not sure. I . . . I just don't know how my day is going to go."

Rebuffed. Quietly. "Oh. Okay." Rachel wasn't going to push it.

The conversation waned, and after promising to visit with the kids "soon," Melinda ended the call.

Rachel thought about her mother. Tall and slim, with even features, once-vibrant hair she kept shoulder length, and brown eyes that seemed to know too much, Melinda had been a loving mother all those years ago. Back then she always had a quick smile and a wink whenever Rachel had caught her sneaking a cigarette. "Don't tell Dad," she'd warned, but had laughed because at that point in time Ned Gaston had been hopelessly in love with her . . . but that had been long ago, before the marriage had cracked and long before her only son had been taken from her, shot dead by—

"Oh, stop it!" Rachel yelled aloud, and Reno, who had settled onto his bed near the back door, gave out a sharp bark. God, what was wrong with her? "Yeah. Sorry." So now she was apologizing to the dog? *God, Rach, you are really losing it. Try to treat today just like so many others, will you?*

But as she stared at the coffee stains all over the bills and junk mail, she knew she was kidding herself.

CHAPTER 6

Rachel wasn't home.

Her car wasn't parked in the garage and she didn't answer the door.

Cade didn't think twice, just pulled his key ring from his pocket, inserted the house key he'd used for years, and stepped through the front door and into the house he'd once called home. "Rachel?" he called, passing through the living area with the attached dining room to the kitchen, where her tablet and cell phone were charging on the table.

No wonder she hadn't answered.

He tried again. "Rach? It's me."

She'd be pissed as hell to find him inside what she considered her turf, the house he'd given her in the divorce. No strings attached. No clause in the decree declaring that she had to sell when the kids were in college, no lien against any equity. Nope. He'd figured she deserved it.

"Rachel? Are you here?"

Obviously not. And yet he felt as if he weren't alone. He stopped and listened. Nothing. Other than the soft hum of the refrigerator and the whisper of a breeze slipping through a partially open window near the table.

Huh.

The kids were in school and even the dog was

missing, along with the car. He started to leave, but paused, glancing at the familiar objects. Her favorite cracked coffee cup now in the sink, the faded message "World's Best Mom" barely visible. The kids' artwork from years before, still on display on a bulletin board, the cracked linoleum flooring that she hated and he'd promised to replace in the small kitchen, the dog bed near the door.

He felt a stupid wave of nostalgia. He'd wanted to tell her about Violet himself, and when he'd gotten no response to his calls and text messages he'd stopped by on his way to the station.

Hopefully, she'd return his call when she got home.

But, by then, it would probably be too late.

Reporters had already started gathering at the Sperry house by the time he'd left. The image of Violet's broken body still hung with him, and his quick interview with Vi's husband, Leonard, brought him to the same conclusion Kayleigh had come to: innocent. Or up for a damned Academy Award. Leonard Sperry had been a broken man, unable to stop the unending flow of tears and barely able to communicate as he'd sat in the police car. He'd been murmuring, "No, no, no . . . oh, Vi . . . no, no," and working his hands, alternately glancing out the window and then at the floor of the cruiser.

His story hadn't altered. He'd been in Bend

with friends. Come home early. Found her on the floor, the dogs locked upstairs in the bedroom. He couldn't think of anyone who would want to harm her or him and, no, he knew she wouldn't have done something like take her own life by throwing herself over the railing. Leonard seemed to think she must've stumbled down the stairway, though, from first glance at the scratched railing, Cade suspected otherwise.

Cade checked the calendar hanging on the cupboard near the back door, a Grumpy Cat calendar with notes scribbled all over it. Rachel, a true techie, still marked appointments on a hanging paper calendar. "Just so we're all on the same page," she used to say even though she kept a digital calendar on her phone and computer as well. Or at least she had when they were married. And there it was. Today's date. The day Luke had died . . . and now, the same could be said of Violet Osbourne Sperry. Both violently. Twenty years apart. For a second he wondered if there was any connection, but he dismissed the stupid thought as quickly as it had come. A coincidence. Like people born on the same day.

Well, not really.

He glanced at Rachel's phone and picked it up, then noticed that the screen was lit. As if someone had just been using it.

But no one was in the house.

Or . . .

The muscles in the back of his neck tensed. Again, he had the sensation he wasn't alone, but as he walked through the first floor and swept his gaze through the rooms on the lower level, he saw no one, not in the living and dining areas nor in the mess that was his son's bedroom. He paused for a second in Dylan's space, noting the empty bottles and wrappers and mussed bedding. Clothes were tossed over the two chairs in front of a space-station of computers.

But no one hiding in here nor in Harper's somewhat more organized chaos.

Then what?

It was the smell. The hint of cigarette smoke? Or his imagination? No one that he knew of smoked. Not Rachel. Not the kids . . . well, that he knew of. And besides, the odor was so faint . . . nah.

He even ignored the tightening in his chest and went upstairs for the first time since he'd left. The rooms had been changed, bedding and towels more feminine than when he lived here. But her robe was the same, a ratty old blue thing flung over the foot of the bed. He touched it. Swallowed and in his mind's eye remembered how they'd made love the first night they'd bought the new mattress. The kids had been gone for the night and they'd spent the hours here, under this slanted ceiling, making love like teenagers. He remembered the taste of her skin, salty with sweat but smelling of that cologne that drove him crazy, how slick she'd been when . . .

Shhh.

Click.

What? He froze at the familiar sound, the sweep of the back door opening and closing before the latch caught.

How was that possible?

Before he finished the thought he was down the stairs and into the kitchen. The back door was closed but he walked through, into the backyard, and saw that the gate was ajar, moving slightly.

Had it been that way a moment before?

He didn't think so and it seemed unlikely.

Sure enough it moved with the wind, unsecured. Which wasn't the way Rachel ever kept the yard. And why the hell was the back door unlocked? Ever since the kids were young and the dog a pup, she'd been a nut about keeping the backyard secure, buttoned up tight.

His feet crunched on the wet gravel walkway. Pushing through the gate, he caught a glimpse of someone walking away, a block beyond, a man in a dark jacket and black pants, watch cap pulled low and hurrying beneath the branches of the fir trees from neighboring houses.

Had he been in the yard?

Or was he just a neighbor out for a walk?

Time to find out. Cade started running only to see the guy fumbling in the pocket of his jacket.

Oh, shit, did he have a weapon?

Slowing, his eyes trained on the man, Cade was ready to leap over a fence and dive into a nearby hedgerow until he spied the man withdraw a key fob and point it at a sedan parked on the street. The car bleeped, lights flashing as Cade called out, "Hey!"

About sixty, unshaven, and wearing glasses, he stopped and turned. Bushy gray eyebrows pulled together beneath the watch cap. "Can I help you?" he asked.

"Maybe." Cade reached the car, a white Buick. With out-of-state plates. Idaho. "Do you live around here?"

"Eight or nine blocks over." He hitched his chin toward the main road. "On Toulouse. Frank Quinn."

"Cade Ryder."

If the name meant anything to him, he didn't show it. "I'm over here looking for my dog. A damned beagle. Got out again and took off after a squirrel or something, I don't know." Lines of worry furrowed his brow. "I'm going to have to get a tracker for him or build a brand-new fence. Don't suppose you saw him."

"Sorry." Cade shook his head. "But I thought you might have been by that house, there, the cottage with the red shutters?"

"I was . . ."

"In the backyard?"

"No. But I peered over the fence."

"Didn't go through the gate?"

"Nope." He scowled. "Why?"

"The gate was open."

"Was it?" He rubbed his jaw, scraping his whiskers. "I don't think so. I leaned against it, y'know, to look over."

"But you didn't unlatch it?"

"No. Didn't want to risk trespassing. Well, unless I'd spied Monty. Then I would have."

"Did you see anyone else?"

"In that yard?"

"Coming out of the house?"

"Nah. And I would've noticed, cuz I was lookin' for . . . well, speak of the devil—" His worried face cracked with a relieved smile as a small beagle appeared from the bushes of a house three doors down. Baying, he came running, bounding over puddles and splits in the sidewalk where tree roots had lifted and broken the concrete.

"So, the prodigal dog returns. You little pain in the ass!" Quinn said, leaning down for the dog to jump into his waiting arms. "You know you're a bad boy?"

White-tipped tail wagging like a whipsaw, Monty licked Quinn's silvery-stubbled jaw.

"Yeah, as if *you* was lookin' fer *me*," he said, opening the car door and setting the dog behind the wheel before shooing him over to the passenger side. "He'd drive if I let him, but I make him settle for shotgun."

Laughing at his own joke, Quinn slid into the car, then drove off.

Innocent.

Cade made his way back to the house and his pickup parked out front. Maybe he'd imagined it all. Maybe his nerves were jangled from the article in the paper about Luke Hollander's death, and then the homicide scene. Maybe everything was fine.

Then again, maybe not.

Rachel picked up a bouquet of daffodils from a roadside stand, then drove to the cemetery. The day was gray, which seemed fitting, and although the rain had subsided for the moment, the ground was sodden. The long, wet grass soaked the edges of her tennis shoes as she wended through the markers to find her brother's headstone, marking the spot where his ashes had been buried.

A landscaper's truck was parked on one of the gravel lanes at the perimeter of Edgewater Pioneer Cemetery, and a man with a shovel was digging around one of the pine trees that marked the periphery of the graveyard. In another tree a bold gray squirrel scolded from the pine's gnarled branches.

Melinda Gaston was already here, a solemn

figure standing on the rise where Luke's ashes were buried. In a long black coat and boots, her head bent, she seemed older than her years. The fingers of one hand curled over the handle of a folded umbrella that she was using to prop herself up as she stared down at her son's grave.

"Hey," Rachel said as she approached and saw that her mother had been crying, her eyes red rimmed though she managed a thin smile.

"Hi." Melinda blinked, then turned to stare again at the ground where a bouquet of white roses marked Luke's grave.

Rachel added her drooping daffodils. "This is always such a hard day."

"Yeah. I know."

"I told myself I would stop coming."

"But . . ."

"But I guess I'm not ready." She cleared her throat and added, "I wonder if I'll ever be."

"I hope so."

"Me too."

A gust of wind, thick with moisture, blew past, toying with the hem of Melinda's long coat, billowing its skirt around her slim legs. After a beat, her mother said, "You know that I don't blame you, don't you?"

"Yes."

Melinda had said as much over the years.

"Try believing it."

"I do."

Her mother eyed her. "Then you should quit blaming yourself."

"I don't." The lie came easily.

One of Melinda's eyebrows cocked, and though she still used the umbrella for support with one hand, she grabbed Rachel's fingers with her other, then squeezed gently. "I felt that I lost two children that night, you know, both my son and daughter. Luke . . . he was gone, yes, but you retreated."

That wasn't quite true. Rachel had drawn away from her family, yes, guilt propelling her. And most of her friends had abandoned her after that night, caught up in their own lives. Rachel had found comfort and strength in Cade Ryder's arms when he'd come back to Edgewater.

"You and I . . . we lost more than Luke," her mother said, nearly inaudibly as the wind kicked up again.

"I'm working on that."

"Well, work on it a little harder, would you? It's been twenty years. Time to let go." Then she placed a gloved hand to her lips, kissed her fingers, and touched the edge of the gravestone. "You need to move on." She was nodding. "And so do I." Hesitating, she bit the edge of her lip, as if something were on her mind.

Rachel asked. "What?"

"He's out, you know," Melinda said softly as rain began to fall again. Big, fat drops that reminded Rachel of tears.

God's tears, her grandmother used to tell her. For the fate of humanity. Rachel had never believed it.

"Who?" she asked, eyeing her mother. "Out from where?" What was Melinda talking about?

"Bruce."

"Bruce?" Rachel repeated before she understood. Bruce Hollander was Luke's biological father. Rachel had never met the man, a convict who'd been sent to prison before Rachel was born. Her dad, Ned Gaston, had worked the Hollander case as a rookie detective. "Oh."

"Right. 'Oh.' "

"He contacted you?"

"No. He can't. Or he's not supposed to and so far he hasn't. I heard it from my attorney, who had been informed by Bruce's parole officer."

"Does Dad know?"

Melinda lifted a shoulder and her face, if possible, grew grimmer. "I don't know."

"You didn't tell him?"

A beat. More raindrops. "We don't talk much."

The understatement of the year. "Maybe you should work on that."

Melinda only whispered a noncommittal, "Mmm."

Together they moved away from Luke's final resting spot and she watched her mother cross the wet grass to the parking lot, where she'd left her car. Rachel had parked on the street, and as she climbed into her Explorer, she looked back at the cemetery and remembered that day so long ago, when the shock was still fresh, her life in chaos as they'd laid her brother to rest.

It seemed like a lifetime ago in some ways, though some details of those days were still vivid and painful.

She watched her mother drive away and noticed the landscaping truck was gone as well. She was alone.

On the seat beside her, Reno whined. "It's okay," she said, reaching over to pat his neck, only to feel the stiff hairs at his nape at attention. "What?" The dog was staring through the rain-spattered windshield, eyes trained on the rise where Luke's ashes were buried.

Rachel felt an unwelcome chill. "You see the squirrel?"

But no . . . the chattering had stopped, the gray squirrel was gone, and the cemetery was silent aside from the plop of raindrops and the rush of the wind.

Her throat went dry. She stared at the lonely hill and saw no one.

And yet . . . she had the feeling that she wasn't alone.

"You're spooking me," she whispered to the dog and felt his shoulder muscles bunch. "It's nothing."

Just an empty graveyard on this gloomy day in

May. Nothing, not one thing out of the ordinary. But as she started the Ford, its old engine turning over and catching, she couldn't quite convince herself. She reached for her phone, realized she'd left it charging in the kitchen, and pulled away from the curb.

As she did she noticed in her rearview mirror that a white car that had been parked farther down the street did the same. It followed her for a few blocks, caught behind her Explorer at the light. The driver was hunched over the wheel, his dark cap visible as the wipers slapped the raindrops off the glass, a dog on the passenger seat with its long snout sticking out of the partially open window.

Nothing. It's nothing. Your nerves are shot.

The light turned green and she turned right, heading back home to grab her phone and make some calls before the meeting tonight. The white car followed and she tried to make out the driver—a man—but did she know him?

It's just a stranger in a car you've never seen before, but no big deal. Get a grip, Rachel. It happens all the time. Every damned day.

But her heart was racing and she hit the gas.

The white car followed, increasing its speed, but keeping the same distance between them.

That was weird, right?

Or not.

At the next intersection, rather than driving

directly home, she turned away from the town, toward the highway, and sure enough the white car followed.

Don't panic.

But she was and she took a corner a little too fast, her vehicle sliding, tires screaming.

Pull yourself together!

When she reached the highway, she barely stopped, just rolled through the light and punched it, the Explorer leaping forward and roaring away.

Around a wide corner, she saw the back end of a lumbering travel coach, coasting along at forty. Through the rain, she saw no oncoming car, so she hit the gas and passed, the driver honking irritably. As it turned out the coach was following a slow-moving pickup. She sped past both the coach and truck, then caught her wild eyes in the mirror.

The road crested, and barreling in the opposite direction was a huge semi.

What're you doing, Rachel?

Her heart knocked and she could barely breathe. She was a mother, an adult, a . . . She glanced in the rearview and saw that the white car had peeked its nose out from behind the RV, but ducked back as the driver saw the semi.

"Good. Stay there," she said, then caught herself.

What was wrong with her?

She took in deep breaths, switched on the radio, and with one eye on the mirror turned at the next country road and drove into the hills, losing the white car.

If it was really following you.

She glanced at her reflection again. "Don't do this," she warned, then saw, in her sideview mirror, the white car turn off of the highway.

CHAPTER 7

Violet is dead?

Oh. God.

"No," Rachel's voice squeaked. She stood in the kitchen, her jacket dripping, staring at the messages on her phone. From Cade, from Lila and Mercedes, all saying the same thing, all relaying horror and shock.

No, no, no. It just couldn't be. She'd seen Violet not long ago at the gas station . . . her car idling, facing the opposite way, while Rachel was tanking up. Violet, a small dog on her shoulder, had managed a thin wave. Rachel had been in a hurry . . . always in a hurry, at that time, late to pick up the kids at school. She didn't even remember waving back.

And now she was gone?

Rachel slid into one of the kitchen chairs and fired up her computer, but information, so far, was sketchy. Just a report that Violet Sperry had been found dead in her home by her husband early this morning. The police had been called and were making no comments as to the cause of death, only to say it was "unexpected" and "under investigation." What did that mean? That foul play was suspected? That she'd been the victim of what? Homicide? Suicide? What?

She dialed Cade's cell, and when he answered on the first ring, she said, "Hey. It's Rachel. Got your message about . . . about Violet. What happened?"

"I was called to the scene this morning," he said. "Violet was dead, had been for a few hours. Her husband found her in the house."

"I can't believe it."

"It's true."

"How did she die?"

"We're still waiting for an autopsy. County jurisdiction, but I'll be informed."

"So not natural causes?"

"No."

"Was it murder?" No reason to beat around the bush.

"It looks like."

"Jesus, Cade," she whispered and she felt her blood chill in her veins. "Why?"

"We don't know."

Of course. Rachel leaned against the counter. She'd been the daughter of a detective, then the wife of one; she understood. "How . . . how is her husband? Oh, God, I don't even know him. He's the furniture guy, right?"

"Leonard Sperry. Yes, works with the family business." He sighed. "I talked with him. He's not doing so great. In shock."

"I bet," she said. "Aren't we all?"

A pause. Then, "I wanted you to know so I came by. Earlier. To tell you in person. You weren't there." Something in his voice caught her attention.

"Running errands. Actually limping. The Explorer had a flat. Fixed now."

He hesitated again. What was that all about?

"And . . . ?" she encouraged.

"And I was worried about you. Wanted you to hear it from me and so . . . I let myself in."

"You let yourself . . . you mean, you 'let yourself in' as into the house?" she asked, stunned. "*My* house?"

"Yeah."

She couldn't believe it. "Really? You knew I wasn't here and you just walked right in? How?" But she already got it. He had a key. She'd never changed the locks because if he needed to get in for the kids . . . oh, hell. "Wow, Cade. You . . . you can't just come busting into *my* home. You know that."

"I said I was worried. One of your classmates was dead, probably murdered on the anniversary of your brother's death, there was the article in the newspaper, and . . ."

"And you think I'm so . . . mentally unstable, so crazy, I couldn't deal with it," she charged, her temper skyrocketing.

"That's not what I said."

"It's what you thought!" she spat out with more venom than she'd expected. *Calm down. Don't add fuel to the fire.*

"You don't know what I thought, but I can tell that you're just fine."

"That's right. I am," she snapped, then caught herself and said, "No . . . I mean, I'm sorry. Overreacting. You're right; everything today is . . . shocking. Terrible. Ramped up because of the day, probably." With difficulty she tamped down the fury that had spurted through her veins. He was just trying to help. And Violet was dead. Killed. Calmer, she said, "I'm surprised you came into the house. That's all. We had a deal, right? Only if there was an emergency."

"And your friend's death doesn't qualify?"

She wasn't going to be baited. "Look, you can't come in here, Cade. Unless you think there's a danger to the kids. Got it? We're divorced."

"I know."

She glanced around the room with the new knowledge that he'd been in here. Maybe looking at her phone and computer and God knew what else. Taking the phone with her, she made her way along the short hallway to the kids' rooms and the stairs. Had he gone up to her bedroom? The room under the eaves they'd once shared.

She was more in control now, her voice low and cold and steady. "This is my space, Cade. Mine and the kids'. One I carved out when you . . . when you left, so you can't just walk in here uninvited." She pushed her hair from her eyes with her free hand.

Her comment was met with silence and she closed her eyes for a second. Counted backward, mentally ticking off her heartbeats as she controlled herself.

"I was just worried," he finally said, his voice clipped. "That's all. I know this is a tough day for you, and then on top of it, Mercedes writes that story, the first of a series about Luke, and Violet Sperry dies. Both were friends of yours."

"Okay," she said. "Okay. Look . . . I don't want to fight."

"Could have fooled me."

"Well, I was pissed," she admitted. "We agreed to have boundaries."

"I was concerned, Rach, that's all. But I guess I shouldn't have been. You can obviously handle this and whatever else comes your way." With that, he hung up, the disconnect a distinct *click* in her ear.

You're an idiot, that horrid voice reminded her. *He's the kids' father; he was concerned, that's all. You don't have to always act like a damned shrew.*

"Wounded party," she said aloud, arguing.

Fine. Then victim.

"No!"

So we're back to crazy person whose temper controls her tongue?

"Oh, shut up!" she said aloud and stormed back to the kitchen, where she opened the refrigerator, eyed the bottle of wine, and slammed the door shut. She still had a couple of hours before she picked up the kids, and then later, she was off to Lila's for the damned meeting.

Lila.

"Ex-Stepmommy Dearest and ex-BFF all rolled into one." She shook her head. "Awesome."

Pull yourself together; let it all go. For God's sake: Violet's dead. Possibly murdered! Remember: It was Violet's testimony that helped convince the judge that you weren't responsible for Luke's death. She provided one of the reasons for "reasonable doubt," though the case never went to a jury.

A new sadness chased away her anger at Cade. It was true. Violet, deeply myopic and not wearing glasses in the dark cannery that night, had sworn she'd seen a flash from a gun's muzzle just before Luke fell, and the flash had been *near* Rachel but not from her own gun. Violet's shaky testimony coupled with the fact that there was no gunshot residue on Rachel's hands or clothes had helped her defense.

Some people thought she'd somehow washed her hands clean on the way to the station, that with her father's help she'd twisted the evidence to her advantage, which was wrong. She'd been numb after Luke had collapsed, yes, and had been grateful that her father had been first on the scene. But as much of a kaleidoscope of blurry, painful images and emotions as that night had become, she hadn't cleaned up. Those tissues her father had given her, to wipe her eyes and blow her nose . . . they hadn't been treated, and even so, they wouldn't have destroyed the gunpowder residue.

But then, what did she really remember?

Don't go there.

Not now.

Not ever.

It serves no purpose.

Just get through this miserable day.

Blam!

The back of Dylan's head slammed against his locker and his teeth rattled in his jaw.

"Just do it," Brad Schmidt ordered. His face was pressed nose to nose with Dylan's, his strong fingers holding Dylan's shoulders in a death grip, his beefy body nearly on top of him. The rest of the hallway was deserted except for Dash Parker, the lookout, standing at the juncture to the science wing.

"I can't, man." Dylan's back was pressed up against his locker.

"You have to!" Schmidt's pupils dilated. His breath smelled of pizza and the pores on his nose seemed enormous. "You promised." He gave Dylan a shake for emphasis. In a letterman's jacket, black T-shirt, and camo shorts, Schmidt was furious, the nostrils on his nose flaring, his skin turning red.

"I'll get caught."

"Then find a way to not get caught. Okay? You're a smart little shit. You'll figure it out."

"No, I think . . . I think my mom is on to me."

"Then be fuckin' careful, got it?" Another hard shake and it was all Dylan could do to stand his ground, to not pee his damned pants. Schmidt had a temper, a legendary temper that had only helped him become an all-conference tackle on the football team. "We had a deal."

"I'm telling you, I can't."

Brad's thick lip curled over his teeth and his dark eyes narrowed. "Who're you more afraid of, Ryder? Me? Or Mommy?"

"She can be pretty badass."

"Not as badass as me, I'll bet." The thick fingers dug deep into Dylan's muscles. "Remember that."

"Hey! Schmidt!" Parker hissed, his head whipping around. He was tall and lean, a defensive end in football, third base in baseball, an all-around jock, and a sycophant of Schmidt's, which made him worse in Dylan's opinion. "Walsh is coming!"

"Sheeeit."

Marlene Walsh was a no-nonsense vice principal. Dylan had been busted by her on more than one occasion for cutting class. So far, nothing more serious. But Parker and Schmidt, who both, it was rumored, had scholarships to local colleges, couldn't afford trouble. Or so Dylan hoped.

"This isn't the end of it," Schmidt growled. He pushed Dylan hard against the locker again, then took off at a dead run, with the faster Parker leading the way to the staircase at the far end of the hall.

Damn it, Dylan thought, caught between the ends of the hallway, one with the stairs at the front of the building and Schmidt, the other with the ever-approaching Walsh. He heard the steady click, click of her heels as she headed this way. He wiped the sweat from his upper lip, turned, and opened his locker. Then, thinking about what was inside, he grabbed his algebra book, slammed it shut, and turned, facing the corner just as Walsh appeared.

"Well, Mr. Ryder," she said on a sigh and glanced at her watch. "What're you doing skulking around the halls when you should be in class?" She was a petite woman with gray streaks in her short blond hair, rimless glasses, and a perpetually benign expression. Today, she was dressed in a red blazer with black pants and a white blouse.

Dylan wasn't fooled by the smile that rained on him right now. Rumor had it that she'd earned a black belt in tae kwon do. He believed it.

Beneath her harmless facade, there was an inner toughness; he could feel it.

"I've got study hall," he said and tried to get past her.

"And you have a hall pass?"

"No . . ." Couldn't lie about that.

"I see."

He tried and failed not to let his shoulders slump.

"You know, Mr. Ryder, you're skating on thin ice. If I'm not mistaken, this is the second time this semester when you've been out of class without a pass."

How did she know these things? How could she keep track of it all in her head? There were like eight hundred or so kids in the school and she knew how many times he'd cut?

"Come with me." She hiked her chin toward the front of the school, to indicate the staircase where Schmidt and Parker had fled. "Let's call your mother," she said. When he didn't respond as he glumly tagged after her, she added, "Or maybe your dad."

Dylan died inside. His parents, independently and together, would kill him if they found out he was ditching class. "I, um, it's not my study hall."

"I know. You're supposed to be in Mrs. Marsden's English."

Oh. God. "Yeah."

They reached the administration area and Walsh led him between two desks to her private office, a small room with a single window looking out to the front lawn. Her desk was neat, a few piles of perfectly stacked papers and her computer monitor along with a handful of pictures of her husband and daughter on one corner. Dylan knew. He'd been here before. Her framed degrees hung on the wall behind her.

"Sit," she said, indicating one of two visitors' chairs wedged between a bookcase and her desk.

He did and tried not to slouch as she took her own chair behind the desk.

"So, Mr. Ryder, how're we going to change this behavior?"

He hated the "we" almost as much as he detested being called "Mr." It all seemed so phony, and come on, there was no "we." He met her gaze. "I won't cut again. I promise," he said, and she brushed off his words with a wave of her hand.

"We've been here before. That's what you said in . . . October, I think." She adjusted her glasses, then typed on her keyboard and studied the computer screen. "Oh, wait. I'm mistaken. It was the first week in November. And then again in February. And now, here we are. Again. Three strikes."

He didn't know what to say, but she filled in the awkward gap. "As you have probably heard, the school district is retrofitting those old wings of the school with cameras, and it just hasn't happened yet because of budget problems and getting the right technician and all kinds of red tape."

So what, he wondered but was smart enough not to say it.

"I hear you're good at that kind of thing. Mr. Tallarico says you've got a natural talent for computers and cameras and all things technical."

"Yeah?" he said slowly. Where was this going?

"So I was thinking . . . maybe you could help us out."

His mind was racing. Was she offering him an out? "So, you wouldn't call my mom, then?" How lucky was this?

"Oh, no. I'm calling her. Of course." Again she offered him her trademark humorless smile. "This is, after all, your third offense." She leaned back in her chair. "So, what do you say?"

"Uh . . . sure. I guess." He kept expecting some trap, something more than a call to his mom, but it didn't happen.

"Good." Walsh gave a quick nod, as if agreeing with herself. "You can start on Monday. Come and see me after school." She stood then and the grilling was over as she said, "I'm trusting you'll head straight to Mrs. Marsden's class. You won't pass 'go,' you won't 'collect two hundred dollars,' and you'll avoid Mr. Schmidt and Mr. Parker as best you can."

His mouth almost fell open. She *knew?* Without cameras, how . . . ? He didn't wait around and ask, but nearly knocked the chair over as he scrambled to get out of the tight, airless office. His mother was going to go through the roof, he decided, but for the moment, he'd avoided a serious beating from Schmidt.

Right, and what are you going to do about him?

Dylan didn't know, but he told himself as he hurried to English class, he'd figure out a way to get Schmidt what he needed. Then, maybe he'd be free. The school year was almost over and Schmidt was heading to college. Hopefully, he'd be smarter in the future and stop stepping into jams like this.

Really?

Cuz everyone knows.

You've become the supplier, and face it, you like the money.

Once Schmidt leaves, there will be another bully. And then another one for the whole time you're in this sucky high school.

How the hell are you gonna get out?

"Crap," he muttered under his breath as he reached the door to room 107. He'd find a way.

Somehow.

He'd have to.

CHAPTER 8

Rachel picked up the kids at school, and if they noticed her bad mood, they didn't say a word on the way home. Harper was deep into her phone, texting while seated next to Reno in the back seat. Dylan, ever-present earbuds in place, looked out the passenger window and kept to himself. The only indication that he wasn't in his usual fantasy world was the fact that his head, deep in the hood of his sweatshirt, wasn't bobbing to the music only he could hear.

Maybe his confrontation with the school administration had made an impact.

Rachel hoped so.

Her own day had gone from bad to worse with the pall of Violet's death hanging over her. Her front tire had gone flat on her way back from the cemetery, then her aging workhorse of a printer had finally given up the ghost in the middle of printing notes for the damned meeting tonight, and finally, to top things off, the school had called to report that Dylan had been caught cutting class.

". . . and don't know what's going on with him," Mrs. Walsh had said, and Rachel had pictured the tiny administrator frowning with concern. Or mock concern. Rachel hadn't been sure which.

She sometimes suspected Marlene Walsh enjoyed her authority and ability to discipline. "But this is the third time and that's cause for suspension."

"Doesn't that seem to defeat the purpose?" Rachel had pointed out. "If he's cutting class, then why would you reward him by letting him out of school?"

The administrator had paused for a beat. As if she hadn't thought of this before, but Rachel suspected differently. "Yes, I know. It's all school policy. But I've devised an alternative solution." She'd then outlined her plan, a far better idea in Rachel's opinion. Would it work? Who knew? Both of her children were pulling away from her, and the little boy who had worn his heart on his sleeve while growing up and who had confided in her had become secretive, as had his sister.

Now, she parked in the carport and let Reno sniff around the backyard as her kids filed through the back door and she followed. Once they were in the house, Harper still texting as she headed down the hall to her room, Dylan shedding his backpack by the door, Rachel let the hammer fall. "Mrs. Walsh called today."

Dylan froze as Harper went into her room. Then he slowly removed his earbuds as Rachel went on. "She told me that she caught you in the hall when you were supposed to be in class."

"Oh. I was getting my algebra book."

God, did he look guilty.

"I know. But you were ditching English."

"Uh. Yeah."

Overhearing the conversation, Harper had returned to the hallway, idling as Rachel asked her son, "What were you thinking?"

"I dunno."

"Oh, come on, Dylan." Rachel didn't bother hiding the exasperation in her voice. It had been a helluva day and she wasn't up to teenage subversion. "There was a reason you ditched."

He hesitated, a tic appearing near his temple, then came up with a lame excuse. "I didn't have my report ready."

"So you didn't go to class? Because of an unfinished assignment? That's how you handled it?"

He tried to shrug it off, but she was sure he was lying. He'd been a bad liar as a little kid and she'd hoped that trait would stay with him, but now she wasn't so sure. Lies came more easily to him these days.

"This is the third time, Dylan. Mrs. Walsh was going to suspend you."

Another lift of a shoulder. "But she didn't."

"Yet."

"I just have to do some stuff for her." He started to open the refrigerator door, and she slammed it shut before he could peer inside.

"I'm serious. There are only a few weeks left of school this year—the least you could do is finish your assignments, turn them in, and stay in class."

His eyes darkened and she thought he was going to say something to her. Instead his jaw tightened and he glared. "I will."

"Wait a second," she said. "Is there something else going on?"

He looked away as Harper cast her brother a glance of . . . sympathy? Conspiracy? *Warning?*

"You know something about this?" she asked, turning her attention to her daughter. "Harper?"

"No." She replied quickly. Too quickly.

"Then why do I have the feeling you're holding out on me? That you're *both* holding out on me?"

She waited.

No one said a word.

The refrigerator hummed.

Outside in the yard, Reno gave a sharp bark.

Another knowing look passed between brother and sister.

"What?" Rachel said, glaring at her children, a new fear knotting her stomach. *"What?"*

"Mom, it's not a big deal," Harper finally said. "Kids cut class all the time."

"Not my kids."

"Oh, right. Because you never did anything wrong in high school. I forgot you were an angel. Just perfect."

Rachel blinked. Saw the insolence in Harper's eyes. She didn't say it, but it was there between them. *You were accused of murder, weren't you? You were caught sneaking out and your brother died because you shot him. And now you're all freaked out because Dylan cut one stupid class.* She heard the accusation, the rationale as clearly as if Harper had spat the words out.

"This is *not* about me. So let's get back to the point. What's going on?"

A disgusted look tightened Harper's features as she held her mother's stare. But her throat worked and she broke first, her gaze moving to Dylan. "Are you going to tell her?"

"Tell me what?" Rachel demanded.

Dylan shot his sister a thanks-for-nothing look.

"Tell me what?" Rachel repeated.

"Thanks," he threw out at Harper, then blew out a huge sigh. "Okay. Fine. I—I . . . some older kids are hassling me."

"What do you mean 'hassling'? You mean like bullying?"

"No! No! It's not like that." Another angry glare sent to Harper. "I made a mistake, okay? I, um, I gambled with them and lost. They want their money."

"They?" she repeated. "As in more than one?"

He licked his lips. "One."

"Who?" she demanded.

"Oh, man. I don't want to say."

"It's Brad Schmidt," Harper said.

"I don't know him."

Harper glanced at her phone. "You wouldn't. He's a loser. Thinks he's a tough guy. Football player. I hate him."

"Oh, good." None of this sounded right. "I need to talk to him."

"No!" Dylan was shaking his head. "Mom, you'll only make things worse."

"So what is this guy threatening to do to you?" she demanded, worried. "What?"

"It's . . . it's my fault. I shouldn't have placed the bet. I know. I won't do it again and this will all go away."

Rachel wasn't so sure and was having trouble not panicking. Who was this kid, this Brad? Was he violent? Would he hurt Dylan? "Mrs. Walsh knows about this?"

"Yeah," Dylan admitted. "Well, most of it."

"So you were gambling with him. How's that work?" Visions of casinos with slot machines and roulette wheels and craps tables spun through her mind. The bright lights of Las Vegas. Or maybe it was local. Whatever kids did.

"It . . . it was kind of an online thing."

That made more sense. Dylan was forever hooked into his computer or his iPad or some game system. "We were playing a game. A war game. Interactive. For money. You pay for hits. I lost."

That was almost the truth, she thought. But not quite.

Rachel turned to her daughter. "You knew about this?"

"I knew he got into some trouble with a couple of seniors."

Her focus swung back to Dylan. "What were you thinking?"

"He wasn't. It was stupid," Harper said, stating the obvious. "Now they want to be paid."

"So they're what? Threatening you?" Rachel was playing this out in her head.

"Not really." But he looked scared.

"How much?" Rachel asked, stepping back and folding her arms over her chest.

He swallowed. Licked his lips.

Her stomach dropped.

"A hundred," he whispered.

"Dollars?"

"No, euros." Harper rolled her eyes. "Of course dollars."

"Okay," Rachel said to Dylan. "So what're you going to do?"

"Pay them back."

"With what?"

"I have some . . . My birthday money and . . ."

He was always broke.

"Would it help if I loaned you the money?" she asked, immediately thinking this wasn't the right way to handle the situation. He needed to learn this lesson. Fast. She couldn't enable him. And yet . . . "And I mean *loaned*. I'm serious. You would have to pay me back. ASAP. Summer is coming, so I'll expect you to do yard work and help with cleaning the basement, whatever."

His eyes brightened a little. "You'd do that?"

"Maybe." She couldn't let him off too easily. "But you'll have to let your dad know. And if this kid gives you any more trouble—"

"He won't, Mom. Really."

She glanced at Harper. "Yeah," Harper agreed, "Schmidt is a bully, but he wouldn't do anything to, like, mess up because he could lose his scholarship."

"He'd lose it if I made trouble?"

"Don't, Mom, just don't!" Dylan said, shooting his sister a dark look. "And please, can we just keep Dad out of this?"

"Nope."

"Oh, man, really?" Dylan groaned and rolled his eyes. His whole body slumped. "Why?"

"Because he's your dad."

"But . . ." Was he really going to argue about it?

"Hey—what is this?" Harper said as she picked up the newspaper still open on the table. The article about Luke Hollander's death was front and center. "Does Lucas know about this?"

"I don't know. Probably," Rachel said. *The whole damned town would have read it by now.*

"Wow. Oh, wow." Harper was scanning the article. "He's gonna freak. It's online, right?"

127

"Everything's online now."

"Yeah, then he'll see it." She shot her brother a look.

"What?" Rachel asked.

"Nothing," she said. "It's just that he doesn't like to talk about it, y'know. It makes him feel weird. Different."

Even though Lila had mentioned how difficult it was for her son in the article, Rachel hadn't dwelled on how the newspaper piece might affect her nephew, the boy who'd never gotten the chance to meet his father. But she knew how it was when someone felt different. Hadn't she witnessed Luke's own emotional response when anyone asked about his father, his "real" father, meaning Bruce Hollander? Luke had always tried to hide the fact that his biological father had been serving time in prison. Whenever anyone had questioned him about Hollander or whenever his father had tried to get in touch, Luke had become angry and sullen, horrible to live with.

It had been a weird dynamic for their little family.

It was probably just as difficult for Lucas. Possibly worse.

Harper finished reading and glanced up to meet Rachel's eyes. "It's hard for you, too, huh?"

"For all of us." Rachel nodded, then fought the tightness in her throat when she caught a bit of empathy in her daughter's eyes. Over the

years the subject had come up; the kids knew the sketchy details and Rachel had left it at that. Now, compliments of Mercedes Pope, they might learn a helluva lot more.

Today, it seemed, was a turning point.

For all of them.

And worst of all, Violet Sperry had been murdered.

CHAPTER 9

By the time Rachel was ready to leave for the meeting, Violet's murder was all over the news.

Flanked by her kids as they stood in the living room in front of the flat-screen, Rachel felt her keys dig into her tightly clenched hand as she watched the press conference where the sheriff himself spoke first into the camera.

Roberto Valdez was a tall, fit man with military-cut brown hair starting to gray, a firm jaw, and near-black eyes that were deep set and didn't falter as he stared into the camera. Standing on the concrete steps in front of the flagpoles and the department's headquarters, Valdez, in uniform, made a brief statement before the public information officer took over. A forty-something woman whose brown hair was clipped at her nape, Isa Drake seemed less grim than the sheriff, though her answers were short and concise:

"Yes, it was definitely a homicide."

"No, there are no suspects or persons of interest yet, but it's still early in our investigation."

"More details will follow, as Sheriff Valdez mentioned."

"We are encouraging anyone with information to please come forward."

The kids stared at Rachel as she turned off the TV.

"So you knew her?" Dylan asked.

"Yes." Listening to the report, hearing the account on the news had only made it more real.

"Like, she was a good friend?" he asked.

"Not close, but we hung out sometimes." Rarely.

"Weird," he said.

"More like freaky," Harper said. "Who do you think killed her?"

"I don't know," she said.

"You must have an idea." Her son, again. "Who, Mom?"

"I don't know." Rachel checked her watch. "How could I know?" she admitted as much to herself as to the kids. "Come on, let's get a move on. We're already late."

She expected everyone on the committee had been held up. She'd received a dozen or so texts about Violet over the course of the afternoon—group texts, which she despised, her phone pinging as each person weighed in. Worse yet, it was a group Lila had created and some of the respondents came in as unfamiliar phone numbers rather than names, which meant she didn't really know to whom she was replying. So she didn't.

They made their way to the back door and the dog bounded behind them. "Not this time," Rachel said.

"Still talking to the dog." Harper let the screen door slam shut behind her.

"Hey!" Dylan called after his sister. He was hoisting his backpack to his shoulder. "We all talk to him. You too!" He seemed to have forgiven Rachel for the earlier grilling. At least for the moment. But as his backpack wasn't completely zipped, she saw inside, her gaze landing on a brown box. "What's that?" she asked.

"What?"

She pointed. "The box?"

"Oh." He flushed, zipped the pack. "Lucas needs a new mouse for his computer. I had one, so I told him I'd bring it."

That didn't sound quite right, but Dylan added, "He's got another one ordered. He's just borrowing this one until it gets here. No big deal." And he was out the door.

No big deal.

She wondered, but let it go.

The trip to Lila's house took less than twenty minutes. She'd let Harper, who had gotten her license just two months earlier, drive, and her daughter tended to be a lead foot.

Which ran in the family. Still, her fingers had curled over the armrest for most of the ride.

With a little difficulty, Harper parked on the street in front of Lila and Charles Ryder's house, a three-storied Victorian built on the steep hillside in the late 1880s. The house had been home to the Ryder family for generations and was the very house where Cade and his brothers had grown up, the place where his mother had died.

Rachel hated it.

"Let's go," she said. As she glanced up at the turret with its 360 view of the city, a flash of memory came to her, of sneaking up the stairs to that small private space with Cade. No one had been home at the time. Through the windows, the lights of the town had glimmered to the dark expanse of the river. Her throat closed as she thought of the way he'd kissed her that night, the way her heartbeat had pounded in her ears, the warmth of his breath against her nape, the tingle of her skin as they'd tumbled to the floor and the breathless feeling of elation that had followed their lovemaking.

All shattered when, six weeks later, she'd learned she was pregnant.

Now, she took the keys from her daughter, then gathered her bag, with her laptop tucked inside, as her kids piled out and walked up the series of stairs leading to the sharply gabled Victorian with its wraparound porch and sweeping view of the town and river.

The front door opened before she could push the bell, and Lila stepped onto the porch, a white cat streaking out behind her. "Oh, crap! Sammy! You get back in here!" But the cat was long gone, slinking from the porch and into the surrounding shrubbery. "Fine," Lila muttered, visibly irritated. She turned back to Rachel. Her usual smile was missing, but as always she was dressed as if she expected to meet a prospective real estate client: heels, expensive slacks, a long tunic, and bracelets that jangled over her wrist. She gave a quick hug to both Harper and Dylan and said, "Lucas is upstairs in his room with a friend. Why don't you go on in?"

The kids shot inside and were hurrying up a sweeping staircase when Lila pulled the door shut behind them, trapping Rachel on the porch. "Can you believe it?" Lila asked, obviously distressed. "Violet? Dead? I mean murdered?" She was shaking her head, her big eyes as cloudy as the day. "Who would do anything like that?" She blinked, then reached into the pocket of her slim gray slacks, retrieving a single cigarette and lighter. "I shouldn't, I know. I quit years ago, but . . . Violet." She lit up quickly and drew a deep breath before saying in a cloud of smoke, "I just don't get it. Why would anyone . . . ?"

"I don't know."

She thought for a moment, waving the smoke away as if the odor wouldn't cling to her tunic or hair. "I just saw her, y'know? She'd come into the real estate office, supposedly interested in property near the river, but the real reason was to let me know that no matter how much I harassed her, she wasn't going to be a part of . . . this." Lila motioned to the bay window of the living room, where the reunion committee was meeting. "Not only did she refuse to be a part of the planning committee, she made it clear that she wasn't even going to attend the reunion."

"Did she say why?"

"Oh yeah." She took another pull on the cigarette, again shooed the smoke away. "High school 'is over.' " Lila made air quotes. "Like she thought we were all going to relive our days at Edgewater High."

"Well . . . some people would."

"The idea was just to catch up with old friends," Lila snapped. "But she thought I was 'harassing' her into coming."

"Did you? Harass her?"

"No, Rach. Of course not!" She rolled her eyes, then added, "I just kind of, you know, 'urged' her to be a part of it and maybe she felt pressured, but really?" She let out a sigh and glanced over the rooftops of the houses lower on the hillside to stare at the darkening waters of the Columbia. "I guess we'll have to . . . oh, you know, include her in the remembrance table."

That was where Lila went? Dismissing Violet to discuss the reunion and the table for classmates who had died?

Another drag, then Lila dropped her cigarette and crushed it, kicked the butt swiftly under the rail and into the bushes flanking the porch. "I don't suppose the police have any idea who would do something like this . . . ?"

"I wouldn't know," Rachel said quickly. As a cop's daughter and wife, she'd learned to keep her mouth shut. Even if she was no longer married to Cade, her lips were sealed.

"Oh, right . . . Well, maybe Mercedes will know something. She's probably got sources in the sheriff's department. I know she's already got a junior reporter on the story."

Mercedes. Rachel flashed on the article in the *Edgewater Edition* and the fact that there were more stories slated. "She's here already?"

"Yes. But antsy. Always on her damned phone. Always working." Lila found a shaker of Tic Tacs in her pocket and popped a couple of orange tablets, crushed them between her teeth. "She wants to talk to you."

"I know."

"You may as well tell your side of the story," Lila confided, stepping to the door. "She's going to publish the series whether you contribute or not. For the record, I was against it, but—" She shrugged. "You can't fight city hall or the press."

Can't you? Rachel thought and, in this case, silently vowed to try.

"Aren't you about outta here?" Patricia Voss, the other detective in the department, poked her head around the edge of the partition separating Cade's desk from hers. A large woman with clipped gray hair, zero makeup, and lines creasing her face from years in the sun, she made a big show of checking her watch.

"In a few." Cade leaned back in his chair, a cup of this morning's coffee still congealing on his desk in front of a picture of his kids. At the time of the photograph, Harper had been about eleven, a gawky tween in shorts and a jacket, trying to hide behind a curtain of hair and looking as if she'd rather be anywhere than the focus of her parents' attention. She'd been standing on the rocky shores of the river with Dylan next to her. In a sweatshirt and jeans, his uncombed hair a wild riot, Dylan had grinned without any inhibitions. He'd been shorter than his sister and skinny, freckles cast over his nose, his teeth still seeming too big for his face.

A lot could happen in six years. Some good things. Some very bad.

Tricia's voice brought him back to the present.

"It's supposed to get down to the low forties tonight." She was slipping her arms through the sleeves of her rain jacket. "Can you believe it? This is supposed to be May, for God's sake." She threw a disgusted look through a window to the gloom of the evening.

"Spoken like a true transplant from California."

"In the forties, Ryder," she repeated. "Like in ten degrees above freezing."

137

"I know."

"Brutal."

"If you say so."

"I do." She zipped her jacket, then squared a cap on her head before offering him a piece of advice. "Go home, Ryder. Enough with all the work. I've got ninety jobs around here, and even I can leave."

"Ninety?" he questioned. She did do double duty. In the small department, Tricia not only was one of the two detectives, but also worked as a backup patrol officer if two or more of the regulars were sick. "I thought two."

She gave a snort of disgust. "Yeah, well, I just happen to be the one who holds this department together, if you haven't noticed." Shaking her head, she added, "Who do you think does the real work around here? Who cleans out the coffeepot and starts a new one? Who cleans out the refrigerator? Geez, you people are pigs."

"Careful," he warned. "Not all cops like to be referred to as—"

"Oh, can it, Ryder. You know what I mean. And this crew?" She motioned around the large room divided by now-empty cubicles. "They're the worst. Not just the men, mind you. The women are no better!"

He laughed. "Wow. You're in a mood."

"Always. As bad as all this is, it's worse at home."

He doubted it.

Sketching a quick salute, she added, "See you Monday."

"If you're lucky."

"Funny guy," she muttered, making her way toward the back door. "Real funny guy."

"Some people think so," he called after her, but she was out of earshot. He rotated the kinks from his neck and looked at the file on his desk. Dusty and yellowed, pulled from the archives of closed cases and marked HOLLANDER.

He'd never gone over it before, though he'd glanced through the digital files years before, then chastised himself. What was done was done; everyone thought Rachel killed her brother in a horrible accident. She'd said as much that night, though later she'd been confused and the case had been muddled with conflicting testimony from eyewitnesses, especially Violet Osbourne and Annessa Bell, both of whom were friends. Coupled with that, the inconclusive evidence had been a little compromised as the first officer on the scene had been Rachel's father.

"A shitshow from the get-go," Ned Gaston's partner at the time had said and been quoted.

So why look at it again? It was over. Closed. Had gathered dust for two decades.

Maybe it was because it was the anniversary of the tragedy.

Maybe it was because he'd felt there had been loose ends never tied up.

Maybe it was because it was a helluva coincidence that Violet Osbourne Sperry, a key witness in the investigation, was killed twenty years to the damned day that Luke Hollander had been shot.

Maybe he was just a damned fool.

Whatever the reason, he knew by just going over the case he was stepping on an emotional land mine.

Well, so be it. He glanced at his watch and considered calling Kayleigh about any updates to the Violet Sperry homicide.

It's not your case.

Yeah, he knew that, and yet . . . he leaned over his desk and returned to the stack of old notes and reports on the Hollander homicide. Up first, the autopsy report, which included notes, a body sketch showing all of the wounds, and then pictures of the body.

His jaw clenched as he remembered Luke in life—vibrant, cocky, athletic—and then there were the pictures of his body. He skimmed the report, noting that Luke was pronounced DOA at the hospital and the death certificate was signed by Richard Moretti, M.D.

Cade eyed the signature; he hadn't known that Nate Moretti's father was the attending physician, but there it was in black and white.

No big deal, he thought, sitting alone at his desk, as most of the personnel in the station had left for the day. The hospital Luke Hollander had been rushed to was no longer in existence, like so many of the businesses that had once thrived in this community.

As far as he knew, Dr. Richard Moretti was still around, working at a clinic in Astoria.

Cade thought about Violet Sperry and Luke Hollander. Both died on this date, twenty years apart. Two people who went to high school together. Two people who'd been at the Sea View cannery the night Luke was shot—Luke the victim, Violet one of the witnesses who had seen what had happened in that dark warehouse.

So what?

This was a small town; people were bound to cross paths.

Just a bizarre, tragic coincidence.

Nothing more.

Or so he tried to convince himself.

He closed the file, locked it in a drawer.

The Luke Hollander case was closed. Long ago.

Violet Sperry's homicide was fresh.

But unrelated.

And, again, remember: Not yours.

"So what?" he said aloud.

Jurisdiction issues hadn't stopped him in the past.

He was pretty sure they wouldn't now.

CHAPTER 10

Rachel followed Lila into the house, walking across the marble floor of the expansive foyer, where the stairs swept upward and an antique chandelier Cade's mother had restored glittered grandly. Suspended from the ceiling three stories overhead, the crystal fixture had been Sandy-Lou's last renovation to the old house before cancer had claimed her, a sparkling reminder of the frailty of life.

At least that's how Rachel saw it as she stepped into the living area, where the committee members were gathered, preparing for "the best reunion this town has ever seen," according to Lila.

Yeah, right.

She took a deep breath, looking past the eclectic blend of period pieces, antiques, and modern furniture that she'd seen during other visits, to the baby grand piano, positioned near the bay window, and the hardwood floors that gleamed, shiny and cold. The walls had recently been painted a dusty rose that Lila had discovered and referred to as "period authentic." Lila's new sound system was cranked and Rachel heard the familiar refrain from a song from her school days. The retro music seemed forced, almost haunting.

Of course, Mercedes was the first person she saw.

Perched on the edge of a curved couch, Mercedes was in a deep, whispered conversation on her cell. Short. Curvy. Exotic looking. And smart as a whip. Her black curls were tossed over her shoulder as she talked, her eyebrows pulled together in concentration. Rimless glasses were propped over the bridge of her nose. Her skin was still flawless, a smooth mocha color; her eyes big and expressive; her lips compressed. With her free hand she typed on the keyboard of a laptop propped open on the glass table. Rachel remembered her—the girl who was always whispering, listening for gossip, the editor of the school paper.

She glanced up, caught Rachel's eye, and the corners of her mouth tightened almost imperceptibly as she quit typing long enough to pick up a can of Diet Coke and take a long swallow.

"I want to talk to you," she mouthed, still listening to whoever was on the other end of the call.

Great.

Rachel's stomach clenched as she scanned the faces around her. All of these adults had been there that night, every last one of them. Her gaze shifted to Nathan Moretti, seated a cushion away from Mercedes and engrossed in his iPad.

He glanced up. "Hey, Rach!" He slanted her that friendly smile that he'd flashed her on the day Luke had died.

Oh, God.

Her heart nearly stopped at the memory.

Twenty years ago today Nate had been behind the wheel of his black BMW, parked in the driveway near the huge pine tree, obviously waiting for Luke. The window of Nate's Beemer had been rolled down and he'd caught sight of Rachel hurrying across the patchy lawn.

"You comin' tonight?" he'd asked.

"Shhh!"

"Oh, I get it, Mom doesn't know, right?" He'd laughed.

"No—I, I can't." She'd shaken her head vigorously as she'd reached his sports car.

"Afraid?"

She hadn't been able to admit it. "No." Would he just shut up? She'd cast a worried look at the house.

But that hadn't been Nate's style. "Oh, come on. It's gonna be awesome." He'd glanced at the house where she and Luke resided, a fifties ranch home like all of the others on the street. "You'll have a blast, I promise."

Before she could argue, Luke had

hurried out of the front door, his backpack slung over one shoulder, his blond hair tossed by the breeze as he'd loped down the cement walk.

Nate had leaned out the driver's window as a squirrel began to scold from the gnarled branches of the pine. "Tell your mom you're staying with a friend," Nate had suggested. "Call Lila. She'll cover for you!"

But she'd just come from Lila's.

"I'm trying to talk Rach into coming tonight," Nate had said to his friend as Luke opened the passenger door.

"Is that right?" Luke had paused outside the Beemer and leaned on its roof to study his half-sister's face. "You really gonna do it?"

"I don't know." Rachel had squirmed.

"It'll be fun."

"If you say so."

"Hey, I've even got an extra gun." With a glance at the house to make sure their mother wasn't peering through a window or walking out the front door, he'd unzipped his backpack and withdrawn a small black case. "Inside. Extra ammo included, no charge." He'd tossed the case over the roof of the car and, panicked, she'd caught it.

"I don't know. I've never—"

"Doesn't matter." Nate had started the engine, but he'd still been staring at her, his dark eyes twinkling with mischief. "Come on, Rach. You'll like it. Have a blast. Get it?" he'd teased, his trademark smile slowly widening. "Promise. You'll never forget it."

Well, amen to that.

Truer words had never been spoken.

She remembered Nate reversing out of the driveway, the tires of his car squealing against the street just as the sound of the garage door grinding upward had reached her ears.

Mom!

Rachel's heart had nearly stopped.

Frantically she'd hidden the gun case under the rhododendron flanking the pine just as Melinda came into view. In jeans and a sweater, Melinda had shaded her eyes with one hand. "About time you showed up, Rachel. I've been waiting."

"Sorry. I . . . I lost track of time."

"With Lila. Doesn't surprise me," her mother had said, and then catching sight of the blush climbing up Rachel's neck, she'd added, "Is something wrong?"

"No. Nothing." Rachel had hurried into the garage and slid inside the

146

passenger seat of her mother's Camry. Craning her neck to look through the back window, she'd spied her mother staring thoughtfully down the street to the intersection where Nate's car was disappearing around a corner.

Could she do it? Could she lie to her mother? Her dad—a cop? He was a detective, good at ferreting out fact from fiction. Her palms had begun to sweat as she'd turned around in her seat and peered through the bug-spattered windshield to her father's workbench, stretched against the far bare wood wall.

She'd swallowed against her dry throat as she heard her mother's footsteps on the gravel drive before the door groaned open and Melinda slid behind the steering wheel. A bemused smile on her face, she'd glanced at her daughter and started the Camry's engine. "Do you have a crush on Nate?"

"What? A crush?" Rachel had blurted. "God, Mom, this isn't nineteen sixty."

"It's okay," Melinda had said with a knowing expression. "We've all had them."

"I don't have a 'crush' or anything else on Nate Moretti," she had said and turned away, hiding the fact that she was scared spitless, her short breaths actually fogging a small corner of the window as Melinda backed out of the drive.

"All right. Fine. No crush. Or whatever. Oh, shit!" She had hit the brakes. The Toyota had ground to a quick stop as a kid on a bike flew past behind them, inches from the bumper. "Damn it. That Farello boy's going to get himself killed! Did you see that? He didn't stop, didn't see me. Holy God. And no helmet! What's his mother thinking?" Letting out a frustrated breath, she'd slowly hit the gas again, backing out into the street.

Do it. Right now! Rachel had blurted, "Is it okay if I sleep over at Lila's tonight?"

Her mom's expression had tightened. She didn't like Lila, though she'd never admitted it, only remarked on more than one occasion, "That girl had better watch herself or she'll end up in big trouble." Lila had always dated older boys, some lots older, and now she'd settled on Luke. That fact had really gotten under her mother's skin. But at the moment, Melinda had seemed to think she was connecting some romantic dots. "Oh, I get it," she'd said. "You're planning to meet up with Luke and Nate."

Rachel hadn't said anything to change her mind, and at the cross street, her mother had warned, "Be careful, Rachel. Stay out of trouble. Okay?" Melinda had shot her daughter a worried glance.

"I will," Rachel had promised.

But it had been a lie. A horrid lie.

"Hey, you okay?" Lila said now, snapping Rachel back to the present, to the meeting and the strains of a familiar song. Wilson Phillips was singing "Hold On," a popular song from grade school, the harmonized strains drifting from hidden speakers. Of course Lila would be playing the songs that brought back all those wretched school day memories.

"Rachel. I asked if you were okay?" Lila repeated.

Her heart pounded in her ears. *No. I'm not okay. I'll never be okay. I have horrible night-mares, I lost my job, my kids worry me to death, our classmate was murdered, and it's the damned anniversary of the day I shot and killed my brother.* "Fine," she forced out with a weak smile. "I'm fine."

"Really?" Lila rolled her expressive eyes. "Give me a break. Because none of us are 'fine' tonight. I don't know if we ever will be again." Frowning she added, "Annessa couldn't even pull herself together to make it. She claimed she was too upset. And that she's having a problem with her kid."

On that issue, Rachel could relate.

"I don't know why Annessa couldn't get it together for a couple of hours," Lila said. "Geez! Talk about a prima donna. And come on, it's hard on all of us. We've all got teenagers with issues."

Annessa Bell had belonged to the popular group in high school, one of the rich kids. She'd moved away for years but with the passing of her father had come back to Edgewater to claim her inheritance, or so the rumor mill had it, even though, according to Lila, her husband was "rich enough that she could afford to loan money to God."

Lila let out a disgusted breath. "I just don't get it. Annessa doesn't have a corner on being upset. We're all shocked and a little freaked out. You'd think she might want to come and talk it out with people who knew Vi."

"Everyone handles grief differently," Rachel said.

"Yeah. Maybe you should give Annessa a break," Nate said, coming to their missing classmate's defense. "She probably has her own issues to deal with. She's married to a guy twice her age."

"And that's a problem?" Lila threw back. "So am I, and Chuck and I, we're happy. Make that very happy."

Nate shrugged one shoulder. "Just saying, you never know."

"Well, if you ask me, she's weird about the reunion. Annessa should be embracing the community, but she spends all her time working. Can you believe that? With her money? Ever since her husband's corporation bought property around town, she spends all her time visiting the sites. I've seen her car at the cannery, St. Augustine's, and Reacher's farm. Did you know he bought that, too?" Lila's lips pinched together in disapproval.

Rachel offered, "It probably has more to do with trying to get a vision for the new construction."

"Whatever. The point is she should be here tonight. She's in charge of the money, you know . . . keeping track of who's paid and who still owes and . . . well, she sent a spreadsheet, so I guess that'll have to be good enough." Obviously irritated, Lila reached in her pocket again, but this time didn't come up with a cigarette.

Watching her, Rachel recalled that Annessa and Lila hadn't liked each other much in high school, but that was long ago. Lately, though, Lila had been pissed that Annessa and her husband hadn't used Lila as a real estate agent when they had purchased various properties in the area, including the old cannery and St. Augustine's hospital with its now-closed private school.

Lila gave up her rant. "Nothing I can do about

it." She touched Rachel on the shoulder. "All this talk of Vi. It's depressing and just . . . just awful." Lila gave a little shudder, her bracelets rattling. "I need a glass of wine. You?" she asked Rachel.

"Not now." She shook her head.

"What about a double shot of whiskey?" Nate suggested.

"Oh. You want?" Lila asked, brightening a little. "I've got . . . scotch, I think. Chuck always keeps a bottle of Glenlivet—"

"No." Nate held up his hands. "I was joking. I'm good. Really."

But Lila was already moving away, hurrying past the pillars separating the living and dining areas. At the far end of a long table, Brit Watkins was huddled with Reva Santiago and Billy Dee Johnson around an open laptop. Reva wore a sleek black suit and a white blouse, her black hair cut in layers to her shoulders. Billy Dee was dressed more casually in sweats and a T-shirt, as if he'd just jogged off the practice field. His bald head shined in the glow of another chandelier as he picked up one of Brit's catering menus. Brit appeared uncomfortable in the straight-backed chair. The trio, in deep discussion over their tasks of planning food, drinks, and games or contests, had not seemed to notice that Rachel had arrived.

"She never listens, does she?" Nate asked, shoving his hands into the pockets of his slacks and hitching his chin toward Lila. Still tall

152

and lanky, his hair as brown and thick as she remembered, Nate would probably be a candidate for the most unchanged since graduation. A few faint lines were visible near the corners of his eyes, the beginnings of crow's feet, but other than that, he looked about the same as he had when they'd graduated.

"Never."

Lila was already filling two glasses at a mirrored sideboard that was laden with trays of food, gleaming stemware, and open bottles of wine, soda, and hard liquor.

In the middle of the display, three white candles had been lit, tiny flames flickering around a small bouquet of violets in a glass vase, obviously a tribute to Violet Sperry.

Geez. Lila must have moved on that quickly.

Sadness crawled through Rachel all over again.

Lila was returning with the drinks and had caught Rachel's gaze. Handing a short glass to Nate, she explained, "I felt I had to do *some*thing." She touched the rim of her wineglass to Nate's, then took a long drink of wine. "I couldn't just ignore the fact that she'd died today."

Rachel didn't say anything.

"Right?" Lila prompted.

"I guess."

"She was killed, Rach. Murdered. In her own home. Last night, or early this morning. I just thought . . . you know, we needed to make some kind of statement. We couldn't ignore it. She graduated with us."

"Sure." That was so Lila. "It's just . . ."

". . . so weird, I know." Another big gulp of wine.

"Rachel!" Brit scraped her chair back. She'd finally noticed that Rachel had arrived and was blinking back tears as she awkwardly made her way around the end of the table. "It's horrible. Horrible."

"Unbelievable," Rachel said, and to her surprise Brit hugged her for a second, pulling her close despite her baby bump.

Brit dabbed at her eyes. "Sorry. I'm emotional. Pregnancy hormones, y'know."

"We all feel it," Rachel said, hiding her surprise at being hugged by a woman who usually could barely scratch up a smile for her.

Nate agreed. "It's sick," he said.

From the corner of her eye, Rachel noticed that Reva and Billy Dee had abandoned their spots at the table and were walking toward the group. Reva carried a glass of red wine, and Billy Dee came around the other side of the table.

Oh. Great. She knew she shouldn't have come. Within half a minute everyone on the committee was clustered in the living room.

"I saw her at the dog groomer's, the one with that stupid play on words—what's it called?

Oh, Doggie Bartique, the one on Third Street—just last week. My schnauzer needed his nails clipped," Reva reported as she joined the others in front of the cold fireplace. "Anyway, she was there with her three dogs and we waited at the counter, making small talk, you know. I can't believe it. Now she's gone. I hadn't seen her in years—I mean years—and there we were talking about the stupid dogs. It's surreal, y'know. Why would anyone . . . ?" Her voice faded and for once Reva seemed at a loss for words. She was pretty and smart, a woman who'd always used her good looks and brains to her advantage. She'd been a cheerleader, of course, and in the choir and drama club. Their senior year raven-haired Reva had sung and danced to deliver a stand-out performance in *Bye, Bye Birdie*.

And, for a while back then, before Lila had turned his head, Luke had dated Reva. Exclusively. Reva had been head over heels for him.

Now an attorney, Reva was as slim as she had been in high school, but her features had sharpened with age. If she still harbored any bad feelings for Lila, she did a damned good job of hiding them. Then again, she'd been a pretty good actress twenty years ago.

"Maybe she wasn't targeted." Billy Dee rubbed the back of his neck, and despite the cool temperature, he was sweating, beads visible on his bald pate. "Could've been a random thing. Y'know, a burglary gone bad."

"You think?" Nate asked, not hiding his skepticism.

"Who knows?" Billy Dee shrugged his shoulders. "These days that kind of shit happens."

"Makes sense to me," Reva agreed. "I'd actually rather believe that than think someone wanted to kill her specifically."

"Now wait a second. Can we let this go for a few minutes and maybe, you know, talk about the reunion, the reason we're here?" Lila asked. "This is too morbid. And we don't know anything anyway."

"It's just hard to concentrate," Brit said.

Billy Dee nodded. "Maybe I will have that drink now," he said and made his way to the makeshift bar, his bald head gleaming under the lights. He'd been a runningback in high school before an injury had sidelined him, an injury that had shattered his ankle and put him in the hospital for a week, all compliments of Luke's tackle in practice. The injury had knocked Billy Dee off the team for the season and, he'd complained later, cost him an athletic scholarship to the University of Colorado. Now he was a teacher at the high school and a football coach for the ever low-flying Eagles.

Despite Lila trying to put everyone on the committee back on track, the conversation about

Violet continued as Bon Jovi played in the background.

There were more questions than answers as they tossed around theories and anecdotes, remembering things about Violet, remarking about when they'd seen her last, wondering how she'd died and why. Had her attacker known her? Was murder the intent? Or was Billy Dee right when he'd suggested the botched burglary? Had she been sexually assaulted? Could her husband be behind it?

"It's all such a shame," Brit said. "A horrible tragedy, and I kind of know Leonard. He comes into the shop before work for coffee and a scone or something. We don't talk much, but I can't imagine him killing Violet. No." She shuddered visibly. "I heard he found the body. He was supposed to be on a fishing trip. Came home early."

"Supposed to be?" Nate asked. "You mean he wasn't?"

"Oh, no, no, no. I don't know anything about it. Just what people say when they come in." She let out a breath. "And that's all just coffee shop talk."

"Gossip," Mercedes said from the couch as Lucas walked into the room.

He glanced at his mother, who gave a quick nod, and then he walked to the buffet and began filling a couple of plates.

Reva swirled the ruby wine in her glass. "The police always look at the family first. And I think they were having money problems. When I saw her at the dog groomer's, Vi was kind of pissed. And she mentioned that Leonard wanted to buy the store from his parents but they were at some kind of impasse. She didn't seem all that crazy about the idea, but then, who knows?" She shrugged her shoulders. "But I bet Leonard is suspect *numero uno*."

Mercedes clicked off her phone and stood, circumventing the coffee table to stand with the rest of the group in front of the fireplace. "Reva's right. The cops always suspect the husband, or if the husband is killed, then the wife, or maybe a whacked-out kid, whoever's in line to inherit. Wait 'til they check the will."

"They didn't have kids," Lila said. Then, eyeing Mercedes, she asked, "When was the last time you saw her?"

Mercedes lifted a shoulder. "Last week. I tracked her down at the furniture store."

Nate lifted his chin. "Tracked her down?"

"I was trying to get an interview with her, for the series. Since she was one of the witnesses at the trial, and she was on the scene when Luke was killed, I thought it would be interesting to see what she had to say now."

"Let me guess," Reva said. "She shut you down."

Mercedes's stony expression acknowledged nothing. "She didn't want to talk about it. The damnedest thing, you know," she said, her gaze moving back to Rachel. "No one wants to be interviewed."

"I wonder why?" Reva tossed out. "Geez, did you stalk her?"

Mercedes opened her mouth, then closed it. "I just needed a little information. It's my job."

"So we've heard." Nate took another drink.

"And just so you know, the next article is coming out next week." Mercedes was staring straight at Rachel. "The Tuesday edition."

"Listen, could we please all get back to work?" Lila said. "All this talk about Vi isn't going to bring her back."

Billy Dee made his way to the table, and Reva followed.

Mercedes stepped closer to Rachel. "I've been trying to reach you. I've texted and called and all I've gotten is radio silence."

"Because I don't want to talk about it." Rachel was going to add lamely that she'd been busy, but Mercedes didn't give her time.

"I just want to ask some questions about Luke's murder. For my series."

"Yeah, Mercedes, I get it! We all do," Rachel said, a little louder than she'd anticipated, and Brit's eyebrows shot up. Lila's head swiveled in her direction.

"You didn't call me back."

"I know that too," Rachel said, the room seeming to shrink a bit.

"Why?"

God, why would Mercedes corner her with everyone else around? Even Lila and Billy Dee in the dining room had turned to look at the small group near the couch. "Nothing to say."

Mercedes wasn't buying it. "Oh, come on. You were accused—"

"Look," Rachel said sharply, cutting her off. "I don't want to talk about what happened to Luke. Okay?"

Mercedes asked, "Can I quote you on that?"

"No!"

"Jesus, Mercedes, give it a rest, would ya?" Nate said. "Have a little respect. This isn't the time or place."

"There is no time or place with Rachel," Mercedes pointed out, bristling.

Lila touched Mercedes's arm. "Come on, Mercy, let it go for now. It's a tough day for those of us close to Luke anyway, and now, with what happened to Violet, everyone's . . . they're just not themselves. You and Rachel can figure this out another time."

Mercedes's eyes flashed. "I've got tomorrow open. Or Sunday before noon. Work for you?" she asked Rachel, putting her on the spot.

"I don't know."

"Don't you?"

"I keep a calendar at home."

Mercedes glared at her. "You have a calen on your phone or iPad or whatever. You're techie."

Rachel stood her ground. "I am and I do, but I can't give you an answer right now."

Mercy wasn't about to give up. "Then—"

"For the love of God, didn't you hear Lila?" Nate threw up a hand, his drink sloshing over the rim of his glass. He didn't care, just glared, flush faced, at Mercedes. "Violet's been killed, damn it. So stop. Just stop!"

"Stay out of it," Mercedes warned.

"Let's all take a breath." Lila stepped between them. "Sort it out later. We've got work to do." Then she noticed her son was still loading up and lingering at the buffet. "Isn't that enough?" she asked.

Lucas looked up, caught her eye, and mumbled a quick, "Yeah," before heading back upstairs.

When Rachel looked back at Mercedes, the petite woman was still eyeing her intently. Back in high school, Mercedes Jennings had been one of the rare girls who hadn't fallen for Luke Hollander, a girl who had called him out for being a phony. Now, she finally said, "Okay, Lila and Nate are right. This isn't the time and we do have work to do. I'll call you and we'll set it up."

Rachel waved her off, but Mercedes couldn't stop.

"So check and see if Monday works for you, Rachel. We can meet at the office or I'll come to your house. That might be better. I'll bring a photographer. Name the time."

"Monday doesn't work," Rachel said quickly.

"You don't know that," Mercedes objected.

"Back it up!" Nate's face was flushed with fury. "You need to learn that no means no."

Brit was suddenly on her feet, closing up her laptop. "I can't handle this. Can't concentrate. It just feels wrong tonight with everything that's going on."

"But we have to," Lila insisted.

"I can't. Being here, talking about high school with Violet . . . I'm outta here."

"No, no. Brit, listen. Try to put your grief aside, will ya?" Lila was getting pissed. "Violet would have wanted us to—"

"Bullshit!" Mercedes said. "Violet wanted no part of this reunion. You said so yourself."

"I was still trying to talk her into it," Lila admitted. "The ironic thing about it was that I was going to put her in charge of the remembrance table and now . . . now she'll be a big part of it."

"You know what's more ironic?" Mercedes threw out to the group. "How about this? Violet was murdered on the very date Luke Hollander was killed twenty years ago."

"Whoa. Wait." Nate's gaze drilled into Mercedes. "That's right, but . . . so what? You're trying to connect the murders? That's crazy. It's been decades."

Rachel felt her insides begin to shred. She had to get out of here. Fast.

"I don't know exactly what I'm going to do, but I am going to report on it. Of course. I've already got someone tracking down the lead investigator on Violet's case, Detective O'Meara."

Kayleigh. The shredding cut deeper. She let out her breath, refusing to think of Kayleigh O'Meara, and how her husband had fallen in love with his smart, redheaded partner.

Water under the damned bridge.

CHAPTER 11

B *lam! Blam! Blam, blam, blam!*

Kayleigh maintained her stance, protective glasses in place as she aimed and fired at the target, her shoulders jerking with each blast of her pistol, her jaw locked. She was wearing ear protectors that blocked out everything but the satisfaction of hitting her mark, the outline of a man's torso suspended at the far end of the shooting range. She'd managed to tune out the other shooters in the indoor shooting range and was totally focused on the target positioned near the far wall. Her shots were on target, three a little off center, just where a man's heart would be hidden under protective ribs.

She fired off several more rounds before she was satisfied that her aim was true. By the time she was finished, most of the tension had drained from her body and she felt reenergized. It had been a long day, and she hadn't wanted to return to her apartment on a Friday night. Alone.

Camille, a friend she'd known since her freshman year at Washington State, had phoned to say some friends were getting together for drinks and appetizers at O'Callahan's. Kayleigh was familiar with the Irish pub located on one of the piers. Still, she had declined.

"Why?" Camille had demanded. "Got something better planned?"

"Have you seen the news? I'm working on a homicide."

"Yeah, and I have a shitty job and a shittier boss who wants me to work late but I told him, 'Forget it.' It's the weekend! Let's have a few drinks, catch up, and un-freakin'-wind. You're not going to bring that dead woman back, you know. Dead is dead."

"That's not what I'm trying to do."

"Okay. Fine. I don't think a couple of hours with friends will stop you from finding out what happened to her."

Maybe. Maybe not. The first hours of any investigation were the most critical.

"Come on, Kay!"

She hadn't let Camille persuade her. Instead she'd worked until after eight and then had come to the indoor range to let off some steam and let the case sink in.

But now as she zipped her jacket and stepped outside, she noticed the fog rolling in from the ocean. She wondered if she should change her mind and see if she could connect with the group, friends from college. Most married. Some with children. But why the hell not?

She could use a break.

She'd spent hours going over interviews and evidence, feeling the clock ticking, the killer getting away.

All the while trying to push aside the impact of seeing Cade again.

Big mistake.

She'd called him because he'd lived in Edgewater most of his life. Also because he was one of the best detectives she'd ever worked with.

And because you wanted to see him again. Be honest, Kayleigh.

Angry with herself, she unlocked her Honda with her remote, slid inside, and started the car. Yeah, she admitted to herself as she drove off, then turned on the radio and cranked it loud. She had used the excuse of Violet Sperry's murder to contact Cade, to see him, to check her own reaction to him as well as see what his was to her.

And she'd felt crappy about it.

Not that she couldn't use his insight, but because her ulterior motives were a little underhanded and disingenuous. Not her favorite traits, she thought, cruising along 101, the shops brightly lining the main artery cutting through Astoria.

She'd fallen for him three years earlier when they'd worked a case together, here in Astoria. He'd been separated from his wife then and the murder investigation had gone on for months.

It had happened during those long nights of a stakeout, when they'd spent hours alone together, the night surrounding them as they'd sipped coffee in a car, or in the apartment across the street, trying to catch a view through the windows of the suspect's house. That was when she'd fallen in love with him.

It had been stupid.

He'd been married; she'd known it.

And though he'd admitted to being separated, he'd never once said he planned on divorce. . . . She had fantasized, of course, even though she told herself now that she'd fought her attraction to him.

Had she?

Or was that just a lie she told herself to feel better about the whole doomed situation?

Tonight, she would unwind. For an hour or two. Tonight she'd put Violet Sperry's homicide on the back burner and she would definitely stop thinking about Cade Ryder even though he was now, indeed, divorced. Had been for nearly a couple of years.

"Still off limits," she reminded herself as she drove under the ramp to the Astoria-Megler Bridge, the tall, four-mile span that linked Oregon to Washington at the mouth of the river.

O'Callahan's was located on the riverfront, tucked between a restaurant and bookstore in what had once been a series of warehouses and was now one big mall, a hodgepodge of stores on three levels.

She parked, locked the car, then dashed across the parking lot to the wide glass doors that were the main entrance. Inside reclaimed wood floors gleamed beneath industrial lights suspended near the exposed air ducts. She made her way down a short flight of stairs to the Irish bar and stepped inside, where the lighting was dim and the conversation humming. Customers lined the bar, where two bartenders poured drinks, chatted, and laughed in front of tall mirrored shelving holding dozens of gleaming bottles. Two flat-screen TVs were positioned overhead, a baseball game in progress.

Kayleigh spied Camille seated in an oversized booth in a rear corner. Wild streaked curls framed her heart-shaped face. She was sipping from a small copper cup, her lips a glossy pink. With her were three men and two women, heads bent over their drinks. Kayleigh took a step toward them, then stopped. Maybe this was a mistake. She could spend the next hours piecing together the case, follow up on . . . *Oh, crap!* One of the guys was Travis McVey.

Her ex.

The man she'd dated before stupidly falling for Cade.

Her heart sank.

Damn you, Camille.

A roar went up at the bar as one of the players cracked a line drive. Travis looked up, then over, his eyes finding Kayleigh. The back of her throat went dry.

They'd lived together six months.

And she'd walked out on him, never really explaining. She hadn't had the heart to tell him she was in love with another man. In love with a married man. And a man who hadn't felt the same, not that she'd known it at the time.

Camille, too, caught a glimpse of her and began waving frantically, motioning her over, chatting up her friends, all of whom looked in her direction.

Decision made.

Mercedes was glaring at Rachel again. "I'm just saying, it's a pretty major coincidence that these murders are on the same date."

"You're right, a coincidence," Nate said. "An ugly one, but nothing more. Geez, Mercy, you're suspicious of the whole damned world."

"That's my job."

"Then your job sucks." He drained his glass as Reva reached the group.

Brit was on the verge of tears again. She flung a glance at Reva. "You got this?"

"Yeah."

"Good." Sniffling, Brit hurried into the dining area and scooped up her notes and tablet.

"Look. Anything you all decide is fine with me." Her gaze found Reva's. "Just let me know. Text me."

"What? No!" Lila had followed her to the table. "Brit, you can't leave," she said in a soothing voice. "We need you."

"You don't. Reva and Billy Dee can handle it." Undeterred, Brit slid her phone into the pocket of her maternity jeans.

"She's right. We're okay," Billy Dee said.

Brit tried to swallow back her tears. "I really . . . I really need to get back to Pete and the kids."

"But"—Lila held up her hands—"if you stay a few more minutes, we—"

"I just can't," Brit said, pushing past Lila and hurrying into the foyer and out the front door. It closed with a definitive thud.

"I should go, too," Rachel heard herself saying.

"No way. You just got here." Jaw set, her cheeks coloring, Lila tried to take charge. She stood in the archway to the foyer as if blocking everyone inside. "Listen. We're all upset. I get that. Me too. God, yes. But we have to get through some of this work. Come on, let's just get to it and make it a short meeting so everyone can get back to their families. Okay? Really. We don't have time to reschedule." As a Realtor, she was used to dealing with arbitration and bringing two opposing sides together. "We just need to get this done. Right."

"Shit, I guess," Billy Dee said. "I dunno."

"You do. Just a few more minutes and then we'll wrap it up for the night." Lila was insistent.

"Yeah, I don't want to postpone," Reva said as she and Billy Dee headed back to the far end of the dining room table.

"Fine." Mercedes threw a dark glance at Rachel. "You're working on the last of the classmates we can't locate. You got some?"

Under her breath, Reva said, "She's such a bitch," as she walked past to join Billy Dee at the dining room table again, but Rachel didn't know if she was talking about Lila or Mercedes, or possibly both.

"I heard that!" Lila said.

"Rachel?" Mercedes prodded as she took her seat on the couch again.

"Yes. I've got a few." Rachel pulled up a tufted ottoman, sat on it, and opened her laptop while Nate refilled his glass. "I've got names, addresses, e-mail, and phone numbers. Everything but social security numbers . . . a hacker's dream."

Mercy arched an eyebrow, but didn't comment. She was still pissed.

Rachel looked down at her laptop and clicked onto the file. "There're, let me see . . . still nine MIA, but I think I'll be able to track most of them down. I've actually got information on them, but haven't received responses to the e-mails."

"You texted?" Nate took his seat again and sipped from his glass.

"When I could."

Lila asked, "Is anyone definitely not coming? Did anyone respond and say that they just weren't going to make it?"

Rachel checked the files on her laptop. "I've got about six who are definite no's at this point."

"Who?" Lila demanded. It was her contention that everyone should attend.

"To start with, we've got two who are serving time. Larry Gorse is in the Washington State Penitentiary in Walla Walla and then there's Lavonne Tinker. She's in Billings, Montana."

"For what?" Lila asked.

"Larry was in for aggravated assault. Almost killed a guy," Nathan said. "I saw Larry's brother a few years back and he gave me the word."

Almost killed a guy . . . Rachel felt herself go cold inside. She had killed someone. Her own brother. Everyone in this room had been there.

"It was on the news even though it happened in Washington," Mercy said. "I ran a few lines about it in the Past and Present column. And Lavonne tried to run over her cheating husband with their minivan, complete with car seats. Thankfully, the kids weren't with her, but it put him in the hospital and she ended up in prison."

"Okay, cross Larry and Lavonne out," Nate

said, then needled Lila. "Hope you didn't want them to head any of the subcommittees."

Lila rolled her eyes, and they got down to business. Finally.

As promised the meeting wrapped up quickly. Within forty-five minutes, Rachel was climbing the stairs to get the kids. She gave a quick rap with her knuckles on Lucas's bedroom door before pushing it open to find the dim space illuminated only by dueling computer screens. Eyes adjusting to the darkness, she spied Lucas and Dylan each wearing headgear complete with microphones and speakers. Lucas was seated in a rolling chair facing a large screen while Dylan sat on the floor, his laptop balanced on his thigh, where he was obviously playing some interactive video game that included abandoned buildings, a military force, big guns, and lots of blood.

Dylan's back was propped against the foot of the bed, on which, in the dim, eerie light, she saw Harper and some boy she didn't recognize. They hadn't heard her. They were locked in a tight embrace, lips parted and kissing wildly, one of his hands in her hair, their jean-clad legs entwined.

"What the hell's going on here?" Rachel stepped into the room, knocking over a cup of half-drunk soda as she slapped on the light switch.

Immediately the room was illuminated.

"Mom!" As if she'd received an electric shock, Harper jettisoned away from the boy, nearly a man by the looks of him. Her feet hit the floor and she stood, thankfully, still in her clothes, blinking against the light. Her flushed face instantly turned ashen. "What're you doing here?"

Rachel ignored her daughter, her focus laser sharp on the unknown kid—was he a kid? His beard shadow was pretty thick. "Who are you?"

"Xander." He rolled off the bed on the near side and Rachel tried not to notice the bulge in his jeans, evidence of his hard-on. At least he had the decency to look embarrassed and tried to hide his arousal with the hem of an oversized sweatshirt.

Dear God.

Rachel turned her glare to her daughter. "What is this, Harper?"

Dylan turned his head, as if suddenly realizing there was more going on in the room than the war game he was playing. He pulled off his headgear and scrambled to his feet, all the while shooting worried glances at Rachel.

"Mom," Harper said, her voice thin, her chin lifted defiantly. "This is Xander Vale. He's . . . he's a friend of Lucas's and . . . and mine."

"Good friends, obviously," Rachel said dryly. When Xander took a step forward and extended his hand, she took it for the briefest of seconds.

What to do next? No parent manual for this one.

"Nice to meet you," he said, this near-man in a gray U of O hoodie, torn jeans, and bare feet. Apparently he was attempting, and having some luck at, growing a beard. A beard! His eyes were dark and there was a hint of arrogance beneath the veneer of embarrassment.

I don't trust you, she thought. *Not one inch. What are you doing with my seventeen-year-old daughter?*

"Get your things," she said to Harper, her voice tight.

"Back off," Lucas grumbled as Dylan nudged him with the toe of his running shoe. "I hit you! You are done, man!"

"Hey!" Dylan said into his microphone.

"What—?" Lucas snapped, yanking off his helmet. "What's your problem?" Then, from the corner of his eye, he caught sight of Rachel and realized the lights were on and the jig was definitely up. "Oh."

"Yeah. 'Oh,' " Rachel said, and for the first time caught a whiff of marijuana smoke. Great. She motioned to both her kids. "Now," she said. "Downstairs. Move it. Your dad's on his way."

"Dad?" Harper nearly squeaked out the word and she glanced around the messy room frantically. "My stuff is in the car."

"Get it." Rachel was in no mood for any kind of excuse.

Eyes wide, Harper said softly, "You're not going to tell him about . . ."

"About Xander?" Rachel asked. "Oh, yeah. You bet I am. Not only that, but you"—she pointed at the man/boy and looked him straight in the eyes despite the fact that he stood six or seven inches above her—"you, Xander Vale, are going to meet him."

Harper let out a little sound of protest. Her makeup was smeared and she appeared so damned young.

In the ensuing silence, Rachel kept her eyes on Xander and was vaguely aware of sounds drifting up from downstairs, music punctuated by voices floating up through the vents. With a tenuous grip on her emotions, she said, "Harper's dad is a great guy." Glancing at her daughter, who was frantically shaking her head, Rachel added, "I hope she didn't fail to mention him." She tried to maintain what little of her cool she still held on to.

The boy, staring at the floor, plunged his hands into the front pocket of his sweatshirt and had the good sense not to try to argue or butt in.

"Cade," she said. "That's Harper's dad's name. Detective Cade Ryder." She waited just a second, hoping to let that final bit of information sink in. The kid, to his credit, stood his ground. "As I said, he's a cop. And trust me, he's going to want to meet you."

176

CHAPTER 12

Cade had barely closed the door of his truck when he saw his ex-wife and kids fly out of the front door of his father's house and gather on the porch. Another kid was with them as well. Not Lucas. Maybe older. In an Oregon sweatshirt, jeans, and flip-flops, the boy looked to be pushing twenty or twenty-one. So not a boy. Beside him a white-faced Harper appeared positively apoplectic. Dylan was sullen and distant in his earbuds, and Rachel's expression told him she was pissed. Make that really pissed.

Great.

Another family trauma.

How many had this old house witnessed? How many while he was growing up? Cade hated to think.

"What's going on?" he asked as he mounted the familiar steps and felt a cool breeze ripple off the Columbia and blow inland. The door to the house was open, the foyer chandelier aglow, a patch of light silhouetting the group gathered just beyond the threshold.

"This," she said, indicating the boy he didn't recognize, "is Xander Vale." She yanked the door shut, throwing the porch into semidarkness, the only illumination cast by the interior lights through the transom, sidelights, and windows. "He and Harper were getting pretty friendly upstairs in Lucas's room." She shot the kid a hard glare.

Vale stood his ground.

Harper seemed to wither.

Cade felt his muscles tense.

Rachel was just gathering strength. "And, though I can't prove it, I think there might have been some marijuana involved."

It was the big kid's turn to blanche. "No—" he said, and met Cade's gaze. "No weed."

Marijuana would change things. In Oregon it was still illegal for minors.

"Seriously," Harper said, finding her voice. "We were not smoking."

"But you and Xander were . . . together?" Cade glanced at his daughter.

Harper crossed her arms over her chest and, with her chin set, met his gaze defiantly.

Xander Vale said simply, "I like Harper."

Cade nodded, glanced at his daughter. *God, how did she get to be so grown up?* "I like her, too," he said, trying to remain calm.

"It was going far beyond 'liking' her," Rachel said sharply.

"Mom!" Harper said, mortified.

"Harper, you were making out with this guy"—she jabbed an accusing finger toward Vale—"with your brother and Lucas in the room and me just downstairs! So don't act like you're embarrassed now. For the love of God, what were you thinking?"

"Mom! Stop!" Harper yelled. "God, please just stop!"

The Vale kid winced in the half light, and Harper looked like she wanted to sink through the floorboards right then and there. Cade didn't blame her even though he wanted to throttle Vale right then and there. Instead, jaw tight, he stuck out his hand. "Cade Ryder."

Vale hesitated, then shook his hand warily.

Harper fought tears.

Dylan moved his head to the beat of some song only he could hear through his earbuds, though Cade caught him sneaking glances at both of his parents and Xander Vale. Maybe his son wasn't as out of it as he let on. Cade hoped so.

Vale said, "Look, Mr. Ryder—"

Rachel cut in, "*Detective* Ryder," and shot Cade a hard glare, silently reminding him to be the father here. And maybe a hard-nosed cop to boot. As if he'd forgotten his role.

Not likely.

Vale swallowed hard. "She, your wife, she did say you were a . . . with the police."

Cade nodded. "I am."

"Ex-wife," Rachel clarified, then to Harper, "Geez, didn't you tell him anything about you? How long have you been . . . dating . . . or seeing each other or whatever it is you call it?"

Vale slid his glance to the side. "We . . ."

Inching her chin up a fraction, her backbone ramrod stiff, her hair catching in a gust of wind, Harper said, "We met last week."

"Last week?" Rachel's jaw dropped. "Holy . . . When?"

"We were at a baseball game. Lucas brought him."

Rachel shook her head. "This is ludicrous. You met him last week and tonight you were . . . Oh, geez, honey, what were you thinking?"

Cade doubted much thought had gone into the encounter. He remembered what it was like to be young, how hot one's blood could flow, how quickly emotions got out of hand, how he and Rachel hadn't been able to keep their hands from each other's bodies, how all they'd thought about was being together, alone. And what had happened? Barely a year out of high school Rachel had gotten pregnant with the very daughter she was now trying to warn.

"How old are you?" he asked Vale as a car turned the corner, a white sedan. Reminded of the Buick with Idaho plates he'd spied earlier, he watched, tensing, as the sedan drove past, engine purring, headlights washing beams over the street before heading downhill. An older Ford Taurus. Oregon license plate illuminated. Not the same vehicle.

"Just turned twenty," Vale was saying. "I, uh, I

go to U of O, down in Eugene. I was just up here hanging out with Lucas. We played ball together. I'm in pre-law. His old man, er, his dad said I could work for him this summer full time. I work there now, part time."

My *old man,* Cade thought.

"Harper's seventeen," Rachel said in a low voice. For a second her eyes narrowed on Vale; then she glanced at her ex, as if he could solve this problem.

Cade had been a few years older than Vale was now when he and Rachel had first gotten together. He'd been to college, served as a Marine. But he'd fallen for a teenaged girl. "Look. I think what Harper's mom is saying is that if you want to date our daughter, ask her out."

"*She* wouldn't let me go," Harper spat, shooting her mother a hard glare.

"Probably not," Rachel agreed.

Cade held up his hands. "Let's just slow this train down, okay?"

"Nothing happened, Dad!" Harper cried. "Nothing. We just kissed."

"Okay."

Vale gave a quick nod. "She's right. Nothing happened." But his dark eyes smoldered and Cade didn't trust the kid as far as he could throw him.

"Let's just keep it that way, okay?"

"Yeah." The kid gave a quick nod while Harper, mortified, glared at her father.

Dylan, embarrassed, on one foot then the other, caught his attention. "Can we just go?"

"Yeah," Cade said. "You got your things?"

"In Mom's car."

"Transfer them. I'll be right there." Then as Dylan hurried down the steps and bounced across the yard, Cade eyed Harper and Xander. "We all understand each other here?"

Harper nodded stiffly.

Vale said, "I'm cool."

"Good." Cade doubted it; he'd been in the throes of teenaged lust. "Cool" wasn't a part of it. Worse yet, Harper was casting the kid a sly, adoring glance. As if Xander Vale were God's gift.

Yeah, that was a problem.

Cade said, "Okay. Let's go, then."

Relieved, Vale lifted a hand in Harper's direction, turned, opened the door, and zipped into the house to take the stairs two at a time.

Athletic. Good looking. Slightly rebellious. Older.

Trouble.

"This is not over," Rachel warned and Cade didn't know if she was talking to Harper or him, or both. He decided the statement was probably all inclusive.

"Can we just leave?" Harper whispered.

"Yeah. Okay." He glanced at his ex-wife, and she didn't argue. To Harper, he said, "I'll meet you in the truck. I want to talk to Mom a sec."

"Oh, great," Harper mumbled, rolling her eyes before heading to his pickup.

"Deal with this," Rachel ordered, pointing at his chest. "I'm serious."

"I know. I will."

"Good." She started to follow after the kids, but he caught her by the arm and spun her back to face him.

"What?"

"We were that age once," he reminded her and she looked at his fingers, clenched as they were on her wrist.

"Exactly." Her gaze met his. "And I got pregnant."

"And it wasn't the end of the world." He let go.

"She's only seventeen. I was older. But let's not have her replay our mistakes, okay? She's got a whole future ahead of her."

"You've talked to her?" he asked.

"What? About sex? What do you think?" She shook her head, the auburn strands of her hair catching in the light cast through a nearby window. "From the time she was in sixth grade. Of course. Have you?"

"Not really."

"What about Dylan?" she asked.

"He's just—"

"Fifteen," she shot back, her face in shadow. "How often did you think about sex at his age?"

Too often. All the time, in fact.

His face must've given him away.

"Yeah, I thought so. So there ya go," she said.

"I will. I'll talk to him. Tonight."

"Good. I've already brought it up. We had a discussion. He hated it, of course, but it had to happen. Face it, Cade, we don't just have to worry about our daughter. Right? Dylan could be sexually active for all we know."

"God, I hope not."

"Me too. But . . ." She let her voice trail off and he stared at her profile—narrow nose, big troubled eyes, dark lashes that brushed high cheekbones and lips that were now pursed in thought.

"Let's take it down a notch, okay? Not go all parent-ballistic on them? Try to have a reasonable discussion."

One dark eyebrow raised. "Is that what I'm doing? Going 'parent-ballistic'?"

He actually felt his lips twitch. "Well, I wouldn't say you were exactly the calm voice of reason."

She didn't seem amused by that. "Okay. Then that's your role, okay? You be the super dad who talks things out and keeps his cool. That's on you. But you might want to know that Dylan's in trouble at school."

"What?"

She told him about his son cutting class and

trouble with an older kid who was bullying him over some bet not being paid.

"I'll get to the bottom of it."

"Good. Do that. I'd prefer not to have Marlene Walsh on speed dial." When he didn't respond, she clarified, "She's the vice principal."

"Got it." He paused, sensing there was something more. Something she was holding back. "What?"

She opened her mouth, hesitated, then said, "I'm just upset. Everybody"—she motioned toward the big house and the people inside— "all of us knew Violet and . . . well, it's a shock."

"I know." In the half-light she appeared vulnerable, the girl he'd fallen in love with. Hurting. He thought about pulling her close, but knew she'd reject him. Thankfully, the door flew open.

"Everything okay out here?" Lila asked, stepping outside.

"Just dandy," Rachel said, and for a second he thought she was going to let things lie. But that wasn't Rachel. She tilted her head and said, "You could've told me Lucas had a friend over."

Lila shrugged. "I did. When you first got here. Xander goes to school at Oregon, but practically lives here when he's not in Eugene. Uses the apartment Charles has for out-of-town clients. What's wrong?"

"Nothing," Rachel shot back, then said, "Unless you mean everything." And she swept into the house.

"Is she okay?" Lila whispered to Cade.

"Right as rain." The lie was easy. He didn't want anyone, especially not Stepmommy-Dearest, to know anything private about his kids or his ex-wife. Besides, he never had trusted Lila, not when she was pretending to be Rachel's good friend and certainly not as his father's second wife. There was just something about her that made Cade wary.

"We're all . . . you know. Unnerved. Upset. Freaked out. Whatever you want to call it. About Violet."

Rachel returned and swept past them. "If the kids need me—"

"They'll call," he said, but his ex-wife, purse and laptop tucked under her arm, keys in hand, was already down the steps and hurrying across the damp grass to her Explorer.

Lila's eyes narrowed and she was about to ask him another question when he spied from the lights of the house Mercedes Pope beelining toward him.

"Hey," she called. "I wanted to talk to you. About the Violet Sperry homicide. That's what it is, right? A murder?"

"Yeah." That much was out. There had already been a press conference. "Not my jurisdiction.

You'll have to talk to someone at the sheriff's department."

"Who? And don't tell me the public information officer. I know that."

"Then the officer in charge. Detective Kayleigh O'Meara."

CHAPTER 13

Rachel was still fuming when she pulled into the carport and cut the engine. Her whole life seemed to be unraveling. She was divorced, out of a job, her son in trouble at school, her daughter rebelling with a boy she sensed was trouble.

And then there was Violet.

Dead.

No, murdered.

She looked through the windshield to the fence that separated this covered area from the backyard. Listening to the engine cool and tick in the darkness, she said a silent prayer for the girl who had been one of the witnesses at her trial, the myopic eighteen-year-old who had sworn there was another shot that night.

And she'd been right. There had been tons of other guns going off, along with firecrackers and other fireworks. . . . It had all been so stupid.

But it couldn't be changed.

"Move on," she said and opened the Explorer's door, the cool of the evening fresh against her face. She used to love the darkness when twilight bled into night, but that was before her sleep was interrupted by night terrors.

As she was walking into the house, her phone

went off and she recognized her father's number on the screen.

"Hey, Dad," she said, letting herself inside the back door only to hear a rapid-fire click of toenails as Reno scrambled down the hall and into the kitchen.

"Hi." He spoke in his usual low tone as she took the time to pat Reno's head, then let him outside.

"I didn't hear that," she admitted as she watched the dog streak into the backyard. "Just got home. Reunion meeting. Had to let Reno out." She flipped on the back porch switch, illuminating part of the yard while the rest remained in shadow. She dropped her bag on a kitchen chair.

"I was calling to say I'm sorry to hear about your friend. Violet."

She imagined him in his house seated in his recliner facing the flat-screen that dominated one wall. He'd put on weight since he'd retired and had quit shaving every day. More than that, he seemed to have lost his drive, his will to get up every morning and face the day. With the divorce and retirement, he seemed to have lost direction. "Thanks. It's . . . it's sad. Beyond sad. Weird, y'know, and there I was with a bunch of kids from the class—well, I guess we're not kids now—and we all talked about Violet. No one can believe it."

"I know. It doesn't make any sense, but then what do I know?" He hesitated and she knew he hated not being a part of the investigation, no longer being a cop. "They're not saying much on the news about what happened." And then she heard it—that click of a beer tab being pulled. "Just that it looks like foul play was involved, a homicide."

"You know how the police work. How they don't say everything."

"They've already asked the public to come forward." A pause, and she imagined him taking a long swallow from his can. Then, "You'd think that someone might know something. Hell, everyone and his dog has a phone with a camera in it. And with all the security cams on buildings or for home protection and traffic cams, someone probably caught an image."

"Edgewater isn't Chicago, Dad, or even Portland. Lots of people around here don't even lock their doors."

"Damned fools."

"They think they can protect themselves."

"As I said, damned fools." She slid her gaze to the backyard, watched the dog sniffing the bushes, trotting in and out of the light cast from the porch lamp. "So . . . how're ya holding up?" he asked. "Tough day."

"Yeah. I'm okay." Well, that was a little bit of a stretch, but no reason to worry her father. He had enough and this day was hard on him, too, having been the first officer on the scene to find that his daughter had shot her half brother. She still remembered him whispering into her hair, "We'll get through this, honey, don't you worry," as he'd helped her into the back of the police cruiser. Although he'd been shell-shocked, he had taken charge. But things had never been the same. Never.

How could they be?

"Well, I just called to say I was thinkin' about you."

"Thanks, Dad."

"See ya later." And he clicked off, leaving her standing in the middle of her kitchen, staring out the window, phone in hand. The night of Luke's death had been the beginning of the end for so many things, including her parents' marriage.

So you not only killed your brother, you ruined your parents' marriage.

"Stop!" she said aloud.

Besides, that wasn't quite right. Rachel had sensed there was trouble between her mother and father before that night, an unnamed tension that she couldn't quite put her finger on. But it had been present in the sharp glances, long silences, and tight lips.

Looking into the darkened backyard, she watched the shadow of the dog as he sniffed around the fence, ferns, and firs before he came barreling back to the porch and whined to be let in.

"About time." She opened the door and he shot inside.

She poured herself a glass of wine and savored the first sip of the merlot. What was it about her? She wouldn't drink with friends but once she was alone . . . but then were her classmates really friends? Not for twenty years.

She wondered about Harper and Xander Vale. How far would they have gone had she not interrupted them? Surely they'd have put on the stops with the others in the room. But Dylan and Lucas had been wrapped up in their game . . . and that brought her to her son. Trouble at school. Then there was the Xanax—missing tablets or not? Was that the real reason Dylan had been in the altercation? Did it have to do with drugs? She'd been certain she'd smelled marijuana.

"Don't do this," she said aloud and took a gulp from her glass. The kids were with Cade now. Their father. She hoped to hell that Cade would talk to Harper and get through to her.

Yeah, right.

What were the chances of that?

And as for Dylan?

God only knew. Cade could handle him for the weekend.

Tonight, though, she had another project.

It was simple: Check out Xander Frickin' Vale.

Another long sip, then she topped off her glass, grabbed her laptop, and, with Reno at her heels, headed upstairs. In her bedroom she stripped off her clothes, tossed them into an overflowing laundry basket, then slipped into a pair of comfy pj's.

As the dog curled onto his bed, she headed across the landing to her office, which was located on the other side of the staircase. Like her bedroom, the office was tucked under the eaves, an attic conversion complete with built-in file cabinets, bookcase, and a long desk-height counter stretching beneath the single window. She set up her laptop next to her much larger desktop. She was good with technology and had honed her skills at finding out about people. She'd done work in HR at her last job along with bookkeeping, and then there was her side business, which, if things didn't improve on the employment front, she'd have to expand.

So how hard could it be to find out some details about Vale?

She cringed inwardly, but just a little. Was she crossing some forbidden line, breaching her daughter's privacy?

Hell no!

What about Vale's?

She figured he gave that up when he started French kissing her daughter.

Another long swig and she went to work, her fingers flying over the keys. Within seconds she was searching for anything she could on Xander Vale. His profiles, his conversations, his photos. She found him on Snapchat, Instagram, Twitter, and Facebook, to begin with, and his privacy settings were set low if at all, so she could snoop around easily.

She scanned each screen eagerly, digging for anything she could find on the mystery man, who turned out to be not that much of a mystery. The long and short of it was that he'd grown up in Portland, gone to high school at Wilson, and was currently a college junior majoring in general studies. There were pictures of him partying, of course, at football games, downing cans of beer with various girls, none of whom was her daughter.

Typical college boy.

His parents still lived in Portland, were still married, and had two other younger kids: a boy and a girl. Xander had been an all-league football player in high school.

Now he was enrolled in college, at the University of Oregon. That would put him down in Eugene, hours away, for most of the week until the end of the term in mid-June. Unless he was taking online classes.

And what had Xander said? That he was working part-time for Chuck, that he was going

to spend the summer working full-time in Edgewater?

"Not good." She took a sip from her glass and discovered it near empty, which explained the slightly warm, buzzy feeling running through her veins.

Maybe Harper's hot romance would flame out by summer.

"If only."

Unlikely. It was already late May. Summer was just around the corner.

From the bedroom, Reno gave out a low growl.

Rachel spun in her desk chair and knocked over the remains of her wine, the glass toppling, the dregs of wine sloshing onto her desk. "Crap!" Again Reno growled and this time she looked across the landing to the other side of the house where the dog, tail stiff, hackles raised, stood facing the window.

"It's nothing," she said, as much to herself as Reno, even though she couldn't help but feel a little niggle of anxiety, a tremor of fear as she righted the glass, sopped up what she could of the wine with some tissues. Then she snapped off the lights, crossed the landing in the darkness, and peered through the glass.

It took a second for her eyes to adjust as she stared into the backyard.

Nothing.

The landscape was calm.

Right?

Or did a shadow move in the darkness of the yard below?

She squinted, the dog tense beside her.

Was that a figure crouching or the arborvitae moving in the breeze? Every muscle in her body tensed. Did it straighten, hidden in the shadows as it was? Oh, God. For a millisecond she was certain she saw the silhouette of a man and Luke's image flashed through her brain; Luke as he might have been had he lived . . .

"No!" she said aloud.

Get a grip.

There's no one out there. No. One. What happened twenty years ago is over.

But the hairs on the back of her neck lifted and her skin prickled and her heart began to pound. The image wavered, then disappeared—a shadow, a puff of smoke, nothing more.

It isn't Luke. It isn't Luke's ghost. It's your own damned mind conjuring images that don't exist!

She bit her lip and saw no movement, heard nothing but the deep rumble in Reno's throat.

Snapping the blinds closed, she said, "It's okay," to the dog, who hadn't let down his guard. Reno whined a bit and still stared at the window. But it could have been anything that had caught the dog's attention: a squirrel, or the neighbor's cat, even a skunk or raccoon.

Or nothing at all.

"We're fine," she said and walked into the bathroom, where she leaned over the basin and splashed cold water on her face.

"There's nothing out there," she said, lifting her head to stare at her reflection in the mirror over the sink. "Nothing!" Her imagination was just running wild. That was all. "Pull it all together." But the pale image staring back at her, water running down its cheeks and chin, looked scared as hell. "You can't do this," she warned the woman in the mirror. "You're a mother. A single mother who needs a job. You cannot fall apart."

She gripped the edges of the sink and, closing her eyes, concentrated on her breathing.

In.

Out.

In.

Out.

When she felt calmer, her rational mind taking over, she returned to the bedroom and opened the blinds again.

The yard was empty.

The dog now nuzzling his bed in the corner before curling into it.

Everything was back to normal.

But the man outside, the ghost . . .

"Oh, for the love of God, Luke is not a ghost!" she muttered, angry at herself. This was insane. She was just stressed about the kids, about not having a job, about the anniversary of Luke's death, about the articles in the paper, about trying to get along with her ex, about every damned thing.

Get a frickin' grip!

She let out a breath as she walked into the office, nervously peered through the front window to see the street was empty. "Good." Taking a deep breath, she let her gaze travel to her computer, open to Xander Vale's Facebook page. The big man-child was still staring at her. "Stay away from my daughter," she said and then heard herself. Dear God, when had she become her own mother?

Wow. She wiped the remaining drops of wine with a clean tissue, wadded it, then tossed it in the trash. Then she closed down her search of Vale, making sure it was erased from her browsing history.

Just in case.

The dog began to make a racket again as she walked back into the bedroom, where Reno was on his back legs, trying to peer through the blinds. "Enough! Reno, down!" she ordered as her phone began to chime and vibrate on her nightstand.

Immediately, she thought something had happened with the kids. Who else would be trying to reach her, as it was nearly midnight?

She glanced down at the screen and noted it

wasn't Cade's number that flashed on the display. In fact, it wasn't any number she recognized.

The text was a simple message, three little words. Yet they had the power to send a chill down her spine.

I forgive you.

What?

Who? Who forgave her? For what?

Dread crawled through her as she waited. A minute passed. Then another. She'd thought that someone would type in that they'd sent the message in error, but when that didn't happen, she texted back:

Who is this?

Again she waited.

The dog crouched on the floor, nose on the wall, eyes at the shuttered window.

She licked her lips as the seconds strung into minutes.

"Fine." She called the number back and listened as the phone rang and rang and rang.

No answer.

Her heart was pounding and she told herself she was being ridiculous. It was a mistake; that was all. But the house seemed suddenly empty and the ticking of the clock downstairs seemed to resonate. Again Reno began to whine.

"Hush!"

She chanced another look, parting the blinds with her fingers and surveying the yard.

Nothing. No ghostly image crouching in the night.

"Don't freak," Rachel warned herself, but it was too late. Her nerves were strung tight, a headache beginning and the feeling that something was very, very wrong burrowed deep in her soul.

CHAPTER 14

The kids were asleep, Harper on the twin in the guest bedroom, Dylan on a daybed in the den. Cade grabbed a beer from the fridge and sat down at his laptop in the living room, some old cop drama playing silently on the television.

Though he'd left the physical file for the Hollander case at the office, he still could access digital files and he just wanted to check a few loose ends before he called it a night.

He'd found that Richard Moretti was going to be at the hospital on Monday, so he thought he'd try to locate the doctor and ask him about the night of Luke Hollander's death. The discrepancy in the file was just a note. One of the EMTs who'd been in the ambulance had claimed that Luke was alive when he'd been left at St. Augustine's, but that note had been crossed out and the ER doctor on duty, Moretti, had written that Luke had been DOA: dead on arrival. He'd been shot in the neck, clipping an artery, and he'd bled out, despite the best efforts of the emergency crew.

It wasn't much, but a little detail that caught his attention.

Also, he knew from conversations with Rachel

that after Ned had gotten his daughter into the police car, he'd followed in his own vehicle, and had made a stop at the hospital to check on his stepson, but it had been too late. Luke had already been gone.

So as Rachel waited at the police station under the wary eye of a female officer, Ned had gone home to break the news to his wife and take her to the hospital before they'd both returned to the police station.

Only then had Ned made his statement, which meshed with that of the second officer on the scene.

Cade took a swallow from his bottle. He knew the rest of the story. Rachel had been arrested, a case had been brought against her, but she'd been acquitted. Her father had been her most vocal supporter.

He thought about Ned Gaston, the father-in-law who'd sat in this very department. Cade and Ned had never been close, but maybe that wasn't a surprise. Ned and Melinda had split within a year of Luke's death and soon thereafter Rachel had gotten pregnant. With Harper.

One strike against Cade.

And there had been many more over the years. Not only had Cade and Rachel divorced and she'd accused him of an affair with Kayleigh, but also there was the fact that Cade was now, essentially, doing Ned's job.

Nope, there was no love lost between him and his ex-father-in-law.

But that still wouldn't keep him from talking to Ned about Luke Hollander's murder. He glanced at the newspaper lying on the coffee table and read the article about the homicide again.

This piece was pretty straightforward, just the facts as they had been reported and, to Mercedes Pope's credit, she didn't embellish the facts, or report rumors, or write anything that was too inflammatory.

But what was next? How could Mercedes sustain a series about the homicide and keep readers interested by merely repeating what everyone already knew?

By changing her reporting and inflating the petty drama?

And embellishing the story of Violet Sperry, a girl who'd been at the scene of the homicide, whose testimony had been crucial in the trial of Rachel Gaston, and who was now dead, the victim of another homicide, twenty years to the date of the first one.

Surely that new mystery wouldn't hurt circulation.

Not that Cade believed Mercedes Pope was behind either of the murders.

He was just damned sure she'd exploit them in order to sell a few more copies of the *Edgewater Edition*.

Click-click.

Shivering in the darkness, the air rushing through the building cold as death, Rachel squeezes the trigger.

Click-click-click-click.

She shoots again and real bullets whizz through the old cannery, though the muzzle of her gun remains dark as she squeezes off the rounds.

Bullets keep flying. Not pellets, as Luke had promised.

Her insides freeze.

This wasn't right.

Click-click.

Luke had said it was safe.

Luke had lied to her, but why? This was a game. It wasn't supposed to be real.

"No," she whispers, but she can't stop shooting; she just keeps squeezing and the damned gun goes off, round after round.

Click-click.

"No!" Rachel cries. She turns, trying to run, trying to throw the gun away. Down the chute to the river, that's it. Her heart thundering, her teeth gritted, she hurls the damned gun, throws it into the chute that opens to the Columbia. Hears it clatter against the rusting metal sides.

But when she looks at her hands again, the gun is still clutched in her fingers.

The same pistol?

Or another?

Real?

Or fake?

Panic strangles her.

She hears a sound behind her, the scrape of a shoe.

Spinning, she fires again, and again, and again. Click. Click. Click!

Luke appears before her, staggering back.

No!

He is bleeding as he falls, his face ashen.

"Oh, God. Luke! No, no, no!" She watches in horror as she sees the light in his blue eyes dim, his lids close.

"No . . . no . . . I didn't mean to—" Sobbing, she kneels beside him. He can't be dead, can't be. She feels as if her soul has been scraped raw as she touches his face. Cold. So cold. "I'm sorry. Oh, God, Luke, I'm so, so sorry."

At that moment, his eyes open and he stares at her. "Where did you get the real gun?" he whispers.

"From you. You gave it to me."

"Did I? I don't think so." Before her disbelieving eyes, his face begins to rot, his skin curdling away from his teeth, blood oozing, his nasal cavity exposed, his eyes bulging.

She screams and scuttles away, across the old plank floors, scrambling to her feet as she hears the others. Laughing. Screaming. Running.

Yet over it all the decaying, horrific thing lying before her whispers in a hoarse voice, "I forgive you."

What? No!

"Stop!" She pulls the trigger. Hard. On purpose. Aiming for the creature that had been Luke.

Click. Click. Click!

"I forgive you," the thing says again, his hideous voice a rasp, yet somehow ricocheting off the walls of the cannery.

"Stop! Just stop!"

Rachel's eyes flew open.

Her own words echoed in her head even as they jarred her awake.

Sweating, breathing hard, her heart pounding a frantic tattoo, she was lying in her bed, not at the cannery. Twenty years had passed. Luke was long dead. She was safe in her own bedroom. There was no gun. She wasn't going to shoot anyone, ever again. There was no gun. She wasn't going to shoot anyone. Not ever!

Pushing her hair from her eyes, she felt beads of sweat on her forehead. In fact, her entire body was moist. *Get a grip. For the love of God, Rachel, pull yourself together.*

At the foot of the bed Reno was curled in a ball, but he'd lifted his head to stare at her. As he always did when the onslaught of night terrors caused her to cry out. "Sorry," she said as if the dog could understand.

But she *was* sorry. So damned sorry. For everything that happened that night. If only she hadn't gone to the cannery. If only she hadn't gotten separated from Lila. If only she hadn't had the wrong gun.

What was it Luke had said in the nightmare? When she'd accused him of giving her the deadly, real pistol.

Did I? I don't think so.

She'd wondered about that. . . .

If only she'd known more about guns. . . . Hell, she'd been a policeman's daughter. She should have had some insight into what was real and what was not. But the truth was she'd never held a pistol before that night. Ned Gaston had seen enough damage with firearms to never allow one in the house. He'd even kept his own service weapon at the station.

"Don't do this," she told herself, speaking to the dark room. It was over. Long over. Luke was dead.

She eyed the clock: 2:47 a.m.

Her phone was on the nightstand and she checked it.

I forgive you.

The cryptic message was still there and had slid into her subconscious and her dream. Unfortunately, it had become part of her nightmare.

Click-click!

She froze.

Waited.

Click-click-click!

What the hell? Cautiously she threw off the quilt, crossed the room, and paused with her hand on the doorknob. Did she hear footsteps? Anything other than the—

Click-click!

From the bathroom.

Steeling herself, she turned toward the bathroom, with its partially open door. A soft breeze slid into the room as she entered and sensed no one. She slapped on the light switch. As she did, the shade moved in the window, slamming against the sill twice.

Click-click.

No wonder.

Because she'd cracked the window a couple of inches during her last shower, the shifting air was sucking the shade in and out, making the recurring sound she'd transferred to the firing of a pellet gun in her dream.

She caught sight of her reflection in the mirror over the sink: white pallor, wild eyes, mussed hair, her own fears visible.

"Oh, crap," she said and shook her head, talking to the woman in the glass. "Harper's right. You are a freak."

The reflection still looked scared as hell.

"Get it together," Rachel grumbled before shutting the window and starting back to the bedroom. But she knew sleep would be elusive, if not impossible, and still she was on edge.

If she'd left this window cracked, what about the others?

She had a routine she followed when locking the house for the night. She'd start in the basement, check the windows, cellar door to the stairwell, then head to the first floor, where she'd do the same, and finally double-check every room on the top level. She always stopped to engage the security system, but then reminded herself it wasn't working, hadn't been for months.

Rachel slid into her slippers, threw on her robe, and, with Reno on her heels, went to the basement where she noted everything was secure. The door to the outside was locked and bolted, the windows were pulled tight and latched, one in the laundry room and two more in the storage area, which was overflowing and had been since they'd remodeled the attic into living quarters. No matter how often she sorted and organized the tax records, old schoolwork, clothes that no longer fit, and a variety of old electronic equipment, the pile of plastic crates and boxes seemed to grow. She made a mental note to have Dylan work on it next weekend. He was always rooting around down here anyway.

On the first floor, she checked both the front

and back doors and the windows in the dining room, kids' rooms, and kitchen as well as the living room and bathroom. As Reno brushed past her in the kitchen to get to his water dish, she noticed the old copy of the *Edgewater Edition*, the pages folded open to the article about Luke's death in the cannery. Damn Mercy. Like a fishing hook dragging her deep into the sea, that resurrection of the details of Luke's murder was taking her into dark places she'd tried for years to put behind her.

The night terrors. The guilt. And now Violet's murder and the unsettling text message.

She tossed the paper aside, realizing she needed to do something about it. The newspaper retrospective was making it all worse.

She had to talk to Mercedes, hold her to the facts and convince her to let the painful story go. Rachel couldn't stop the nightmares or the horror over Violet's death, but this news series, this was a devil she could grab by the horns.

CHAPTER 15

Going to O'Callahan's hadn't been her smartest move.

Drinking her first mojito hadn't been wise either.

The second drink had been a mistake.

And the third? A definite disaster. Maybe even a catastrophe, Kayleigh thought as she woke up on Saturday morning, her head pounding, her thirst reminding her she hadn't tied one on like this for years. The room was shadowed, only the barest light of early dawn sifting past a rolling fog and the sheer curtains.

After consuming the three—or had it been four?—drinks, she'd made the smart decision not to get behind the wheel. Rather than call an Uber car she'd made the not-so-smart decision to allow a much more sober Travis McVey to drive her home.

So now she had two headaches, the one pounding behind her eyes, and the one snoring softly beside her.

"Idiot," she whispered.

She wanted to close her eyes and her mind to the night before, but couldn't. *What's done is done,* her grandmother used to say. *Deal with it.*

She rolled out of bed, threw on last night's

jeans and a long-sleeved T, then made a quick stop in the bathroom to wash her face and brush her teeth. Afterward she downed a cup of water and snapped her hair into an unruly ponytail.

Now or never.

She found McVey right where she'd left him, lying on his back, his body half out of the rumpled sheets, his eyes closed, dark lashes lying against bladed cheekbones.

God, she was a fool.

He was naked, of course, his one bare leg exposed, one of his arms folded over his bare chest.

Oh, geez.

What were you thinking?

That was the trouble. She hadn't been.

"Hey, McVey," she said, poking his shoulder. "Rise and shine."

"Wha—?" He blinked his eyes open, stared up at her, and smiled widely, then, as the situation hit him, the grin disappeared. "Oh, Jesus."

"Yeah. My thoughts exactly."

Neither one of them had ever expected they'd wake up in the same bed again. But last night things had changed. She remembered kissing hot and hard, their tongues colliding as they'd fallen onto the couch. Her hands had slipped beneath his shirt to touch rock-hard muscles and she'd let go, wrapping her arms around him, feeling his hands on her buttocks. A zipper had hissed

212

down and then suddenly he'd stopped. He'd wrapped his arms around her, held her close, and whispered into her mussed hair, "I don't think I can do this, Kay."

"What?" she'd murmured.

"You'd hate me forever."

"I already do," she'd teased and had kissed him again.

"No, that's the problem. You don't."

"So you're rejecting me?"

"Never." He'd stared at her a second. "Go to bed, Kayleigh."

He'd been right. She'd known it then just as she knew it now. Even though the effects of the drinks hadn't worn off last night, the weight of his words had gotten through. "I don't care," she'd said, and she'd meant it then.

He'd groaned, held her tight, and carried her into her small bedroom. They'd tumbled together onto the covers and she'd thrown all caution to the wind, crossing a bridge she'd thought was long broken.

Now, as more light made its way into the room, his gaze locked with hers as he, too, remembered, one big hand rubbing the beard shadow of his jaw. A strong jaw. In a handsome face. That she'd once thought she'd loved. A long, long time ago.

Before Cade.

"What were we thinking?" he asked, raking stiff fingers through his hair.

"Thinking didn't have much to do with it."

"Seemed like the right idea last night."

"Lots of things did."

"Amen to that." His eyes, deep set and intelligent, held questions that he didn't voice. But he obviously noted that she'd pulled on her jeans and shirt and had picked up her jacket, found on a hook near the door. "Looks like you want to get going."

"Lots to do. Big case."

"Yeah." He stood up then and she turned away as she caught a glimpse of his long legs and tight buttocks.

She felt a little catch in her throat. Which was just plain ludicrous. "I'll be in the living room." Was that even her voice—so breathy? What the hell was wrong with her?

As she walked into the living area, Kayleigh heard the metallic sound of a zipper. She went directly to the front door, where her bicycle was propped against the wall, to wait. When she turned and saw him, dressed and carrying the running shoes he'd kicked off with such force one had hit the closet door, causing it to rattle, she felt her throat go dry.

She had loved him and a bit of her heart cracked.

But she didn't want to remember their short period together, so she pushed any memories far into a dark corner of her mind as he sat on the edge of the couch and tied the laces, then slapped his legs and stood. His hair was still rumpled, the edges of his mouth remaining hard as he said, "Okay. Let's go get your car."

"Good idea."

Minutes later he was driving her through the awakening town, a handful of cars rolling down the streets, headlights and taillights glowing through the heavy mist oozing in from the sea.

"I could buy us coffee," he said, nodding toward a kiosk where cars were collecting near the corkscrew ramp leading to the bridge that seemed to disappear into the mist.

"Maybe another time."

But they both knew it would never happen.

"Okay." He pulled into the near-empty parking lot of the riverfront mall and parked. As she reached for the door handle, he said, "It was good to see you again, Kayleigh."

"Yeah. You too." She stepped outside before she said anything further, anything she might regret. "Thanks."

He, too, had gotten out of the car, letting it idle. "Bye."

She managed a quick wave, and as she unlocked her car, she wondered what the hell she was doing. What she'd done. What she'd wanted to do. She and McVey were long over; that romantic ship had foundered before it had ever really set sail. So why did she still feel a distant yearning? Why the hell had she so willingly—no, make that so *urgently*—made love to him?

Before the thought took root, she turned on her wipers and glanced in the rearview mirror, but his image was clouded by the condensation on the window.

"A good thing," she decided. She could only make out his silhouette as he leaned against his car, watching her drive off. She caught a glimpse of her own troubled eyes in the reflection. "God," she told the woman staring back at her, "for a smart woman you're an idiot when it comes to men."

Forget Travis McVey.

Oh, and while you're at it? Forget Cade Ryder, too.

The downtown block seemed as lifeless and tired as Rachel felt late Saturday morning as she strode toward the newspaper office, determined to straighten out one thing in her life.

Time to face Mercedes and deal with the stupid articles she was running on Luke's death.

God, why now?

Couldn't Mercedes just let the past lie?

Of course not.

As the sky darkened, Rachel steeled herself, then pushed open the door to the newspaper office, on the first floor of a two-story downtown building. Some of the buildings on this block had been refurbished, but not the offices of the *Edgewater Edition*. The same gold logo was emblazoned on the glass window, and inside the faded wood floors and oversized desks that had been there when Rachel was a kid, visiting for a class field trip, were still in place, the large room separated by half walls of cubicles.

"Can I help you?" asked a girl working on a laptop at her desk. Her brown hair was cut short, her face round, and she smiled as she looked up.

"I'm here for Mercy," Rachel said, not breaking her stride as she passed the young woman's desk.

"Wait. You can't go back there."

"Don't worry. We're friends." *At least, we used to be, before she cracked open my worst nightmare and served it up to the whole damned town.*

"But you're not supposed to go back there."

"It's okay. Really. She wants to talk to me."

"No worries," came a voice from behind a screen. "I'll handle it, Alexa." Mercy's head arose from the divider, a bland expression on her face as she tucked her reading glasses into her hair and motioned Rachel into the cubicle. "I'm surprised you came in."

"Me too." She eyed her once-upon-a-time friend. "I felt like I had no choice. That you backed me into a corner."

"We all have choices, Rachel." Mercy waved her into a single visitor's chair and Rachel sank

217

into it as Mercy sat behind the desk. "I just want the truth."

"You just want to sell papers."

"Okay. That too."

"And it doesn't matter that a lot of people are upset about it."

"News is news."

"Even if it's old news?"

"Not so old now," Mercy said. "Violet was there that night, and now someone's killed her."

"So?" Rachel said, stunned at the obvious track of Mercedes's thoughts. "You're trying to link the two deaths?" That didn't make any sense.

"I'm just saying it's a coincidence, that's all."

"You're pissing a lot of people off."

Mercy let out a short, humorless laugh. "Oh, I know." She retrieved a newspaper from the stack on her desk. "Lila's decided to be outraged. It wasn't evident at the reunion meeting, but you must've got her going or else she stewed on it and got pissed. Anyway, she's called me and demanded that I stop writing about it. And she got her husband to send me a 'cease and desist' e-mail. And that's just for starters. Then there's Annessa. She might not have come to the reunion meeting but she's damned certain that the articles about Luke's murder will have a negative impact, bad publicity for the building that she and her husband now own. She sent me a furious text and threatened legal action."

"She could have a point."

"Maybe, but this is the type of story that will bring subscribers to the paper. This next week I've got several other articles about the Sea View cannery. The history, including the heyday of the plant when it was a primary source of income in the town, and the decline of the industry. And now I've got the Violet Sperry murder angle, as well. I can tie her to the cannery. These are solid pieces, and together, they've got everything readers want: drama, tragedy, survivors. And it all happened right here in Edgewater."

"You sold out the friends you grew up with."

"Oh, come on, Rach. None of us are really friends anymore. Acquaintances, yes. And we share a history. But, really, I'm not out to hurt anyone, and I didn't publish anything that I can't back up with my notes. My goal is to bring out the truth from that night. That's the mission of a journalist: the quest for the truth."

"I call BS."

Mercy lifted a diet cola can on her desk, and then, realizing it was empty, tossed it into a blue bin. "You're entitled to your opinion."

"Don't dismiss me. I have two kids in high school who have already heard that their mother is a murderer, thanks to the last article. How do you think they feel? You've got a kid, Mercy. Are you going to let Daisy read your account of that night in the warehouse? How's it going to go down when her friends ask her if her mom was really an accessory to murder?"

"I was never formally charged with anything."

"And I was acquitted of all charges. And yet, here I am." Rachel jabbed a finger into the stacks of freshly printed papers. "I'm the killer who got away, in the world according to Mercedes Pope. What am I supposed to tell my kids?"

Mercy sighed. "What you've always told them. Look, I'm sorry if this embarrasses you."

"You think I'm embarrassed?" Rachel's voice rose, indignation burning through her. "That's not even close."

Mercedes lifted both hands. "Okay, so now, here's your chance to tell your side of it. I've wanted to interview you for days, so let's get down to it. Tell me everything you remember about that night. And since I'm doing a piece on the victim, on Luke, I'd like to hear what your home life was like. How you all got along, that sort of thing. Luke wasn't Ned's biological son, so there must have been some tension there."

"What? No!"

"His real father is a felon, right? Didn't he beat his wife, your mother, Melinda Hollander? And I heard that your dad was the cop who put Bruce Hollander away."

"That's . . . that's ancient history. No one's interested in it."

"Let's get this on the record." To Rachel's

horror, Mercedes actually turned, found her phone, and hit the record button.

"No!"

"I just want some perspective," Mercedes insisted. "To tell the story of the boy who lost his life in the cannery. Who, exactly, was he?"

For a second Rachel was stunned into silence as she thought about Luke as he truly was: complicated. Popular but secretive, an athlete who stood toe-to-toe with his stepfather if need be, a kid with a great sense of humor, a boy who loved to tease and taunt, though he always, *always* had his sister's back.

"I'm not talking about Luke."

"Then talk about that night. Let's hear your side."

Rachel stopped short, shaking her head as she stared down at the phone. "My 'side' is in my statement to the police. From twenty years ago. It hasn't changed and I'm sure you've got a copy."

"But I'd like your perspective now and how you look back on it. Maybe you remember some details that weren't in the original report. You know, tell me what you think, what you remember, now that your dad isn't a cop and looking over your shoulder."

"My father had nothing to do with it. What I said was the truth."

One of Mercedes's eyebrows cocked a fraction.

"We're all more careful when our parents are around. Especially as children."

Rachel stood then. "My story hasn't changed." Placing both hands firmly on Mercedes's desk, she looked squarely into the other woman's eyes. "And if you print one word that differs from what I said in the original police report, I'll sue you, Mercedes, and you can quote me on that." With that she turned and left.

"I'm quivering in my boots," Mercy called after her, and even had the audacity to laugh.

"You do that," Rachel ground out quietly as she flew out the door, turned away from the shop window, and collapsed against the stucco wall. A heavy mist was falling, quickly soaking into her hair. She hugged herself, trying to stop the tremors that rose from the cold deep inside her. So much had been ruined, and she didn't know when she'd have the energy for damage control.

After these stories went out, would she ever find another job? Would she lose clients from her small business?

Would the kids lose respect for her? Not that they treated her too well as it was, but she couldn't stand them using this as an excuse to make bad choices.

Would the kids be ostracized at school?

The rain began in earnest, and she pressed back against the building, wondering if she should make a run for her car or wait until it blew over. Suddenly she wished she had the kids this weekend. She'd make them some comfort food—tomato soup and grilled cheese—and try to have one calm afternoon in a week of constant turmoil.

Just then Rachel noticed a shadow moving across the street in the narrow alleyway between two buildings.

Someone stood there, his face in shadow. He seemed to be wearing a dark jacket, with the collar turned up and a baseball cap pulled low.

Was it just someone having a smoke?

No. He was simply standing there, watching her.

She glanced right and left to see if there was someone else he was keeping an eye on. Nope. She was the only person outside in the gray drizzle.

Icy fear, cold as the rain penetrating her scalp.

She told herself she was imagining things, that there really wasn't anything sinister about him, that she needed to keep her cool. But her skin prickled as she wiped the gathering moisture from her face and then cupped a hand to her forehead to shield her eyes and focus her gaze on him. A passing truck blocked her view momentarily.

And then he was gone.

The alley empty.

Leaving her to wonder if he had ever been there at all.

CHAPTER 16

Monday morning the sky was clear, a few stars fading, the air fresh as Kayleigh let herself in through the back door of the cedar and stone building housing the sheriff's department. A skeleton crew was manning the phones and desks until the shift change, so the offices were quieter than during the day, just a few voices and footfalls audible over the rumble of air running through ducts overhead.

Shedding her jacket in her locker, she was already mentally going over the Sperry case as she made her way to the lunch room. After picking up her car on Saturday morning, she'd spent most of the weekend reviewing notes and interviews on the Sperry homicide, studying evidence and checking alibis, and allowing a little time for watching football.

So far, Leonard Sperry's story was holding up. His fishing buddy had come through with an alibi, confirming Sperry's whereabouts near Bend in Central Oregon. Motel and restaurant receipts had placed him 250 miles from his home. The police were still waiting for cell phone records, but Kayleigh assumed the information from the phone company would confirm his alibi.

Meanwhile Sperry had provided a copy of

his wife's will, which indicated everything s
owned was to be left to him. For good measu
he had supplied his will as well, and the revers
was true: Had he predeceased her, she woul
have inherited all of Leonard Sperry's worldly
assets. They'd also provided a caveat that should
they die together, everything was to be divided
among ten charities.

They hadn't had children and the only sibling
either of them had was Leonard's estranged
brother in Arizona, outside of Phoenix. Neither
he nor their parents were mentioned in the wills,
as both Violet and Leonard had assumed they
would outlive them. Sperry had supplied copies
of their life insurance policies, two on Violet's
life to the tune of over three hundred thousand
dollars, enough for Leonard to buy out his
parents, or take a world cruise or whatever.

In the lunchroom, where Drummond, a wiry
deputy with a flat-top haircut straight out of the
fifties, was leaning over the sports page at one of
the round tables, she listened to the hiss of the
Keurig machine as it spat out her single cup. As
she added cream to her coffee, she made a mental
note to double-check that Leonard didn't have
a girlfriend tucked away somewhere. He didn't
seem the type and had appeared convincingly
grief stricken and horrified at his wife's murder,
but really, who knew what went on behind the
closed doors of a marriage? Theoretically it was

possible Sperry could have hired a killer to do his dirty work, pay the murderer off out of the insurance proceeds, and still pocket a lot of cash.

All tax free.

But it felt wrong.

She just couldn't see Leonard Sperry as the mastermind to take out his wife.

At least not yet.

Blowing on her cup so that the coffee would cool, she made her way to her desk, a neat and tidy space, not one picture resting on it nor pinned to the padded sides of the cubicle. Kayleigh liked to keep her work space clean and impersonal, almost sterile.

Quickly she scrolled through her e-mail. With any luck, today some footage from cameras in the area surrounding the Sperry home would come in soon. And Violet Sperry's gun. Where the hell was it? Part of the robbery, the only object taken? Seemed unlikely. Violet's laptop, money in her dresser—those valuables had been left behind. Only the gun was missing, according to the husband.

In her mind's eye Kayleigh imagined Violet hearing a noise, maybe the dogs alerting her, and grabbing her gun, going to investigate, and ending up confronting the intruder. In the ensuing struggle, the gun went off and the killer tossed her over the rail, then left in a panic that things had not gone as planned.

So what had been the plan?

And why the tape over her eyes?

Had he slapped it there and intended to kidnap or rape her, but she drew the gun and he was forced to kill her by pushing her over the railing?

She bit her lip, replaying the scene over and over in her mind.

Why was the tape placed over her eyes? Why not over her mouth, to cut off her screams?

Had the killer entered the bedroom, caught her unaware, and taped her eyes shut so she couldn't identify him later? Then somehow she grabbed her gun . . . but the dogs . . . and she would have woken. . . . No.

The struggle had happened outside the bedroom; that much seemed clear by the damage to the railing. Kayleigh only hoped that Violet had fought hard to fend off her attacker and that if she had, she'd managed to claw at him, collecting hair or skin beneath her fingernails. If so, the scrapings could be analyzed for DNA.

"And then we'll get you," she said, as if the killer could hear her.

A hand slapped her desk and she jumped, nearly spilling what was left of her coffee.

"Mornin', sunshine," Jerome Biggs said, and she realized she'd been at her desk for over an hour; the day shift was clocking in, voices and laughter breaking what had been near silence.

"Don't feel like sunshine."

"Rough weekend?" He smiled, a big, toothy grin that flashed white against his dark skin. Once a basketball player, now a detective, Jerome was her partner who had been on vacation the past week.

"Busy," she said, and for a second she remembered the weight of Travis McVey's body lying naked and sweating atop hers.

Oh. Good. Lord.

"Let me guess, workin' your tail off down here. Sperry murder."

"I worked from home, but yeah. Since you were off having the time of your life on vacation last week, let me catch you up."

"I don't know if painting the house in this weather counts as 'having the time of my life,' but yeah, I heard we caught the case. Bring me up to speed."

So as he leaned a hip against her desk, Kayleigh told him all the details with one exclusion.

She didn't mention that she'd called Cade Ryder to the scene.

She didn't need the lecture about jurisdiction, or crossing all kinds of lines, both professional and personal. Biggs would find out soon enough.

But for now, she kept that bit of information to herself.

Hands shaking, Rachel stared at the bottle of Xanax tablets and wondered if it was worth it to finally relax and get some sleep. She put the bottle on the shelf in the medicine cabinet, pressed her palms to her chest, and tried to take a deep breath.

She had to get a grip.

The last two nights had begun okay but disintegrated into night terrors that kept her from falling back to sleep. Now here she was on Monday morning, a basket case when she should be online looking to send out a new wave of job applications or, at the very least, drumming up customers for her freelance business.

She would be relieved to have the kids back this afternoon, grateful for the company and the routine of corralling them. Last night had been particularly bad as she'd been pulled from another nightmare by the frantic barking of the dog, who'd been pawing at the bedroom door to get out.

"Reno, stop!" she'd ordered, pushing back the covers in a mixture of annoyance and alarm. She hadn't wanted to get out of bed, but usually the dog didn't go off unless something was wrong.

Groaning, Rachel had forced herself to her feet and found her slippers, knowing she'd have to check the house from top to bottom. As soon as she opened the bedroom door, the dog disappeared down the stairs, as if honing in on a target.

Oh, God. Was someone in the house?

Pausing to grip the banister at the top of the staircase, Rachel had listened cautiously but heard only the staccato bark of the frantic dog. Pulse thrumming in her ears, muscles taut, she had hurried down.

"What's wrong with you?" she'd called as she found the dog pacing at the front door, sniffing at the threshold.

Was someone there?

Biting back fear, she'd ignored her accelerating heartbeat and reached for the door handle to ensure the bolt had caught. It was locked, thank God, but that didn't stop the dog from letting out a new string of guttural barks.

Reno was on alert. Nose to the door, he was ready to bolt outside. His flesh quivered, the fur on the back of his neck stood at attention, and he let out a high, nasal whine when she refused to open the door.

As if he'd scented a squirrel or raccoon or some other night creature daring to cross his yard.

"Oh, geez." She let out a sigh. "Stop it."

But the dog wasn't about to give up and started scratching frantically at the door, ready to bolt outside and scare off or kill the invader.

"You're being ridiculous. Stop it! Now," she'd ordered and stood on her tiptoes to peer through one of the three small windows that ran across the top of the door. She half expected to see a coyote scurrying through the shadows. Instead she caught a glimpse of a smallish dog hurrying past, a man in dark clothes, cap over his ears, holding the animal's leash in one hand, and something else—a bag of some kind—in the other.

Just a guy walking his dog.

At three in the morning?

Who walked their dog in the middle of the night?

She felt a frisson of fear scuttle down her spine as she watched the man glance back at the house, then hustle his dog into a white sedan parked three houses down. Within seconds he was driving off, taillights disappearing as he rounded the corner.

"It's nothing," she'd told the dog, but didn't believe it for an instant.

It was odd.

Out of the ordinary.

What had her father said about things that seemed out of sync? That if something seemed wrong or out of place, it usually was.

She heard his advice as if he were standing next to her: "Pay attention, Rach. It's the little inconsistencies, something a bit unusual, a tiny detail that a person remembers that often is the start to cracking a case."

Her calves had begun to ache from the strain of standing on her tiptoes, so she'd lowered herself and tried to twist the knob and open the door. It didn't budge. Locked securely. She started her security ritual, heading down to the basement to double-check that every lock was engaged, every dead bolt thrown, every window unmoving until she was certain the house couldn't be breached. Although she knew the house was secure, she didn't feel safe. Not tonight.

"We'll be fine," she'd told the dog as she'd settled into bed again.

But she'd known it was a lie.

Now, her body was riddled with exhaustion, jacked with stress.

Anxiety was nothing to sneeze at; nothing to ignore. Rachel knew it. But as she stared at the pills in her medicine cabinet, she couldn't get herself to pop one. She'd been off the Xanax for weeks now and taking the medication seemed like a step backward. Even though she realized that wasn't the case, she didn't want to lean on any more medication. She palmed the bottle, counted the pills, making certain no more had gone missing. All accounted for, but maybe she should have pushed the kids harder. Was she too loose with them? A bad parent. Well, she'd have a look in their rooms today, before they got home. A parent's prerogative.

She recapped the bottle and threw on running clothes, snapped on Reno's leash, and headed out.

Her nerves were still jangled from lack of sleep, and throughout the weekend she'd felt a trepidation about her solo runs in the early morning, but she refused to be intimidated. Couldn't allow it. With her dog by her side and pepper spray in her pocket, she headed out the back door and pushed through the gate into the street. Reno kept pace as she ran downhill toward town, where a lingering mist still clung to the river. The air was crisp, the sky a promising, bold blue, and she suspected the mist would burn off by noon.

The cool air should have cleared her head, but instead the text floated through her mind.

I forgive you.

Received twenty years from the day of Luke's death.

Of course she'd first thought of her brother; he was the one person whom she'd so horribly wronged, but he was long dead and she didn't think St. Peter was handing out cell phones at the pearly gates. Nope. The text was from a living, breathing person, either a mistake or a prank.

And she was leaning toward the idea that it was sent in error. She avoided a puddle and kept running, thinking of anyone who might have sent it. One of the people at the reunion meeting? Someone close to Luke?

Lila, who'd been left to deal with having his baby?

Mercedes, who was hell-bent to write her series about his death and was pissed that Rachel hadn't agreed to an interview?

233

Nate, his best friend, who had seemed so untethered after Luke's death?

Her own mother?

No, no. Not Melinda!

His father then? Out of prison recently.

What about a half dozen others . . . friends who were close to him?

But why wait all these years and then suddenly now try to freak her out?

Who hated her that much?

She passed by the cannery, didn't stop, just circled back and ran directly home. She smiled as Reno trotted the familiar path to the side gate and back door. Sliding the lock closed, she pushed off her sneakers, let Reno off his leash, then reached for a mug.

After coffee, a shower, and a cup of yogurt, she sat at her computer for a while, going over responses to her resumes. Two. One that, should she get the job, would require relocation to Seattle.

No thanks. Not until Dylan had graduated. If then.

The other with a note that the position she'd inquired about had been filled.

"Two strikes," she said. Lapsing back to her former worries, she wondered about telling Cade about the text message. As a cop he could make inquiries.

It wasn't a threat.

Just forget it.

She had work to do. The kids were gone. Wouldn't be home until after school, so despite all of her lectures about privacy, she braced herself for the invasion of her kids' rooms. Determined to get to the bottom of whatever her son was hiding, she ignored all the crime scene tape and "Do Not Enter" warnings posted over Dylan's door and started searching.

She didn't know what she was looking for.

She hated to think what she might find. A cache of some kind of contraband? Drugs? Weapons?

She felt like a thief slipping into a house that was still occupied.

Ludicrous as it was, her heart was pounding and she was jumpy, though she had every right to search his room. This was her house and, more importantly, he was her son; she was responsible for his health and welfare.

She did worry that he had probably set up cameras in the room and even now could be watching her on his phone.

Tough.

The room was a sty, but that would be something he'd have to do himself once he was home. She was laying down the law.

So she didn't pick up the cans and plates and trash on the floor. Nor did she change his bed or even straighten the covers, even though she'd checked between the mattress and box springs, then under the bed. Years of dust had gathered there, along with more cans, bottles, and dirty paper plates that had been stashed out of sight. She viewed the bottom side of the box springs.

Nothing.

She opened the vent from the furnace.

All she found was a fork that had slipped through the slatted cover.

His bookcase was cluttered, but hid nothing. His nightstand drawer was stuffed with a box of Band-Aids, a half-finished assignment for a class he took in grade school, a TV remote, lip balm, a pack of tissues, a bag of cough drops, and various game controllers. The area around his computers showed nothing out of the ordinary and, of course, the computers were all password protected so she couldn't check what he'd been doing online.

His chest of drawers held folded clothes, nothing hidden beneath or behind.

In the closet his hamper was full of dirty, wrinkled clothes, and there were boxes of old toys and treasures that, she assumed, he no longer noticed. Some shirts were draped on hangers. There were a few small, empty boxes. Overall, nothing out of the ordinary.

She saw that his shoes were kicked into a corner and that's when she noticed a slight bulge in the carpet, just inside the bifold closet door, a little lump no bigger than a mouse. She bent down and ran her hand over the bump.

Thankfully it didn't move. Didn't appear to be alive.

With a little more inspecting, she saw that the carpet wasn't tacked down just inside the door. Instead it was taped, and within? A sock containing a thick roll of money: ones, fives, tens, and twenties. Eight hundred and thirteen dollars. Even though he supposedly owed a hundred dollars to that bully Schmidt for some kind of computer bet and acted as if he couldn't pay it, the kid was willing to work off a loan with Rachel.

"Not good," she said aloud, her dread mounting. She tucked the sock and money in the back pocket of her jeans, then continued searching the closet, half expecting to find a stash of weed, pills—God knew what kind of drugs—in the toes of his shoes or pocket of a jacket. She thought of the pills from her own bottle of Xanax, pills that she'd thought had gone missing, and the way Harper had shown her disdain.

We didn't steal your damned drugs. What do you think we'd do with them? . . . Sell them at school?

Dylan had appeared stunned, as if it had never crossed his mind. Or had she misread his guilt?

She went over his room again, locating nothing more, then wracked her brain for other possible hiding spots.

The back porch where he kept his bike? She

quickly made a check, but it turned out to be clean.

The shed next to the carport, where his skis and skateboard and camping gear were tucked away?

Nothing there either.

She stood for a second in the drive, as sunlight pierced the high, slow-moving clouds and a crow cawed from the house's eave.

Maybe he was hiding something at Cade's? Would he dare mess with a cop's instincts and leave anything under his father's nose?

No—primarily because whatever it was wouldn't be handy.

This business with Dylan was bad, but she sensed there was a lot more going on with her daughter.

Harper was seventeen; nearly on her own. Rachel felt worse about searching through her things, but did anyway, in both Harper's bedroom and bathroom. She didn't find anything unexpected. No weed. No cigarettes. No hidden half-drunk bottle of booze. No unexplained stash of money. No contraceptives, which, considering how things were playing out, might not be such a bad idea.

So they were destined to have one of those mother/child talks both kids hated once they got home. In the meantime, she had a website to update and a job search to continue.

She walked to the kitchen to grab her phone,

and just as she was about to grab it from its charger, it started vibrating on the counter. She picked it up and noticed the phone number on the small display was unfamiliar, no name attached to it. She thought of the text she'd received, but that was a different cell number completely; she knew—she'd memorized the digits.

"Hello?"

"Hi. This is Rachel, right? Rachel Ryder?" a woman asked, then didn't wait for an answer. "I thought I should call you."

"Sorry, who is this?"

"Oh. My. It's Ella Dickerson. From across the street. Jim's wife."

Rachel's heart sank as she pictured her neighbor, a white-haired woman pushing eighty who was always working in her yard and complaining about one thing or another. There was her arthritis, her children, or her husband, whose latest offense, or at least the most recent one Rachel had heard about, was purchasing a seventy-two-inch flat-screen, "to watch more sports, if you can imagine. I swear they're on twenty-four/seven!" Ella was the neighborhood busybody who knew everything about everybody on the street.

"Your front door," Ella was explaining. "I mean, have you seen it? Oh, dear. You'd best take a look. I assume it was vandalized and I thought you should know if you hadn't seen it, but if you have, then—"

"What are you talking about?" Rachel asked, already walking through the house.

"I was afraid you hadn't seen it. I said so to Jim. I saw it when I went to pick up the paper this morning. I told Jim that you couldn't possibly know—"

"I don't get what you mean." Rachel unbolted the door and flung it open to find out what the nosy neighbor was talking about.

She took one step onto the porch, then stopped, her heart plummeting as she saw the single word, scrawled in red paint on her black door:

KILLER

CHAPTER 17

Cade pushed the speed limit on his way to Rachel's house. When she'd called he'd immediately heard the strain in her voice, the edge to it. "I think you'd better come over here." She'd sounded wound tight.

"Why?"

"Just come, Cade. Are you working today? Can you come now?"

"On my way."

He didn't like the way she sounded.

At her house he caught sight of Rachel standing on the porch by the front door, an ugly message painted on the panels behind her.

"Oh, Jesus." He parked on the street and jogged up the walkway, aware that the neighbors across the way, an older couple, were in their yard watching the drama unfold. Cade eyed the door and his insides clenched. "What happened?"

"I don't know. I didn't see it until the neighbors called. I didn't notice it when I went for a run this morning, but you know when I leave the house I go in and out through the back door. Anyway, Mrs. Dickerson called to tell me something was up and I came outside and found this."

Painted in a crimson shade that made him

think of blood, the message was like a shriek in a horror film: KILLER.

Rachel was ashen faced, but holding it together. "I was going to start painting over it, but I thought I should call someone. . . ."

"You were right." He was already whipping out his phone and tamping down his fury. "Vandalism is a crime. Not a prank. But I think someone other than your ex should take the report." He made the call, and Voss, who was on duty and in the area, promised to be at the house within ten minutes.

"Officer Voss is on her way," he told Rachel as he stuffed his phone into his pocket and eyed the vandalized door. "So this happened last night?" he said, pointing at the entrance to the house.

"I think so."

He glanced across the street and saw the Dickersons hadn't left their stations in their yard. Standing side by side on the other side of a short wrought-iron fence guarding a row of azaleas and rhododendrons, she in a long housecoat, he in a T-shirt and jeans, held up by suspenders, they watched the drama unfold.

Rachel, obviously aware of the Dickersons, and now a bike rider doing a double-take as he saw the door, touched him on the arm. "Maybe you should come inside."

Once they were in the hallway where Reno greeted him and the door with its ugly message pulled firmly shut, he said, "So tell me."

"The long and short of it is that I had a bad dream, about Luke."

Of course. He didn't say it.

"But that's not the worst of it."

"Meaning?"

"Odd things have been happening. I keep hearing things, seeing things, and it's not just me. Reno does, too," she said, amping up a bit. "And . . . I received a weird text. . . . I mean, it was as if Luke had sent it. I know that's impossible—crazy—but . . . here, let me show you." She patted the back pocket of her jeans and then frowned. "I guess I left it . . ." She walked quickly down the hallway and into the kitchen and he followed. "Here . . ." After retrieving her cell from the counter, she studied the screen, punched out some commands, found what she was looking for, and handed the phone to him.

"I forgive you," he read the text aloud, his insides chilling. He glanced up at her. "Who sent it?"

"Don't know. I tried to text and call back—no one responded."

"Could be a mistake. Sent to the wrong number." But he didn't believe it for a second, not with the message—the vile accusation—sprayed across the door.

"I don't think so." She glanced out the window. "I should tell you I saw something last night."

"What?" *Real? Or imagined?*

The doorbell sounded, and the dog started barking.

Patricia Voss had arrived.

Good. He wanted to hear it all, but thought it would be best if someone else heard the story. Someone with a little distance, someone who hadn't spent nights beside her in bed as Rachel woke with night terrors, someone who hadn't had to calm their children when their mother was half crazed with fear, someone objective and professional.

"Reno, hush!" Rachel opened the door, quick introductions were made, and Voss set up a recorder to take Rachel's statement. They were in the living room, where the clock ticked over the fireplace, nearly buried in the framed pictures of Harper and Dylan crowded upon the mantel. Cade felt an uncomfortable pull remembering when some of the photographs had been taken. Christmas when the kids were just starting elementary school, Harper missing teeth, Dylan sporting a buzz cut that Rachel had hated.

He stood near the couch where Rachel sat, Voss in a winged-back chair at one end of the coffee table, the dog finding a spot on the corner of the rug.

"You have any idea who would have done this?" Voss asked, her pen poised to take notes to back up the recording.

Rachel shook her head. "No. But I think maybe I saw him."

"Him. A man?" Voss asked and Cade felt his jaw tense.

"It was last night, well, around three in the morning." She explained about having a bad dream, being awakened by the dog's barking. Downstairs, she'd looked through the windows in the door to see a man and a dog getting into a car at the end of the street.

"A dog?" Cade repeated, feeling a jolt.

"Can you describe the man?" Voss asked.

"No, it was too dark; he looked . . . average, I guess, and he was carrying something. And, like I said, he was walking his dog."

"What kind of car?" Cade asked, already guessing.

"Don't know. Just what looked like a white, or maybe silver, sedan."

He pressed her. "You get the plate number or notice if it was from Oregon?"

"No."

Of course not, but his mind was spinning ahead. "And the dog? What kind was it? What breed?"

"I couldn't say. Small or medium sized, I guess, and light colored."

"Could it have been a beagle?"

She lifted a shoulder. "Again, it was dark, but maybe. About that size."

"You know anyone named Frank Quinn?" Cade asked.

"What?" She looked up at him, her lips turned into a frown as she slowly shook her head. "No."

"He lives on Toulouse Street," Cade said.

"I said I don't know him. Why?"

"The other day when I came over?" He explained about the guy looking for his dog, a man who drove a white four-door sedan with Idaho plates, and as he spoke he noticed the panic starting to rise in his ex-wife's eyes.

"I have no idea who he is," she said. "You think he's the same person?"

"Maybe." He kicked himself for not delving deeper into Frank Quinn. "Tell Voss about the text."

"What text?" Voss asked.

"This one." Rachel found her phone and handed it to Voss.

" 'I forgive you'? From who?"

"That's it. I have no idea." Rachel repeated to Voss what she'd already told Cade, including explaining that she'd tried to contact the caller by phoning and texting back with no response.

Pushing her hair out of her eyes, she sighed. "It came on the anniversary of my brother's death. Twenty years ago."

"I read about what happened in the paper." Voss's eyes narrowed. "So you think whoever called you is forgiving you for being involved in his death?"

"I don't know."

Voss pressed. "Who would need to forgive you? Someone who thought you were guilty, right?"

Rachel's face tightened. "I guess."

"Who?"

"I don't know." Rachel looked away. "I mean, Luke's dead so it can't be him." She didn't seem convinced.

"Of course not," Cade said.

"I know, but I had this feeling . . . I don't know. It sounds crazy, but that someone wants me to believe it's him."

"It wasn't Luke," he said firmly. She couldn't go down that impossible track.

"I know." Her voice was a little sharp. Defensive.

Though it had been twenty years, she'd never really gotten over her half brother's death; she'd always blamed herself.

"It's probably someone who took Luke's death personally," Voss thought aloud as she underlined something in her notes. "Someone close to him?"

Immediately, Cade thought of Lila. Good old Stepmommy. Mother of Luke's son. But why? Yeah, there had been some tension between Lila and Rachel over the years, family stuff, but nothing that would lead to this. And why now? No.

"We'll check with the cell phone company," Voss was saying. "If it was accidental, which I doubt, or if it was some kind of a sick prank, we'll figure it out."

"But if it's a burner phone?" Cade wasn't liking the turn of his thoughts. He wasn't buying into the "mistake" theory. Especially not with the grotesque message spray-painted on the door. Someone was trying to freak Rachel out, and he thought it might just be Frank Quinn.

"You know the drill. If it's a burner we'll try to track it down from the store where it was purchased. If there's no record of who bought it, no credit or debit card receipt or check, if the guy used cash, hopefully there will be camera footage of the buyer. And we will double-check all the security cameras in the area that might have images of the man and his dog."

"What if it's a burner app?" Rachel asked. "You can do that, y'know. There are apps that disguise your number, make it impossible to trace."

Cade had heard of them. "There has to be some kind of trail, digitally."

Rachel shook her head. "I think everything can be encrypted."

"I'll dig deeper on Frank Quinn. Find out if he lives in the neighborhood or owns a Buick with Idaho plates," Cade said. Again he thought of Violet Sperry, murdered in her own home, and his blood turned cold. Was there a connection?

Voss said, "Didn't I see a camera on the porch?"

"Not working," Rachel admitted.

Cade winced inside. He should have dealt with it when he still lived here.

"It's old school," Rachel said, "put in by the people who owned the house before we did over twenty years ago. It wasn't working, always going off, so I canceled the service and was going to install a new one, connected to an app on my phone." She smiled weakly. "I just hadn't gotten around to it."

Voss gave a curt nod. "You might want to make that a priority."

Amen to that, Cade thought. They went through a few more questions, and the tech came, dusted for prints, and left, with Voss taking off a few minutes later.

Which left him alone with his ex-wife. In the living room they'd once shared. It felt right but different. Odd. She hadn't changed the room much other than painting it a lighter color, a neutral gray, rather than the tan it had been. She'd also filled the space where his recliner had sat with a smaller chair.

"You okay?" he asked.

"Do I look okay?"

"Uh, no. You look like—"

"Hell. I know. I look like hell."

"You don't—"

"I do. Crap." She raked her fingers through her hair and stood. "You know, ever since Luke died, I've had these nightmares."

"Yeah." He was nodding, had lived through them.

"And I've always told myself to somehow put it behind me; that what's done is done, to move on. And I've tried. But this . . . Mercy dredging everything up again in the paper, and the reunion meeting with all the people who were there that night, and now . . . this." She held up her phone, then pointed to her door. "It's freaky."

"You're right and I don't like it."

"And then there's Violet." Shuddering, she sat down again and tucked her feet under her. "Is there any news about what happened to her?"

"Not that I know of."

"Well, it's disturbing. Worse than disturbing." She was rubbing her arms as if suddenly chilled.

"I know," he said.

"I'm afraid it makes me like a, you know, a crazy, overprotective mother."

He slanted a smile and took the chair Voss had vacated so he could look out the window to the Dickersons' now empty yard. "The kids might agree with that."

"Do you think it's true?" she asked and turned her eyes up to him as Reno stood, stretched, then wandered toward the back of the house.

"Crazy? No. Overprotective?" He held up his hand, then tilted it. "Sometimes. A little." But even as he said it, he thought again about Violet Sperry and her bizarre death. There was probably no connection to what was going on here—God, he hoped not—but he didn't want to just dismiss

250

the thought. "We all need to be careful." He didn't want to alarm her, send her over the edge, but he couldn't pretend that the Sperry murder wasn't cause for serious concern.

"The last thing I want to be is overprotective. After growing up with my own parents." She rolled her eyes. "I swore I'd never be the hovering, nosy parent my mother was, and as for my dad, I saw what being married to a cop was like, how he wasn't home for a lot of the holidays or major events."

He felt his insides turn to stone. How smart had his own choices been, he wondered. "Sometimes history repeats itself. The choices we make."

There was a bit of a hesitation before she said, "Then I guess I should make better ones."

"Maybe we both should."

She stared at him a sec, then changed the subject. "How was your weekend with the kids? We all left on bad terms Friday night. I wasn't happy with either of them. Dylan because of him ditching class and Harper because of . . . you know. The new boy or man or whatever in her life!"

"Dylan's been fine; if it bothers him that he's in trouble at school, he doesn't show it and won't talk about it. Harper says you blew things all out of proportion, that she was just kissing Xander and that she's . . . Let me get this straight." He thought for a second. "Oh, I remember. Same old line I said way back when. Harper claimed that she was almost eighteen and when she turned eighteen she could do whatever she wanted."

"Like eighteen changes everything. The magic now-I'm-an-adult card." She smiled. "She'll find out. But I can't push back too hard against this boy because it'll just drive her further into his arms. Ugh."

"She wants to go to a concert with him in Portland next weekend. Saturday night."

Rachel let out a sigh. "No."

"Why not?"

"It's two hours away, for starters."

"She's gone before."

"But we've known the kids, the parents."

"Lila vouches for him."

"Since when do you trust Lila's judgment?"

"Okay, point taken. But Harper's seventeen. She'll be eighteen in October."

"Which she so often reminds us."

"Off to college."

"Not until next year," Rachel said, then skewered him with a glare. "You're promoting this? I can't believe it."

"He might not be so bad. I figure you've probably already checked him out online, looked into his social media accounts."

She ducked that one. "It's not about bad or good, Cade, you know that. We've been over it before. I just don't want her to make a mistake she can't unmake."

"Like you."

"It was different! I wanted to marry you. I wanted your baby! It just came in the wrong order."

"Is that so bad?"

She folded her arms and stared at him. "I want my daughter to have more options and it's not like she's in love with Xander Vale; they're just in lust. Hot for each other." She crossed her arms under her breasts in anger, unaware that she was lifting them. "I just hope they *think* before they act."

"Harper's not an idiot."

"Neither was I. Except when it came . . . when it came to you."

He let out a derisive laugh. "Me too. You know, she's texting all the time and when I ask her about it, she's always texting 'a friend' or she'll cop to communicating with Lucas, but I'm pretty sure it's Vale."

"When has she ever texted Lucas?"

"They were pretty tight as kids," he reminded her. Back in the days when he and Rachel were still married and Lila and Rachel had been close. Since the divorce, things had changed for all of them.

"And now she's got a renewed relationship with him."

"Looks like."

"Because of Xander Vale."

"Probably. You remember how it was. When we were in 'lust' and hot for each other."

She actually blushed. "As I said, 'options.' Like college. So she can get a bigger view of the world than just from Edgewater, Oregon. It wasn't the worst thing that happened to me, okay, I'll admit it. Having Harper and marrying you, ending up with Dylan. I wouldn't change a thing. Well, not most things anyway." She looked away, no doubt thinking about his betrayal. And then, as if the conversation had gotten too deep, she waved in the air as if to dismiss her words. "So, look, don't worry about the door, okay? I'll deal with it," she said with more resolve than he'd seen in her in a long while. "I panicked after Ella called, but I'm okay now." She glanced at the door. "Nothing a can of spray paint can't cover up until I can paint the whole thing. I was thinking of changing the color anyway."

"And the security alarm?"

"My . . . *our* son owes me and he's got the skills, I think. Maybe even the equipment."

He withdrew his keys from his pocket. "Any kind of guard dog?" he asked.

"Reno?" She let out a humorless laugh, and the dog, hearing his name, wagged his tail, then circumvented the coffee table to stand next to Rachel and place his head on her lap. She scratched him behind the ears. "Not much of one."

"Maybe you should upgrade."

"Yeah, right." To the dog she said, "Don't listen to that. He's just kidding."

His phone buzzed in his pocket and he checked the screen. A text from the precinct. "The job," he said to her, standing. "The boss wants me in early."

"Then you'd better go."

"You'll be okay?"

"Never better," she said, though they both knew it was a lie.

"I can come back, help clean up the door. I've painted a few panels in my day."

"No, I've got this," she said firmly as she stood. "You need to get to work."

"Forget work." He paused, knowing she wanted to handle things herself; it was her thing. "I've got time coming. I have no problem calling in."

"No. I'll be fine." She flashed him one of her rare smiles and her gold eyes gleamed for a second. "Remember: I've got Reno."

"Guard dog less than extraordinaire."

"Exactly."

He didn't like it but saw she couldn't be moved. "Okay. Fine. But I'll be by to make sure the security system is online."

"Really, Cade, you don't need to do this."

"Yeah, I think I do," he said and decided to be brutally honest. "My kids live here with my ex-wife, and contrary to what she may believe, I care about her, want her safe."

Rachel drew in a long breath. "Oh . . . I don't think that . . ."

"I don't care what you think, Rach, it's the truth." She looked about to argue again, so he started for the door. "In the meantime, keep the dog on alert and the doors and windows locked."

CHAPTER 18

Dylan was sweating bullets.

His knee was twitching and he kept glancing at the clock, ticking off the seconds of the school day, maybe of his life.

His mom was on to him.

He saw her poking around his room this morning, finding his stash.

Shit! Shit! Shit!

Ten minutes left in class. Then he'd have to avoid that moron Schmidt and his goons, then deal with the smug assistant principal.

He felt as if the walls were closing in on him, that he had nowhere to turn, no one to confide in.

"Dylan?" Tori Suzuki's voice brought him back to the present, at his terminal in the library media room, where he and the rest of the class were supposed to be finishing their English essays.

He looked up and caught her smiling at him from the next computer terminal. "Sorry to bother you, but . . ."

Dylan's heart jolted. When Tori smiled at him, with her dark eyes and pretty face framed by shiny black hair, he could barely concentrate. She had a boyfriend, so he didn't think she was actually flirting with him, but she always sat next

to Dylan if they were in the media room during second period, and he was good with that.

"What?" he asked, keeping his voice low so the library monitor wouldn't pounce on them. Exams were proctored, but since it was harder to cheat on an essay, no one watched too closely.

"I was wondering if you could show me that trick you know to make your essay look a little bit longer? Without changing the margins."

He got it. If the essay wasn't five pages, you couldn't get an A. And it was easy enough to put all the punctuation in thirteen-point type for starters. He had a few other tricks as well.

"Sure."

She leaned in, so close he could smell her perfume. He tried not to notice; he couldn't get distracted by anything, not even Tori.

He swallowed hard.

"You think you could set it up for me?" she whispered.

"Sure," he said again. As if it were the only word he knew. Girls like Tori made him nervous, even nice girls who already had a boyfriend. He shot a glance over his shoulder to see if anyone was paying attention. Nah. Holding his breath, he leaned over to her keyboard and opened the systems file. A few changes, probably less than sixty seconds, and he was done. "Try it that way."

She opened her file, scrolled through it, and

flashed him a bright smile. "Wow! Perfect! It's five pages now. That's amazing."

Dylan nodded.

"Thank you *so much!* You're so good at that." She paused for a second, then whispered, "Hey, is it true? What they're saying about your mom?"

"My mom?" Where was this going?

"You know, what was in the paper? That she . . . that she was arrested for murder." Her almond eyes rounded a bit and he felt cold inside. "And it's online."

He knew. He'd already read it himself, but the article was pretty straightforward; just gave the facts on a homicide that was as old as dirt.

So Tori was suddenly interested in him so that he could help her do her homework and because his mother was some kind of psycho or something, possibly a killer? Suddenly he looked like some kind of bad boy? Edgy? Really?

"She didn't kill anybody," he said under his breath and felt heat crawling up the back of his neck.

"I know, I know, but wow. Arrested for murder. Can you imagine?"

"No." He felt suddenly defensive.

"It's kind of . . ."

Don't say "cool."

". . . interesting." She flashed him another smile. He'd known about the article and had wondered if it might be a big deal here at

Edgewater High, but Tori was the first to bring it up to him. If anyone had read it or cared, he hadn't heard about it.

Until now.

"If you say so."

"At least you can say your mom's not boring." Tori picked up her things. "My mom's an actuary. Ugh." She rolled those incredible eyes, then pulled her phone from her pocket, studied the screen, and didn't look back at him as the tone sounded, signifying the end of class and the end of the day.

He grabbed his backpack, keeping with the mob of students. It was too bad that he couldn't even think that she might like him just a little if only for the wrong reasons.

Slipping into the hallway and losing himself in the throng of teenagers walking, shouting, laughing, and banging lockers, he felt a little niggle of pride. She was right, though. He might not be good at a lot of things, but he understood computers, inside and out. He had mad skills, but word was getting around. She wasn't the first kid to ask for his help, and that wasn't good. He had to keep a low profile. Not show off. Now more than ever since Walsh was on his case. He was scheduled to meet with her right after school.

In the hallway, he skirted the area near his locker and kept up with a group of kids heading toward the main doors near the admin offices.

He kept looking over his shoulder for Schmidt, but he was nowhere to be seen. Good. As long as Dylan kept with large groups, he should be safe.

Maybe.

The secretary waved him into Mrs. Walsh's office. "She'll be right back. She told me to let you go on in."

He stepped into the small room and wondered how long she'd be gone. If he had time to—

With a quick look over his shoulder he saw the receptionist was busy at the counter. Before he could talk himself out of it, he shoved the door so that it was barely open, just a crack, then moved around the desk. Not bothering to sit, he pushed back the chair, leaned over the keyboard, and checked Walsh's computer terminal.

Of course it wouldn't open. He needed a password.

The screen saver, a picture of the front of the high school, stayed in place, mocking him. Softly, hardly daring to breathe, he pulled open her drawer, searching for a card or something where she might have jotted a note. On first sweep, nothing. He swept his gaze across the flat surface of the desk, even picked up a picture and checked the back, anywhere she might keep her password. No hint in the drawers. Nothing on her neat desk.

He was really sweating now.

He didn't have much time.

If he could figure it out . . .

Come on, come on.

The picture of her daughter . . . God, what was that girl's name? Beth? Bethany? Brittany? She was a few years older than Harper, had graduated the year before he'd become a freshman. So she was like nineteen, maybe? He tried a combination of each of the names, backward and forward, with each of the two years when the daughter might have been born.

Nothing.

He bit his lip.

Thought hard.

Felt the sweat bead on his forehead.

Come on, Ryder, think. You can do this.

Glancing up, he saw the girl at the counter gathering her things. Crap. The receptionist was about to return to her desk, and might peek inside and catch him.

His heart was racing.

Calm down!

Only a few more seconds.

If he knew more about Marlene Walsh, like her husband's name or if they had a pet, or the year Walsh herself had been born or graduated from high school or college . . . He needed more information to get in.

Not that it was that big a deal. He knew he could hack into the school's system; it wasn't that tough, but it would be so great to be able to log on as if he were the friggin' vice principal.

That would give him a sense of satisfaction, kind of a behind-her-back-but-also-in-her- face move. Major bragging rights and . . .

Footsteps clicked outside the door.

His heart nearly stopped.

Crap!

He looked up.

The receptionist was turning back to her desk.

He scrambled back to the chair behind the door just as it swept open, yanked his phone from his back pocket, and pretended to be texting.

"Dylan." Marlene Walsh smiled that same plastic grin she used when addressing the student body in one of her stupid "Rah-rah Edgewater Eagles" speeches that made him groan. So phony. "Sorry I'm late."

"No prob." He actually stood. Something his dad had taught him a long time ago.

"Sit, sit." Waving him back to his chair, she swept around the desk and stopped on the far side to eye her chair.

Jesus, he'd forgotten to push it back under the desk.

Her neatly plucked brows puckered as she sat, scooting it closer to the computer monitor.

She knows! She can feel you were there.

He tried to keep cool as she adjusted her reading glasses onto her nose and typed quickly onto her keyboard. *Beth2018Anne.* At least that's what it looked like.

That was her daughter's name. Beth Anne! Now he remembered. And if the school required her to change the password every so often, he bet she just put in a different year or something and kept the letters the same . . . 2018, the year after Beth Anne had graduated? Who knew? And really, who cared?

She pressed her palms to the desktop. "How long have you been waiting?"

He lifted a shoulder, attempting to appear bored. "I dunno. Maybe a minute or so."

"Hmm." She didn't believe him. But she kept typing. And now he could feel his shirt sticking to his back. "Okay, let's see . . . I've been going over your records." She glanced at him. "Not attendance, we've been through that, but performance."

He felt a little tingle of dread raise the hairs on the back of his neck. What was this all about?

She eyed the screen, as if studying it for the first time, but Dylan figured this might be for show, that she already knew what she was going to say. "Since you started at Edgewater High last year, your grades have slowly declined."

So what else was new?

"But your test scores? Not at all. They're above grade level, especially in math and computer science." Her eyebrows knit over her glasses and her mouth turned down. Another practiced look. "In fact, your schoolwork doesn't come anywhere close to where your tests indicate you should be."

She looked at him and he lifted a shoulder again. He got it; she was saying he was a slacker.

Turning away from the monitor, she leaned across the desk. "You know, Dylan, you have tremendous potential."

Yeah, yeah, he'd heard it all before.

"In fact, Mr. Tallarico has requested you to be his TA in computer science next year. That's a spot usually reserved for a senior." She paused, waiting for a reaction, but he just slouched in his chair. "So why the disparity?" she asked, though he thought it was a rhetorical question. She really didn't expect him to answer and he didn't. Leaning back she asked, "How're things going here, at school?"

"Okay."

"No problem with friends, other than with Mr. Schmidt?"

"Yeah. Fine."

"What about at home?"

"What?"

"You live with your mother." Not a question.

So here it was. The big *D* word. His parents were divorced. Which wasn't a big deal; lots of his friends' parents had split up.

"Most of the time, yeah." He looked up and held her gaze.

"But you see your dad." Another too-kind smile.

"Oh, yeah."

She frowned a little. "Everything okay at home?"

"Yeah." He said it with a little more enthusiasm. What was she getting at? He added, "We're good. Real good."

She waited a few seconds, then pushed herself to standing. "Okay, then, but just so you know, you can always talk to me or Miss Lindley."

The school psychologist? Oh, geez. "Don't need to," he said, feeling his back muscles tighten.

"Fine. Just as long as you know. Now, maybe you can help us sort out the mess with the security cameras. As I understand it, the problem lies in storage of the data on the computer. Mr. Tallarico has already started looking at it."

Oh. So he wasn't on his own. No surprise. But too bad. He would love to have some time alone with the school security system.

As Mrs. Walsh rounded the corner of her desk he noticed for the first time the newspaper folded neatly near her in-basket. Suddenly he understood.

She'd read the article about his uncle being murdered, about his mom being charged. Just like Tori Suzuki. Great. Of course, the vice principal would think it messed him up. That's why she brought up the school psychologist.

As if that was ever going to happen.

No friggin' way.

• • •

Patient: "I lied. I lied to everyone."

Therapist: "That night?"

Patient: "Yes. And now. I'm lying to them now. To my friends. To Luke."

Therapist: "Tell me."

Patient, worried: "I've never told anyone. I've tried, but I couldn't. I can't. I still can't."

Therapist: "Let's go back. To that night in the processing plant."

Patient: "I don't want to."

Therapist: "It's your decision."

Patient, voice tremulous: "Okay. I will." A pause. The patient visibly shudders. "I'm here, now. In the cannery. It's dark; so . . . dark. I think I smell fish . . . no, just the river. Wet. Dank." The patient concentrates, eyebrows knitting. "People are here but I can't see them, just hear them. Lots of them. Guns going off. And firecrackers. Someone's laughing. But I'm scared. Luke! I need to find Luke. Before it's too late."

Therapist: "Too late for what?"

Patient: "Before someone else finds out!"

Therapist: "Finds out what?"

Patient, frustrated, voice cracking: "About my lies. To him. To my parents. To my

267

friends. To everyone. But mainly . . . mainly to him."

Therapist: "Where are you, in the building?"

Patient: "I'm walking, my gun in my hand, but it's dark. So dark. I can't see. People are running. People are laughing. I hear someone climbing the ladder, the rungs ringing, and then . . . and then . . . I shoot."

Therapist: "And then what?"

Patient, agitated, eyes wide, nearly frantic: "And then Luke falls! He's been hit! There's blood everywhere. Oh my God! He can't die. He can't! I need to talk to him, I need to explain . . . I have to save him!"

Therapist: "And can you?"

Patient, in a panic: "No! There's too much blood. Luke! Luke!"

Therapist: "Let's come back now."

Patient, determined: "No! I can't leave him. I won't!"

Therapist: "It's time. You're returning."

Patient: "No, Luke, please, please."

Therapist, taking control: "You're surfacing."

Patient: "Luke, oh, God, Luke. Forgive me!"

Therapist, more firmly: "You are leaving

the cannery and Luke. For now." The therapist hides frustration and keeps a steady voice. "On my count."

Patient, taking short breaths, nearly hyperventilating: "But—"

Therapist, rock steady: "Three. And you're leaving the building, going away from the riverfront and Luke, and leaving the past behind."

Patient, still frantic: "I don't know. I could save him—"

Therapist, in control: "Two. And you're nearly awake."

Patient: "There's so much to tell him." The patient's still worried, but coming around.

Therapist: "One."

The patient's eyes open and blink, adjusting to the soft lighting and soothing music in the tiny room. A bit of incense tinges the air with oleander as the patient stirs and focuses on the therapist.

Therapist, smiling with relief, voice soft and steady: "And you're back."

Patient, breathless, still worried: "I couldn't tell him. I didn't get the chance."

Therapist: "You will. Maybe in the next session."

Patient, sighing: "Maybe. But I've been living with this for so long."

Therapist: "It takes time."

Patient, wryly: "And time wounds all heels, isn't that what they say? Well, this wound, this pain has been around too long. It needs to go away."

Therapist, taking a peek at the clock on the antique desk: "It will."

The leather of the recliner creaks as the patient adjusts the chair to a sitting position. "I hope so." The patient stands. "God, I hope so."

CHAPTER 19

Over the years Rachel had learned that she had to pick her moments, so she waited until both of the kids were home from school Monday evening. Dinner was in the oven, lasagna; the security system had been reconnected; and they were settling in for homework.

Dylan hadn't said much about his extra time at the school doing Mrs. Walsh's bidding, just that it was "okay." And Harper had spent a couple of hours working on some project at a friend's house, supposedly studying.

Neither kid had asked Rachel how her day had gone, though if they had, she wouldn't have told them about the front door. The new coat of black paint had dried, and she figured that threat could wait for another day.

Now, though, it was time for the truth about what her son had been up to.

Harper was already on her phone in her room, the door only slightly ajar, and Dylan was heading to his when she stopped him. "We need to talk," she said. "In the living room."

"About what?" He didn't seem surprised and didn't argue, just walked down the hall in his bare feet.

"This." She pulled the sock with the money

out of her pocket and noticed his jaw tense. Not surprise. Anger. She'd thought he would be shocked and he definitely wasn't. "Sit."

He dropped onto a corner of the couch.

"Want to explain?" she asked.

"No." Rebellion flared in his eyes.

"Well, you're going to or I'm going to expect the worst." She emptied the sock and dropped it and the damning bills onto the coffee table. "Talk."

"Geez, Mom, it's not what you think."

"Which is?"

"That I'm selling drugs, right? Isn't that what you think, why you brought up the Xanax?" He rolled his eyes. "I'm not that stupid."

She resisted asking, "And just how stupid are you?" Instead she said as she sat in a nearby chair, "Convince me."

He hesitated, looked out the window, and sighed through his nose as Reno trotted into the room to take his spot in the bed near the fireplace.

"You said you were broke, that you needed money to pay off the kid that was hassling you?"

"Schmidt," Dylan supplied.

"Right. You borrowed a hundred dollars from me because you owed him some 'gambling debt.' " For emphasis, she made air quotes.

"Yeah! And I'm paying it back! Geez, Mom, didn't I help you with the security system? Didn't

I say I'd mow the lawn and do whatever stupid job you have?"

"But you already had money. More than enough. This money." She pointed a finger at the uneven pile of small bills. "Where'd you get it and don't . . . don't even say anything about saving it from your birthday or whatever. Everything you take in goes to some kind of equipment for either your computer or your game system or something."

"It's my business."

"And mine." Trying to cool off a little, she said, "So what's going on, Dylan? What're you into?"

"Not drugs!" he yelled, then more calmly, "Okay?"

"Then what? And don't try to convince me that you're into some online betting, because I'm just not buying it."

Arms folded, foot bouncing nervously, he didn't answer.

"I'm not the enemy, you know," she said.

"Then why are you acting like it? Interrogating me?"

"Because I'm scared, Dylan. You're doing something behind my back, something you don't want to talk about, something you want to keep hidden. So I'm worried that you're in trouble."

"I'm not."

She hadn't heard Harper come out of her room nor walk down the hall, but she showed up and stood half in the hallway, half in the living room. "Tell her," Harper said, staring at her brother.

"What?" He was shaking his head, his eyes round.

"Tell her that you help kids on the side, y'know, with computer stuff." She was staring directly at her brother. "Admit that you're a geek, probably the best one in school."

Dylan was as white as a sheet.

"So you do what you did this afternoon for Mom or for Mr. Tallarico after school—you fix computers and all kinds of electronic stuff. For other kids." She came into the room, stood near the fireplace.

"But—"

"Tell her, or I will," Harper said, her gaze still firmly holding his. "Well, fine," she said and finally turned her attention to Rachel. "He's kind of got this side business going; it's not that big of a deal, but word is getting around, and he helps kids get their gaming systems or computers or whatever working again."

This didn't sound right.

"He's done stuff for me, with my phone when I couldn't figure out an app, and he's helped Lucas and Xander, and my friend Julie, lots of kids." She waved a hand as if to include the entire student body of Edgewater High. "Sometimes it's behind the parents' backs. Like a kid got a cell phone from a friend or whatever."

"Stolen."

"No!" She shook her head fiercely.

"Uh-uh." Dylan was in quick agreement.

Rachel was trying to piece it all together. "Is that why the Schmidt kid was on your case?"

Dylan nodded, glancing at his sister as if she would back him up.

"How?" Rachel asked.

"Something I did for him didn't work and he . . . he wanted me to fix it right then and there, so I cut class and met him, but I didn't have all the right equipment. I wanted to bring it home and he was pissed off—er, mad at me. Said he'd already paid and . . . and so . . ."

"But why wouldn't you tell me?"

"Because you freak out about everything, *every*thing. You're a walking basket case."

Rachel protested. "I'm not—"

"Seriously, Mom," Harper said, "it's like we can't tell you anything or you'll go all . . . weird and hyper and suspicious."

"Is that true?" Rachel said, turning to her son. Beyond him, through the window, she saw Ella Dickerson in her yard, down on her hands and knees, pulling weeds. "Am I that bad?"

Dylan swallowed and glanced at his sister before meeting his mother's eyes. "We just don't want to, you know, upset you."

She wasn't certain she was getting all of the truth, and she was suspicious that they'd somehow both worked together, double-teamed her with the story, but part of it was right.

"We hear you, Mom," Harper said softly, and for the first time since she'd entered the conversation, her daughter seemed totally sincere. "At night, when you have those dreams. We hear you walk around, talk to yourself, even scream sometimes."

Her heart sank. The last thing she wanted to do, the very last, was worry her children.

"It's not your fault," Harper was quick to add. "I—we know that, but it's . . . scary."

"Yeah," her son put in. "Kinda freaky, Mom."

Her heart squeezed painfully. "Oh. God. I don't want to ever . . ." Rachel felt horrible and wanted to apologize all over the place, but she couldn't help but wonder how this conversation had turned around, to the point where instead of dealing with Dylan's obvious lies, she was now feeling as if she'd failed as a mother. She looked from daughter to son. For once they seemed absolutely sincere. Still she was suspicious. Even now they might be hiding something. But what? "Okay. Well." She slapped her hands onto her thighs, then stood. "This has been . . . enlightening. And maybe we should all work on being more truthful."

"And calm?" Harper suggested.

"Yeah. That too." Rachel felt that this would be a group hug moment if her life were a television sitcom or drama, but as it was, Dylan said, "Can I go now?"

"Yeah. But no more secrets and no more cutting class. You can set up something here, or meet kids before or after school."

"Okay. But can I have my money back?" he asked.

"Yes. Sure. It's yours," she said, "except for the hundred dollars you owe me, right?"

"Right," he said, scooping up his money and heading to his room.

"Thanks," she said to her daughter, but didn't feel the relief she'd anticipated.

Harper nodded. "You're welcome, but, Mom, really, don't go through my room again, okay? And don't tell me you didn't, cuz I know you did. I can tell. Besides, we're not having any more secrets. Right?"

"Right."

"And going through my things, that's like illegal, right? An invasion of privacy or something?"

"Not illegal." Rachel shook her head and tightened the band that was holding her hair away from her face. "But next time, I'll let you know."

"No. Not another 'next time.' I need my own space. I'm almost—"

"Eighteen, I know. And from that point on you think you'll be totally independent. But you'll still be living with me."

"Or Dad. I could live with him." Harper elevated her chin just a fraction.

Rachel's heart twisted, but she hid it. "Yeah, that's always an option."

"Or get an apartment." A little more defiance.

"You think you could afford one?"

"With a roommate."

Uh-oh. Where was this going? A roommate like Xander Vale? Rachel didn't go there. No reason to give Harper any ideas that she might not have come up with on her own. "And you'd need a job, maybe two jobs to make ends meet, on top of juggling school, so you should probably wait. It's a lot cheaper here."

"But it's like I live in a prison." Harper flung out her arms dramatically. "You won't even let me go to a concert. Because you don't like Xander!"

"I don't know him."

"Exactly!" She reached into her pocket, read a text on her phone screen, and repeated, "A prison."

Rachel gave her a you've-got-to-be-kidding look. She couldn't wait until Harper was living on her own and learning the real lessons in life, but not yet; she was still so young, naive in so many ways. So she said, "You're right, it's a prison and I'm the warden."

"You know what I mean!" She actually looked up from the screen.

"Yeah, I do. I remember saying the same thing to my mother and I'll give you the same advice she gave me: 'Deal with it!'"

He was late.

Again.

Annessa walked through the old school with its unused classrooms, forgotten hallways, and dirty windows, many of which had long been boarded up. St. Augustine's elementary, once filled with laughter, shouts, and running feet, was now quiet, deathly quiet, empty and cold, smelling of disuse.

Her husband, Clint Cooper, had bought the place, along with other properties in town. Since she'd moved back to Edgewater to deal with her ailing parents, he'd thought it would make her happy to purchase some of the "historic" places around the area, to "revitalize" a town that had suffered with the times. To that end, Clint had purchased a farm outside of Astoria; a sawmill not far from Astoria; the old cannery on the waterfront; and St. Augustine's, which consisted of this school, a small church, and an attached hospital.

"Let's make Edgewater a destination, y'know?" Clint had said, thinking he would please her. "We can turn the old school into a hotel, the chapel a restaurant, and maybe condos in the hospital." He'd been on the deck of their penthouse, smoking a cigar, the lights of Seattle shining

279

a bright backdrop. As he'd told her about his plan, he had grown enthusiastic. "How about refurbishing the Sea View cannery into a mall loaded with quaint shops? Condos too, being as it's on the river, great views, fantastic wildlife! I know the building would have to be razed, but we can go off the footprint, make people think it's just as it was. The history of it all, the jobs it created, and then there's that murder that took place. Adds to the mystique, y'know."

"I was there," she'd reminded her husband, who was drawing on his cigar, the tip glowing, smoke coiling over his balding head. "No mystique. It's horrible."

"People like horror." And off he'd gone, dreaming of building something unique.

What he didn't realize was that she didn't care about Edgewater. So the town was dying, so what? Yeah, she'd go back, look after Dad now that Mom had passed, but it was temporary. Or that had been the plan. *Her* plan. But where she'd seen duty her husband had glimpsed opportunity.

A mistake.

And being here now, in the old school, was a little unnerving. She walked into what had been a bathroom for primary students, with its low sink and row of stalls. *Girls' bathroom,* she thought. No stained urinals still hugging the walls. She caught sight of her reflection in the dusty, cracked mirror. Tall and slim, her hair glossy and almost black, her eyes, with the aid of colored contacts, an intense turquoise. Still attractive. Even wealthier than she had once been. Far wealthier.

And lonely as hell.

No children.

Grown stepchildren, and young stepgrandchildren who didn't know her and didn't care to.

An aging lion of a husband who cared more about his latest golf score, his next development, and the figures in his bank accounts than his trophy wife.

Clint just had never "got" her. Didn't understand.

Never would.

Thirty-two years was a helluva age difference. For God's sake, she was avoiding her twentieth high school reunion and he was collecting social security! A thought that hadn't occurred to her fifteen years ago when she'd been swayed by his money and Clint, at fifty-five, had still been dashing, trim, and worldly and . . . and it had all been a load of crap.

So here she was, waiting for a lover who didn't care any more for her than her husband did.

Disgusted with herself, she heard the steady drip, drip, drip of a pipe that hadn't quite been turned off, and she walked into the hallway again, remembering wearing uniforms and running out to the play yard, where there had been a covered area, a tetherball pole, four-square courts, and a few pieces of aging and probably unsafe equipment. Now, as she peered through a locked door, she saw only rubble in the open area where she'd once screamed and laughed.

Her first eight years of school, well, nine, counting kindergarten, before she'd been enrolled in public school. Edgewater High.

Twenty years past.

She probably should have gone to Lila's reunion meeting, but the truth was she couldn't stand the woman. Nor had she felt any different twenty years ago when Lila had been jealous of her and her father's money. And for her part, Annessa, studious, hadn't liked the flinty blonde who had flitted from one boyfriend to the next, always looking for someone a little more popular or wealthy or cool or whatever. Lila had flirted with just about any boy, or man, for that matter, as she'd always gone for someone older.

In that regard, Annessa had been surprised when Lila had settled on Luke Hollander. He wasn't wealthy and he was only a couple of years older and no longer a football star. Yet, Lila had set her sights on Rachel Gaston's brother and become Rachel's best friend.

For a while.

Anyone with any brains could see that she was only using Rachel to get close to Luke.

Probably Rachel had known it, too, because their friendship had seemed to fade with time.

Annessa smiled at that. Well, who could blame Rachel? Lila had become her damned stepmother-in-law.

Sick.

Using her key, she unlocked a door to the school yard and stepped outside. It was twilight, the gloom settling in.

The area was completely enclosed, two sides blocked by the wings of the old school. The third boundary, directly across from where she stood, was the old chapel, now crumbling under a sloping roof, its tall spire and silent bell tower knifing into the dusky sky. The final wall of the school yard was a high wooden fence with a locked gate leading to the parking lot of the hospital.

She remembered third grade when she'd fallen from the monkey bars and sprained her ankle. Sister Mary Rosarius, the meanest nun in the school, had hustled her through the gate and along a covered portico to the hospital, all the while muttering that Annessa would be fine, that she shouldn't be a baby and should stop crying. "Oh, now, don't blubber. Say a prayer with me," she'd ordered, walking fast, the skirt of her habit swishing with her strides. "Hail Mary, full of grace. The Lord is with thee. Blessed art thou amongst women, and blessed is the fruit of thy womb, Jesus . . ."

Annessa hadn't prayed and she hadn't stopped sobbing.

Now she stepped into the yard, where a few insects buzzed in the coming night and a lone security lamp offered dim, uneven light over the tufted dirt where once there had been grass. Shards of broken glass glinted in the bald patch of earth.

She'd spent many hours here, laughing and playing and scheming with her friends. She remembered the bells in that spire tolling for mass, or to signify the end of the school day. Father Timothy had been the principal, and though there were a few nuns employed at that time, most of the staff were laypeople.

She recalled . . .

Scraaape.

What was that?

She froze.

Was it a shoe scuffing the earth behind her?

Whipping around, Annessa expected to see him crossing the patchy yard, a devilish smile slashed across his jaw, his mischievous eyes sparkling.

But the space beneath the porch was empty. Devoid of life. Quiet and still. Grimy windows dark.

Jesus.

Her nerves tightened. She licked her lips. Eyed the entire yard, with its misshapen pieces of broken equipment and shadowy areas where blackberries and weeds had taken root. Her throat was as dry as dust.

They'd gone too far this time. These clandestine meetings always had an edge to them, a little bit of danger that made the sex all the more potent. Cheating on their spouses wasn't enough; they each liked a little more adrenaline in their bloodstream.

But this—what they'd planned tonight—had crossed a line.

Another line, she reminded herself as a bat flew toward the old tower.

The hairs on her arms lifted and her pulse pounded in her ears.

"Are you here?" she whispered.

She waited.

No response.

Just the wind rustling a piece of paper that danced across the broken concrete walkway.

Annessa was already tense.

She'd read about Violet Sperry's death, seen the report on the news, heard gossip in the coffee shop.

All she knew was that Violet had been killed by an unknown assailant, murdered in her home. Here in sleepy Edgewater, where the news was so slow that the local paper had to dredge up the fatal accident that had taken the life of Luke Hollander. Her insides turned to ice. She'd been there that night, in the cannery. The noise. The confusion. The sounds of firecrackers booming, or had it been real gunfire? Along with the steady click of pellet guns, the shouts and screams. She'd witnessed Luke go down, seen him bleed out, thought his sister, Rachel Gaston, had actually shot him until she realized she hadn't been sure. Hadn't the spark from the real gun been off to Rachel's side . . . or had she been mistaken? She hadn't been certain then, and she sure as hell wasn't now.

She pulled her jacket around her more tightly and wondered how long she would have to wait.

Not long.

She wasn't going to waste her time.

Creeaak.

The sound echoed through the yard and she shot a quick look over her shoulder to spy the broken, lopsided merry-go-round slowly spinning, rotating on its ancient spindle, casting a moving shadow beneath the solitary lamp.

What the hell?

The merry-go-round was turning from the wind?

But the breeze was slight, not strong enough to push the old structure on its rusting pivot. For a second she thought of the ghost stories they'd told one another as kids, insisting that the chapel was haunted.

"Just kids being kids," she whispered now, but her skin was prickling and her nerves were strung as tight as the strings of Sister Catherine's cello.

It's nothing.

But she decided it was time to go. This was a ridiculous place to meet, anyway.

Why had he even suggested it to begin with?

Why had she agreed?

Oh, yeah, because they each had a connection here, to this complex, and they'd both gone to elementary school here.

So what? She was out.

She reached into her pocket for her keys.

The merry-go-round slowed, groaning to a stop.

Her heart began to race.

She started for the door to the school and heard the clank of chains. *What?*

Turning quickly, she swept her gaze over the entire yard to land on the pipe structure from which the swings were suspended. Of the three swings, one was broken, missing its seat, the second unmoving, and the third swaying slightly, its chains rattling as if someone had just gotten off.

That was it.

She was out of here.

Now!

Even if he was here, trying to scare her, she was over it. Their romantic trysts had been sexy and wanton, wild and dangerous, but this, being scared out of her mind like this? When someone she knew had just been murdered?

Nope.

She'd been an idiot to agree to it.

Walking quickly, she made her way to the door she'd used to enter the area, grabbed the big handle, and tugged.

The door didn't budge.

What?

But she'd just unlocked it. . . .

She pulled again.

Nothing.

Crap!

If he was out here and this was supposed to be some kind of a joke, she'd kill him. She decided to tell him so. "If you think this is turning me on with all this cloak and dagger stuff, you're wrong."

No response.

Fear skittered up her spine.

Did something move over by the chapel door, in the alcove of the doorway? Her heart clamored.

She fumbled with her keys, forced the right one into the door.

The lock clicked open.

Thank God!

Thump, thump, thump, thump, thump, thump!

Faster and faster.

The sound of bats flying, whirring overhead?

No!

Footsteps, running. Gaining speed. Tow.
She pulled the door open, and—

Bam! A big gloved hand shoved it closed.

The razor-sharp edge of the door scrape
finger, digging into her flesh. "Ow! Shit!"

"Nuh-uh-uh," a voice growled at her ear, w
and heavy and not the one she'd expected.

A new fear slithered through her.

Who was this guy?

He pressed his body against hers. She felt him
hard against her back. Felt his damned erection
pressing into her buttocks through her clothes,
gloved hands tangling in her hair, tightening.

No, oh, God, no!

She started to scream, but he slammed her
forehead against the door so hard her nose
cracked. Light flashed behind her eyes. Pain
screamed through her brain. Blood gushed.
Stunned, she sagged. Her knees buckled and she
would have sunk down but his body kept her
upright, pinned to the door.

Her scream was faint. A moan. She heard her
keys, jarred from the lock, clink against the
concrete

*Don't pass out, Annessa. Do not! Fight!
Scream! Yell!* This guy was going to rape her or
kill her or both. She opened her mouth to scream
again. Tasted blood running down her throat.

Who was he? Why was he doing this?

Fight, Annessa! Fight, damn it!

Despite his weight pressed against her, she tried to twist, to squirm out of his grasp, but she could barely move. Her arms flailed uselessly; her legs were pinned against the metal door.

Another attempted scream.

Big gloved hands encircled her throat.

Don't panic! Just get free. Somehow, get away! Now!

He shifted; her legs moved. Frantically, she kicked and swung with her arms, her hands batting wildly as she tried to scream but only wheezed as his steely fingers gripped harder. Dug into her flesh. Crushing. Woozily, she realized she was being lifted off her feet. She kicked wildly! Lost a shoe. Heard it thud against the door.

Kick him! Hit him! Bite him! Get him off you, Annessa! Don't let him win. Do not!

Fight with all you've got. He's going to kill you!

She struggled.

Her lungs burned.

The other shoe fell away.

Frantically, she tried and failed to drag in even the slightest amount of air.

Nothing!

Oh, God.

Her lungs felt as if they would explode.

Blackness pulled at her consciousness.

Please, God, don't let me die this way. Help me!

She swung as hard as she could but her arm dropped uselessly.

The fingers around her neck pressed harder.

Through the pain she realized she was about to pass out. There was nothing she could do but give in. As the blackness came, the old prayer whispered through her. *Hail Mary, full of grace. The Lord is with thee. Blessed art thou amongst women. . . .*

CHAPTER 20

Her bedroom was dark.
Quiet.
Other than the frantic beating of her heart.
Come on. Do it. Now.
Holding her breath, Harper slid open the window and braced herself. She hardly dared breathe. Waiting expectantly, she didn't hear a siren shriek or see lights flash on in warning. It worked! Dylan, that cretin, had done what she'd asked and disconnected the security alarm's circuit running to her room.

Thank God!

She let out her breath slowly, still not convinced that she wouldn't be caught sneaking out. But Reno didn't start barking madly, nor did her mother's feet hit the floor of her bedroom overhead.

So far, so good.

Heart pounding, she slipped on her running shoes, hoisted herself up on the windowsill. Balancing there, she turned herself around and slid down the side of the house. Then she pushed the window almost all of the way closed, paused just long enough to text again. Once she hit SEND, she took off, running along the hedgerow to the back of the house and then sprinting down a side street, moving quickly, just as she had in the hundred-yard dash when she was running track.

The spring air was cool, the night clear, darkness crouching beyond the lights of the town. She felt wild and edgy as she ran, her hair streaming behind her. The doubts that she was doing the right thing shrank, just as Lucas said they would. Her cousin had introduced Xander to Harper even though she'd claimed she wasn't interested. "He's too old, in college. God, he lives like, what? A million miles away."

"It's only about three hours, maybe a little longer, and so what?" Lucas had said, his blue eyes glinting. "He's a good guy. Yeah, he can get his wild on, I guess, but he's up here all the time, working or interning or something for my dad. He saw you when your mom brought you over to the house once, a couple of weeks ago, and thought you were hot, wanted me to set you up, I guess. And it's not that big of a deal. He just wants to meet you; it's not like it's forever or anything."

"Mom would kill me," she'd argued, but she'd been intrigued.

"She doesn't have to know." Lucas had grinned then. He'd been enjoying this, and for as long as she could remember, he'd been at odds with his own mother and stepfather—her grandfather. Always giving them fits and loving it. "Come on,

Harper, what've you got to lose? Aren't you tired of always doing what your mom thinks is best?" He'd let out a snort of disgust. "Besides, you may not like him. This all might be a big waste of time." He'd lifted a shoulder and Harper had decided he was right. She and Lucas weren't all that tight, but in this case, she thought, he had a point. And because of it, she'd met the most wonderful guy in the world. Her soul mate.

She raced under a low-hanging branch, fir needles brushing her hair.

Would he be there? Waiting, as they'd planned? Oh, God, she hoped so. Staying out of the pools of light cast by a few street lamps, avoiding buckles in the sidewalk, she ran around the corner and spied his Jeep idling by the curb, no lights visible.

Her heart soared.

She watched as the passenger door opened, the overhead light offering feeble illumination, but enough that she recognized Xander as he leaned across the seat, his near-black hair falling over his forehead, his teeth flashing in lips that slanted into a quick, heart-stopping grin.

God, she loved him.

"You made it," he whispered as she slid into the interior and pulled the door shut behind her.

"Yeah. Piece of cake. Let's go."

"You're sure she won't check on you?"

"She never does. Not after what she calls her

'perimeter check,' when she's going upstairs. Every damned night. It's an OCD thing." She glanced up at him. "Or maybe something worse, but then she leaves us alone until it's time to get up."

"Good."

He kissed her first and she melted inside at the touch of his warm lips. His teeth flashed in the darkness. God, she'd really done it. As dangerous as it was. She'd snuck out in the middle of the night. Her mother would kill her if she found out, but Harper couldn't stand it anymore. She was being treated like a prisoner in the house, and her mother just didn't get how she felt about Xander. He was different from the boys in high school. Smarter. Funnier. More worldly. He made her previous boyfriends—both of them—seem like junior-highers in comparison.

She felt better already, just being with him.

He slipped the Jeep into gear but paused. "I don't want you to get into trouble."

"Too late."

"You're sure?"

"I'm here, aren't I? And, oh yeah, I'm sure." Of course she wasn't, but she wasn't about to let him know that.

"All right." He kissed her again, then flashed a conspiratorial grin her way. With the lights still off, he pulled away from the curb. At the cross street, he turned on the headlamps, then drove them out of the neighborhood and through the sparse traffic to the place they'd agreed to go: her grandfather's little retreat at the law offices and Xander's crash pad when he was working for Charles Ryder.

The studio apartment was used infrequently for guests or clients of the small firm, or, once in a while, for Charles, if he was working late. However, this time Xander had use of the studio when he was working for the firm, either in the office or doing odd jobs, which included some repair work to the building. Xander had adjusted his schedule so that he had more free days during the week as well as time on the weekends.

Which was perfect!

It was only natural that he'd want Harper to spend some time alone with him there. So far she hadn't, but tonight . . .

She swallowed hard, her heart beating like a drum, and wondered if she was making an irreversible mistake.

But she wasn't going there. Not now. She was with Xander and she wanted to be here, with him, and no matter what, she had the right to live her own life, to fall in love with whomever she pleased. No, she wasn't going to second-guess herself. At least not tonight.

He parked in the lot that separated the law office from the property to the west, the old St. Augustine School.

He led her to the back door and inside to a staircase. Up the stairs they hurried to the second floor and her grandfather's little apartment, one room with a connecting bath and a kitchen stretched along one wall. A television was aglow in the corner, some late-late show turned down low. A café table with two tall chairs sat in a spot near the single window, with its view across the parking lot to the fenced school yard next door, the school property.

A single lamp burned near the sofa, but he snapped it off, picked up the remote, and killed the TV as well. The room became darker, the only bit of shifting light coming from the partially open window, where a security lamp offered a cool blue aura, and a soft breeze entered, dissipating some of the smell of a recently applied coat of paint.

Wrapping his arms around her, he drew her close. Then he kissed her. Gently at first and then more urgently, in a way that made her tingle all over, a way that caused her bones to melt. His tongue was pure magic, touching and flicking with hers, and she kissed him back, closing her eyes and losing herself.

This was what it was like to be in love. Real love. Not puppy love or whatever you called it.

He bent his knees and they tumbled onto the makeshift bed, a small part of her wondering if she was making a mistake, but just a very small part.

This was sooo right.

"I'm glad you're here," he said, kicking off his shoes.

"Me too." She toed off one Nike, then the other, kicked them away.

He kissed her again, his hands slipping under her sweatshirt and up her abdomen, his fingertips brushing across the top of her breast. Within her bra, her nipple tightened. She was breathing faster than normal as he yanked off his hoody and T-shirt, exposing a ripple of muscles on his chest and abdomen.

"C'mon," he said and helped her out of her sweatshirt and began kissing the top of her breasts. A low moan escaped her throat as he skimmed the lace of her bra with his tongue, his warm breath piercing the sheer fabric.

Deep inside, she began to ache, to want.

She reveled in the feel of his weight as he rolled atop her, pinning her down with his hips and levering himself on an elbow to stare down at her.

This is dangerous! a part of her brain was screaming as he turned her slightly, reaching behind and unhooking her bra, tugging on the scrap of lace until it fell away.

No, no, no! This is so right. Meant to be, an arguing part of her mind replied.

Harper ignored her doubts and told herself to just trust him. To love him.

She felt his gaze skate down her body.

His face was in shadow, the whites of his eyes visible, the scent of him filling her nostrils as the room closed in on her, growing more intimate, making her feel that they were alone in the universe, two like souls.

"I love you," he whispered across her breast, the warm air inviting, his words seductive. He touched the very tip of her nipple with his tongue and she felt the slow-growing need deep within, a pulsing desire. Instinctively, she reached up, laced her fingers through his thick hair, and pulled his head closer, forcing her breast into his mouth, arched her back, felt the hardness beneath his jeans.

This was right, so right . . . and . . . and . . .

Creeeeeak, the sound like a heavy bough swaying in the wind rippled through the room.

Harper froze.

Her heart thudded as she strained to listen.

"Help," a weak voice reached through the room.

He, too, became a statue. "Did you hear that?"

"Yes."

They waited.

Nothing.

"What was it?" he asked.

"I don't know."

His brows slammed together and he looked worried. He turned his head to stare at the window, then slowly rolled out of the bed. "Sounded close." He headed for the window.

Creeeak!

Harper went completely cold inside.

The disembodied woman's voice said more loudly, "Please . . . help me."

"Jesus. Let's go," Xander said with a glance through the glass. Then he scooped his sweatshirt from the floor and yanked it over his head.

"Go?"

"We've got to help her, whoever she is." He flung back the hood. "No. Wait." Pointing at Harper, he said, "You stay here. I'll go."

"No, I'm not staying here alone." The idea was impossible. "We . . . we should call the police."

He slanted her a look. "Don't you think your dad might take the call? Is that what you want to do?"

"No, but—" She scrambled to find her bra, located it on the floor.

"Stay here. Lock the door. I'll go check it out and if I have to call the police you'll be okay. Just don't open the door. I'll text you."

"No!" She was already hooking the clasps behind her back, snapping her bra into place. "If you're going, I'm going."

"I don't think that's a great idea." He stepped into his shoes.

"Better than me being here. Alone."

"Shit." He looked about to argue but the voice

came again. This time weaker. "Help. Please, someone help me."

"I'm going with you," Harper said, pulling on her own sweatshirt. "Don't argue." She scrambled to find her shoes. One was under the bed. . . . Oh shit, where was the other one? She switched the bedside lamp on, blinked in the sudden brightness, but caught a glimpse of the toe of her shoe poking out from beneath the coffee table.

"Then stick close." He was already at the door as she yanked on her shoes.

"Jesus." They started for the stairs.

She was one step behind. Outside, they raced across the parking lot, scaring a marauding cat into hissing and dashing across the street.

Xander eyed the tall fence. Over six feet, it surrounded the property that had once been St. Augustine's church, school, and hospital.

"It's too high," she said.

"Nope. Just wait here."

"What? No!" She was frantic. For a wild, horrifying second she thought he was leaving her.

"I'm just going to move my Jeep."

"What?"

He loped to his rig, climbed inside, switched on the ignition, and then reversed to the spot near where Harper was standing. "I'll climb over first. Then you."

Before she could ask any questions, he had

made his way onto the hard top of his Jeep and placed his hands on the top of a post, then vaulted to the other side. He landed with a hard thud.

"Come on," he called to her in a low voice.

Great. Harper didn't like the idea, but wasn't about to be left, so she did the same, scrambling onto the roof of his Jeep and standing up to peer over the fence. Xander was in the school yard, looking up, arms outstretched. "Come on," he whispered and motioned quickly with his fingers. "I'll catch you."

This was nuts.

Crazy.

But she placed her hands on the post, hesitated an instant, then swung one leg over the top of the fence, straddling it for a second, then finally getting her second leg across. As she let go to drop to the ground, she felt strong hands at her waist, just before her toes touched the uneven ground.

"See, easy peasy. Come on." He took one hand and they skirted the quiet school yard, where beneath the gaseous light of the lone security lamp, she spied pieces of broken play equipment, clumps of weeds, and piles of junk scattered between the school, hospital, and church.

Fear skittered up Harper's spine.

This was wrong. So wrong.

She strained to listen but now heard nothing but an occasional car passing on the street and the soft sough of the wind over the frantic beating of her heart.

Where?

Where was the woman?

Maybe she'd left.

Perhaps she hadn't been here in the first place.

And then she heard it. No words. Just a low moan that seemed to crawl through the night air.

Xander took her hand and pulled her toward the chapel. He placed a finger to his lips and she moved along beside him, trying desperately to tamp down her fear.

Creeeak!

That awful sound again. But there were no big trees, no strong wind.

Oh. God.

Fear chasing her, Harper kept up with Xander as he crossed the yard. They should leave. Now. Just call the police and let them take care of whatever they might find. An injured person? Or a crazed lunatic? What?

The door to the chapel hung open, sagging on one hinge, revealing the stygian darkness inside.

"I don't think—" she started to whisper, but Xander gave a quick shake of his head and stepped through the opening.

Her throat dry, every nerve strung tight, she followed, through a small, rotting vestibule and into a larger space, what had once been a nave, a few pews remaining on either side of the aisle, the altar still intact. Above it all, a huge cross was still suspended. Though not Catholic, Harper sketched a sign of the cross over her chest.

What would it hurt?

A rat scurried across the dusty boards of the aisle and Harper let out a sharp scream.

"Shh!" Xander pulled her farther inside.

She held fast to his big hand, squinting to see in the dark.

What if someone else was here? Watching them? Maybe from the tiny choir alcove over the vestibule or . . .

Creeeak!

Her stomach dropped.

This was all wrong. Fear sizzled through her and she was sweating nervously, seeing images in the cracked stained glass windows, imagining killers lurking between the broken pews or behind the altar.

Xander pulled out his phone and turned on the flashlight app.

Another groan echoed through the vast space and Xander released her hand to sprint forward.

"No!" she cried after him, thinking that an attacker might be nearby, watching and waiting. With Xander's phone as a beacon, an attacker could zero in, find them, hurt them. They could be walking into a trap!

Screw it!

She whipped out her phone and punched in 911.

If she got into trouble—and she would—tough!

"Oh, Jesus!" Xander said as another raspy groan seemed to ooze through the chapel. He took off, running to one side of the altar, through a door that hung awkwardly on only one hinge, his footsteps pounding loudly as if he were climbing stairs.

"Nine-one-one. What is your emergency?" an operator asked.

"Someone's hurt. In the church at St. Augustine's. This . . . this is Harper Ryder and I'm here and someone's hurt . . . on Hawthorn Street. I don't know the address, but send someone fast. . . ."

"Holy shit!" Xander said. "It's a woman. Oh, God. Lady, I'm here, I'll help you."

Harper was already dialing her father's cell as she climbed the few steps to the bottom of the bell tower. Then she stopped, her hand on the phone freezing, her eyes bulging.

From a long rope, a woman was hanging upside down by one leg, her hair sweeping the floor of the tower, her eyes blindfolded as she groaned and spun slowly.

"For Christ's sake, Harper, help me!" Xander ordered. "We have to get her down!"

She dropped the phone.

CHAPTER 21

It had been years since Cade had been involved in a stakeout, and here he was at 1:13 in the morning parked a few doors down and on the opposite side of the street from the cottage where Rachel and the kids lived. His old house. He felt a lot more nostalgic about it than he'd ever felt about the massive Victorian where he'd grown up, the home now occupied by his father, Lila, and Lucas.

"Small town," he reminded himself and sipped from his cup of rapidly cooling coffee. He'd been here for nearly an hour, and so far he'd seen nothing out of the ordinary. His vigil wasn't official business, just a man watching his ex-wife's home because he couldn't sleep and because of recent events that included a murder along with the vandalism and an anonymous text.

Being here wasn't stalking, he told himself. He was just looking out for his kids' and their mother's safety.

The area was quiet, a few street lamps casting pools of light on the roadway, several unoccupied cars parked on either side. He cracked the window and heard the soft hoot of an owl hidden in the thick branches of the fir trees high overhead.

The cottage, like the other homes along the

street, was dark, only the faintest glow emanating from the dining room window along one side. He remembered how she'd always insisted on leaving the light on over the stove in the kitchen. Some things never changed. Some things were always changing.

Earlier this evening Rachel had called and told him that Dylan had jerry-rigged the old security system and he could see that Rachel had handled the message on the front door, the cruel message covered by a thick coat of paint.

Still, Cade hadn't been satisfied that she and the kids were safe. Not with Violet Sperry's brutal murder unsolved, and the weird text Rachel had received and, of course, the vandalism to her home with the single word: KILLER.

Was someone just trying to freak her out? Get his or her jollies from terrorizing his ex-wife? A cruel prank that preyed on her fears? That was bad enough and it made his blood boil, but it could be the start of something more dangerous, a warning of more dire, perhaps deadly things to come.

He snorted.

He was starting to be as paranoid as she was.

But, he told himself, his eyes scanning the street, with good cause. He saw a movement in the shrubbery, a dark shadow, and felt himself tense until he realized the motion in the leaves was an oversized racoon. Standing on his back legs, the critter stared straight at Cade's truck with his masked eyes before waddling away, deeper into the shrubbery guarding the fence line.

Cade had spent the day trying to track down the elusive Frank Quinn, who didn't have a driver's license or registration for a white Buick, nor did he live on Toulouse Street. Though there were four Frank Quinns in Portland, two on the other side of the mountains, one in Bend, and another living outside of Pendleton, none was the man he'd met on this very street last week. He'd even checked dog registrations in Chinook County—again no Frank Quinn, nor F. Quinn.

He'd thought the name was an alias and kicked himself for not taking a picture of the guy or asking more questions at the time.

He saw a light go on upstairs in the office overlooking the front yard. Her silhouette was visible beyond the shade, and for a second he felt like a voyeur, a teenaged boy trying to gain a peek of the girl next door taking a shower. He watched as the light snapped off, replaced by a blue glow—her computer. And he imagined her in an oversized T-shirt, her hair pulled into a messy bun that was falling loose after hours of restless sleep, a yawn parting her lips.

God, he missed all that.

He missed her.

He missed living with the kids—being a part of his family.

"Get over it." He'd blown that once-in-a-lifetime opportunity.

He wondered if she'd gotten another text that had woken her.

Or had it been another one of her nightmares?

Or just her ongoing battle with insomnia?

He'd been such a fool.

"Too little too late."

Staring at the house, watching and waiting, he remembered the good times . . . and the bad. When he'd married Rachel she'd been pregnant and scared, and he hadn't realized how deeply scarred she was from the tragedy of the night her brother died. Yeah, it all came back to Luke's death and that stupid, dangerous game the group of kids had been playing.

She'd always blamed herself.

Despite the fact that most of the people in that darkened cannery had testified that they didn't think Rachel could have fired the gun. Violet Osbourne and Annessa Bell had both claimed they weren't sure that Rachel was the killer.

He finished the coffee and saw the computer light dim in the house, but the street remained quiet. He thought of how it had all fallen apart. There had been fights, of course, especially about her ever-increasing paranoia. With motherhood came a whole new raft of fears. She'd overprotected the kids, he'd thought, and the kids had rebelled. Rachel probably hadn't been able to stop herself and the nightmares had increased. She'd been freaked out that something would happen to a member of their family and hated the fact that he was a detective, as her father had been. She blamed her father's job for his drinking and the dissolution of her parents' marriage. She'd been certain the same fate would befall them, and because of that, her fears of divorce, she'd almost put the wheels into motion.

Yeah, Ryder, but you were the driver, weren't you?

His partner at the Chinook County detective division had moved on and had been replaced by Kayleigh O'Meara and they'd spent many a night on stakeouts like this one, getting closer, enjoying the camaraderie and the hours alone. She'd broken up with a boyfriend—Travis Mcsomething or other—and Cade's marriage was crumbling. He'd confided more than he should have on those long, dark nights, and he'd recognized that she was starting to fall for him. He should have put the brakes on, headed her off at the pass.

But he didn't.

Once in his old sedan, Kayleigh had been bold enough to kiss him and he hadn't stopped her. Her warm lips felt like heaven after weeks of being shut out from a wife who was falling apart. One kiss led to another, and soon they were fumbling at each other's clothes before he came to his senses and stopped the madness. "I can't," he said, breathing hard, looking away from her. "And . . . and we need to pay attention here." They were on a stakeout of a suspected drug dealer, in a sketchy area southeast of Astoria near the bay, a small, one-story house tucked among similar crumbling residences, some abandoned and boarded, trash littering the cracked road. There was a chance that this was a meth lab, a small operation but one that might lead to others, part of a larger system.

He straightened his clothes, and from the corner of his eye he saw her do the same, her lips pursed, as she swallowed hard. Embarrassed. As he was.

"Look, I'm sorry," he said.

"Don't be." She stared straight ahead through the bug-spattered windshield to the house with a single lamp glowing in a cracked window. "My mistake."

"Kayleigh—"

"Don't. Just don't." Her lips had barely moved, but in the weak streetlight he saw that her eyes were glistening, a tear starting to slide down her cheek.

"Oh, God, I . . . I don't know what to say. I'm married."

"Are you?" She swung her head around to stare at him. "Really? All you've done for the past month or so is talk about how miserable you are, how miserable *she* is, how you don't know what to do."

He couldn't deny it. He'd crossed a line. But he wasn't going to cross another.

"I thought your marriage was over; Jesus, Ryder, I usually don't make this kind of mistake!"

"Neither do I."

"Oh, shove it." She sniffed loudly, but her eyes, almost luminous in the night, glared at him, her pain turning to a palpable fury. "I'm sick of this. Really sick of it. I'll ask for a new partner in the morning."

"You don't have to—"

"Yeah," she said, cutting him off and pulling her sidearm from its holster. "Yeah, I do." And with that, she opened the door and slid out of the car. "I'm over this."

"What're you doing?"

"Finding out if we're wasting our time out here." She closed the door and, in a half crouch, ran toward the house.

"No. Oh, fuck!" Frantic, he called for backup as he exited the car, closed the door, then took off after her. What the hell was she thinking? Not only might she blow their cover, but she was going to get herself killed in the process! And if these guys were cooking meth . . .

And they were. He smelled it, that acrid odor filtering through a crack in the windows somewhere. Maybe from the attic where one small dormer peeked from the dilapidated roof, the glass of the window nonexistent.

Kayleigh had made it to the broken-down fence of the backyard and was slipping past a leaning post when he heard the creak of a door.

Oh, crap!

A second later a scrawny man with thin, stringy hair stepped onto the porch to light a cigarette. Beside him, a beast of a dog, gray and bristly, wandered into the yard only to stop suddenly, turn, and bark wildly. A sharp, loud warning.

No!

Cigarette dangling from his lips, the man turned, peering in the direction of Kayleigh just as the dog spied Cade. Snarling, it leapt from the porch and the man twitched, his gaze shifting from the fence to the street. He raised his gun.

"Police!" Cade yelled. "Drop your weapon."

"You heard him!" Kayleigh screamed. "Drop it. Now!" She was aiming straight at the back porch. Then, "No! Cade! Watch out—!"

Blam!

A gun fired.

Cade's body jerked, then spun. He took a wobbling step backward before he stumbled, his pistol clattering to the broken pavement. His knees folded and he felt a sharp, burning sensation on his neck. He'd never seen the man on the porch lift his weapon, but Cade had gone down, the world spinning as more gunshots blasted and somewhere far in the distance the sound of a siren wailed through the night.

He found out later a second shooter had been in an attic window and had fired at him, while stringy-hair and the dog had backed down. The dude had dropped his weapon and commanded the dog to "stay," rather than risk shooting an officer. Kayleigh had gotten off several shots, hitting the assailant in the window. Both of the suspects had been arrested, charged, and convicted and were now serving time, their small operation shut down, the link to the larger system never discovered.

Now Cade stared at Rachel's house, dark again, Rachel having, he presumed, turned off the computer and returned to bed. Not that she would sleep; he knew better. When she had the nightmares she had trouble finding sleep again. He knew. He'd been there. Had held her and whispered that "everything's all right," and that she needed to "calm down" as he'd kissed the top of her head and felt her trembling in his arms.

He checked his watch and found it now after 4 a.m., the neighborhood calm. Not even the raccoon disturbed the stillness. He stretched the muscles in his neck by rotating his head, then settled back against the seat. That stakeout had been the beginning of the end, he thought.

When he'd opened his eyes, he'd found himself

staring up at the can lights in the ceiling of the intensive care unit of the hospital.

A male nurse was in the room with him. His name tag read Ari Granger, RN. With stern blue eyes, a soul patch, and the brisk demeanor of a bartender, Ari checked Cade's vital signs. Cade winced.

"What happened?" he asked, his voice gravelly and dry. For a second he wasn't able to remember anything.

"EMTs brought you into the ER. Gunshot wound. You've been in surgery." Another grave look.

Cade tried to shift in the bed and changed his mind when the pain flared through his back.

"How's your pain on a scale of one to ten? I can give you something for that," Ari said.

"Not . . . not good." Cade stopped moving to help the agony subside. "My back . . ." The top half of his body felt raw.

"The bullet lodged close to your spinal cord. Another inch and I don't think we'd be having this conversation right now. But if you rest and follow the doctor's orders, in a few days, you'll walk out of here a whole man. For now, you need rest. Here, let me give you something for that pain," he said, and added a dosage into Cade's IV.

"Point taken. Is my partner okay? Kayleigh O'Meara?" he asked as the memory of the scene at the meth house started to return.

"She's out in the waiting room, I think. You thirsty?"

Cade nodded, increasingly aware of the dryness in his throat and the burning pain spreading through his back, shoulders, and chest.

The nurse disappeared for a minute or so it seemed, then returned with water in a glass with a bendable straw. "Dr. Kendris will be in sometime this afternoon to discuss your prognosis."

Cade sucked the ice water through the straw, soothing his parched tongue and throat. As his memory returned with a slow clarity, he recalled the fuckup at the stakeout, how he'd given in to temptation with Kayleigh, and how he'd almost let his marriage go.

What had he been thinking?

"My wife?" he said, but the nurse had disappeared through the door again. Of course Rachel knew he was here. She would have been the first one notified. He thought to call her but his damned cell phone wasn't anywhere in sight, and the old landline phone sat across the room on the windowsill. Pushing his palms into the mattress, he tried to sit up, get up, get to the phone. But failed. He was sleepy again. Succumbing to the pain medication. He closed his eyes and was gone again.

When he reopened them, it seemed like a moment had passed, but he sensed more time than he imagined had lapsed.

Someone squeezed his hand.

He blinked.

Kayleigh, her green eyes dark with guilt, her face pale. "So you decided not to leave us after all," she said. "You scared the hell out of me. Out of all of us." She cleared her throat. "I . . . I . . . shit, I don't know what to say. I made a mistake. Nope, I made a lot of them last night. I, um, I'm sorry. God, so sorry."

He paused a second, then had to ask, "Is Rachel here?"

Her eyes slid away. "Not sure. But she's been called."

He wondered if she'd show up. Their last fight . . .

"So, seriously," she said, clearing her throat. "How are you feeling? Are you in any pain?"

"I think I'm on pretty good meds. Just can't move much. I need to get up and—"

"Don't think so, Detective." She attempted to put on a brave face, lighten things up. "I'm pretty sure you've got doctor's orders to stay put." Her auburn hair, which she usually pulled back, hung down loose and thick now, falling onto the hospital gown over his chest as she leaned in. "You stay where you are and follow every single doctor's order, Ryder. You just scared the hell out of me, and I'm going to make it my personal mission to make sure you take it easy until you're back to one hundred percent."

"You don't need to do that."

"Too bad. Already decided." Some of her guard had fallen away and he witnessed a deeper emotion in her eyes, something neither one of them wanted to acknowledge.

"Kayleigh, don't," he whispered just as the door to the room opened and Rachel appeared, looking frazzled and rushed, her jacket billowing, her dark hair springing from its ponytail.

Everything about her said: *I'm here for you. I dropped everything. I rushed over.*

But in the next heartbeat the intense desperation in her eyes gave way to shock and pain as she took in the scene.

Kayleigh dropped his fingers as if they'd burned her.

"What the hell?" Rachel whispered, her eyes wide.

"I was just leaving." Kayleigh started for the door.

"Cade?" Rachel said, then shook her head slowly as Kayleigh's footsteps echoed down the hallway.

"Hey, Rach." He almost added, *I know this looks bad,* which was the truth, or *It's not what you think,* which was a little bit of a lie, all things considered, but he didn't want to stoop to clichés.

"Hey, Cade," she responded, not getting too close to the bed, her chin set, her gaze damning.

"You take care, okay?" And then she'd turned and left.

They'd tried to patch things up. He'd moved back home, but their marriage had never been the same. A few months after the shooting, once he'd been on his feet again, he had quit his job with Chinook County and taken this job with the Edgewater PD. He'd hoped to create a more normal life. He'd thought that he would be able to repair the cracks in his marriage, that he would become an active father on a more regular schedule.

Six months after the shooting, Rachel had asked him to move out, though she seemed to think he was the one who wanted to separate. Again. Theirs had never been an easy, steady union. She'd filed for divorce. He hadn't fought it.

And he'd learned the hard way that whatever doesn't kill you makes you stronger.

CHAPTER 22

It was late.

Ned should just shut off the damned TV and go to bed.

But he knew he wouldn't sleep.

Not that he ever did.

Instead he tossed the newspaper he'd been reading into the trash, then walked to the kitchen, delved into the refrigerator, and cracked another beer. Over the sink, where several dirty plates and a couple of glasses resided, he looked out the window at the dark yard, but all he saw was the headline, in bold type, burned into his brain:

TWENTY-YEAR-OLD MYSTERY STILL HAUNTS TOWN

"You bet it does," he said to himself and saw the ghost of his reflection. He noticed that his jawline wasn't as tight as it had been and he scowled, then looked past the watery image to watch a stray cat tiptoe along the boney laurel that marked the edges of the yard. The scrawny thing sniffed the night air and cast a thin shadow in the fake light from Ned's back porch.

He took a long swallow from his can, then snapped the blinds shut.

The night of Luke's death had changed his life forever. Changed Melinda's and Rachel's, too.

Disturbed, he walked back to his sparse living room and retrieved the paper, stared down at the smaller print.

WHO KILLED LUKE HOLLANDER?

"Jesus," he whispered, and it was half prayer as he remembered that night, the confusion of the dark interior of the cannery, the kids shouting and running, firecrackers or something going off and, of course, gunfire.

A genuine clusterfuck, if ever there had been.

He felt a deep sadness and more than a little guilt for how he'd handled the situation, first cop on the scene and the one who had ultimately helped his daughter into the back of a squad car.

It seemed like a million years ago.

And it seemed like yesterday.

He'd hoped it would slowly disappear, the pain subsiding, time dulling its edges, and it had. Until now. Until the renewed interest due to the article.

And not just one.

A series.

"Great," he muttered, scratching his chin. "Just great." That night had killed whatever hope he'd had of repairing his faltering marriage. Luke's death had shattered Melinda. The fact that her daughter had been accused of the murder had caused an emotional chasm so deep, no amount of penance, tears, or family counseling had been able to bridge it.

And really, who could blame Melinda, he wondered as he settled into his recliner in his small living room. Certainly not he. No, Ned Gaston, the cop who had put her first husband away on assault charges, a man she'd thought was her hero, had certainly proved himself fallible, or worse. Melinda had learned that sorry fact too little, too late.

And so their marriage had died, along with her son.

Another swallow and he told himself again that he should give up the booze, but hell, it was only beer and light beer at that.

If he could change things, God knew he would. His connections to what remained of his family, his daughter and grandkids, were frail at best and sometimes seemed to be unraveling.

Probably his fault.

He needed to try harder. Hadn't Rachel told him that over and over again, that if he wanted to know his grandkids he needed to make an effort? Harper would graduate from high school next year, was about the same age Rachel had been when Luke had died. And Dylan, that kid was only a couple of years behind. It was probably already too late.

"Shit." Another deep swig.

He'd observed that Melinda and Rachel had a decent if far from perfect relationship. All things considered, that was more than he could ask for.

Melinda still blamed him for Luke's death. He knew that. He'd heard her arguments: Ned should have been around, more invested in the marriage and family. Ned should have been more of a positive influence on Luke as his biological father was an ass-wipe and a felon. Ned should have been more of a hands-on father to Rachel, more of a loving, faithful husband to her. Maybe then her kids wouldn't have lied to her, Melinda had rationalized, maybe they wouldn't have been at the cannery that night, maybe the tragedy that had ripped their lives apart would have been averted.

"Maybe," he said, pointing his remote at the oversized flat-screen.

But he didn't believe it for a second.

He wondered if the article in the newspaper would stir any interest in the police department. Probably not. The case had been long forgotten.

Until now.

Shit.

He didn't like that pot being stirred. His family, fractured as it was, couldn't take the hit.

Nor could he.

He hesitated a second, staring at the TV as the late-night host interviewed some beautiful young star he didn't recognize, then reached into the side pocket of his chair and pulled out his laptop. Unbeknownst to anyone currently working in the department, he could still access the Edgewater PD database.

Before he'd retired, he'd dated the secretary/ computer whiz for a while. He'd spent a lot of time with her at the office, then later after hours, often at her house. He'd found passwords that were long out of date, but had learned how to access her account and knew where she kept her list of user names and passwords. Whenever he was blocked, he logged in as if he were she, remotely, and checked her own password manager and, presto, he was in. He felt a little bad about using Donna as he had, but a guy had to do what a guy had to do.

He finished his beer, crushed the can, tossed it into the trash along with the newspaper, and logged in as D. J. Larimer in the department and tried the latest password she'd concocted using a combination of her mother's birth date, a symbol, and an old family pet's name. He entered 19Rosco46* and was in. A smile crept across his jaw, and not for the first time he was thankful that the sleepy little police department was small enough not to have up-to-the-second technology. At least so far. He started searching and, as the late-night host paused for a commercial break, whispered, "Thank you, Donna Jean."

Cade rubbed the kinks from the back of his neck as he stared at his ex-wife's cottage. So far, the night had been quiet and he wondered if he was wasting his time. He checked his watch. Almost two. He'd give it another two hours, then go home and sleep for a few before work. He was used to little sleep and was fortunate enough to be someone who could catch up on hours lost by logging in more hours the next night.

So far.

He kept telling himself that the text Rachel had received might have been in error or some kind of stupid prank, but why the message "I forgive you"? Didn't make sense. And the vandalism on the door? That, too, could be a nasty prank spurred by the article in the newspaper; God knew there was a lot of hate to go around these days. He wondered if Frank Quinn was involved—and was that even his real name? Had he been at Rachel's house? With the dog? Or was that a cover? Was Quinn the person who'd marred the door? If so, why?

He slouched in the pickup. Then there was Violet Sperry's murder. Who would kill Violet and why now?

He kept coming back to the article in the newspaper and the twentieth anniversary of Luke Hollander's murder.

Were all the events, including that long-ago homicide, connected?

He didn't know, and it didn't seem likely.

Yet the murder, vandalism, and weird text had happened over a matter of only a few days.

Coincidence?

He didn't think so.

He would contact Kayleigh in the morning and see how her investigation was going, and then talk to Richard Moretti, the doctor who had declared Luke DOA at the hospital. And while he was at it, he needed to talk to Ned Gaston, his ex-father-in-law. Ned wouldn't want to talk about the long-ago murder of his stepson, or the fact that his only child had been the primary suspect in the homicide, but if the events were somehow related, and they seemed so, then Cade would need Ned's insights. Like it or not, Rachel's old man had been first on the scene.

He yawned, leaned back, and felt his cell phone vibrate. Glancing at the screen, he saw Ed Nowak's name and number as he answered. "Ryder."

"Nowak here. I'm down at St. Augustine's," he said curtly, all business. "You'd better get down here. We've got a victim. Deceased. Homicide. Strung up on a bell rope and blindfolded."

"What?"

"There's more. Hell, Cade, your daughter and her friend discovered the woman."

Harper? "Wait—what?" He glanced back at Rachel's cottage. "My daughter?" But that was impossible. Harper was right here, in that house . . .

"That's what I said. She's here with a young man. Xander Vale. They are both fine. Got that? Your kid is okay."

Cade threw another look at the house. No way would Rachel have let Harper be with that kid at two in the damned morning. And on a school night . . . Wait. Oh Jesus. "Who is it? The victim?"

"Still working on that."

"But Harper's okay?"

"Yeah. Didn't I just say that? She's gonna be okay."

"Fuck." He was already starting his truck while dread seeped through his guts. "I'll be there in ten."

He made it in seven and parked half a block away from the school complex as the street was cordoned off. Police cars, lights flashing, blocked one entrance to the street, while another was barricaded at the far corner. In between, taking up a full city block, was the St. Augustine property and the two-story building owned by his father. Only a parking lot separated the two. An older Jeep had been parked against the aging plank fence while two rescue vehicles had been backed to the gate.

What the devil had Harper gotten herself into?

Cade was out of his truck in an instant and

327

running to a spot where a huge gate to the school yard hung open, the chain that had held it closed now broken.

Inside the complex, he found Nowak huddled with several other people, one he recognized as his own daughter. "What the hell happened here?" he demanded and Harper seemed to shrink. Xander Vale, one arm draped over Harper's shoulders, stood rigid, his face white, his demeanor grim.

"Daddy!" Harper flung herself into his arms. "I'm sorry. I'm so, so sorry."

"Shh. It's okay," he said, holding her close, knowing he was lying. Whatever had happened here, it was not okay. Definitely not okay.

"But I saw it. I saw her . . . oh, God! It's horrible!"

"Shh. Slow down." Wrapping his arms around her, he breathed into her hair. "It'll be all right, just calm down, okay?" He waited for her body to quiet, the sobs to slow, the tears to stem.

"But she's dead. She's *dead*." Harper was shaking. "They couldn't save her." Crying, hiccuping, and sobbing nearly hysterically, Harper clung to him. "We tried to save her. We did. Really. Xander cut her down. But it was too late." Her voice was a squeak, and as Cade held her, he stared over Harper's head to Vale, whose jaw was clenched. Though Vale appeared to wish he was anywhere else in the whole damned world, he stood his ground while other police personnel and rescue workers moved through the dark school yard. Their flashlight beams cut swaths of illumination over the mounds of dirt and broken equipment.

Cade's gaze narrowed on Vale. "What happened?"

"It's like she said—"

"From the beginning," Cade cut in, and the kid stiffened.

"These two," Nowak said, hooking a finger at Harper and Xander, "heard moaning, came to investigate, and ended up finding a woman hanging upside down from the ropes of the bell tower. Gruesome, just like she said. Look, I called Voss, too. She's inside."

"Good."

"I figured—"

"That because my kid found the body, someone with a little more perspective should be involved."

"Yeah."

Cade didn't blame him. Protocol. No blurred lines. Not like Ned Gaston handling a case involving his stepson and daughter.

Nonetheless he needed answers. Cade stared straight at Vale. "I want to hear it from you. Start with how you got here."

"It's my fault," Vale said.

"Your fault?" Hell, was the kid going to confess?

"Whoa. Not about what happened, but that we're here," the kid clarified, obviously stricken at his choice of words. He held up a hand. "I mean it's my fault because I talked Harper into sneaking out. We met at the corner of Height and Grange a little after midnight, I think. We texted and I picked her up and brought her up to . . . to my apartment." He hooked a finger to the building next door where the law offices of Charles H. Ryder were housed.

Cade felt sick inside. He knew that apartment. Well.

"We just got there when we heard something, someone crying for help. So we came over here, climbed the fence, and found her in the chapel. She was hanging facedown and . . . suffering."

"It was awful!" Harper said, her voice high.

"Yeah." Xander Vale was nodding, his expression grim. "I cut her down and Harper called nine-one-one. They got here fast."

"Not fast enough," Nowak said. "She was too far gone. The EMTs worked on her, but it was too late."

"Anyone know who she is? ID?"

Nowak nodded. "Phone and driver's license in her back pocket. Annessa Cooper. Got a car registered to Clint Cooper, a Mercedes, parked two blocks over on Chinook." Nowak looked at him. "Must be the husband. Isn't he part of some financial group buying up properties around here? I read about it. Like from Seattle or Tacoma or someplace up there?"

"Yeah. I think so," Cade said slowly, his gaze moving to the spire of the chapel, his stomach turning a little. The name meant something to him. "Annessa was local. Originally from here. Last name of Bell." Was it possible? Another class-mate of Rachel's, an alumni of Edgewater High, murdered? Within a week of Violet Sperry's death?

"You said she was blindfolded?"

"Tape," Nowak clarified. "Over the eyes."

Like Violet.

Fuck.

Cade's arms tightened around his daughter. He thought of the two murders and the weird text Rachel had received, the vandalism on the house. Connected? Possibly. Certainly more than coincidence.

"Look, you said you got statements?" he said to Nowak. "Let's get these two home."

He felt his daughter tense. "You're not going to tell Mom, are you?" Harper asked, drawing away to stare at him with a newfound worry in her eyes. "Dad, please—"

"I'm pretty sure that can't be avoided." He kept his gaze on Vale. "As a matter of fact, I think both of you should be there when I do. Give me ten minutes to check out the scene before we head out." He turned to Nowak. "You'll stay with them?"

"You've got it." Nowak gave a curt nod.

"Okay." To Harper, he said, "I'll be right back, okay? I just have to check out a few things. Stay with Officer Nowak."

"I'll be here," Vale offered, as if that were any kind of comfort.

"I won't be long," he told Harper.

"Okay, Dad." His daughter moved away from him, looking small and pale.

"Ten minutes," he repeated, then headed across the uneven ground of the old school yard. Voss was over by the school, her flashlight illuminating the patches of grass and dirt.

"We think the attack started here," she said. "You can see signs of a struggle." She ran her flashlight's beam onto a door and the broken cement of the porch where there was evidence of blood and scuff marks in the dust. "One shoe here." She illuminated a red high heel. "Another here." Not far away, the mate of the first shoe lay on its side.

"Then he dragged her this way." She ran the beam over the ground where shallow, parallel ruts were scraped into the bare earth—a trail leading across the yard. They disappeared in the spots of grass only to show up in other spots of wet earth. "Her heels are scraped, so it looks like he dragged her." Voss was slowly walking toward the chapel. "He probably picked her up and carried her from here. The door was pried open and there are no drag marks inside the building."

Cade nodded, reviewing what she'd told him, trying to envision the crime as it had been committed.

A fierce attack.

Brutal.

The killer had been determined.

He glanced up at the spire of the church, and then let his gaze move downward in the night sky to the fence at the back of the chapel. Just beyond the fence, he could see the roof of the building next door, his old man's law office. A muscle began to work in his jaw. He knew the place well, especially the apartment where Vale had taken up temporary residence.

Hadn't he used that very spot himself when he was younger?

Hadn't he and Rachel spent nights alone up in that studio?

Doing the same things his seventeen-year-old daughter was doing with Xander Vale?

What goes around, comes around.

Son of a bitch!

"In here," Voss said, urging him on.

They stepped through the door and into an anteroom. Lights were visible on one side of the altar, shafts falling through an open doorway. Following the beam of Voss's flashlight, they walked carefully down the aisle and around a corner to the base of the bell tower, where the woman lay crumpled on the floor of the square space. A severed rope was still tied around one ankle. Her hair fanned out on the ground around her, and her eyes were glassy and fixed, bits of some gooey substance clinging to the skin near her eyes.

"Tape," Voss said, as if reading his thoughts. "It was over her eyes. As she was still alive, Vale tore it off her face before he tried to revive her." She motioned to the side of the enclosure where a wad of blue tape was tacked to the wall. It appeared to be identical to the tape they'd found slapped across Violet Sperry's face.

Evidence.

Destroyed.

Two rescue workers, a man and a woman, were bending over the woman.

"No one would have been able to save her," the male hypothesized. "Once the killer strung her up, she was probably too far gone." A lanky twentysomething, his face pockmarked from acne in his youth, his hair trimmed tight on the sides giving way to a thick tuft of red on top, he nodded as he stared at the lifeless woman. "Looks like a ruptured trachea, broken windpipe."

"Hyoid fractured?" Voss asked.

"Probably," the female EMT agreed. "Have to wait until the autopsy for the actual cause of death. ME's on his way."

"Crime scene team, too. They should be here any minute," Voss said, then added, "It looks like Vale's story holds up. He had a knife, gave it up." She cast a glance up at Cade, her face in weird shadow cast by the eerie lights. "The kids were lucky they didn't surprise the killer."

"Not for her," Cade said, glancing down at the corpse.

The male EMT stood up and scrabbled in a front pocket for a nonexistent cigarette. "As I said, nothing they could do."

Cade looked upward to the dark recess of the tower overhead and imagined the brute force required to carry the victim here, presumably as she fought back. He wondered about the adrenaline rush firing the killer's blood. Why had the killer brought her here? Why string her up? Why not leave her at the site of the attack, across the way at the school?

Premeditated.

This wasn't a random killing.

"She have any valuables on her?"

Voss nodded. "Wedding ring set, lots of diamonds in the setting, credit card and forty dollars in her back pocket along with her driver's license. Robbery wasn't the motive."

That much he knew just by considering the brutality of the crime, the way the body was staged to be found.

"Her husband been notified?"

"Yes, she's married. Is that a lucky guess?" Voss asked.

"I knew of her. Small town."

"We reached the husband, but he's in Seattle. On his way back here now."

"You found her cell phone, right?"

"Yeah. Checking the recent calls and contact list already."

"Good." He glanced down at the body one last time. "I gotta go."

On the way back to the parking area he said, "I'll be back once I get Harper home and settled, make sure she's all right."

"Got it."

They reached Nowak, who was leaning against his car. Harper was huddled against Vale and she looked young and scared out of her mind. He didn't blame her. He said to his daughter, "Okay, you ride with me. And you?" He met the younger man's disturbed gaze. "You come to the house. In your own vehicle." Then, thinking twice, "If you're okay to drive."

"I am." The kid seemed calm, so Cade took him at his word.

For now.

Just before he climbed into his truck, he texted Kayleigh: Check out homicide at St. Augustine's chapel. Could be connected to Sperry murder. Busy now. Will call.

He pocketed his phone and got behind the wheel. Before he switched on the ignition, he turned to look at his daughter, huddled against the passenger door in the dark. God, she looked vulnerable, even though she was trying to hold herself together. "You okay?" he asked.

"No." She blinked, sniffed, then rolled her eyes. "Are you?"

"No, not so much."

"I'll never be okay again," she whispered and stared out the window.

His heart cracked a little. Never had he wanted her to experience anything so traumatic. Reaching across the cab, he held her as close as her seat belt would allow. "You will be," he said. "It'll be different; never the same. But we'll both be okay."

She shuddered. "I don't think so."

"Give it time," he suggested and released her. "You're tougher than you think."

"If you say so. Come on. Let's go. Get this over with."

He started the engine and the headlights came on automatically, cutting gold swaths into the dark night.

Harper let out a long sigh as he put the car into drive. She whispered just loud enough so that he could hear, "Mom is gonna so freak."

"She'll be all right."

His daughter threw him a disbelieving glare.

"Oh, yeah? When was the last time she was 'all right'?" She made air quotes, then slouched deeper into the seat. "Trust me, Dad, you'll see. She won't be anywhere close to all right."

CHAPTER 23

"Annessa is dead?" Rachel whispered, trying to get her head around what she was being told, here in the middle of her living room, by her ex-husband.

He'd texted, then shown up at the door with Harper in tow, Xander Vale making an appearance a few minutes later, just as she'd woken Dylan per Cade's demands. With a barking Reno at her side, Rachel had met them at the door, and her daughter had almost fallen into her arms.

At first Rachel had held Harper as if she'd never let go. As the news had sunk in and she'd realized the depth of the trauma Harper was dealing with, Rachel had squeezed her, then finally released her. "Thank God you're okay," she'd said as they'd both battled tears and Harper had bravely dashed hers away.

Now Xander, Harper, and Dylan sat on the couch, ashen faced and looking as if they wanted to drop through the floor. Dylan's hair was mussed, but his eyes were wide as quarters, on alert, despite the fact that he'd been yanked from his bed. Harper wiped away tears, scared as hell and lost in her personal nightmare, while Xander stared at the floor, hands clasped between his knees.

Shocked beyond belief, Rachel tried to control

the trembling that rippled through her body as she lowered herself into her favorite chair. She was still struggling to digest the horrific news.

First Violet and now . . . Annessa? Rachel couldn't believe it. Another classmate. Another young, vibrant woman.

Dead.

Murdered.

And her girl had witnessed the horror, watched a woman die from wounds inflicted by some monster. Rachel was torn between wanting to scream at Harper for being so foolhardy and, relieved that she was safe, holding Harper tight to protect her. Harper looked so young, so innocent . . . so vulnerable. Oh, God.

"Just start at the beginning," Rachel said once her initial shock lifted and her heart rate returned to nearly normal. She listened as Harper explained how she'd slipped out of the house, met Xander Vale, gone to the apartment owned by Chuck Ryder's firm, and then heard the moans coming from outside the window. The kids had followed the sounds to St. Augustine's, where they'd found Annessa barely clinging to life and hanging upside down from the bell tower in the long-closed chapel. Desperately, they had tried to save the near-dead woman, calling 911 as they'd cut her down. But Annessa had died before the paramedics had arrived.

Rachel fought desperately to hold herself

together as she struggled to make some sense of the story.

To be calm when she was frightened out of her mind.

What if Xander and Harper had heard those cries for help while the killer was still there? Would they have become his next targets? Would they, too, have ended up swinging from bell tower ropes? Would they have survived? Her throat tightened and she gripped the arms of the chair at the thought of what might have been. Instead of one victim, there could have been more, including Harper.

Her soul turned to ice and she had to battle the panic that threatened when she let her thoughts venture down that dark, crooked path.

She couldn't go there . . . wouldn't. Instead, she considered how the night had unfolded. "What were you thinking?" she asked her daughter, then caught Cade's slight shake of his head, warning her this wasn't the time or place to chastise their already terrified child. "Never mind, we'll go into that later," she said, taking his cue and seeing Harper swallow and fight tears. Shaking inside, Rachel said, "I'm just glad you're safe."

Tears began to drizzle down Harper's cheeks all over again. She sniffed and brushed them quickly away, tried vainly to look tough.

"Look, honey, why . . . why don't you just go

341

to bed?" Rachel suggested. "We can all talk again tomorrow."

"I don't want to talk about it. Ever."

"Shh. Your mom is right." Vale placed an arm around Harper's slim shoulders, then whispered something in her ear and kissed her hair. So tender it almost broke Rachel's heart. Almost. He looked up and held Rachel's gaze.

"I am sorry for all of this," he said, his voice rough. "It's my fault that Harper snuck out. My idea. It . . . it won't happen again."

Harper looked up through her tears and pressed a palm to his chest. "No. It's not your fault. I came because I wanted to be with you."

"We can discuss all this later after we've all had some sleep," Cade said. "The important thing is that you tried to help and you're safe. We'll have a better perspective in the morning."

Rachel couldn't have agreed more. Now that her daughter was home and unhurt, she just wanted Vale out of her house, needed time to get her own head on straight.

"You can go," Cade said to Vale, "but you're probably going to be contacted by the department again. There're bound to be more questions."

Beside him, Harper groaned. "We already told them everything we know."

"Right, but there'll be a follow-up interview," Cade said. "You might remember something else."

"I don't want to remember any of it," Harper

342

said as Vale rose to his feet and she joined him. With Harper at his side, he made his way to the front door.

"Me neither, but we're gonna have to." He looked into the living room and muttered a quick, "Thanks," though he didn't explain whom he was thanking or why. He didn't kiss Harper again, just slipped outside, pulling the door shut behind him. Cade walked to the door and twisted the dead bolt into place.

Harper glared at her parents. "You can't blame him," she said. "He tried to help that woman."

"We don't," Cade said, but Rachel wasn't so quick to acquiesce. If it hadn't been for Vale wanting to sneak Harper away, they never would have been in this situation. Yes, Annessa would still have been killed, but her daughter would have been safe and spared the trauma of watching someone die.

Just as you did.

She remembered looking down at Luke on the grimy floor of the darkened cannery and watching the light go out of his eyes as he'd slipped into unconsciousness only to die soon after.

Now her own daughter knew the same gut-shredding terror of watching someone die.

Her insides shriveled as she heard a beeping noise and realized it was the security system. She shot to her feet, ran to the back door, and punched in the code to shut off the alarm.

Returning to the living room, she found Harper leaning over the back of the couch to peer through the front window and stare at the disappearing taillights of Vale's Jeep. With a heartfelt sigh, Harper slid onto the cushions and turned, meeting her mother's eyes.

Rachel's heart twisted. "I'm sorry you had to go through this."

"We all are," Cade agreed. "Now, before you all go to bed, one last thing."

"Uh-oh," Dylan said under his breath.

He focused on his daughter. "How did you get out? The security system was in place and your mom said it was still turned on when she got up and checked. Did you turn it off, then reset it?"

"No." Harper bit her lip. "I, uh, I asked Dylan to disengage the circuit to my window."

"What? And you did it?" Rachel said, staring at her son in disbelief. "But that's the whole point of the alarm, to keep you guys safe."

"And to keep us in." Harper folded her arms over her chest, back to being rebellious again.

"Yeah." Rachel was nodding. "At night. Because it's dangerous, Harper. You should understand that after what you went through tonight. Don't you see, I'm . . . we, your father and me . . . we just want to keep you safe."

"But—"

"No 'buts' about it," Cade said, staring his daughter down. "We don't know what's happening, but this is the second murder in Edgewater in under a week."

"It has nothing to do with us."

"You don't know that," Cade cut in and pointed at the door. "This house was vandalized—"

"What do you mean?" Harper asked.

Rachel explained about the door and when it had been marred.

"Seriously?" Harper was stunned. "I didn't even notice."

"I know," Cade said. "It happened the other night. Your mom painted over it and didn't want to upset you."

"Geez." Dylan slid a glance at Rachel.

Cade went on. "That's not all. Your mom got at least one kind of freaky text. The text might be nothing, but we don't know that. Not yet. That's the point. We, all of us"—he motioned to indicate the entire family—"need to be extra vigilant. So you don't sneak out again. And you"—he turned his gaze on his son—"you don't need to be sabotaging the security system. What were you thinking?"

Dylan didn't answer.

Rachel couldn't believe it. "Let me get this straight. You made a separate circuit for Harper's room, one you could disengage at will?"

No response.

She went on, "Did you do the same to your room, too?"

Dylan studied the floor and Rachel's eyes narrowed. "It didn't take you long to do it. I was right there." Another worrisome thought crawled through her brain. "Please don't tell me this is what you do for other kids," she said, horrified at the thought. She paused to fill Cade in, explaining about searching both kids' living areas and being accused of invading their spaces. "And I found an unexplained stash of money in Dylan's room. Harper said it was for fixing his friends' computers and the like, but I think there's more to it."

Dylan glanced up, then down again and swallowed as if there was something stuck in his throat.

"We'll need a list of any security systems you altered," Cade said, obviously trying to keep a lid on his own anger.

"I didn't do anyone else." Dylan finally met his father's gaze.

"He's not lying," Harper said.

Rachel wasn't convinced and drilled her son. "Then what is it you're into?"

"Geez, Mom," Dylan said. "What I told you before. Computers. Gaming systems."

"Why am I having trouble believing that now?" Rachel glared at her kids. "Do you know what happens when you pull stunts like this, both of you? You lose our trust."

"And it's going to take a while to gain it back," Cade said.

"So do we have to start all over with our security system?" Rachel asked, ready to tear her hair out in frustration. "Or is it secure again?"

Dylan nodded. "It's all working. I hooked it up again when Harper texted me that you were bringing her home. It's just a simple switch."

"That you'll remove," Cade said.

"Yeah."

"Tomorrow."

"Yes!" Dylan's temper flashed.

Cade repeated, "And tonight, now, everything's secure?"

"God, Dad, yeah. Go check for yourself!"

"I will. But you show me."

Dylan rolled his eyes but led them all into the kitchen, then the pantry, where the system control box was located. He walked them through the system, explaining that it was now "live," that all the doors and windows were engaged.

"Okay, disconnect it for now, and I'll turn it on after Dad leaves," Rachel said.

"See how hard it is?" Dylan said sarcastically, tapping in the code.

Cade pointed to one of the tabs that was marked FDC. "What's this?"

"The camera for the front yard. It means front door camera," Dylan said.

"Was it working the night the door was vandalized?" Cade asked.

Dylan shook his head. "Nothing on this system was."

Cade's face fell. "Too bad. We might have been able to ID the guy that sprayed the door if he'd been caught on camera."

"Yeah, but the image might have been all grainy. This system's a dinosaur," Dylan said. "You might not even be able to get parts for it."

"Time to upgrade," Cade observed. "You can get digital systems that are easy to install and record and connect to your phone."

"We will. But not tonight," Rachel said, suddenly bone weary. "You two"—she waved a finger between her children—"go to bed. School tomorrow."

"You're making us go?" Harper let out a disbelieving huff.

"Yep." That might not be true. Though her daughter deserved a tough punishment for sneaking out, she had been through a horrid trauma, one to which Rachel could all too easily relate. Was it punishment enough? Probably. Still, Rachel needed to make a stand.

Tomorrow.

Dylan shot down the hall like a bullet, Harper following more slowly. Rachel waited until she heard both their bedroom doors close before saying to her ex, "Welcome to my nightmare."

"Mine, too. And I'm serious about that security system upgrade."

"Got it. I am, too."

"Good." He was walking toward the front of the house again.

"I just can't believe that Annessa's gone," Rachel said as she kept step with him. "That someone would do that. Leave her for dead suspended in the bell tower. Why?"

"Don't know. Yet. But we'll find out."

"I hope so. Does her husband know?" Rachel asked.

"Uh-huh."

"You think it's connected to what happened to Violet?"

"Yeah." He thought for a moment. "You know what struck me? Not just that they graduated together, or that they may or may not have been friends. The thing is that both women were at the cannery that night and both testified on your behalf."

"That's pretty random," she said, but felt a little drip of fear slide through her. "I mean, it all happened twenty years ago."

"And now it's being dragged up in the newspaper, right? And you're having your high school reunion, bringing all the players together?"

"I don't think either Annessa or Violet planned to come."

"Even though they still live in the area?"

"Maybe that's why," she said sarcastically. "Anyway, it really pissed Lila off. She wants to make the reunion one of the best ever or something along those lines. You know Stepmommy-Dearest. Always wants the biggest and best; to make a splash."

"Watch out, your claws are showing."

She narrowed her eyes at him. "Just sayin'."

They'd walked to the living room again and he stopped near the door. "Is there anything else that links Violet and Annessa?"

"Oh, geez, I don't know. I haven't kept up with either of them." She thought for a second. "All I know is that they both moved away for a time, got married. Neither had kids and they ended up back here. Violet came back because of her husband's business—Leonard Sperry and the furniture store—and Annessa's husband, whatever his name, Cooper—"

"Clinton."

"Clint. Yeah, that's right, he's some big developer who bought some property around here. Annessa moved back here pretty recently, in the last couple of years, to help out with her parents. They were in their seventies and . . . I don't remember but I think they're both gone now, but don't quote me on that. I could be wrong.

"Anyway, Annessa and Violet didn't run in the same circles in high school, and I don't think they became friends recently. At least I hadn't heard that they connected."

"But they were both at the cannery that night?"

It wasn't a question and they both knew what night he was referring to.

"Yeah." She eyed her ex. "But a lot of people were."

"I know."

"So what? Are you trying to freak me out? Because if you are, it's working."

"No." He took a step toward her, and for a second she thought he might cross the room and wrap his arms around her. Instead, he stayed near the door. "I just want you and the kids to be careful." He reached for the knob, then pointed at Reno, who had curled into his bed near the bookcase. "I'll be back. Keep the dog on alert, reset the alarm, and lock up the house."

"I will."

"Good."

And then he was gone.

No kiss.

No arms wrapped around her.

No hint of the intimacy they'd once shared.

Which was a good thing; what she'd insisted upon.

Right?

Why then the tinge of disappointment when she threw the dead bolt on the front door?

"Because you're an idiot," she whispered before engaging the alarm system near the back of the house, then starting her nightly routine of double-checking all the locks on the doors and latches on the windows.

CHAPTER 24

Kayleigh was waiting for him. Cade recognized her slim form in the strobing lights of the cruisers barricading each end of the block in front of St. Augustine's.

He parked and ducked under the crime scene tape, thus avoiding a TV crew that stood by a white news van, the logo of a Portland station emblazoned across the side panels. The reporter exchanged a disappointed look with the cameraman, who juggled a shoulder cam complete with microphone and lights at the ready.

Kayleigh stood, her hair pulled back, a baseball cap low over her eyes as she talked with Nowak and Voss near the open gate. She wore tight jeans and a coat that hit her midthigh. Deep in discussion, Kayleigh looked up as he approached. "Hey," she said. "Got your message."

He nodded. "I see. They bring you up to speed?"

"Yep."

"You all think this murder might be linked to the Sperry homicide?" Voss asked.

"Yep." Cade was certain of it.

Voss snorted. "Makes you wonder what the hell's going on in this small town. No homicides

in twenty damned years and now two within a week."

"Two victims who witnessed the shooting twenty years ago," Cade said.

"Oh, good Lord," Voss said, "you're not trying to link what happened tonight to the Luke Hollander homicide twenty years ago?"

"Not yet."

"I saw you pulled the case file."

"Just brushing up on what happened."

"My ass. I know you, Ryder. You think you're on to something."

"Maybe nothing."

Voss caught his gaze. "All good on the home front?"

"As good as can be expected."

Voss snorted. "What a mess."

Kayleigh didn't remark, but one eyebrow arched beneath the bill of her cap.

"The ME?" Cade asked, turning the conversation from his personal life.

"Been here and gone. Body, too. On its way to the morgue." Voss shook her head. "I'm heading that way. Meeting the husband. He'll ID her, but it's just a formality. She matches the photo on her license, which still lists her residence as Seattle. The husband explained that she hadn't gotten around to getting a new one in Oregon. They weren't sure they were moving here permanently."

"How did he sound?"

"Okay. Considering. But who can really tell on a phone? The wireless connection wasn't all that great. He was already driving south. Has a friend or business partner with him." She checked her watch. "Not much traffic, clear night. He should be arriving soon."

"Have the crime scene guys come up with anything?"

"Not that we didn't already know. Maybe we'll find some clues in the victim's car. It's already been towed to the garage. We're pulling phone records," Nowak said.

"And I'll check the victim's home once we're through at the hospital." Voss was patting the pockets of her jacket, then came up with her keys. "I'd better get moving if I want to beat Clint Cooper to the morgue. God, I hate this part of the job."

"Don't we all," Nowak agreed as she headed toward her vehicle. He slipped his phone from his pocket to check a text. "Aw shit, Elvin Atkins is at it again. Visibly drunk and banging on his wife's door, despite the restraining order." Sighing, he said, "I guess we're done here anyway. Time to wrap it up."

"I want another look," Cade said.

Nowak nodded. "Go for it. Right now, it's the crime team in control, and once they leave, O'Neal will lock things up."

As Nowak departed, Cade and Kayleigh walked through the gate to the yard, where lights cast an eerie pall over the landscape. Two technicians combed the area, searching for trace evidence.

"Your kid discovered the body?" she said as they signed into the scene and put on protective shoe covers before picking a path to the chapel.

"She and a friend, Xander Vale, but the victim was still alive. They called nine-one-one. Couldn't save her." He glanced her way as they slipped inside the church, now illuminated by harsh temporary lights as another investigator went over the pews.

"Is Harper okay?"

"Hope so," he said, not sounding nearly as confident as he had when he'd been trying to bolster his daughter. They made their way to the bell tower, where a technician was finishing, just leaving the area where the victim had been discovered.

"Looks like the victim was attacked by the school," Kayleigh said. "Then once the killer had subdued her, she was brought here to the bell tower and hung upside down." She kneeled down to eye the dusty floorboards of the bell tower, then looked up to the ceiling of the steeple, now dark, where once bells had been suspended. Cade remembered hearing those chapel bells peal as he grew up, the sound carrying through the town just before mass. He also remembered hearing the shouts and laughter of the kids who attended the private school. He'd been in this chapel only a couple of times when he was a kid. His mother had been a nonpracticing Catholic, his father an atheist, so visits to the chapel had been rare.

Cade studied the scene and wondered about the killer. How had he met his victim? Did he know her? Had he lured her here? Why was she at St. Augustine's—an abandoned property—so late at night? And why would the killer take the time to drag her into the chapel? As if to stage her death. Why take the risk?

Somehow, he thought, the little church was significant.

"Are you really trying to connect this to the Hollander murder?" Kayleigh asked, dusting her hands as she straightened.

He shook his head. "Not really."

"The case was closed. They had a confession."

"It was an accident," he said sharply, feeling a need to defend Rachel. Which was ridiculous.

"Then what's the connection?"

"Too many coincidences."

They walked out of the church and back along the fence to the gate, where they discarded their shoe coverings and signed out. A thin fog was rolling in from the west, oozing through the parking lot, blurring the sharp lines of the buildings.

Cade checked his watch. It had been a long

night already and dawn was still an hour off, not a hint of gray light to the east. "Let's talk this out," he said. "I'll buy you coffee at Abe's. Breakfast if you want."

"Coffee'll do," she said and climbed into the passenger side of his truck.

For a second he remembered another time, when they were still partners and the night had closed in on them. There had been one kiss, then another and . . . they'd stopped, both breathing hard, rain drizzling down a windshield that had started to fog. "I can't do this," he'd said, and she'd stared hard into his eyes. "Neither can I." That had been the end of something that had never truly begun. They'd never stepped across that frail boundary of his disintegrating marriage, not before he'd signed the divorce papers and not after. Almost as if they'd known then it was a bridge too far.

He drove to the all-night diner situated on the highway at the western edge of town, a spot long-haul truckers used to spend the night in the oversized parking lot, beyond which fields stretched out to the old cannery site. The restaurant itself was a 1950s cinder block building with a high peaked ceiling and globe lights suspended over a counter that ringed a central kitchen. From behind a half wall, bacon sizzled, coffee perked, and dishes rattled.

They settled into one of the booths near the

back of the building, though it still seemed like they were in a fishbowl, with the floor-to-ceiling windows that rimmed the restaurant. At this time of day, the place was nearly empty.

A skinny blond waitress who was far too perky for five in the morning appeared with a pitcher of steaming coffee in one hand. "Hey there. I'm Livvie. I take it you two need some good hot coffee right off the bat. And how about some breakfast?"

"Coffee for both of us for now," Cade said.

"Chef's got an awesome farmer's breakfast this morning," she said, showing a dimple. "Sausage *and* bacon."

"Just coffee," he said.

Kayleigh nodded. "Yeah, me too."

"You sure? It's the special and really, really yummers."

Kayleigh said, "No thanks."

"Okay." Her smile had never faltered as she poured them each a steaming cup. "But you let me know if you change your mind." Still smiling, she flitted away as an elderly couple entered.

"Effer-frickin'-vescent," Kayleigh muttered, watching the gray-haired couple take a table near the counter where a slowly turning pie display was front and center and the waitress was ready with two plastic menus.

"Yeah, well, Livvie hasn't just come from a grisly homicide scene."

"Lucky for her." Kayleigh tossed her baseball cap onto the seat beside her, her ponytail now messy, hairs springing around her face. "So tell me," she said, pouring cream from a small pitcher into her coffee, "since you're the lifer in town, how does the Cooper murder link to the Sperry? I know the basics: they went to school together, were more acquaintances than friends, didn't seem to hang out, and that's about it."

"You're right. They were both married, no kids and no other connection that I know about."

"But killed within a week of each other, blindfolded with the same blue tape."

"We think it's the same tape."

She shot him a look. "Oh, come on. What're the chances that it's different? Two murders in twenty years, both victims not gagged, but blindfolded with blue tape. Some psychologist would have a heyday with that one." She slid the salt and pepper shakers together and stared at him with hard, green eyes. "Come on, Ryder, it's the same guy, the same tape, and we both know it. We just have to prove it."

He paused, caught on what she'd said. "A psychologist?"

"Let's just hope the techs can find a latent print on the tape."

"And then you've got to hope our killer has prints already in the system."

"If not, needle in a haystack."

He knew it was a long shot and watched as she stirred the coffee, then took an experimental sip. "Yeah, but maybe we'll get lucky with the tape or something else. We'll start with phone records."

Frustrated, she leaned back in the booth. "So tell me why you think these murders have anything to do with what happened to Luke Hollander?"

"I'm not sure they do; it's probably nothing. I just thought I'd review the case. A couple of things have happened that seem to indicate someone hasn't gotten over it."

"Maybe they're just stirred up because of the article in that rag, the *Edgewater Edition*."

"Could be," he said, but sensed it was deeper than some nutcase getting riled from reading a piece in the newspaper. He told her about Frank Quinn, the message on Rachel's door, and the text.

" 'I forgive you'?" she said and sat back against the red cushion. "Someone's gaslighting her, y'know. Messing with her mind."

He couldn't argue the point; didn't like it. "Why?"

"You tell me."

"Don't know, but I'll work on it." He took a sip from his cup as a couple of truckers walked in and bellied up to the counter. "Anything new with the Sperry homicide?"

She scowled. "Nothing that's of any help.

The bullet in the wall was the same caliber as the Sperry gun that's still missing. None of the victim's friends or relatives could say a bad word about her. You know, all of a sudden Violet Sperry became a saint. We're still checking phone records and going through her computers. So far it looks like she was really into her dogs, spent a lot of time on blogs and websites for Cavalier King Charles spaniels. The husband was into online gambling and some porn." She rolled her eyes. "As near as we can tell, the last person to see her was a pizza delivery guy; we found half of a cheese and pepperoni pizza in her fridge. The delivery guy arrived at six thirty-seven, the same time she paid for it with her debit card, according to bank records, which, so far, have shown nothing out of the ordinary. Before that, she went to a yoga class at two, but the instructor says she always kept to herself, just came in and did her routine, then left. No yoga buddies that we could see. Just an ordinary day."

"That ended with her being tossed over the stairs with blue tape across her eyes."

"Painter's tape, by the way. The kind you can get at any paint store or a place like Home Depot. Another needle in a haystack. There were partially used paint cans in the Sperrys' garage, but no rolls of blue tape."

"The killer could have picked one up as he entered."

"Possibly, but it seems random; doesn't make a lot of sense to come to the scene intending to blindfold someone, then think, 'Darn, I forgot, but, oh, hey, here's a roll of tape in the garage.'"

"Point taken. No latents on the tape?"

"Nope. Didn't get that lucky." She was as frustrated as he and now they had a second murder. "So tell me. Quinn. What did you find out about him?"

"Doesn't exist." He finished his coffee. "At least not that I can find. But we're searching for him and his car and his dog."

"Good luck with that."

Livvie returned to top off their cups, then bustled off as the diner began to fill up. Along with the morning crowd came another waitress, who, in contrast to Livvie, looked dead on her feet. She couldn't keep from yawning as she started moving through the tables.

As Cade shifted in his seat the scents of frying bacon, brewing coffee, and warm maple syrup wafted through the restaurant. He was hungrier than he'd realized. When he saw a platter of pancakes and eggs pass, his stomach grumbled. "You sure you don't want breakfast?" he asked.

Kayleigh drained her cup. "Can't. Gotta run." She'd just checked her phone and was reaching for her Mariners cap. "But you? Knock yourself out." Scooting out of the booth, she said, "Keep me in the loop."

"You, too. Wait. Don't you need a ride?" He started to get up.

"No. I'll walk." She paused at the side of the table, fingers resting on its edge.

"I can give you a lift."

She placed a hand on his arm. "Really," she said. "It's not that far and I could use the exercise. Besides, I need to think. I think best when I walk."

"I don't like it."

"Tough." She met his worried gaze, let her hand slide away from his sleeve. "Seriously, I'll be fine."

He hesitated, then saw that she wasn't about to be talked out of it, so he sat again.

Under the harsh globe lights, she looked down at him. "Take care, Ryder," she said in a moment of tenderness, then slipped her ponytail through the opening in the back of her cap. "And thanks for the coffee. Don't forget to leave the server a nice tip."

CHAPTER 25

"Oh my God, oh my God, is it true?" Lila was almost screaming from the other end of the wireless connection.

Seated at her computer, Rachel decided she'd made a mistake answering what she knew was the inevitable call.

Lila sounded as if she was bordering on hysteria. "Is Annessa really dead? Murdered? Oh my God, I can't believe it. I just can't believe it. I was working out, you know, my in-home routine, and the news was on and . . . oh, holy crap, there it was. At first they were saying that the police had to wait to identify the victim until the next of kin had been informed, but then they must've told Clint, because then they said it was Annessa Cooper and oh my God. . . . And it was at St. Augustine's, right *next door* to Charles's offices. And then Lucas came down and said he'd gotten a wild text from Xander saying that he and Harper had found her hanging in the bell tower! Oh my God, oh my God. This is terrible. Horrible. And after Violet . . . oh, wow." A pause as a thought seemed to occur to her. "Wait a second. Are the murders connected? I bet they are, I just bet they are. They have to be! I didn't immediately go there. I mean, who would want to think that a

364

serial killer is here in Edgewater? Killing off the class of . . . oh, they have to be connected."

"Cade thinks they could be."

"Of course they are. So you've talked to him?" She sounded surprised.

"He brought Harper back last night."

"Oh. Oh. Geez, Rach." A pause and then a deep breath. Rachel guessed she'd found another "just for emergencies" cigarette. "Then . . . what happened? The details were sketchy on the news, mainly just that she was found in the chapel. I can't believe it." Another drag and a long breath as she exhaled.

"I did. Yeah. We talked," Rachel said, but decided not to go into detail. "But Cade didn't say too much. Just what you heard on the news."

"This is awful! Chuck is beside himself and Lucas is freaked. Freaked! I mean, you can imagine, it's his friend and cousin who found Annessa. It's his fault that Xander is up here in the first place." She was winding up. "Another classmate? I mean, what are the chances? Does someone have a thing against us? Against our reunion?"

"I don't think—"

"And the committee. What about the reunion committee? Annessa was in charge of the money. . . . Oh no. And she was one of the signers on the bank account. It takes two signatures, you know. But I'm on it and Reva, too . . . oh, God.

This is going to complicate things. I'll have to find someone else to handle the money for the registration. Oh! Maybe you could take charge. You're already trying to find the classmates who are missing—"

"Oh, hey, wait. No."

"But—"

"Lila, stop! As you said, two classmates are dead, murdered, and my daughter discovered Annessa. . . . It's a madhouse around here."

"Oh. Right. Sorry. I heard about the vandalism, but this could be a good distraction for you. It would be easy for an organized person like you."

"Find someone else!" Rachel said with more vehemence than she'd intended as Reno stood and stretched, then trotted to the top of the stairs. "I can't. And I really can't think about the reunion right now."

"But she was a classmate!" Another pause. Another drag. "I don't have anyone to handle the remembrance table and now . . . now we have another name to add. Oh my God, this is so damned sad."

"Very. You know, Lila—"

"And scary as all get-out. To think two members of our class have been killed in the past week. It makes you think twice, you know."

Did she ever. Reno whined and headed down the steps. Rachel pushed back her chair and followed. "You might consider postponing the reunion or maybe not even having it at all," she said as she reached the main floor and lowered her voice as the kids were still sleeping.

"What?" Lila gasped. "No! Are you crazy?"

"Are you? Think about what's gone on."

"But it's the twenty-year reunion. A biggie."

"You could wait until twenty-five."

"No! No way. We've all put too much work into it. Look, Rachel, I realize you're upset with everything that's gone on, but we have to keep going, you know. Just keep going. We're *not* stopping it or postponing it, but we might have to have another emergency meeting. Losing Annessa at this point is a big deal."

"She's not lost, Lila; she's dead. Someone killed her."

"I know . . . I mean, I'm not trying to be insensitive, just practical. So, Friday night here. I'll let the committee heads know." And she disconnected, leaving Rachel with her phone to her ear.

She couldn't believe it. Lila was still going on with life, the damned reunion, as if nothing had happened. Oh, sure, she'd been shocked and upset, but she was willing to brush the two brutal murders under the rug in order to keep the celebration of their class on track. Two murders!

"It's sick," Rachel said to the dog as he pawed at the back door. She let him outside and tried to shake off the feeling of dread that had seeped

367

into her bones. She was dead tired, hadn't been able to sleep, and had decided to give the kids a break, especially Harper. Neither would go to school today; Rachel had already e-mailed their teachers for homework assignments, and so she'd let them sleep, checking in on them twice, just to make certain they were safely in their beds.

They were still asleep, even though it was now after ten.

The day had dawned murky, with a fog that had rolled through the town, thickening as the hours had passed. Now, she could barely see the fence line.

She poured herself a cold cup of coffee from the pot, then heated the cup in the microwave. Her eyes were gritty from lack of sleep, a headache was starting to form, and though she'd tried to answer e-mails this morning and work on updating a website for a local wine shop, she hadn't had the energy. Her mind had wandered back to Annessa and Violet and their deaths.

Why?

Who?

She set her now steaming cup of coffee on the kitchen table and scrolled across the screen of her phone to get online. The Tuesday edition of the newspaper had dropped, and as promised, it was filled with more stories about the cannery. The front page alone had four stories directly or indirectly linked to the Sea View fish-packing plant. The first article that caught Rachel's eye was a bio: "Who Was Luke Hollander?"

The text was thin, as no one from Luke's immediate family had commented on the years Luke was a youth, growing up in the Gaston household. There were no direct quotes from either Melinda or Ned, and Rachel hadn't provided any fodder when Mercedes had pressed during the aborted interview at her office. To help fill in the blanks of Luke's life, Mercedes had relied on information from friends, teachers, and coaches. Some anonymous source described as someone "close to the family" had been quoted describing Luke's home life.

Her mother would be devastated when she read the story.

"Great," Rachel said.

The second article was all about the cannery's history, how the plant had been built near the turn of the last century when salmon were fished in gill nets, before the tuna industry swelled. It mentioned how Sea View had grown to become a major employer in the area and then how it had slowly declined to eventually close, making note that it was the scene of a horrid tragedy twenty years earlier.

A third article was entitled "Waterfront Development Seeks to Restore and Renew." The half-page story was a typical hopeful account of a new developer seeking to restore the old cannery building. That article showed some computer renderings of a shopping mall that reminded her of a tourist attraction from Portland or Seattle, as well as floor plans of apartments in the waterfront building and listed Bell Cooper and Associates as the developer. Clint Cooper was even quoted, bragging that the new shops, condos, and businesses would "breathe new life back to this part of Oregon." He'd obviously been quoted before his wife had been murdered.

But homicide hadn't eluded the *Edgewater Edition*. The final story was front and center, an article about Violet Sperry's murder. The story itself was just a factual analysis of the crime, but Mercy did manage to work in that Violet had been present that tragic night at the Sea View cannery and had been a witness in the subsequent investigation involving the shooting.

"Nice tie-in," Rachel thought aloud.

Next to the text was a picture of Violet Sperry seated on an oversized chair and surrounded by her three small dogs, all with long ears and doe-soft eyes.

Rachel's throat tightened and she had to slide her gaze away from the photograph.

Skimming the rest of the paper, she found nothing on Annessa's murder, of course, as it had happened too late for the paper's deadline. As she looked for an updated version that mentioned

Annessa, a text came from Cade asking about the kids: Harper okay?

Rachel texted back: Still asleep. I gave them the day off from school.

Cade: Good. I left texts for her and Dylan. Will call later.

Rachel: Any news about what happened to Annessa?

Cade: Not yet. Security guys coming?

She cringed inwardly and texted: Decided to order one online—self-install. Should be here later in the week.

Cade: OK. TTYL

She'd lied, of course, but quickly took the time to pick out and order an updated system, one with digital cameras that would work through a phone app. Only when she was done did she realize that Reno hadn't scratched at the door to be let in. Pushing back her chair, she glanced out the slider. Reno wasn't in his usual spot.

She went to the door and called for him, waiting for the dog to appear, but no tawny beast emerged from the yard. "Come on," she said again and gave a sharp whistle.

Still nothing. "Reno? Reno, come!" Her voice was sharp and irritated as she slid into her gardening clogs and stepped onto the wet grass.

"Where are you?" Sleep deprived, she was already on edge, the lack of visibility only heightening her anxiety. And she didn't need to be playing hide-and-seek with a rambunctious dog. "Come on, boy."

Searching the gloom, Rachel walked the line of the shrubs and plants, all the little markers the dog favored, but she didn't see any hint of a wagging tail or shiny eyes peering through the mist.

"Reno?" She was starting to get a bad feeling about this, but steadfastly tamped it down. The dog loved to play catch-me-if-you-can at times. "Come!"

Nothing.

Don't freak.

He's here. He's got to be.

Or . . .

She walked to the side yard and the gate that was rarely opened except when they were mowing the lawn as it was on the far side of the house, and, sure enough, it wasn't latched. The resulting span, a six-inch gap, was perfect for the dog to slip through. Her heart jolted. Not only was the gate never left open, but Reno wasn't likely to roam far. She thought of the weird text and the ugly message written on her door. And then there were the murders. . . .

Goose bumps traveled up her arms.

Don't go there!

"Reno, come!" She moved carefully through mist, squinting at shadows and cursing the ever-changing weather. No sign of the dog in the side yard. Her heart was thudding. She thought about rousting the kids for help, but she didn't want to take the time. And she didn't want to disturb the neighbors.

Her voice was stern, commanding, hiding the panic in her heart. "You come!"

Nothing.

No response.

The garden beds in front of the house were empty. Time to trespass to the Pitts' house. Gingerly, she crept onto their lush grass. She checked the shadows by the rock wall and the fat pots of impatiens on either side of their porch.

No dog.

She moved on to the next house, the Giordanos'. Didn't know them well. She hoped they weren't watching her stalk through their yard. "Reno!"

And then she heard it, a low, anxious moan.

She froze.

Reno? Or . . .

Through the fog, she heard the rustle of leaves behind her. Her heart stilled. Why the devil hadn't she brought her pepper spray or . . . She spun, squinting into the garden, and saw the movement of a tail whipping frantically at the base of a thick hydrangea bush, the silhouette of her shepherd mix visible.

The dog was moaning anxiously, running to the fence, standing on his back legs. He gave a sharp, anxious bark, and from high above, hidden in the fog, came the returning chatter of a squirrel.

"Oh. Geez. You nearly gave me a heart attack," she said. "Reno, come. Now." Two dark eyes appeared as the dog bounded up to her, all innocence and playfulness. "Not in the mood," Rachel said, relief chasing away her fears. "Come on. Let's go." She snapped her fingers and Reno kept up with her as they headed to the front of the Giordanos' property. "You scared the hell out of me, you know," she scolded, but the dog just trotted beside her, tongue lolling, tail in the air.

Rachel moved quickly now, this time in the street to avoid trampling anyone's lawn or flowers. She went back through the side gate and, mentally berating herself for being such a ninny, she secured the latch.

That was when she saw the footprint. Large. Distinctive. The impression of a boot or shoe in the bark dust near the gatepost. It hadn't been there the night the door was vandalized. Right? Surely she would have seen it. She considered all the times she'd felt that she was being watched, that some voyeur was eyeing her, and her skin crawled again.

It's a footprint. Nothing more. Maybe made by Dylan or one of his friends? Even that seems a stretch.

Get a hold of yourself!

Gritting her teeth, telling herself that she was overreacting, she followed Reno to the back porch and into the kitchen again.

Harper was waiting in pajamas, her hair a mess, her eyes sunken. "Where'd you go?" she asked, opening a cupboard and searching for a cup.

"Reno got out. Hey, you, wait!" she ordered the dog, who was dancing around Harper, tail wagging madly. Rachel grabbed a towel she kept on a hook in the closet near the back door for general dog cleanup and attempted to wipe Reno's wet paws. She was only partially successful. "Hold on, Reno. You're making this impossible."

"God, you talk to the dog, like, *all* the time."

"So you've said, over and over. It's normal, by the way."

"Whatever." Harper retrieved a cup.

"Did you leave the gate open?" she asked. "Last night when you were sneaking out? And did Xander come to the house?"

"No."

"I'm talking about the gate to the side yard." Rachel hooked a thumb toward the Pitts' and Giordanos' side of the house.

"I said 'no.' I wasn't near that side of the house. Geez, what is this? The Spanish Inquisition? God." She filled the cup with water and stuck it into the microwave.

"It was open."

"So what?"

"It's never open."

"Oh, geez, don't tell me you're going to flip

out about a gate. It was probably Dylan or one of his dweebie friends."

"Let's not start with insults, okay?"

"Fine. But they are. All of them super computer nerds." Then, "I thought you were going to wake us for school." The microwave dinged and she retrieved her cup and started dunking a tea bag into the water.

"I figured you could use a day off." Rachel leaned a hip against the counter as Reno lapped from his water bowl. "How are you?"

"Fine!" she snapped. "Geez. Dad texted like a million times this morning. I mean, yeah, I'm not cool with what happened. Not cool at all, but . . . I don't need you guys treating me like a baby. It was awful. I hate it, but"—she looked up—"can we just forget it?"

"Okay, then let's talk about you sneaking out to be with a boy."

"Oh. God." Harper rolled her eyes, still frantically dunking the tea. "Really?"

"Really." Then, as this was the moment, Rachel asked, "Are you on the pill?"

"What?" She looked at her mother and shook her head. "Oh, Mom, no, let's not do this."

"Are you having sex?"

"Oh my God! Don't, just don't!"

"Unprotected sex?"

"Stop! Just stop! Just because you and your mom both got pregnant before you were married doesn't mean I will. It's not like some mutant gene."

"But it still happens. I'm just saying, and no judging here, if you need me to—"

"I don't! Mom, I can handle my life! Just drop it."

Rachel realized she was handling this all wrong and took a breath to calm herself. "I can't. This probably seems like a bad time for this conversation, but I'm not sure there's ever a time when it's not awkward."

"I won't get pregnant. Okay? And I'm not going to get some STD, if that's what you're getting at!" Harper was dunking her tea bag so rapidly that water sloshed over the rim of the cup. "Oh, shit . . . crap." She yanked a paper towel from its spindle and started mopping up the mess. "I can't deal with this!" Tossing the stained towel into the trash, she abandoned the tea and headed back to her room.

Watching her, Rachel didn't know whether to throttle her daughter or hold her close and never let go. How much of Harper's attitude was from dealing with the trauma of the night before, and how much of it was just being a self-centered brat?

Probably a little of both.

You're the adult, she reminded herself, but sometimes it just didn't feel like it. She considered tossing the tea down the drain, then picked up the cup, walked down the hall, and rapped on Harper's door.

Her daughter was just yelling, "Could you just please leave me alone!" when Rachel pushed open the door.

"Mom!" Harper, texting, was propped up in her bed, the duvet wrapped around her, her eyes sullen.

"No lectures, okay?" Rachel said. "But you need to quit yelling and acting like a baby. I know you've been through a lot. We all have. But you don't need to berate me or talk badly about your brother and his friends. We need to stick together."

"I thought you said 'no lectures.' "

"That's all of it." Rachel set the tea on her daughter's nightstand. "Just one last thing," she added and Harper's lips pinched. "I get that you want to be treated like an adult. I remember. So . . . here's the deal: You start acting like an adult and I promise I'll start treating you like one."

Harper's eyes narrowed suspiciously. "You think you can really do that?" She let out a disbelieving huff. "Come on, Mom, you're . . . well, you know."

"What, Harper? I'm what?"

Harper's chin jutted. "You're, like, paranoid. You freak out at every little thing. The dog got out and you panicked. I heard you calling for him.

He's a dog. He went sniffing into the neighbor's yard. It's not a big deal."

Rachel's spine stiffened. She'd walked to the door, but now turned and stood in the opening to the hallway. "Things have been a little freaky lately. Weird."

"I know, yeah. I was there!" On the bed, Harper gave a shudder. "I get why you're freaked out. People are dying, being killed. It's scary, but, Mom . . . the dog?"

"Okay, maybe I overreacted," she admitted, thinking of how the blinds rattling the other night had caused her to become frantic, how she sensed someone watching her when there was no one around, how a prank text had caused her to consider her brother reaching out from the grave—on a cell phone no less. How she was always nervous, on edge. But then there were the murders, the vandalism, and now there was the shoe print. She cleared her throat. "I'll work on keeping it more together."

"Can you?" Harper asked earnestly, even ignoring her phone as her big eyes pleaded with her mother.

Rachel lifted a shoulder. "Don't know, but I can give it a try."

Still obviously skeptical, Harper said, "Okay," and as Rachel turned to leave, she added, "Thanks for bringing me the tea."

"No prob." As Rachel closed the door to her

daughter's room, she told herself she had to find a way to get hold of herself. She had let her own worries, her fears and anxiety, get the better of her for far too long. *Be strong. Be strong. Be strong.* She headed upstairs, the mantra playing over and over again in her head, but she knew mind over matter wasn't as easy as it sounded and one couldn't just will oneself not to be anxious, but she would try, just as she had promised her daughter.

She'd just about convinced herself that she would beat this thing when her phone vibrated in her pocket and the same simple phrase that she'd seen before appeared in a text:

I forgive you.

CHAPTER 26

Rachel nearly stumbled on the top step as she stared at the message. Her heart went into overdrive as she made her way to the office and dropped into her desk chair. Frantically, she punched the function to return the call.

No answer.

Not unexpected.

She tried again.

Nothing.

"You son of a bitch," she ground out and texted back:

Who is this?

No reply.

Who are you?

Silence, of course.

Why are you doing this?

But she didn't expect an answer and none came.

So she fought back uselessly and typed:

Stop texting me!

Oh, yeah, like that's gonna stop a freak with his sick pranks. Get real.

She looked out the window to the foggy front yard and now invisible street. Was he even now staring at the place? Hidden by the curtain of thick mist. "You sick bastard." She made her way around the upper story, pausing at each window to look out and check that it was closed and latched. Which of course they all were, as she'd double-checked last night. She did the same on the main floor, ignoring Harper's indignant, "Oh, Mom, what now? You think I'm sneaking out? I thought you were going to start treating me like an adult." In Dylan's room she stepped over trash and some cartons of who knew what to double-check his window, then went downstairs to the basement and pushed aside some boxes she needed to recycle in the exercise room, before determining that her family was safely locked inside.

"This is ridiculous," she told herself as she hurried up the stairs. In the pantry she double-checked to see that the damned jerry-rigged system was engaged. It was, a green light indicating all systems were go.

The place was locked up tight and alarmed, but this ritual of fear was exhausting, she realized as she climbed the stairs to her office one more time. As she reached the top landing, her cell vibrated again and, expecting another cruel text, she pulled it from her back pocket.

She felt a wave of relief when she saw her father's number come onto the screen: Heard about last night. Harper finding the body of that woman. How is she?

Rachel: Bad news travels fast.

Dad: Small town and I have a few friends still on the force.

Of course. Rachel: She's pretty shaken up, but working through it. I think she'll be okay.

Dad: I hope so. Heard about the new articles in that trashy paper today. You okay?

Rachel: I guess. You?

Dad: I'm fine. Tougher than I look. Don't like seeing my family put through this all again, though. Would like to strangle Mercedes Pope.

Despite her worries, Rachel couldn't help but smile. *Get in line.*

Dad: How about your mother? How's she handling all this BS about Luke?

Rachel: Haven't heard.

Dad: Got to be hard on her. Maybe you should give her a jingle?

Because you can't, Rachel thought sadly. *You two can't even be in the same room at the same time.*

Rachel: Good idea. I will.

And then: Hey, maybe we could get together?

She felt like she could talk to her father; right now, she would like to run a few things past him. He was an ex-cop, a once-upon-a-time detective.

Dad: I'm here.

Rachel: I'll give you a call.

Dad: Look forward to it.

As she finished texting, she heard the sound of water running in the bathroom downstairs. Someone was showering. That was progress.

Once more she glanced at the anonymous text and her stomach clenched.

This has nothing to do with Luke.

That was the problem.

In the back of her mind, though she knew it was crazy, a part of her wondered if the message was from her dead brother. Who else would need to forgive her?

Cade?

One of her kids?

Her mother?

Dad?

Who?

Once more, she tried calling the number and once more she was disappointed. Whoever had left the text had intended to and then gone dark. One message she could have believed was a mistake, but two? No way.

Staring at the message, she thought of all the people she'd wronged in her life, and there were quite a few, but she'd never done anything worthy of some weird wireless absolution. *I forgive you.* As if she'd sinned, for God's sake.

The first message had come in twenty years to the very day she'd pulled that fateful trigger and her brother had died.

Coincidence?

If not . . . then who would play such a sick, cruel joke on her?

And why?

And what was significant about this day? It had nothing to do with that long-ago tragedy.

Then it hit her. Both messages had been received upon the publication of the articles about the cannery.

Worse yet, each text had been received after the murder of her classmates, two women who had testified on her behalf. A cold dread curled in her stomach. Was that it? Or was she jumping at shadows, coming to ludicrous conclusions?

Either way, she had to find out.

Jangled nerves be damned, she couldn't let someone threaten her family or control her emotional state.

She grabbed her purse and flew down the stairs, nearly running into Harper, who, dressed in a robe with her hair wrapped in a towel, was just stepping out of the bathroom. A cloud of warm mist seeped through the doorway and a quick glance inside showed the mirror completely fogged.

"Hey, I was just going over to Grandpa's for a few minutes," she said to her daughter as she retrieved her keys from a side pocket in her purse. "Wanna come?" That sounded reasonable. She'd wake Dylan as well. They could all go together.

"Are you kidding?" Harper said, motioning to the terry turban on her head. "I can't. Not now. Besides, I've got *tons* of homework. Sometimes I

think Mr. Gorson piles it on twice as much if you don't show up to class."

Dad lived just across the small town, less than fifteen minutes away. And it was the middle of the morning. Rachel wanted to argue with her daughter, but this was no time to panic Harper. And she couldn't overreact, not because of one text.

Two texts and two murders.

"Mom. We'll be all right," Harper said, as if reading her thoughts. "You've got that security system, right? And the dog's with us? And we're both here with cell phones." She leveled a gaze at her, this girl who had witnessed a horrendous death less than twelve hours earlier. "We'll be fine."

Rachel hesitated.

"Seriously?" her daughter asked when she saw her mother's indecision. "We can always call Dad, too. You know, the cop? And if all else fails, nine-one-one. The station is what? Ten minutes away."

"Okay." Rachel relented. "I won't be gone long. Text me if you need me."

"No worries," Harper said. "Adult. Remember?" She actually floated her mother what seemed like a genuine smile.

"Okay. I'll just give Dylan the word."

"As if he cares, but whatever."

Rachel knocked on Dylan's door and stepped

inside his cluttered room. The window shades were drawn, the room was dark, but he was awake. Sitting in bed, propped against the headboard, he wore a headset and worked the buttons of a wireless gaming controller as he stared at a computer monitor. On the screen a military-style scenario was playing out, armed soldiers hiding behind partial walls, piles of bricks, and huge barrels as the player inched his way through a labyrinthine building.

"Hey," she said.

"Yeah." His gaze didn't shift from the screen.

"I'm heading over to Grandpa's. Be back in an hour. Okay?" She didn't ask him to join her, preferred her kids be together.

"Yeah."

"Aren't you even going to ask about school?"

"Figured you took care of it." He was still working the controller and it bugged her.

"Can you find 'pause' or whatever it is?"

"But I'm in a major battle for . . ." Then he stopped; his thumbs and fingers quit moving, and he actually looked at her. "Sorry."

"That's better. You've got homework. I saw it posted online. Do it. And there's cereal, or toast or whatever you want in the refrigerator, for breakfast . . . or lunch."

"Okay."

"Text me if you need anything. And keep the doors locked."

"Yeah."

"And, Dylan?" she added. "Do something about this room. You and I, we had a deal that you'd clean it up. Part of the arrangement when you got in trouble last week. Doesn't seem like you've tackled it. So, when I get back, I want to be able to see the floor and know that it's been vacuumed and dusted."

"Yeah."

"I mean it."

"Got it."

He seemed to be listening, but sometimes she just couldn't tell.

"Don't go anywhere."

He finally looked at her. "Like where would I go? All my friends are in school."

Good point. She left then and told herself she'd be gone only a half hour, forty-five minutes on the outside. What could possibly go wrong?

All things considered, Cade didn't feel too bad. He'd finished the "awesome" farmer's breakfast at Abe's, gone home, hit the rack, and slept for four hours. When his alarm had gone off, he'd walked through a cold shower, ignored his razor, dressed, and discovered a can of Red Bull that Dylan had left in the refrigerator. After downing the energy drink, he'd sifted through e-mails, texted Rachel and the kids a couple of times, and skimmed the latest online edition of the local paper. On the way to work, he'd bought a cup of coffee and was only slightly jangled as he stepped into the office a little after eleven.

He'd just sat in his desk chair and was logging into his computer when Voss showed up. She was wearing her usual black slacks and jacket, with a gray blouse and a cat-who-swallowed-the-canary smile that was a little irritating considering the amount of sleep he'd had. Or, more precisely, the sleep he hadn't gotten.

"Hey, Sleeping Beauty," she said, needling him a little.

He wasn't in the mood, but let it pass.

"Guess who was the last person Annessa Cooper texted?" Behind her glasses, Voss's eyes glinted.

"From your attitude, I'm guessing it wasn't her husband."

"Nope." Voss wagged her head back and forth, her pleased smile never shifting. "I was thinking she might have had a boyfriend she was supposed to meet, and I was right. Check your e-mail," she said, motioning a finger at his computer monitor. "I just sent you a transcript of the texts we found on her phone. Pretty interesting stuff there." She arched her graying eyebrows.

Cade turned in his chair to face the screen again, then clicked on an e-mail from Voss and scrolled down.

"This is what's called sexting," she said.

He skimmed the lines, long conversations about what one of the texters planned to do to the other. Or, even more graphic, what was happening to their bodies as they communicated. "People really get off on this?"

"All the time," Voss told him. "It's like they touch themselves with their free hand or just imagine the other person and, voila, an orgasm. But look at the end of the communication, the last couple of lines." She rounded his desk and pointed to the screen where the conversation got precise.

Caller: Meet me at St. Augustine's. You've got keys.

Annessa: Why there?

Caller: Old times' sake. Think about what all those nuns would say.

Annessa: Oooh. They'd want to punish me.

Caller: I want to punish you. You've been such a bad, bad girl.

Annessa: Okay. You've convinced me. What time?

Caller: Around midnight. The witching hour.

Annessa: That's weird.

Caller: But you like weird, don't you? You like things a little kinky. This is making you hot already. Just thinking about it.

Annessa: Clint is coming home.
Tomorrow. Early. Possibly tonight.
Caller: Which makes it all the more
exciting. Dangerous. And you like
danger, don't you?
Annessa: You know I do.
Caller: I might come just thinking about
it.
Annessa: Don't. Wait for me.
Caller: Oh, I'll be waiting.

Cade stared at the screen. "So who is the anonymous number? Anyone we know?"

"Oh, yeah," Voss said, nearly bursting. "That number belongs to Mr. Nathan Moretti. Single. Self-employed. Sells medical equipment in Astoria."

And one of Rachel's classmates. Best friend of Luke Hollander and son of Dr. Richard Moretti, the doctor who had pronounced Luke DOA.

"I figure Annessa didn't tag him with a name or have his picture in her phone just in case good old Clint picked up her phone." Voss crossed her arms, pleased with her discoveries. "So I assume you want to interview him."

"Oh, yeah."

He was already pushing his chair away from the desk, grabbing his sidearm. "Want to come along?"

"Wouldn't miss it for the world." She slid her

phone in her slacks pocket and slipped on her shoulder holster. "And by the way, Ryder?"

"Yeah."

"I'm the lead on this one. You just may be a little too close to the investigation. If it weren't for the fact that we're so small, I'm pretty sure the chief would kick your ass off this one." She was reaching for her jacket. "So mind your p's and q's."

"What the hell does that mean anyway?"

"Hell if I know. My translation: Don't get in my way." She slid her arms through the sleeves as they began walking.

"Wouldn't dream of it," he said, in step with her as they walked through the back door near the lunchroom.

"Yeah, right."

CHAPTER 27

Harper waited until she was certain her mother was gone, then strode down the hall to Dylan's room. Now was the time to confront her idiot of a brother. God, what was he doing? She'd lied for him to Mom, covered his ass, but she was worried sick about what he was getting into.

Yesterday at school her worst fears had been confirmed. She'd been coming down the stairs from the theater department with her friend when she'd spied Dylan. And he hadn't been alone. Julie had peeled off for her next class, but Harper had waited and watched from the landing, still a handful of steps above the area in front of the gym, as the two guys had cornered her brother.

Their body language was menacing. A big, hulking guy in gym shorts and a dark hoody scowled at Dylan, while a second skinnier guy in jeans and a fleece pullover screened him from the rest of the hallway. She didn't know the kids— probably sophomores. Definitely not Schmidt or Parker.

But it didn't look good.

God, please don't make me have to run down there and save the little punk's sorry butt.

Dylan dug a hand into his backpack. He

pulled something out and another guy stood up, watching as Dylan handed something over, a small black sack. The kid looked into the bag, poking around a little, as if inspecting whatever was inside, then quickly slipped something to Dylan.

Cash.

Dylan looked at the bills, made a quick assessment, and nodded.

Drugs. Her brother was dealing drugs.

Shit! She'd seen more than one freshman or sophomore slide twenty-dollar bills into Dylan's hand while they passed each other while changing classes. She had thought that he'd been loaning his friends money, but now she knew.

Stupid, stupid, stupid boy! There might be cameras taking all this in, recording him in the heat of the transaction. He was obviously in way over his head.

Dealing drugs on school property. What a moron! Everyone knew that would get you in big trouble. If he thought he could get away with something so dumb and blatant, he deserved to go to jail!

Except she couldn't let him. The idiot didn't have an iota of common sense. Brilliant and stupid, that was Dylan.

Someone had to save him from himself.

Turned out, she got the honors.

She pushed open Dylan's door, with its stupid

crime scene tape that discouraged no one, to find him propped on his bed, gaming controller in one hand, phone in front of him, a sack of Doritos open and spilling onto the bedding, a nearly finished plate of last night's lasagna on the night table.

"Hey!" he said, his head snapping up. "Knock next time."

"I know what you're doing," she said. "And it has to stop."

"What I'm doing? I'm playing a game."

"I'm not talking about that," she said, motioning toward the controller.

He didn't seem to get it.

"I'm sick of covering your sorry ass so that Mom doesn't find out, but I'm not going to do it anymore. You have to get out of it right now."

"Out of what?" But he blanched a little, confirming her worst suspicions.

"Oh, come off it. The drugs. I know you've been dealing."

"What?" he said, shocked.

"Mom is going to kill you if she finds out," Harper warned. "And Dad is going to kill you, and God, you know what? Maybe I'm going to kill you, too!"

"I'm not—"

"Stop it! Don't lie. It's over. I saw you yesterday," she charged, stepping into the room, which reeked of cheese and tomato sauce and teenaged boy.

His mouth dropped open. "You saw what?"

"The deal go down. The two kids by the gym? The black sack."

Dylan was shaking his head slowly, back and forth. "You've got it all wrong."

"Do I? Then explain."

He hesitated. Swallowed hard.

"I thought so," she said as she felt Reno step past her and begin sniffing at the floor.

He leaned back on the bed, closed his eyes, and banged his head twice on the headboard. "God, I'm such an idiot."

She didn't argue.

Sighing, he said, "It's not drugs."

"Good."

"No, not good." He swallowed hard. "It's worse."

"How could it possibly be worse?" she asked, and he bit his lip, looked away. Obviously he didn't want to say. For a second she thought of the two women who had been killed recently. Surely her brother wasn't into anything like that. Her pulse started pounding in dread.

He found her gaze. Held it. His face was white as a sheet. "You can't tell Mom."

"I won't."

"You promise?"

"Yeah, yeah. Sure. I promise." She crossed her fingers.

"I hacked into the school computer system," he

admitted. "I've been selling tests and teacher's notes and even . . . even fixing grades."

"You've done what?"

"You heard me. I could be suspended or expelled or worse. . . . And you're right, Mom and Dad would kill me."

"Only if they found out." The wheels were turning in her mind and her eyes narrowed as she considered all the options. "So then, what was in the bag yesterday?"

He lifted a shoulder. "Just a hard drive I fixed. I work on stuff and sell it. Refurbish it."

"Like to who?"

"I dunno."

"You expect me to believe that?"

"I just don't want to get anyone in trouble!"

"I said I won't tell. So who?" she demanded.

"Just some guys."

She waited.

"Friends. Like the guys you saw me with. Ryan. And Brent, you know, he lives a couple of blocks over, and Xander."

"You sold computer stuff to Xander?"

"Well, him and Lucas, but come on. You can't let Mom and Dad know, Harper. It's got to be on the down low. You promised."

She took another step into his gross room. "Why is that a secret?" she asked. "Who would care?"

His gaze slid to the side and he let out a sigh.

"Some kids don't want their parents to know. It's like spy equipment, or extra cameras with microphones. That sort of stuff. Not really a big deal."

"So what about Schmidt?" she asked. "What are you doing for him?"

"Oh, geez." He was about to clam up again but then rolled his eyes. "He needs his grades lifted in a couple of classes, before the end of the year. And he wants me to make them significant, like from a D or an F to an A. . . . I can't do that. Someone might notice; teachers will know if they double-check. But he needs his GPA upped by too much. I told him I couldn't do that much and he got mad. I paid him his money back, but he's super pissed. Said it's gonna affect him going to college or something, like he has a scholarship or his folks insisted he keep his grades up before they would pay for a four-year school or something."

"Did you do it?"

"Not yet. If I do, I have to wait until the last day that the grades go in, and even then . . ." He leaned back against the bed. "I'm so screwed."

She didn't believe that. Dylan always figured a way to weasel out of any kind of trouble. She thought about what he'd told her. This could be to her advantage.

"You said you wouldn't tell," he reminded her nervously.

"I won't. But I want in." She held his gaze. "I need an A in chemistry."

Aware of the clock ticking, Rachel drove straight to her father's house despite the fog that clouded her vision.

She couldn't be gone long, but she needed to talk to him, and so she sped along the highway, nearly missing the turn onto the county road, and slowed just as she reached his lane. All the while she thought about the murders of people she knew, of the stupid articles in the paper, and of course of Luke and how she'd pulled the trigger and watched him go down.

Don't do this, she silently told herself, hands tight over the steering wheel. She'd held it together for the kids, but felt herself unraveling.

"Get it together," she told herself. Her Explorer shuddered a little on the bumpy, unpaved driveway to his house, where she spied his truck was parked near a shed. She switched off the engine and raced up the back steps, her usual entrance to his home.

As she stepped onto the porch she startled a cat, which scurried out from beneath a stepladder surrounded by a pile of paint cans and drop cloths. "Great," she said, the black cat crossing her path to streak across the uneven yard just as she nearly stepped under the ladder.

With a quick rap on the door, she tried the knob and, without waiting for her father to answer, stepped into the kitchen. "Hey, Dad, it's me!"

"Well, look who's here!"

He walked in from the living room, a newspaper in his hand. "I was just reading about you in this rag."

She rolled her eyes. "Mercedes won't give it up."

He tossed the paper into a trash can standing near the back door. "Try not to let it bother you. She's just trying to sell papers."

Reading glasses were perched upon his nose and he looked at her over the half lenses. "You okay?"

"What do you think?"

"Yeah." He opened his arms wide and she fell into them, grateful for a second of his strength. She'd always relied upon him; probably always would. She squeezed her eyes shut, fought tears, and when she opened them again, looked through the window to spy the cat sitting atop a fence post, black tail curled around his feet, a mist rising around him, the whole scene eerie. "I think I scared your cat."

"Not mine. Stray. I made the mistake of feeding him and now he thinks he lives here. . . . Well, come to think of it maybe he does. So, kid, how're you holding up?"

"Not so good, and I can't stay long. The kids

are at home alone and that's dangerous during the best of times. Now . . ."

"I hear ya. Do you have time for a cup?"

She noted the Keurig on his aging counter. "Sure. A quick one. Got decaf?"

He snorted. "That's not coffee. Just black water. But yeah."

"Okay." He reached into a cupboard for the box of coffee pods, and as he did, he winced.

"What's wrong?"

"Nothing. Just getting old. Strained my shoulder . . . been painting and tiling the bathroom." He found the pod, snapped it into the coffee machine, and pressed a button, only to rub his shoulder. "Gettin' soft, I guess." He rotated his shoulder, then plucked a bottle of ibuprofen from the windowsill and shook two into his palm before tossing the dry tablets into his mouth. "Probably a pinched nerve or arthritis or something. No big deal."

The Keurig hissed and sputtered before he handed her the cup and made another. "Real coffee," he pronounced, replacing the old pod with a new one, snapping it into place and tossing the old one into the trash.

"If you say so."

"Decaf's for wimps."

"Sometimes I am."

He snorted. "I don't believe it."

She heard the ding of a text coming in, then

another, but seeing that they weren't from the kids, she ignored them. She glanced at the clock over the stove, time ticking away, and took a swallow of the coffee as she took a seat at the kitchen table that Ned had refinished himself.

"How's Harper?"

"Dealing better than I thought she would."

He slid a glance over his shoulder as his cup filled. "Watch her. Sometimes it hits later, after the shock wears off."

She was aware of that all too well, she thought, as she ran a fingertip over the old knots and scars of the tabletop.

"How well did you know the victims?"

"Just in school. You remember. Violet more than Annessa. She'd come over once in a while." But as he turned to face her, fresh mug of coffee in hand, she realized he didn't recall her high school relationships. How could he? He was a full-time cop at the time, often worked nights, and the family was breaking up at that point, splintering as he and Melinda were well on their way to divorce. "But I didn't keep in touch. Even though they lived around here, I didn't know them."

"They both stood up for you, if I remember right."

"Yeah," Rachel said, staring into her mug.

"They were there." He took a slow sip. "And now they're dead."

"Killed." It was surreal and horrible and painful. She remembered Violet in the darkened cannery, how she'd refused to wear her glasses and how she'd flipped out in the chaos that seemed to be a war zone, how Rachel had tried to drag her out of the building, where kids were shooting, blasting away, and then Luke . . . falling. Her heart began to pound at the memory, her pulse was racing, and little beads of sweat were forming at her hairline.

"Last night—Annessa's murder—it was too close to deadline to make the latest edition of the newspaper," Rachel said. "But just wait. The murder's already been all over the news. Even though Harper's under eighteen, they'll find her. Mercedes will."

"You can bet on that."

Groaning, she let her head drop to the table in frustration. "Will it ever end?"

"Never," he said quietly, then cleared his throat. "How is Lila handling all this?"

"Lila?" she repeated. "I guess in her usual Lila, over-the-top, near hysterical wanting-to-take-control way. She's already freaked out about the reunion, if you can believe that."

"I can. You know, I never felt she got over what happened."

"None of us really have," she admitted. "But she's got Luke's son. Kind of a living memory, a blessing, yeah, of course, but a reminder."

He nodded, staring out the window over the sink, eyes narrowing.

She followed his gaze, saw he was watching a hawk as it circled, dipping low, visible for an instant, then disappearing in the mist again. But she doubted he was concentrating on the bird. No, she understood, his thoughts were far from this day, to another place and time.

"Your brother and I, we had our share of problems. Butted heads a lot," he admitted, then took a long swallow from his cup, and she noticed how his once-sandy hair had silvered. "Too often."

She couldn't help recalling the fights. The yelling. Often created by Luke's insolent attitude and Ned's mercurial temper, which, in those days, had sometimes been fueled by whiskey. Luke had been quick to raise his fists and Ned had never been known to back down from a fight.

"I was hard on him," Ned said. Regret tinged his words. "Too hard, probably. The kid had it tough. Think about it. Me, his stepfather, the guy who raised him, was responsible for him not knowing his dad." The back of his neck tightened. "Not that Bruce Hollander was any prize." He nodded, agreeing with himself, and then his shoulders slumped a bit. "Still . . . I could've gone easier on the kid. I was the one who arrested his old man for beating on his wife and then ended up marrying her. At the time, Luke was a baby, didn't know any different, but as the years went by and he grew up, figured it out, was teased about his old man being locked up, it was a different story." Another absent swallow from his cup, then, "Ah, hell! Nothin' to do about it now."

"Water under the bridge."

"Is it? I wonder." He turned to face her, blue eyes holding hers steady. "Well, we just have to deal, right? Like we have been all along." He scraped back a chair and sat across from her. "Did you hear he's out of prison? Hollander?"

"Mom told me."

She saw his jaw tighten at the mention of Melinda and wished to God they could just get along.

"You called her?"

"No, she mentioned it the last time I saw her."

"All this"—he motioned to the newspaper in the bin—"it's gotta be tough on her, too." He caught Rachel's gaze and held it. She got the unspoken message.

"I said I'd call her. I will. Promise."

"Has he—Hollander—contacted your mother?"

"Not that I know of. And I think she would have said."

"Good." He took a sip of coffee. "Either way you cut it, Luke wasn't born lucky when it came to the whole male role model thing."

"What're you talking about? You were a great dad."

"Maybe. Maybe not."

She looked at the clock again, then dragged her cell phone from her pocket. "I want you to see something. I got this text message the other day, and right away I thought of Luke."

Her father's eyebrows crashed together.

"I know, crazy, right? But . . . well, it kinda freaked me out."

He frowned at her phone as she handed it to him and he read the message. "Did you call or text back?"

"No response. And the police are looking into it, but Cade thinks it's probably from some kind of burner phone. Untraceable."

"Could be a mistake?"

"Don't think so. Because of the time. The first one came in around midnight twenty years to the very date that Luke died. The night that Violet was murdered. I thought the text message might be a mistake, a weird coincidence, but then I got another one." She scrolled to the second text. "Got it this morning, just hours after Annessa was murdered."

"Someone's trying to get to you."

"He has," she admitted and then told him the rest: sensing someone outside, the footprint, the scrawled message sprayed upon her door.

He returned her phone to her. "You file a police report?"

"Cade insisted on it."

"They find anything?"

"Not yet."

"Jesus. I'd say it was just teenagers—y'know, bored and making trouble—but the murders put a darker spin on it."

"Yeah." She told him about the precautions they were taking, then, seeing the time, got to her feet.

"Anything you want me to do?" he asked as she set her half-full cup in the sink.

"Nah. I just needed to talk it out, y'know." She gave him a quick kiss on his beard-stubbled cheek. "I've gotta go."

"Okay, but you be careful," he warned, "and if you need anything . . ."

"I'll let you know."

He walked with her to the back porch. "You do that. Keep me in the loop."

She sketched a wave and hurried down the two steps and shivered. It wasn't cold outside, just gloomy. She had things to do.

Such as what?

Keep the kids safe?

Get real.

> Patient, lying back in the recliner: "I don't know what's happening."
> Therapist: "What do you mean?"
> Patient: "People are dying. People I know."

Therapist, calmly: "Death is a part of life."

Patient, a little more anxious: "But they're being murdered! Killed."

Therapist: "And how does that make you feel?"

Patient, whispering: "Responsible."

A beat.

Therapist, concerned, leaning forward: "Why do you feel responsible?"

Patient, fighting tears: "Because I think . . . I feel that if it weren't for me, for my lies, they wouldn't have died. It all started with Luke." Tears begin to sprout. "I lied to him, oh, God. I lied to him and I shouldn't have. I want to talk to him, but I can't find him. I think . . . I think he's hiding from me."

Therapist, eyeing the clock: "That's long over."

Patient: "I don't think so and it haunts me. He haunts me."

Therapist: "Luke haunts you?"

Patient: "Because of my lies. You told me I could speak to him."

Therapist, pausing, then: "That might not be possible. You have to let him go."

Patient, swallowing: "I try, but it's hard."

Therapist, relaxing a bit and inhaling the scent of lemongrass from the burning incense: "I know, but you can do it. Now, it's time for you to surface."

Patient: "He would never forgive me."

Therapist: "You can't bring him back. You can't undo what's done, but you can move forward. Look to the future."

Patient, confused: "What? How?"

Therapist: "Just try. First, look back at the past. What do you see?"

The patient is still uncertain.

Therapist, encouraging: "Just look."

Patient, head turning to the left and frowning eyebrows knitting in concentration: "I see dark clouds. A storm over a mountain. Rain and thunder pouring over the valley."

Therapist, leaning in closer: "Good. Now, when you look to the future?"

Patient, head slowly rotating to the right, the knitted brow relaxing, a smile toying on previously downturned lips: "It's bright." Relief is evident. "A warm glow over the mountain, sunshine beaming down on the valley where a river is flowing like liquid gold."

Therapist, pleased: "Then let go of the past. Of the storm. Accept the light. And now it's time to return. Three: You're beginning to surface."

Patient: "But the storm is following. People are dying."

Therapist: "Let them go."

Patient: "But Luke. You're saying I have to forget him. I don't know if I can. . . ."

Therapist: "Two. You're leaving them behind. You're leaving the past behind. You're leaving Luke behind."

Patient, nodding in the chair, hair rubbing against the leather, face more relaxed: "I will."

Therapist, relieved: "Good." A pause. "One. And you're back."

CHAPTER 28

A redheaded twentysomething in blue scrubs with a name tag that read "Will Hart, Customer Service" was behind the counter at Ace Medical Supplies in Astoria. He had been stacking boxes on the back wall behind the register but had turned to face Cade and Voss when they'd entered the small storefront owned by Nate Moretti. The space inside was small, filled with freestanding shelves that displayed neat stacks of all kinds of medical equipment from bandages to blood pressure cuffs to latex gloves to diabetes monitors and more. Against one wall, a row of walkers stood at the ready, crutches stacked neatly behind, all gleaming beneath suspended fluorescent lights.

"Can I help you?" Will Hart asked. A lanky kid, he had a pug nose sprinkled with freckles, dark eyes, and an eager-to-please expression.

"Yeah. We'd like to speak with Nate Moretti," Cade said. "We're with the city police." He showed his ID and badge, just as Voss retrieved hers and displayed it on the counter.

"Oh. Wow." Hart glanced at the badges and swallowed hard. "He. Um. Mr. Moretti's not in right now."

"Do you know where he is?" Cade asked, shoving his wallet back into his pocket.

"No. I mean . . . Oh, geez. Is he in trouble?" Will asked.

"We just want to talk to him," Cade said.

Voss repeated the question: "Do you know where he is?"

Will shrugged. "He didn't say."

"But he called you?" she said.

"Yeah." He was nodding frantically, obviously unnerved at the presence of the police in the store. "But . . . it was kinda weird. First of all, he never misses a day of work. Never. And he left me the message at, let me see"—he fished a cell phone from his pocket and flipped through the screen—"three forty-seven in the morning. Like, who texts then?"

"What did it say?"

"Just that he wouldn't be in today. That he was feeling sick." With some trepidation, he handed the phone to Cade. The message was simple: I've been up all night. Stomach bug. Open up and Wendy will be in around noon.

Sure enough the time was noted as 3:47 a.m.

Hart's response at 8:13 was: OK

Ryder was tempted to scroll up, but didn't. "Who's Wendy?"

Hart's mouth pinched. "My coworker. She'd better show."

"Why wouldn't she?"

412

He glanced over his shoulder as if he expected someone might be listening even though there was no one else in the store.

"Because she's a slacker, that's why. Has she shown up? No. Has she answered any of my texts? No. Do I think she's going to come in and relieve me? Take a guess." He glanced at the clock, which read 12:28. "She's already late. My guess: she's not coming in." His eager, wanting-to-please attitude was quickly disintegrating.

"Well, if Nate calls in, let him know we're looking for him," Voss said and slid her card across the counter.

"I will," Hart said, dropping Voss's card into the back slot of the register just as the front door opened and a white-haired man wrangling a woman in a wheelchair backed into the store.

Cade held the door for him, and the man, in baseball cap and jeans with suspenders over a plaid shirt, spun the chair as he entered.

"Thanks," the woman said. She was in her late seventies, it seemed. With short, snow-white hair, she was wearing a housecoat and one leg was in a cast, propped on the footrest.

"We're looking for Nate," the man said as he rolled his wife to the counter, where Hart waited.

"Get in line," Voss said under her breath as the door swung closed behind them. "Let's go see if good old Nate is home in bed, nursing a bad tummy." She threw a glance at Cade. "Who knows? Maybe he's not alone."

They knew his address and as Voss keyed it into her phone for a GPS readout, Cade slid behind the wheel of the Jeep, a department-issued Jeep that was short on comfort and big on technical equipment. Despite Voss's preference for her phone, he punched the address into the GPS of the Jeep's computer, then wheeled out of the lot of the strip mall.

The fog had settled in rather than dissipating and Ryder, though he wanted to gun it, had to drive slower than usual, knowing though not seeing that he was paralleling the river and that somewhere out there in the mist the old cannery, now invisible to him, lay rotting. He told himself that he was reaching, trying to connect the death of Luke Hollander with the homicides that were happening now; but he couldn't discount the fact that "KILLER" had been scrawled in paint across Rachel's door or that the text she'd received suggested that it had come from someone close to Luke, if not from her stepbrother himself, who was long dead.

Kayleigh was right—some sick prick was behind it, but why? Who would get his rocks off by terrorizing her?

His hands gripped the wheel more tightly and from the corner of his eye he thought he spied the cannery, a behemoth of a building, holding its own secrets, but, of course, that was just his imagination. He couldn't see fifty feet in front of the Jeep, much less across the acres that separated the cannery from the road.

He saw the change in direction on the screen, just as Voss said, "Turn left up here . . . there." She pointed at a crossroad and he waited, making certain no one was coming from the opposite direction.

He headed upward through the hills on the county road, and the fog became less dense. Fir and spruce trees gave way in spots to fields that had been cleared, and fence posts stood like sentinels rising in the mist.

"What d'ya bet he's hiding out?" Voss said. "He knows we're on to him. He's got to know that we'd find her phone and start looking at him. God, can we get a little heat in here?" She fiddled with the control. "End of May and still colder than a well digger's butt."

"You think Moretti's the killer?"

"Who else? If you ask me, they planned to meet at the school yard, things get a little rough, out of hand, and she ends up dead." She nodded, as if agreeing with herself as she peered through the windshield. "Probably a sex game gone wrong."

"Then how does the murder tie to Violet Sperry?"

"Not convinced the homicides are linked."

"Really? No murders in the area for years and

now two, within a week, women who knew each other—"

"Everyone knows everyone in this small town," she cut in.

"—both having blue painter's tape slapped over their eyes."

"Yeah, I know." She let out a sound of disgust. "Okay, I was just screwin' with ya, playin' devil's advocate. But Moretti could be our doer; he knew Violet Sperry as well."

"Wasn't very smart, though."

"When sex is involved, no one's exactly an Einstein." Scowling at the map on her phone, she said, "Maybe he was involved with both of them, you never know."

"No 'sexting' on Violet's cell."

"Well, shoot. Maybe she was just more careful than the Cooper woman was. Maybe her husband kept an eye on her phone and computer. Maybe she was just smarter than Annessa Cooper."

"She still ended up dead."

"Yeah, I'll give ya that. But that's about all."

"The killer had to know we'd find him through the phone records. And he didn't bother to take her phone. No, he wanted us to find her, to know who she was; it was like she was on display."

"In the church."

"In the bell tower," he said, driving around a corner as the road flattened a little. "Her maiden name was Bell."

416

"Oh, geez, now you're really reachin'."

"Am I?"

Voss said, "Slow down, I think you're about at the turn."

He squinted, searching for the lane in the soupy mix, then spied a mailbox. "Here we go." He turned onto a gravel lane where two ruts wound into the fog, the space between the tire tracks filled with weeds and tufts of grass.

"Let's just hope he's home."

Rachel nosed her Explorer into the garage. After cutting the engine, while still behind the wheel, she decided to read through her recent texts. She'd skimmed them, saw that they hadn't been from Cade or the kids, so she'd ignored the rapid-fire messages that she'd received in the past few hours. Now, more carefully she read each short text.

The first was from Mercedes, of course: I heard about Annessa Bell and that Harper found the body. Call me.

"Nope," Rachel said aloud and deleted the text.

The next was from Brit: OMG! Not Annessa too! I just can't believe it. What the F is going on? Is Harper okay?

Lila, of course, had texted several times. The first: I'm still reeling. Do you know anything? Chuck and Lucas and I are horrified! Horrified!!!! Call me! ☹ ♥

The second: Lucas wants to know if Harper's okay. Have you seen Xander? He's a mess!!! This is horrible. HORRIBLE!!! 😞 🖤

And a third: Call me, would you? We need to know that you're all doing okay. I can't believe this. Emergency reunion meeting! FRIDAY, MY HOUSE. 7:30!!! 😺

Really?

Even Reva had weighed in: Just heard about Annessa. Hard to believe. My God, what's happening and really, who's next? This is bizarre and unsettling. I hope your daughter isn't too traumatized. OMG—of course she is. Sorry. Can't believe Lila thinks we need a reunion meeting. The woman is relentless. (Sigh.) Guess I'll see you there.

Deleting the remainder of the texts, Rachel felt a bit of satisfaction watching the stupid emojis disappear. Sometimes the too-cute graphics bothered her—well, make that all of the time. But now, in the wake of tragedy? They just seemed inane.

She climbed out of the SUV and actually saw rays of sunshine piercing the fog. Maybe the weather would actually improve.

Ever since leaving her father's house, she'd been consumed in thought, turning the conversation with Ned over in her mind to the point that she'd nearly missed the turn to her own street.

What had it been that bothered her about the conversation? Yeah, her father had been kind, even insightful, had told her to let things go, but there had been something beneath the tenor of the conversation, something hidden by words, a sense that there was more to it.

Maybe it was because he'd asked about her mother. That was always a tense situation.

"Oh, crap." She'd promised to call.

She found Melinda's name on her contact list and hit the call button. Seconds later she was sent directly to her mother's voice mail. "Hey, Mom," she said as she opened the gate and let herself into the yard. "It's me. Just checking in. Give a call back when you can." She walked up the back steps, unlocked the house, and yelled, "I'm home!" into the hallway as Reno galloped up to greet her. She scratched her dog behind his head and yelled again, "I'm back!" into the house.

Locking the door and rearming the alarm, she waited for a response.

Nothing.

"Harper! Dylan?"

The house was still and she told herself not to worry. So what? They probably had earbuds in or were sleeping or caught up in some television show. With Reno beside her, she stepped down the hallway to Harper's room and pushed open the door. Empty. A feeling of dread slithered through her and she told herself she was being silly. She opened Dylan's door and he, too, was missing, an open bag of chips on his bed, the room the sty it always was. But empty. Silent. His game controller left on a pillow.

This wasn't good.

"Kids?" she said, thinking they might be upstairs or down. But the house was too still, silent aside from the padding of Reno's feet and the hum of the refrigerator. *Don't panic.*

They wouldn't go anywhere.

The house was locked, the alarm set. . . .

Then where the hell are they?

Nate Moretti's house, an A-frame with an addition that extended to a double garage, was tucked into a copse of evergreens. The lane that had wound through a stand of fir and maple opened to a small clearing where the home had been built, probably somewhere in the early seventies.

No light glowed in any of the windows, and in the mist-laden afternoon the house appeared deserted.

Cade rapped on the front door and waited for the sound of footsteps or the woof of a dog, or even a cough.

Nothing.

He knocked again, louder this time.

No one answered.

"Well, damn it all." Voss grabbed hold of the

doorknob and gave it a twist, pushed hard, but the door didn't budge. "Humph."

"Let's check the back."

They did, peeking through windows as they followed a trail of concrete rounds to the back, where the grass was untended. The remains of what had been a chicken coop complete with wire fencing, partially rolled away from the path, stood fifteen feet from the back door, the sides rotting, weeds growing beneath the raised floor, discolored straw littering the area.

"Looks like he could use a gardener," Voss observed. "Or a wife."

"Sexist."

"Truth." She climbed two steps to a back porch that also served as a sunroom, paned windows enclosing the area. She pounded on a screen door that rattled, then tried it, and it opened.

The inside door, however, was locked.

"No luck." She sighed and they both peered through the window cut into the back door. Inside was a kitchen, clean enough, though time-worn, one of the kitchen chairs pulled out a bit, so as to view a small television propped on the table.

"No one's here," Voss said and they moved on, looking through windows and past partially open blinds or curtains but seeing no signs of life.

Next, the garage. It was locked as well, but a window on the side wall gave a view of the dark interior, where a workbench, clean as a whistle, stretched across the back wall, the rest of the space empty.

Cade said, "Not here."

"And not at work. Lied about being sick," Voss said, standing on her tiptoes for a view of the interior and holding on to the outer sill of the window for balance.

"Unless he's at an urgent care. Or at a friend's. Maybe he just took the day off and didn't want the help to know he was playing hooky."

"Or in the wind if he thinks we're on to him."

"If he's the killer."

"Yeah. So far, he's got my vote."

"Pretty sloppy if he wanted to get away with it."

"Like I said, sex game that went a little too far."

"Possibly." But Cade wasn't buying it. Something was off about the idea of Nate Moretti killing both women. "Let's call him." Cade already had his phone out of his pocket. He'd already put Moretti's number into his contacts, but when he punched out the number and was connected, he was immediately sent to voice mail. He left a message, asking Moretti to call him back.

"So back to square one," Voss observed as she let go of the sill and stood flat-footed again. "Unless you want to break in."

"Not yet." They made their way back to the SUV, parked in front of the house. "Let's put a

BOLO out for his vehicle. It's a Toyota, right? SUV?"

"RAV4, 2019, hybrid."

"You've done your homework."

"Always."

"Then let's see if his father knows where he is." He tossed Voss the keys. "I'll run him down." Then he was on the phone again and slid into the passenger seat as Voss climbed behind the wheel.

The day was slowly beginning to clear, clouds and fog lifting, visibility improving as she turned on the SUV, then drove back down the lane. They turned onto the county road and wound through the wooded hillsides before eventually connecting to Highway 30 and heading west to Astoria.

Cade didn't get far with his call to reach Nate Moretti's father. A receptionist who answered the phone at Moretti's clinic told Cade that "Doctor" wouldn't be in until four. Frustrated, he gave Voss the word, and at the next crossroad, she turned the vehicle around to head back to the station.

All the way back to Edgewater with Voss driving so painstakingly near the speed limit that he wanted to scream, he thought about Nate Moretti's disappearance on the heels of his lover's bizarre murder.

Had he met her at St. Augustine's and, as Voss had surmised, their tryst went horribly bad?

Had someone else been waiting for them?

Was he alive, hiding out somewhere? Or on the run?

Or could he be already dead?

Cade didn't like any of the options.

CHAPTER 29

Panicked, thinking she might have missed the kids calling her, Rachel checked her phone again for messages, texts, or missed calls. Nope. The living room was empty. Her heart began to race as she saw her bedroom and office were empty, so she hurried down to the first floor and then to the basement, hitting the switch on the wall to illuminate the darkened area.

No voices. No hum of the old treadmill. No sounds of anyone. But a scent that was unfamiliar. The hint of musk. She froze and realized that some of the boxes she'd piled down here for recycling had been moved—shuffled around.

Or at least she thought so.

But why?

And where the hell were Harper and Dylan?

The musky odor had disappeared, if it had existed at all, but Rachel felt edgy. She stood stock still and listened, but other than the sound of Reno whining at the basement door she heard no one.

Crap.

Once more she looked around. Searching past shelves of boxes of stuff she hadn't thrown out, old lamps, paint cans, and boxes of tile left over from the bathroom remodel, she told herself she was overreacting. She swept her gaze through the three rooms, where, as she'd known the second she'd started down the rickety old steps, she would find no one.

A dark fear drizzled through her blood. As she started up the stairs, she began to text Harper, only to hear the back door squeak open and then the sound of footsteps hurrying inside. Along with the footfalls, she heard voices. Harper and Dylan and someone else, a male voice. Xander Vale, no doubt. He just didn't get the message.

"Mom?" Harper called as Rachel stepped onto the main floor. The back door was hanging open, the security alarm beginning to bleat when Rachel's phone rang. She checked the tiny screen and saw her mother's number.

Melinda was returning her call.

Rachel didn't answer. Not right now, as she spied Lucas, rather than Xander Vale, walking into her kitchen. He was pocketing his phone and keys while Harper carried in a couple of take-out sacks and Dylan in full camo bustled into the pantry to disengage the alarm.

They were safe.

Thank God!

"I thought I told you to stay home," she said to her children and she heard the edge in her voice. Panic with a touch of anger.

"My fault." Lucas flashed a sheepish grin. He wore jeans and a short-sleeved T-shirt despite the cool weather. "I texted Harper. Wanted to see if she was okay. Mom said she . . ." He let the sentence falter.

Rachel caught his drift. But she was still irritated. "You should have let me know."

"I thought we'd beat you back," Harper said.

"Still—"

"Hey, I didn't want to worry you, okay?" her daughter snapped. "I mean, you've been so freaked out, like, all the time, and yeah, I get it. Weird, sick things are happening, but I didn't see how going out and grabbing tacos and Cokes in the middle of the day would be that big of a deal." Her eyes sparked with challenge.

"But after last night—"

"Mom. I get it." She held her mother's gaze and a slow burning blush was climbing up the back of her neck. She was embarrassed? Because she got caught disobeying? Because Lucas was observing the fight? Or because she thought her mother was a nut job, completely unhinged.

"Fine. Next time, please just let me know," Rachel said, backing off slightly. "You scared me, is all."

"Everything scares you!" Harper's chin inched up a fraction, almost daring her mother into a battle.

Her phone began ringing again.

"Let me get this. It's Grandma. Calling me back." She clicked on her cell, then, phone to her ear, walked into the living room, where she would have a little more privacy. "Hey, Mom."

"Got your message," Melinda said.

"Yeah, I was just checking in." Rachel sat on the arm of the couch to look out the living room window, where the fog, thinner now, partially obscured the Dickersons' front yard.

"I heard about your friend."

Technically Annessa hadn't been her "friend," but she let it pass. "I know. God, it's so awful."

"And Harper was there?" How had she heard that already? Not that it mattered. Edgewater was a small town and news traveled through the stores, coffee shops, restaurants, and small businesses like a wildfire caught on the wind.

"Yeah."

"Traumatic for her." A pause. "Is she okay?"

Stretching her neck, Rachel looked down the hallway to the kitchen, where Harper was seated at the table, Lucas at the door, Dylan out of sight, probably standing around the corner next to the refrigerator or stove. "It's hard to tell. She says she is, and she seems as normal as can be expected, but it was rough on her. I kept both of them home from school today." As she watched, Harper grinned widely and gave a short laugh. She handed Lucas her phone as she sipped from a straw stuck into a cup with the logo of the local Mexican take-out spot. Probably not part of her proclaimed detox regimen.

Lucas took one look at Harper's cell and his face split into a wide grin that reminded Rachel of Lila. Luke's son definitely took after his mother's side of the family.

"I don't blame you for letting them stay home," Melinda was saying. "With everything that's happening here, keep them close. It's all just so hard. For all of us."

"You read the paper today?" she asked her mother.

"Yeah, yeah, I did. I told myself not to, that I'd just be upset, but . . . anyway, of course I did, and yes, it was upsetting." A long sigh. "It's nothing compared to the murders, of course. Those families are in so much pain and I know what that's like, but . . . ."

Rachel said, "It still stings, though."

"Stings like a bitch and Mercedes Jennings—er, Pope—keeps calling me and wanting me to submit to an interview for that damned paper, but I just won't." Melinda was firm.

"Don't blame you."

"I think it's odd that she's so focused on what happened to Luke," Melinda confided. "Because he told me once that she didn't like him."

"Yeah." Rachel sighed and shook her head. "She's one of the few of my friends who wasn't half in love with him. God, they all fell all over him, like he was God's gift or something."

"Maybe he was," Melinda murmured.

Rachel cringed.

"At least Lila Kostas thought so," Melinda said bitterly.

Rachel kept her voice low. "At least she gave you a grandson."

"Yeah, well, there is that." Melinda's tone was flat. She'd never been close to Lucas. She'd lost a son. Lucas had lost a father he'd never known. But instead of bonding with her first-born grandson, Melinda had chosen to distance herself from him and his unwed mother, not even sending Lila a note of congratulations when she married Chuck.

Their family was absurdly complicated, Rachel would give her mother that much. At least Lucas had connected to his cousins. Here he was now, laughing and joking with Harper and Dylan.

Rachel hazarded another glance into the kitchen and saw Dylan reaching into the open sack, pulling out a wrapped taco, then wadding the empty sack and throwing it at his older cousin, who caught the incoming ball easily, then hurled it back with some force.

"I guess we'll muddle through," Melinda said.

"We have to. By the way, Mom, you said Luke's dad was released from prison."

"That's right."

"Has he tried to contact you?"

A pause. "Why would you ask that?"

"Just curious. I mean, he was Luke's father."

She could almost feel her mother bristle over the connection. "A father in name only. The man's a beast, Rachel. Someone who talked with his fists. I'm grateful that Luke never knew him. God knows what would have happened. . . . Oh, Lord . . ."

Yeah, the worst had happened. Luke had died. And Bruce Hollander hadn't been involved.

"You didn't answer my question."

Her mother hesitated. "I got a text from him, at least I think it was him. He said it was. I didn't respond. Blocked the number."

A text? Rachel's pulse jumped. "What did he say?"

"It was nothing. Came through on the anniversary of the day Luke died. He identified himself and said he was sorry. Nothing more. I figured he was in some kind of twelve-step program and I was one of the steps."

"Do you have that number?"

"I deleted it."

"But could you find it . . . isn't there something under 'recently deleted' on your phone? Or something like that?"

"Maybe, but why? I haven't had contact with him for over twenty years. There's just no reason."

"There might be, Mom," she said. "I've, um, I've had a couple weird texts and the first one came in on the anniversary of Luke's death."

431

"What? Oh, that's horrible. What did it say?"

" 'I forgive you.' "

"For what?"

"Didn't say. But that was it. Both times." Rachel explained about the two missives she'd received from the unknown person.

"Wow. You know, I don't know Bruce any longer, but I'm not buying that he's a changed man. I don't think twenty years in prison necessarily turns a person around, but that just isn't his style, or it wasn't. He wasn't into subtleties, not when I knew him, when I was married to him. And if it were really him, and he was, you know, reaching out to you like he did to me in whatever program he might be on, why not be up front? Why the cloak-and-dagger stuff? The anonymity. That's not part of any program I've ever heard about and certainly not his style. At least it wasn't in the past." She hesitated. "I'll try to locate that number, though."

"Good." If she did, Rachel intended to pass it on to Cade. ASAP. They talked a little more, and when she hung up, she spied Ella Dickerson in her yard, gardening gloves covering her hands as she knelt near a bed of roses, all starting to bud. The kids were still in the kitchen, which smelled of cumin and hot sauce. As she walked down the hall, she saw that Lucas was shoving his phone in his pocket and fiddling with his keys.

"I was just heading home," he said as she entered.

"Don't leave on my account."

He shook his head as he reached for the door. "It's not that. Mom is kind of nervous these days and I have a final I should be studying for." To Harper, he said, "See ya," then cast a glance Dylan's way and hitched his chin. "We need another game."

"Yeah." Dylan nodded, pointing at his cousin. "You've got it."

"I'll go out with you," Rachel said as Lucas opened the back door, then to the kids, "Just turn off the alarm for a second. I need to take Reno outside."

Hearing his name, the dog scrambled to her side. She snapped his leash onto his collar and walked out the back and around the house to Lucas's car, parked on the street. It struck her that Lucas was nearly the same age Luke had been at his death, so walking with him across the grass brought back unbidden memories of her brother. Though Lucas was slightly shorter and more muscular than Luke had been, his hair was almost as blond. As he folded himself into his black Porsche, she remembered Luke getting into Nate Moretti's BMW on that fateful afternoon.

Her heart ached with the old, familiar pain. Forcing the memory back to the farther reaches of her mind, she asked, "So how're you doing with all of this?"

Seated inside, he looked up at her through the open window. "All of what?" he asked, then caught her drift. "Oh, you mean the articles in the paper? And the people being killed?"

"Yeah."

He frowned, more serious than usual. "It's weird."

"That's an understatement."

"Okay, freaky weird." His eyes narrowed. "Do you think—I mean, is it possible that the people who've been attacked, that they had anything to do with my dad?"

"I don't know," she admitted, keeping Reno tethered in one hand as the dog sniffed around the grass near the curb. "Maybe. Maybe not. Why?"

"Just something Mom said. You know. About what happened. About how those women . . . that they were witnesses to him . . . to him dying."

"A lot of us were."

"I guess so." And then he squinted at her and she saw the never-asked question in his eyes. *Why did you do it? Why did you kill your own brother, the father I never had the chance to meet?*

"You know, Lucas," she said, her fingers curling over the edge of the sports car's door, her throat closing, "I'm sorry about your dad. Really sorry for my part in it, sorry about . . . about all of it."

His lips folded in on themselves. He didn't ask why, just gave a quick nod. As if he knew what she was talking about. "Don't worry about it," he finally said and started the Porsche's huge engine.

Reno jumped back, and as Lucas pulled away from the edge of the street, heading back to town, Rachel crossed in front of her house to the Dickersons' place. Ella was still on her knees, eyeing Lucas's sports car speeding away, then barely stopping at the far corner before roaring out of sight, disappearing into the rising mist. "It does no good to spoil a kid," she said, pushing herself to her feet and dusting her gloved hands free of damp bark dust.

"Probably," she agreed, then got to the point. "You have a good view of my house and I was wondering if you saw anyone hanging around."

"I told the police everything I know about what was written on your door." Adjusting her glasses, she added, "I was the one who told you."

"Yeah, I know and thanks. I hadn't seen it."

"Horrible stuff. Sometimes it makes you wonder what the world's coming to."

Reno pulled at the leash. "Sit," Rachel ordered. "But I mean not just that night, but others. Have you seen anyone hanging out by the side gate, for example?" she asked, pointing to the strip of grass that led to the back gate on the side of the house abutting the Pittses' place.

Ella took off her gloves. "Well, yeah."

The back of Rachel's mouth went dry. "Who? When?"

"I don't know, it's usually dark. I've seen someone there a couple of times, didn't think anything of it. There's a lot of coming and going at your house. Teenagers. Cars." She shrugged. "I never said anything because I thought you knew. I thought they were probably friends of your kids."

Really? "What time . . . when?"

"Oh, gee, the last time was probably the night before last." She screwed up her face as she thought. "Sometime after midnight or thereabout."

"Sunday?"

"Yeah." She nodded. "Pretty sure."

"A boy?"

"Or man . . . maybe even a tall woman."

"Could you identify them?" Rachel asked, her pulse jumping as she stared at her own house with its discolored door, the horrid word illegible, but the mismatched paint a scar. Tomorrow, she'd repaint the entire thing.

"Don't think so. It was dark, not foggy like today, but deep night. Anyway, all kids look alike these days—boys and girls in those oversized hooded sweatshirts and jeans with holes in the knees. It could even have been your son. Never saw the face, y'know."

She didn't know, but one of her children had used a window to sneak out, so it wasn't too hard to believe that her son, too, might have been going in and out of the house at will. She thought of all the nights she'd thought she'd seen someone lurking in the backyard, the times that Reno had acted as if someone was out there. She'd thought she was going out of her mind, when really . . . her own kids might have caused all her trauma.

"Say, did you know that woman who was killed?" Ella asked. "I watched the noon news. She was about your age and they said she'd grown up around here."

"She was a classmate."

"And the other one, too. The one who was murdered last week?"

"They both graduated with me."

"What do you think happened?" The older woman's eyes gleamed at the prospect of gossip and Rachel didn't want to get into it.

"I don't know," she said, then added, "I have to get back. The kids are home and I have to make sure they're doing their homework. Thanks!" Before the older woman could ask another question, she tugged on Reno's leash and they crossed the street to go inside and confront her children, one or both of whom were still lying to her.

CHAPTER 30

Cade had driven back to the crime scene for one last look and then spied his father's Mercedes parked in the lot next door. He let himself into the office and with a quick wave to Doris, Chuck's receptionist and secretary, he headed straight to his father's office.

"Oh, Cade, please wait." Doris snapped the headset from her perfectly coiffured gray hair.

"It's okay, Doris. I've got this." A fixture who had been with Chuck since Cade was a teen, she looked positively stricken that he wasn't waiting as commanded in the small reception area.

Instead he strode into Chuck's office. Charles Ryder was now the lone attorney in the building, his partner having retired several years earlier.

Cade found his father dressed in slacks and a white dress shirt, sleeves rolled up. His face was perpetually tanned, his graying hair thinning, and lately he had been wearing glasses, but he was still fit, his body the lanky shape of a long-distance runner's. He was putting, hitting a golf ball across a long green mat laid over the carpet to a hole complete with auto return. The ball hit the right spot and the device shot it back down the length of the mat to where Chuck stood still in putting stance. He captured the ball with the head of his putter and lined up again, barely glancing up, not wanting to break his concentration.

"Busy day?"

"Just wrapped up with my last client ten minutes ago. Thought I'd hone my short game before I headed home. And, to tell you the truth, I figured you'd be showing up," he said, and with a short, sharp stroke hit the golf ball to send it rolling dead center to the return device. It popped back and this time Chuck straightened, cupped the ball with the head of his putter, tossed it into the air, and caught it deftly with his free hand. He rested the putter against the bookcase and dropped the ball into a dish holding several others.

"You expect me to believe that you were waiting for me?"

"Oh, no, no." He swatted the air as if he could dismiss the idea. "Of course not. But I'm not surprised you're here considering that a homicide happened right next door. I'll cut to the chase. Of course I don't know anything about what happened at the property next door last night." He sat on the overstuffed arm of a leather couch that had been in the office for as long as Cade could remember. "But before we get into that, how's Harper?" His face creased with genuine concern.

"Dealing."

"Is she?" Sucking in a breath through his

teeth, he shook his head. "Pretty tough. And she shouldn't have been there. It's Xander's fault she was even here in the first place." He scowled darkly. "You give a kid a break—a part-time job and a place to live when he's here—and what does he do? Brings your seventeen-year-old granddaughter up to it in the middle of the damned night!"

He slapped his knees, stood, then walked to his desk, rolled back his chair, and dropped into it. "Sit, sit," he said, waving Cade into one of the side chairs. "Drink?"

"Still on duty."

"I'm your father."

"Doesn't matter."

"Well, hell, I'm having one." He reached behind him to the liquor cabinet, found a decanter of scotch, and poured himself a healthy shot into one of the short glasses that were on display. "Anyway, I sent Vale packing. Told him that I'd give him decent references but that he had to find another job." He took a swallow from his glass. "I'm sure Harper's going to be upset, but hell, I can't have that." Another long swallow. "So did I cover everything you needed to know?"

"Just about. But have you seen anyone coming or going at the property next door?"

"Just people from Bell-Cooper, and that's a pisser, let me tell you. I had been trying to buy that property for years but got nowhere with the archdiocese, and then this yahoo from Seattle comes down here and starts buying up everything. You know he's got a deal for Reacher's farm and the old Galloway sawmill, even that damned cannery—Sea View—and God knows what else? The whole thing has had Lila tied in knots. You know she didn't get the listings to begin with, nor did Annessa, who was supposed to be a friend of hers, use her to do the purchasing?" Pointing a finger at Cade, he said, "Lila's a helluva real estate agent, as you know. She should have had those sales and boy was she mad when she didn't get a one! I don't blame her. Some friend." He clucked his tongue. "Well, I guess that's neither here nor there now. The poor woman's dead. I just can't imagine."

"You never saw a silver Toyota? A RAV4 hybrid. 2019?"

He shook his head. "I don't really pay all that much attention, but no, I don't think so. Let me ask Doris." He pushed a button on an antiquated intercom. "Doris, would you mind coming in here a second?"

"I'll be right there," was the metallic response, and true to her word, she appeared in the doorway. As ever, she was dressed in a pantsuit, this one black, with a pink blouse and a scarf in hues of gray.

Cade posed the same question to her and her face pulled into a wrinkled knot of concentration.

441

"I don't think so, but my desk doesn't face that direction, and even if it did, there aren't any windows on that side of the building, at least not downstairs. You have to be on the upper floor to really see much because of the fence." She shrugged. "Sorry."

"No worries."

"Anything else?" she asked Chuck. "If not, I'm going to take off. The kids and grandkids are coming over tonight. Pinochle, you know." She brightened at the mention of her family.

"God, that's right. It's Tuesday, isn't it? Sure. Go, go. That's fine. I'm about out of here, too. I'll lock up. Thanks, Doris."

"Good night," she said to her boss, then gave a nod to Cade and bustled out of the office.

"She's retiring next year," Chuck said thoughtfully. "She'll be hard to replace."

"You'll figure it out."

"Guess so." He finished his drink. "What about Rachel?" he asked. "Lila said she's looking and I think she worked for an attorney in Astoria."

"Years ago."

"She's good with computers."

Cade wasn't going to douse Rachel's chances but it seemed more than a little incestuous to have his ex-wife working for his father.

"I'd see the grandkids more."

"Maybe."

"Worth a shot."

"Give her a call," Cade said, but didn't expect Rachel would jump at the chance to work for her ex-father-in-law and Lila's husband.

"Got anything else on your mind?" Chuck asked. "If not, I'd better get going, too. It's family night at our house as well, but with Lila's mood, it won't be all that fun, let me tell you. And then there's Lucas." He pushed himself to his feet. "If it were up to me, I'd see that he went off to a four-year university, just like you and your brothers did, but Lila won't hear of it and I don't suppose the kid could get in on his grades." He rubbed the back of his neck. "I really thought Vale was a good influence on him. Too bad about that."

"Yeah. Probably for the best. Let me know if you think of anything that you might have seen that's out of the ordinary."

"Will do," his father promised, and as Cade walked to the door, he saw his father pour himself another drink and then reach for his putter again. In no hurry to go home.

Kayleigh was frustrated. Seated at her desk in the office, scrolling through the reports on her computer screen, only vaguely aware of the noise and activity of the station around her, she reread the interviews of everyone who knew, lived by, or was related to Violet Sperry. Nothing. She also studied the preliminary autopsy report, and found nothing new, nothing to work with.

The investigation was heading for a standstill.

She could feel it in her bones.

The neighbors had seen nothing. The victim, according to everyone, had no enemies. Her husband, Leonard, had an airtight alibi and no greedy children were around to be on the suspect list. Violet's handgun was still missing, no one in the area had cameras that might have viewed a suspicious vehicle being driven or parked in the area, and so far there was no physical evidence collected at the crime scene—no blood that didn't match the victim, no latent fingerprints, no discarded cigarette butt or gloves left in the bushes—and no evidence of any affair. No texts or phone calls to an unknown number.

All they had so far was the damned painter's tape.

And, oh, another dead body, too, whose eyes had been taped over until the kids had come and tried to save her. Xander Vale's prints were all over the wad of blue tape left at the scene, but he'd tried to rescue Annessa Cooper rather than kill her.

The two crimes had to be connected, the killer the same, but while Violet Sperry's body had been left in a pool of her own blood from the fall that had broken her neck and cracked her skull, ribs, pelvis, both of her ulnae and radii, as well as her right fibula, Annessa Cooper had been carried and dragged from the spot where the attack had taken place near the doors of the school to the bell tower of the old chapel and hung from the long-forgotten ropes.

Why?

Why one and not the other?

Violet's death had been fairly quick after a struggle. It could be the killer had planned to take her somewhere else, to display her as he had Annessa, to not murder her quickly, but let her suffer until she was found, but the fight had turned violent and deadly.

Annessa had been at the school to meet her lover, it seemed, according to the texts in her phone. The conversation had been with Nate Moretti, a classmate who had known both women, though he seemed to have no connection to Violet Sperry other than having gone to school with her way back when.

She bit her lip and thought, hearing some commotion in the hallway and a deputy swear about having to go and deal with traffic as someone had hit an elk. "Highway thirty, about six miles out of town, the animal died at the scene, the driver is okay, rescue on its way, traffic backing up. Shit." It sounded like Claire Donahue had taken the call. "I hate this part of the job," she was saying as her footsteps pounded a quick beat down the hallway. "Azure, are you coming with me? For the love of Mother Mary, I don't know why that damned herd doesn't stay down in Gearhart where it belongs!"

"I'm in," Trace Azure said, his voice a deep baritone and sounding faintly amused at his partner's frustration. "Let's roll."

Donahue muttered loud enough for anyone within fifteen feet to hear, "Effin' elk."

"So where do you think you are? Effin' New York City? Deal with it, Donahue," Azure said, making a point. Chinook was a large county, primarily rural, with a few small towns in its boundaries, Edgewater being included. Their voices faded and the backdrop of ringing phones, low conversations, and shuffling footsteps returned to its usual dull cacophony.

Kayleigh tried to get back into work, still going over the reports, hoping for something, any damned thing she might have missed on her first quick scans.

Cade had called and reported Moretti was MIA. Great.

Kayleigh's first thought had been the wronged husband might have sought out his vengeance on his wife's younger lover, but it turned out Clint Cooper, too, had an iron-clad alibi. He hadn't even been in the state. And, once more, no fortune-hungry kids were waiting for her to die. Annessa Cooper's stepchildren by Clint's first and second marriages wouldn't get a dime until Clint himself kicked off.

She drummed her fingers on her desk, then caught herself and stopped, only to pick up a pencil and twirl it nervously. She was antsy because of too little sleep and too many unanswered questions. Where the hell was Moretti? Had he been scared off last night? Was he in hiding, in fear for his life after what he'd seen, the attack at the school? But why then not call 911 or try to break up the assault himself?

So what was the connection?

And why the staging? Why leave her alive? Had the killer been scared off? Had he been confronted by Nate Moretti?

She came back to the same thought over and over again: the victims graduated together from Edgewater High twenty years earlier and they both had been at the abandoned fish-packing plant when Luke Hollander had died. They'd both been witnesses on Rachel Gaston Ryder's behalf.

But that seemed far-fetched.

Who would care after all these years?

Nate Moretti? Reportedly Luke Hollander's best friend? Why would he suddenly go homicidally berserk? Because of the articles in the paper? She snorted at that thought. Because of the twentieth anniversary of the homicide or was it because of his upcoming high school reunion? She almost smiled. A lot of people hated reunions and didn't want to be reminded of high school, but killing classmates seemed a little on the extreme side.

She wondered about Harper. Poor kid. No teenager should have to witness the horrifying death of another at such a young age. Well, never, of course, but death happened, often at the hands of another person. Seeing the girl at the scene, so young and broken, beyond upset, clinging to Cade, had gotten to Kayleigh. Watching the interplay between father and daughter had only confirmed to Kayleigh that her decision had been right, that breaking it off with Cade before it had ever really gotten started had proved to be the only path to have taken.

But it was still hard. Painful.

Observing him comforting his daughter had torn at Kayleigh's heart, had caused her to want Cade Ryder even more than she had before. Why?

Because you're an effin' cretin when it comes to Cade Ryder.

She tossed her pencil onto her desk in disgust and watched it slowly roll to the floor, then picked it up and stuffed it back into the mug of writing utensils she kept near her monitor.

She needed to do something. Get out of the office. Away from the desk. Clear her mind. Get a fresh perspective. She was tired from lack of sleep the night before and nothing was happening here. Her phone buzzed and she saw it was Travis McVey. For a second, in her mind's eye, she saw his bare chest and ropey arm muscles, remembered how it felt to have him turn her easily in the bed and run his hand down her spine and over her rump. She felt a little shiver of desire deep inside but quickly shut it down. "Not now," she said and let the call go to voice mail. Then added a silent: *Not ever.*

CHAPTER 31

At 4:47, Cade was done waiting.

Still at his desk in the office, he put in another call to Dr. Richard Moretti's office and was told that "Doctor" wasn't returning. Yes, the receptionist had assured Cade she'd handed him the message, but mentioned that the doctor had been called to the hospital. She assured Cade that Moretti had his number.

"Tell him it's important," Cade said and heard a pat, if distracted, "Of course," as she disconnected.

Frustrated, he called the medical supply store Moretti owned.

The phone was picked up by a bored woman who sounded as if she was chewing gum as she said bluntly, "He ain't here. Ya wanna leave a message?"

"Already did." And he explained.

"Okay. Got it," she said and hung up.

"Strike two." He glanced at his desk, noted the faded manila file folder on Luke Hollander's death, and wondered why it still bothered him, why he thought it was important in the recent murders. Yeah, the two victims had been at the cannery the night Hollander was killed, along with a lot of others. Their connection was that they'd both testified for Rachel.

Did that mean anything?

He couldn't see how.

He flipped open the file again, rifled through the statements until he came to those of the people he knew.

Lila Kostas, now his stepmother, had sworn she was at the other end of the cannery at the time of the shots, though she'd admitted she'd been searching for Luke, her then boyfriend.

Nate Moretti, Luke's best friend, had been smoking near a broken window and had seen the cops approach. He swore he hadn't heard the report of a gun, nor seen its flash, but he was too far from his friend.

Reva Augustus, now Santiago, had been "near the chute" where the unused fish guts and scraps had been tossed during the cannery's operation. But she, too, had a link to Luke. She was the girl he'd tossed over for Lila and, according to all reports, had been bitter about it. But she'd done well for herself, become an attorney.

Mercedes Jennings Pope had been hiding out in an upper story, this confirmed by Billy Dee Johnson, who'd been with her when people started yelling, "Cops! Run!" Mercedes had never liked Luke and had made no bones about it. Billy Dee had been his friend until a football "accident" in practice had ruined Billy Dee's chances at a scholarship. Luke Hollander had

451

been the kid who had tackled him, the reason he'd had to settle for community college.

Annessa Bell Cooper had not been far from the spot where Luke had fallen. She'd sworn that she'd seen another flash, behind Rachel, that she thought someone else had killed Luke. Though Rachel had thought she'd shot her brother with the very weapon her brother had handed to her earlier in the day.

That was the hard part to swallow.

Why would he do that?

She could have killed or wounded anyone with that weapon. And it just happened to be unregistered, not linked to any previous crime. Where had Luke gotten it? No one knew; he hadn't confided in anyone, or anyone who would admit to it.

Back then, there was a missing gun: the one that had killed Luke Hollander.

But Rachel's own testimony, that she'd fired while trying to leave the building, dragging Violet with her, had been the reason she'd been arrested. Freaked out at what she'd done, that she'd actually shot and wounded her brother, she'd dropped the pistol after firing.

No other bullets had been found, no casings or shells.

One shot had hit Luke and he'd eventually bled out, being declared DOA at the local clinic that served as the emergency room for the area back then. And the doctor in charge who signed the death certificate? Richard Moretti.

The case had been far from open and shut. Rachel's confession had nearly sealed her fate, but her friends' conflicting testimony and her young age and a soft judge had changed things.

And she'd never gotten over it; never really let it go.

Now, there was another missing pistol: a gun registered to Leonard Sperry.

He glanced at the clock again and put the file away. Moretti wasn't calling him back. "Screw it." It was time to take matters into his own hands.

After shutting down his computer, he grabbed his wallet, badge, and sidearm.

"I'm heading out again," he told Voss, who was sitting at her desk sipping iced tea while tracking down and reviewing footage from security cameras belonging to businesses not far from the crime scene. "Gonna track down Moretti's dad."

"Let me know how that goes. I'm here if you need me."

"I've got this."

She nodded. "Looks like it could be a long night, but I think footage from The Right Spot tavern shows a car like Nate Moretti's parked in their lot until about eleven-thirty last night. A deputy is picking up a copy and taking it to the lab to enhance. Turns out Moretti was a regular, so I've got a call in to the bartender who was working last night to see if he was there. Maybe we'll get lucky."

"Let's hope. We could use a break."

The Right Spot was a dive located about three blocks east of St. Augustine's, a local watering hole where Cade had spent more than one night after his divorce.

She gave him the high sign and he made his way to his truck. No reason to take a city-issued vehicle—after his conversation with the doctor he planned on going home. Eventually. After checking in with Rachel and the kids. He knew they'd spent the day at home and just wanted to double-check on Harper, go see how she was doing, and to make sure Rachel was working to get the security system installed.

But first things first: Richard Moretti.

Sometime during the afternoon most of the fog had dissipated, though a fine layer of mist hung close to the river. He found his sunglasses in the truck's console and slipped them onto his nose and drove into the direction of the lowering sun, toward Astoria and the hospital. He pulled into the parking garage to the area reserved for physicians and settled in to wait, but it didn't take long. He recognized Moretti the minute the doctor stepped off the elevator and with remote key in hand unlocked the doors of a silver Audi. The car's lights blinked.

Cade got out of the pickup, slammed the door shut, and intercepted Moretti just before he reached his car.

"Richard Moretti?" he asked.

"Who are you?" Moretti was instantly wary. On guard. In khaki-colored slacks and a blue button-down, he was tall and slim, the resemblance to his son unmistakable. His dark hair was graying at the temples and wireless glasses sat upon an aquiline nose.

Cade showed his badge. "Detective Cade Ryder, Edgewater Police."

"Oh, yeah." Behind the clear lenses, his eyes narrowed. "You're one of Charlie's boys." He wagged a finger. "Married to Ned Gaston's daughter."

Cade didn't bother to correct him. "I'm looking for your son," he said. "Do you know where he is?"

"Nate? At work, I suppose, or maybe on his way home."

"He didn't show up today. Called in sick."

"Then at his house."

"Don't think so. I went there earlier and no one was around. His car is missing."

"Then out of town." Richard Moretti rolled his palms into the air. "I have no idea where he is, but maybe he decided to go camping, or on a trip, or whatever."

"But he would have told his employees.

Instead, he left them a message that he was too ill to come in today."

"What?" Moretti pulled a face. "That doesn't sound like him."

An older model Camaro sped around the end of the lot and barreled toward them, speeding toward the exit, music blasting from the open windows.

Quickly Cade stepped closer to Moretti's car, getting out of the Chevy's path.

Moretti made frantic pat-pat motions in the air, signaling the driver to slow down, but she didn't see him, was too interested in lighting a cigarette, and then sped across a walkway, leaving a trail of exhaust in her wake. "What's wrong with her?" Moretti said in disgust. "A health care worker at that!"

"Know her?"

Shaking his head, he said, "No. I'm only here a few days a week and it's a big hospital, well, at least by our standards. But I can probably find out by the description of her car." He scowled at the retreating sports car as it sped down the street and rolled to a near stop before the driver gunned it, squeezing into a free space in front of a minivan. "What the devil is she thinking? If she isn't careful, she's going to kill someone. Now"—he turned his attention back to Cade, some of his supercilious attitude dissipating— "let me see if I can get hold of Nate." He slid a phone from his pocket, punched a preset number, and put the phone to his ear.

Cade heard the phone ring, then be answered by the same recorded voice he'd listened to earlier. "Huh," Richard said, then dialed again, and when someone answered said, "Hi, this is Nate's father, Dr. Moretti. I'd like to speak to him." A pause, then, "Well, when do you expect him in? . . . Yes, I know you're getting ready to close . . . but you haven't heard anything. . . . Yes, I'll give Will a call." He disconnected. "Maybe we should go out to his house," he said, the lines across his forehead creasing more deeply. "I'll call Will Hart on the way. He's already gone home for the day."

"Do you have a way to get in?" Cade asked.

"Yeah." The doctor was nodding as he slid behind the wheel. "I know where he hides the spare."

Cade crossed the lot, climbed into his truck, and followed the Audi to Nate Moretti's A-frame in the hills. The house and grounds looked as deserted as ever, and once his dad located Moretti's key, hidden on a crossbeam of the small porch, they walked inside.

"Nate?" Richard called, wasting no time as he walked through an open living room and kitchen, then straight to the downstairs bedroom. "Hey! What's up?" But he was talking to open space. No one answered and the bed, sloppily made, was empty. The downstairs bath and extra bedroom were quiet, no one around. The upper loft, with its steeply angled walls, was used as an office that stretched the length of the building, a window on each end.

Nate Moretti was nowhere to be found.

"Odd," his father said, and tried texting. Without a word he walked through a door off the kitchen, down a hallway that was used as a laundry room, and directly into the garage.

Which, of course, was empty.

"He's gone," he said, stating the obvious. Then, after a thoughtful moment, he strode back through the house to the master bedroom, where he opened a storage closet that was filled with luggage—one complete set, other smaller duffels and bags. "It doesn't look like anything's missing . . . but he could have gone fishing. . . ." He stared into the crammed space for a second, then closed the doors. "If he were really sick, he would have called me." Worry pulled at the corners of his eyes as they returned to the living area. "Let me call my wife," he said, and before Cade could say anything, he'd punched in her number and she picked up.

The conversation was short, the upshot being that she, too, had no idea where their son could be. As he slipped the phone back into his pocket, Cade asked, "What do you know about his relationship with Annessa Cooper?"

"Annessa? The woman who was found yester-day? A classmate of my son's, yes, but what relationship?" He appeared absolutely confused. "Was he in one? You mean romantically?" His forehead furrowed as he thought. "You're saying that he and Annessa were seeing each other?" He thought about it and shook his head. "I, um, I suspected he might have a new girlfriend, but he didn't say anything." Then he sighed. "She was married, wasn't she?"

"Yeah. And now she's dead."

"Oh. Wait. Nate had nothing to do with that. My son . . . he's not a killer. Is that what you're implying?"

"They were supposed to meet. Last night."

"No . . ." He was shaking his head, denial his first instinct, but a wary light entered his eyes. "Oh, Christ." And then when the situation gelled in his mind, his eyes sharpened. "Wait a second. What're you getting at? What, exactly, are you saying, Detective?"

"I think your son is missing because of last night. Either he was involved with Annessa Cooper's homicide and left, or saw something that scared him and he took off, or, possibly, he's a victim himself."

"What?" The doctor was shaken, his pallor washing white. "This can't be," he whispered, but was obviously piecing what he knew together, as he thought about it.

"Come down to the station and tell me every-thing you know that could help in locating your son," Cade suggested.

"Fine," he said. "I'll be there in half an hour."

"Good. And bring your wife." He left the house, climbed into his truck, and drove down the lane, checking in his rearview mirror to see Moretti's Audi following. Moretti seemed to be talking, to no one in the car, probably calling his wife on a Bluetooth device connected to his phone.

Unless Moretti actually knew where his son was and was warning him, but Cade didn't think so; the man was cut off at the knees hearing that his boy was not only involved with a murder victim, but also missing. His phone rang on his way to Edgewater, and seeing it was Voss, he answered, picking it up from the cup holder where he'd tossed it.

"Yeah?"

"You on your way back?"

"Should be there in less than fifteen. Something up?"

"Possibly. I talked to the bartender at The Right Spot, and guess what? He remembers Nate as he's a regular. Nate got caught in a conversation with a guy the barkeep didn't recognize. Nate left, the guy finished his drink and took off. I'm checking the footage now and it's interesting. Nate left the bar alone, left his car there—the time stamp says eleven forty-six—and when he came back, about an hour later, he wasn't alone. A guy was walking close to him. And Nate didn't get behind the wheel. His companion did. You gotta see this."

"Same guy?" Cade asked, and he felt that little sensation that maybe they were getting a break in the case.

"Possibly. Not sure. Both were wearing baseball caps, but the bartender can't or won't say that it's the same guy. He said that he thought the patron who was talking to Nate had been wearing jeans and a jacket and a baseball cap. The guy in the film is wearing a sweatshirt with a hood—a hoodie—though you can see the bill of a cap poking out from under the hood. Face in shadow, of course. I'll have the lab enhance."

"Can we ID the guy who was talking to Nate? He's got to be the last one to have seen him before he went missing."

"If he and our friend in the parking lot are one and the same. But no, not so far."

"No credit card receipt?"

"Nope. Didn't get that lucky. He paid with cash."

"Damn." Frowning, he stared through the windshield and as he swept around a final corner, caught a glimpse of the waterfront and the town of Edgewater spread upon the Columbia's shores.

Ten minutes later he was inside the office and Voss was showing him the tape of Nate Moretti

461

getting into the passenger side of his car, on her computer monitor. He did seem to stumble and nearly fall into the car, his companion helping him in and slamming the door shut before getting behind the wheel. Was Moretti being coerced? Ordered into the car and complying? Or was he not driving because he'd had too much to drink?

"Bartender said Nate left at 11:45, which this tape confirms—see there, 11:46," Voss said as they both eyed the grainy black-and-white footage. "But check this—these guys come back at 12:57. An hour and eleven minutes later. Nate should have been sobering up."

"Mmm. Unless they went somewhere else, drank more or got high. Who knows?"

"Nate seems to lose his balance, the other guy catching him."

"Or forcing him into the car. Could have a weapon."

"The lost hour." She replayed the tape on slow mo. Moretti was recognizable. The other guy, not so much. He was about the same size, slim enough, but his face was in shadow, hidden within the hood of his sweatshirt and the baseball cap.

"So what happened? If Moretti was supposed to meet Annessa Cooper, why's he with this guy? Did they kill her together? Is Moretti a victim? And who the hell is this guy?"

Voss frowned and squinted at the screen. "Don't know."

"Yet," Cade said. "We'll find him."

"Yeah, but will we find him alive, or strung up like his girlfriend?"

Cade didn't want to think too hard about the options.

CHAPTER 32

Sweat dripping from the tip of her nose, Kayleigh pushed harder, riding the stationary bike in the gym, pushing her way through a preprogrammed routine of hills and valleys, her legs beginning to ache after spending time working through a kickboxing drill and weight training before ending up here in a long row of bikes going nowhere. She should have swum laps, she thought, as she'd been a swimmer in college and always enjoyed the feel of cutting through the water, breathing regularly, away from all the worries of the world.

But not today.

Somehow the workout seemed to mimic her life: spinning her wheels and getting nowhere.

She was listening to Axl Rose screaming near the end of "Sweet Child O' Mine" when her phone cut in and she saw Cade's number flash onto the screen. Her stupid heart leapt and she silently cursed herself as she answered.

"Hey, what's up?" she asked, breathing hard, the pounding beat of Guns N' Roses suddenly silenced.

"Thought I'd pull you in."

"On what?"

"Nate Moretti's missing. He's—"

"Annessa Cooper, your victim's lover, yeah, I know."

"He's missing. At least we think so." Then he explained about Nate Moretti calling in sick and not being at home, not answering his phone.

"You think he's running?"

"Possibly."

"Or ended up a victim, too. In the wrong place at the wrong time."

"Again, possibly. I'm on my way to the station. To interview the father. He was also connected to the Luke Hollander homicide."

She made a deprecating noise. "You still trying to link the two? Connecting nonexistent dots?"

"More like filling in very existent blanks."

"Okay, I'll see you there." She clicked off and stopped pedaling, and caught a disparaging glance from a toned forty-year-old guy on a nearby bike. *Oh, get over your bad self,* she thought, as she swiped her face with the towel draped around her neck.

So cell phones were off limits in the gym, so what? Ignoring the pinched-faced woman in her perfectly matched workout wear, Kayleigh half jogged to the showers, where she stripped, stepped under the hot spray, turned the temperature to cold, then turned off the water. Seconds later she'd toweled off. She was dressed and out of the gym in less than five minutes from the time Cade's call had come in. No makeup, wet hair starting to curl despite being swept back in a quick ponytail.

Good enough.

On her way to Edgewater, she thought about Nate Moretti be-ing MIA.

She'd seen the texts, knew he'd been planning to meet Annessa at the school.

Had he bailed?

Had something come up?

Or had he made the tryst and been scared off?

Or become another victim himself?

"Time will tell," she said aloud as she drove along the highway skirting the river. As she approached Edgewater, she saw the old cannery, a blackened building rising out of the mist that had settled over the Columbia, the decrepit old building where, Cade seemed to think, all the horror had started twenty years before.

"Really?" she said aloud and turned her attention to the road again, where the semi she was following slowed as it entered the city limits. She peeled off at the next corner and wound her way through the business district and pulled into the small lot next to the police station.

Inside she found Cade in an interview room with a man and a woman, both of whom looked tense and unhappy, but dressed as if they belonged to some country club set. He was slim and tanned with a full head of hair just starting to turn gray, she as trim as he, her red hair cut short and spiky, a few freckles visible, her eyes wide with worry, her lips trembling slightly.

"Detective O'Meara," he said, "this is Dr. and Mrs. Moretti, parents of Nathan Moretti. Detective O'Meara is with the sheriff's office and she's the detective in charge of the Violet Sperry homicide. There's a chance the murders of Annessa Cooper and Violet Sperry are connected, so I asked her to sit in on the interview. Okay with you?"

"Yes, yes, whatever. Just tell me you've found Nathan," Mrs. Moretti said. She sat in a chair next to her husband's, holding his hand, looking frightened out of her mind.

"Not yet. But we know that he intended to meet Annessa Cooper; text messages were sent between them and we just confirmed that your son's car was parked in The Right Spot's lot that night."

"Oh, dear God." Mrs. Moretti's voice was high and tight.

"But it was gone later."

She blinked and Cade started asking questions:

Did either of them know that their son was involved with Annessa Cooper?

They did not.

Did they have any idea where he may have gone?

Again, the answer was no. "We started calling all of his friends and, well, his work again,

467

anyone we could think of, but no one had seen him since yesterday," Dr. Moretti said. "The last person to have seen him that we know of was Will Hart, his employee."

"I—I just don't understand," Nate's mother squeaked, and while she tried to hold herself together they told them what they knew about their son, that he'd never followed in his father's footsteps and become a doctor, though Lord knew he was smart enough; that he'd never settled down with one girl; that he had a "bit" of a wild streak; and that they had no idea where he might be.

Eventually the two were interviewed separately and Kayleigh sat in on both conversations, but she learned nothing more of importance while she spoke with Nate's obviously distraught mother and worried father. Kayleigh came away from the interviews feeling as if she'd learned nothing more about Nate Moretti's disappearance or the murders of Violet Sperry and Annessa Cooper.

"There was one last thing I wanted to talk to you about," Cade said as he and Richard Moretti were alone in the interview room. The doctor's wife, done with her private interview, had asked to use the restroom, Voss had left to show her the way, and Kayleigh had taken a call and already left.

Leaving Cade alone with the doctor.

"What's that?" Moretti asked, standing near the door, jangling the keys in his pocket.

"It's about the night Luke Hollander died."

"What? Luke Hollander?" Moretti blanched a little. "That's out of left field, isn't it? I'm here because my son is missing."

"But you were the doctor who attended to him that night."

"That's right. They brought him directly to St. Augustine's. It served as an emergency room, or an urgent care for locals back then. I was on call and met the ambulance there."

"You pronounced him DOA."

Moretti paused a second, looked away, remembering. "Yes. That's right. It was a chaotic night. The shooting at the cannery, all the kids involved, my boy included." A muscle worked near his temple. "Ned came in. . . ." He let the sentence trail, remembering.

"Ned took Rachel to the station." Which wasn't protocol.

"Yeah . . . Everything was topsy-turvy that night. Nothing made any sense."

"But Luke was dead when he got there?" Cade asked.

Moretti had been looking at the floor, caught in thought; now his head snapped up.

"That's what you wrote in the report and on the death certificate," Cade pointed out.

He nodded. "That's right." But he said it slowly, as if anticipating Cade's next question.

"But the EMT who was attending swore he was still alive."

"One of them," Moretti said quickly. "The other agreed with me."

"So why the discrepancy?" Cade watched the doctor carefully.

Moretti's throat worked. He scratched his cheek. "As I said it was a crazy night. Kids being rounded up, some brought here, to this station, Luke dead, his sister having pulled the trigger. Ned Gaston, he was a mess."

Cade didn't doubt that. The night of Luke's death was the beginning of the end of Ned's career and had exacerbated the breakdown of his marriage. From the point that he'd brought his daughter into the station, his drinking had increased, his temper flaring more easily, his whole life seeming to crumble. Cade knew. He'd witnessed it firsthand during the tenure of his own marriage. "So what happened?"

The doctor's back stiffened. "Luke Hollander died."

"When?" Cade pushed.

Moretti's mouth opened and closed.

"He wasn't dead when he got there, right?"

"He . . . he was gone."

"Tell me." He wasn't buying the doctor's story.

Moretti's eyes shifted away.

"What happened?"

"He was . . . he was . . . dead."

"Was he?"

"Yes."

"Okay. Good to know. Because I'm reopening the case," Cade said, stretching the truth. "And the EMTs who brought him in, even a nurse on duty, I've already talked to them and they're coming in later, to corroborate your story."

"Why? When you have murders to solve and my son to find? Why would you bother?"

"Because it's all linked together."

"That's ridiculous. Luke died twenty years ago."

"And someone's pissed now. The crimes are linked, Moretti, and your son is somehow involved."

"Oh, Jesus. No. You don't think Nate's . . . He would never harm anyone. No, no, no . . ."

Cade just stared at him. The questions still hanging. "Okay, then, we'll go at it through the staff that was at the hospital that night and the rescue workers. Someone will remember something and maybe, just maybe, it'll help us find your son."

"I don't see how," Moretti said weakly as the sound of footsteps could be heard through the partially open door. He glanced through the opening and his face collapsed as he spied his wife. In a second, he drew a breath. "I don't want

Janine to know," he said. "Let me take her home and . . ."

"Now, Moretti," Cade said and opened the door. To Voss, he said, "We'll just be a minute more. Maybe you can walk Mrs. Moretti to the car."

"Sure," Voss agreed, giving him the what's-up look but touching Nate's mother on her elbow, then saying to her, "This way."

"Richard?" his wife asked.

"I'll just be a minute." He offered her a weak smile as they passed.

Cade pushed the door closed. "So," he said, "did you help Luke Hollander get out of this world, Doctor?"

Moretti's knees started to buckle and Cade caught him.

"Did you?"

"Oh, God." Moretti fell into a vacant visitor's chair. "No," he said, and shook his head vehemently. But his entire body had seemed to fold in on itself and he held his head in his hands. "But . . . but I didn't do everything to save him. He was too far gone, he'd lost too much blood, his brain starved of oxygen, comatose, totally unresponsive. Had he lived, he would have been a vegetable. . . . When Ned said to 'let him go,' I . . . I wrestled with my conscience, with my oath as a doctor, with what was truly life and . . . oh, Jesus . . ."

"You didn't do anything to save him," Cade said, finally getting it.

"He was too far gone . . . and Ned said it would be a living death for Melinda to have her boy alive but not . . . unable to function. . . ."

"So you didn't give him a chance."

Moretti closed his eyes. "I tried . . . I did . . . but . . ."

"You let him die."

Rachel's phone hadn't stopped buzzing all afternoon as text after text had come through:

Lila: I heard Nate is missing! Is it true? I can't believe it. It's like our whole class is under attack. What's going on? Call me!!♥ ☹ ♥♥

She was shocked and would have thought Lila was overreacting to some gossip that had no foundation until she read the subsequent texts:

Brit: Friends of Nate's came into the coffee shop. I overheard them saying that he's missing, didn't show up at work, that the police are looking for him. Do you know anything? ☹

Of course, Mercedes was all over it. Not only had she left a couple of voice messages asking Rachel and Harper for an interview, but also texted:

Do you know anything about Moretti going missing? I have a source who says he was supposed to meet Annessa last night. Is that true? Does this have anything to do with

Annessa's murder? Did Harper see him? I NEED to talk to you! Anytime. I sent you an e-mail, but please, CALL ME!

Even Billy Dee had texted:

What's up with Moretti? What's going on? His dad called me. Said he's missing. Got any info? Kinda worried.

"Me too," Rachel said aloud, then texted Cade:

Just heard Nate Moretti might be missing. True?

After laying down the law when she'd gotten home, her kids had surprised her. Dylan had actually tackled his room, and though it wasn't up to her white-glove standards, at least it wasn't a biohazard waste dump site any longer. Harper was doing homework.

"Trying to get a better grade in chemistry," she'd said when Rachel had checked in on her daughter. Harper actually had been seated on her bed, books spread around her, as she typed on a laptop. "Maybe make the honor roll."

"That would be great," Rachel had said, and as Harper had turned back to her studies, she'd closed the door and stepped into the hall. Since when had Harper cared about her GPA? Probably the end of her freshman year, so why the sudden interest . . . ?

Oh.

It hit then.

Xander Vale was attending the University of

Oregon and Harper's GPA was hovering near, but not quite at, the admission standards. Maybe Cade was right and Xander wasn't such a bad influence after all.

Or maybe you should just trust that your daughter is finally growing up, becoming that adult she's so fond of mentioning.

It was odd, this feeling that both kids were doing exactly as she'd asked.

It was almost as if they were being too good, she thought, then kicked herself for being so suspicious. They'd done what she'd asked and Harper, if a little more serious than usual, seemed fine, her more studious and subdued attitude explained by the ordeal she'd been through.

After glancing at the clock, she warmed what was left of the lasagna in the oven, and after tossing together a quick salad, headed upstairs to check her e-mail. No responses today from any of the jobs she'd applied for and, of course, the e-mail from Mercedes.

"Give it up," she muttered under her breath, then decided, her curiosity getting the better of her, to open and read it:

Rachel,
I would love to interview you for the last of the articles, give you a chance to tell your side of what happened the night that Luke Hollander died. I'm hoping to

get perspectives from some of the other people who were there. I want to do an in-depth feature on who Luke really was, behind the mask of high school athlete (and heartbreaker), and so some insight on his life growing up would help, too. Your mother and father seem to be stonewalling me, but I hope you could add something and convince them to contribute. Please call me.

Mercedes

Along with the e-mail were three attachments, all photographs. One was a family shot that Rachel remembered as being on a Christmas card they'd sent when Rachel was around eleven. She remembered the ugly red sweater that her mother had made her wear, while Luke was in green. At that point in time the family still had been pretty tight and looking at it brought back memories of happier days. The second shot was one of Luke's senior pictures, one where he was staring straight into the camera, a mischievous smile tugging at the corners of his mouth, and the third was of a stranger, a mug shot identified as being Bruce Hollander. "Oh, no," she whispered. Mercy couldn't drag her mother's first marriage into these articles. "Shit." She picked up the phone and dialed.

Mercy picked up on the second ring.

"You can't write about Luke's real dad—I mean, his biological father," Rachel said as she stared at the picture on her computer monitor. She'd never seen a picture of Bruce Hollander before, but now she saw the resemblance to Luke and something else.

"I think I can," Mercedes was saying. "You all keep trying to stop me by giving me nothing to go on and I'm scrambling here. But let me tell you, not only have we sold more papers this week than any other this year, but the online subscriptions have skyrocketed. This is the kind of story people love to read about," she added, sounding pleased while Rachel's stomach was turning.

"But it's my family."

"And it's newsworthy."

"Twenty years ago."

"Maybe, but people love that retro stuff and get off on a bit of a mystery, a little bit of a scandal."

"No matter whose life it harms."

"Temporary," Mercy said. "Until the next big story hits, and with the recent murders, you don't have to worry too much. People will move on. A twenty-year-old mystery won't hold the readers' attention like the new ones."

"Geez, Mercy, the new ones are people you know."

Mercedes sighed. "I can't help that. News is news."

"What if it were your family?"

"I'd report it."

"Sure."

Rachel was still staring at the picture of Bruce Hollander. Something about him bothered her. The picture was obviously old, but she knew how to photoshop in a few wrinkles and less hair, make him more clean shaven. . . .

Her heart nearly stopped.

She'd seen this guy.

Recently.

And she knew where.

She added a baseball cap to the picture and felt the muscles in the back of her neck contract. Yeah, this was the guy loitering around the offices of the *Edgewater Edition*, the man she'd seen watching her. A noise in her head started, like the sound of the ocean. Had he been the person she'd seen walking the dog on the street the night her door had been tagged? But why?

Because he thinks you killed his son.

Mercedes was starting to ask another question but Rachel blurted out, "Bruce Hollander is out of prison now."

"Yeah. I know that."

"Have you interviewed him?"

Silence.

"Have you?" Rachel demanded, her thoughts whirling. Fear sliding through her soul.

"Yeah," she said. As if it was no big deal. This was the man who had beaten up his wife, put

Melinda in the hospital. "He wasn't too hard to track down," Mercy said.

But he's dangerous! A known felon! "Does he live around here?" Rachel's heart was thudding wildly and it was all she could do to keep her tone normal. "Do you have his address?"

"No . . . Just a phone number. He, unlike you and the rest of your family, was willing to discuss his feelings about the son he'd barely known."

"I'd like that number."

"Oh . . . no, I can't do that."

"You've already admitted that you talked to him. It's not like you're protecting a source. You're printing his damned picture in the paper."

"Whoa, slow down. So what? Look, I don't give out addresses or phone numbers. If he asked for yours I wouldn't give it to him."

"Did he? Did he ask for mine?"

"No! God, Rach. Slow down, will you? What's wrong?"

Everything. Every damned thing. My marriage is over, my kids are growing up and away from me. Someone's definitely targeting me. People I know are being killed, damn it, and you're bringing up the worst part of my life, putting it out for public display, so that my children will see it, so that the whole town will read about it, so that I'll relive it.

"I'm fine," she lied.

"I hope so." Obviously Mercedes didn't believe

her, but her voice softened as she added, "Look, Rachel, we've been friends a long time. I was there that night; I saw what Luke's death did to you, to your family. I remember seeing you so upset and your dad comforting you and trying to comfort Lila, who was out of her mind, and I know you think I'm exploiting you and your family, but I'm just telling the story, or retelling it because it's a part of the history of this town.

"That cannery, where it all happened, used to be the very heart and soul of Edgewater. One in three families had someone directly or indirectly involved with tuna and salmon packing back in its heyday. From fishermen to cannery workers to truckers to janitors and inspectors, that cannery along with the sawmill and logging camps, kept this town alive. And then it was over and the cannery was closed, never sold, and a group of kids went down there one night for some fun, and a boy, a local athlete, was tragically killed. It's part of Edgewater's history. Now the cannery is scheduled to be renovated and rebuilt into a bustling new complex of restaurants and shops, condos and businesses, lauded as rejuvenating this town. It's important." She let out a sigh. "Of course, now there's a new angle."

Rachel saw where this was going and she thought she might be sick. "Violet's and Annessa's murders."

"That's right. It's horrible, yes, but news. And

your daughter found Annessa. So it's important that I talk to Harper."

"Important for whom? No."

"I think it should be her decision."

"What? No! God, Mercy, back off. She's just a kid."

"About the same age as you were when Luke was killed."

"I'm aware of that," Rachel said through tight lips.

"This is my job, Rach."

"And this is my life. My kid's life."

"Just let me talk to her. I won't use her name."

"I think it's too late for that." Rachel heard footsteps behind her and glanced over her shoulder. Harper was at the top of the stairs, peering into her office. "Look, Mercy, I've got to go—"

"I'll talk to her," Harper said and Rachel realized her daughter had been listening in the stairwell, hearing her side of the conversation. "Don't hang up."

"No, Harper." Rachel was shaking her head. "I don't think it would be a good idea."

"But I want to."

"No."

"God, Mom, what are you afraid of?"

Everything.

And there it was.

"I'll call you later," Rachel said into the phone,

then cut the connection. "What do you mean, what am I afraid of? Remember last night?"

"Yeah, I do," Harper said as she entered the room and rested a hip against the edge of Rachel's desk. "She's going to print the story. She has to. Don't you think it would be better if she gets the story straight?"

"Fine, yes. Exactly. But from the police. They have a public information officer who handles this kind of thing and releases only what the police want the public to know so that their investigation isn't compromised. That way the case is protected, as are the witnesses, people like you."

"She isn't the only one who called," Harper said, folding her arms over her chest. "A reporter from a news station in Portland called me."

No. "How did he get your number?"

"I don't know," she said, "but obviously, it's out there."

CHAPTER 33

Cade took Rachel's call as he made his way through the front lobby of the station. He wasn't the only one working late. Voss was waiting for enhancement of the film, Kayleigh had called and said she was running down a lead on the painter's tape, and even Donna Jean was at the desk, talking with a short middle-aged woman about a lost dog.

"Hey," he said, thinking about Moretti's confession and what it meant to her, the guilt she'd carried and the implications of her own father's involvement. Richard Moretti, a doctor sworn to care for the injured, and Ned Gaston, a cop sworn to protect lives of the populace, had conspired to let her brother die and allow her to think that she'd shot and killed Luke when he might have survived. Cade wanted to talk it all out with her, but needed to do it face-to-face. For now he paused in the station's lobby and asked, "What's up?"

"Bruce Hollander," she said, sounding frantic. "Luke's biological father! He's out of prison now and . . . and I think, no, I *know* I've seen him. Hanging around. Here. At the house!"

"What?"

"Mercedes sent me a picture of him. It was

old, but with a little photoshopping, to add years, you know, I saw what he probably looks like or what he could look like now and I'm sure he's someone I've seen here and in town!" She was talking faster and faster, a breathless tone in her voice.

"I think he was here the other night. I mean, I'm sure it was him. He vandalized the door, Cade. Bruce Hollander. And . . . and . . . I've seen him at the newspaper office and . . . and I think other places. I've had the feeling I've been followed, and a few days ago, after I visited the cemetery, a white car was following me. I didn't say anything earlier because I was imagining things, freaking out as it was the anniversary of Luke's death, y'know, but then I was talking to Mercy and she said she'd interviewed him and his picture is going to be in the paper, his side of the story and . . . and . . . Oh, God, do you think . . . do you think he might be involved in what happened to Annessa and Violet? Maybe Nate being missing and—"

"Whoa," he cut in, keeping his voice calm. Steady. "Slow down a second, Rachel," he said as he processed what she was saying about Hollander and spotting him and the white car. "I'll come over. On my way. E-mail me the picture Mercedes is going to run in the paper."

"Okay . . . I will. But hurry!"

"I'm on my way." He clicked off, his thoughts

spinning out. Could it be? Was Luke's biological father a possible suspect? Could all the interest in the old crime or the anniversary of the tragedy itself have triggered him? And a white car. In his mind's eye he pictured the white sedan with Idaho plates and the guy who was looking for his dog. As he pushed on the door to leave, he heard part of the conversation going on at the front counter as Donna Jean tried to deal with the distraught woman on the other side, and his phone pinged, indicating a message had come through. From Rachel. With a picture. His jaw tightened as he recognized the photoshopped picture: Frank Quinn, aka Bruce Hollander. And he'd met the man, now a suspect, near Rachel's house.

He was vaguely aware of the conversation going on around him. ". . . I told you, Mrs. Sanders, we're doing everything in our power to locate your dog."

"It's just that he's so friendly, he'd go with anyone," the woman said. Short, middle-aged, wearing a skirt and matching jacket, looking like she'd just gotten off work at an office, she was emotional, fighting tears. "Sometimes he runs off—beagles are known to do that, you know, follow their noses—but Freddy's always come home and it's been a week. I've been to the local vets and the pound and the shelters from here to Seaside and there's just been no one who's seen him." She swallowed hard. "I know it's not usual for the police, but could you please, please do something?"

Cade felt his stomach drop. "Excuse me," he said, and stepped closer to the woman to introduce himself. "I couldn't help but overhear that your dog is missing. A beagle, right?"

She glanced up hopefully. "Yes."

He pulled up the picture on his phone and flipped it around so that the woman could view the screen. "Can you tell me if you've ever seen this man?"

She frowned thoughtfully and began to shake her head, then stopped suddenly. "You know, I may have. Does he drive a white Buick, like a LeSabre? I'm not a car nut, but my husband had one of those back in the day. A ninety-seven. Brand-new, that's why I remember. It was a big deal for us to buy it at the time. But his was . . . stone beige metallic, yes, that's right, that was the color. But what does this have to do with Freddy?"

"I'm not sure," he said, hedging a little as he didn't want to get the woman's hopes up. "But leave your name and number with Donna here."

"Oh, she has," Donna said with a pasted-on smile. "Several times."

But he barely heard her as he pushed his way out the front door and jogged to his truck. He'd call Voss on the way, have her find out from

Bruce Hollander's parole officer where he was, and once he'd made certain that Rachel and the kids were okay, he'd hunt the bastard down.

That was the easy part.

What was more difficult was eventually telling his ex-wife that her father had lied, that he'd been complicit in her brother's death, that he hadn't taken an iota of blame for the tragedy and had let it all fall on Rachel's shoulders.

Until he was certain of the facts and had a talk with Ned himself, Cade decided not to burden Rachel, but eventually, the truth would come out, and then, all holy hell would break loose.

In Astoria Kayleigh had driven through McDonald's and picked up a Diet Coke and a double cheeseburger and a small order of fries. For the moment, she was ignoring all the bad publicity about fast food and sodas. She just needed something on the run, so she was driving, sipping from the ice-packed Diet Coke, and picking at the fries when her phone rang. She swiped her fingers on her jeans and picked up the second she saw Cade's name flash onto the screen.

"I think we've got a break." From the sound of it, he, too, was driving, rushing air and traffic underlying his words.

"What?"

"We're looking for Bruce Hollander, Luke Hollander's father."

"You still think there's a connection between him and what's happening now?" she said, tossing the idea over in her mind again. Was it possible? Maybe. But . . .

"Sure of it. We need to check with his parole officer, find out where he lives, put out an APB on his car, a Buick LeSabre, white, circa the late 1990s. Idaho plates. And he might have a dog with him."

"A dog?"

"Beagle." And then Cade explained his theory, which seemed a little far-fetched, that Bruce Hollander had gotten out of prison and within months moved to Edgewater to wreak his revenge on anyone who was close to the son he'd never really known, especially anyone who might have given sworn statements that allowed Rachel, whom he blamed for killing Luke, off the hook. He was certain Hollander had vandalized Rachel's door, been watching and possibly following her in the Buick with Idaho plates. Cade had even run into Hollander searching for his dog near Rachel's house, and he suspected that the dog, whom he was told was named Monty, was really the missing Freddy.

"I don't know," she said, thinking the motive was thin. "I mean, yeah, if Rachel can ID him on the vandalism, then we can get him there. But the rest? It's a big leap from tagging a door to murdering two people."

"He has a record. Did time for several assaults, the last being to Luke's mother."

"A long time ago."

"Once a thug, always a thug. Prison usually doesn't help."

"Possibly." She paused for a stop light, took a long drink from her diet soda, and tried to piece it all together, but it was ragged, with sharp edges, not melding together in her mind.

"Let's find him and bring him in, see what he has to say."

"Okay. I'd like to be there," she said as the light turned. "By the way, I got a call from the lab, on the painter's tape."

"You located where it was purchased?"

"No. But they found a small hair on it."

"DNA?"

"No, that's the kicker. They don't think it's human."

"What then?"

"Still working on that. Should have an answer soon. But we can't get too excited, yet. If it's from a dog, it could be from one of the dogs Violet Sperry owned. I mean, that's the most likely scenario, but who knows? Maybe we'll catch a break. I'm on my way to the lab now. They already have samples from the Sperrys' Cavaliers, so we should learn something." And if the hair on the tape, not human, wasn't from the victim's dogs? That thought gave her a little tingle, and though she was jumping the gun a little, she sensed she was getting closer to the truth, to figuring out exactly what was going down, despite the missing pieces and jagged edges.

She switched lanes and thought there was a slim chance that the animal hair and DNA would link Freddy, aka Monty, to Hollander. It was a long shot, but worth checking out.

"Get this," Cade said. "It turns out that Luke Hollander wasn't dead when he was admitted to St. Augustine's."

"So we're back to that again—trying to connect what happened twenty years ago to the murders now?" she asked, even though she, too, had experienced similar thoughts, that the tragedy of the past couldn't be separated from the horror that was happening now.

"Yeah, I know, it seems a little far-fetched."

"Try a lot far-fetched." Then she said, "But, I get it. There's something . . ."

"I just can't get away from it. I think it's all starting to link up. Ned Gaston was the first cop on the scene. Got there pronto, said he'd already been called."

"Rachel's dad, yeah, I remember."

"And Luke's stepfather." She heard the edge of excitement in Cade's voice, remembered it from previous crimes they'd solved together. "So it turns out he and Dr. Moretti, our missing person's father, decided not to do everything possible to save the kid."

"Are you kidding me?" She was shocked and eased off the gas, slowing for another red light.

"The rationale, at least Moretti's, was that the kid was too far gone, would have been a vegetable, and Ned Gaston didn't want his wife to have to deal with a bed-ridden, basically brain-dead son."

"You think there's more to it?" she asked, interested.

"I'm sure of it."

"Then let's find out what it is," she said as the light turned green and she hit the gas. Finally, it seemed, they were getting somewhere.

With difficulty Rachel had tamped down her panic attack upon recognizing Bruce Hollander as the man who had been lurking around the house. But her hard-fought rationality collapsed as she heard the approach of Cade's pickup just as the dog began whining to be let out. "Just a sec," she said to the dog, and when her ex appeared at the back door, she flung it wide and let him fold her into his arms as Reno whined and did a happy dance at his feet.

"Apparently he's accepted you," she said, as she extracted herself from his embrace and made a mental note that they were divorced, with a capital D. She couldn't let herself fall into the trap of depending upon him. Not now. Not ever. Besides, she was handling things, had put a lid on her freak-out show on her own. She could handle this. She had to.

As the door was still partially open Reno took advantage of the situation to catapult himself outside and off the porch, did tornado spins, then several laps around the yard.

"How're the kids?" he asked, pulling the door shut, just as Harper came out of her room.

She looked like she'd been crying, her cheeks puffy, her eyes red. Spying her father, she stormed into the kitchen. "How could you?" she said, sniffing.

"How could I what?" Cade asked. "And by the way, 'hello,' too."

"Don't, Dad. Just don't. And don't act like you don't know what's happening. You know! You do. How could you get Grandpa to send Xander away?"

"Whoa, what?" Cade held up his hands, palms out, as if in surrender. "You're blaming me?"

"It's not Xander's fault, you know," Harper cut in, "that I snuck out. That's on me. And what happened to the woman. Wow, that was crazy weird! But you"—she was leveling her furious gaze at Cade—"you were the reason he had to leave! And now he's gone and I don't know when I'll see him again!" She was winding up now, but Cade kept his cool.

"I didn't know Grandpa had let him go—"

"What?" Rachel asked. This was the first she'd heard of it.

Harper focused on her father. "You're Grandpa's son! " she said hopefully.

"It has nothing to do with me. Grandpa didn't like his behavior—"

"It's not his business!"

Cade's eyebrows raised. "It definitely is. Exactly that. Xander worked for him, and stayed in Grandpa's apartment rent free."

"But you're a cop!"

"That's not a part of this."

"Oooh!" She let out a hard, angry breath, but seeing she was getting nowhere with her father, Harper looked at her mother and started to plead her case. "Mom, please. It's like I'll never see him again!" She was working herself up to a fresh spate of tears.

"Of course you will. If you want to and he wants to," Rachel said, weakening a bit; Harper had been through so much. "You'll make it happen. Eugene isn't that far away."

"But I don't even have a car!"

The same old argument. "We said we'd consider it when you graduate, that we would help you."

" 'We'? Since when is it 'we' again?" she demanded, seeming horrified at the prospect of her parents standing together on anything.

"Xander's got a car," Cade pointed out.

"So if he came up here, he could stay with us?" Hope rose in her eyes.

"I don't think that would be a good idea," Cade said.

"I agree."

Harper's eyes narrowed. "Well, what's he going to do? He can't stay with Lucas anymore. Grandpa would have a fit!"

"I'm sure he can figure something out."

Tears threatened again. "I thought you might understand, but I guess you don't!" With that, she turned and fled back to her room.

Rachel took a step toward her, but Cade grabbed the crook of her arm just as the door banged shut. "I need to talk to her."

"We both do, but let her cool off and think about it," he suggested. "Anything else is going to blow into a major fight. Now, tell me about Bruce Hollander."

"Right. God, I'd nearly forgotten about him with all the drama. I have the information," she said, and was one step ahead of him. At the stairs, Cade, spying Dylan in the living room watching TV, hesitated.

"Hey, bud," he said.

"Hi." Dylan rolled his eyes. "I heard what was going on in the kitchen and thought I'd, you know, let the storm pass."

"Good thinking."

"Hey," Rachel said, "let Reno in, would you?"

"Yeah." He didn't move.

"Now?" Cade added.

"Oh. Yeah. Sure." He actually climbed off the couch and turned off the TV before heading toward the back of the house. Rachel continued leading Cade to her office. For a few minutes she'd been caught up in her daughter's teenaged angst, but now, the threat of Hollander returned. Full force.

In the office she rolled out her desk chair and clicked on the information she'd gathered on Hollander, including his picture before and after being photoshopped. Cade told her the department was already searching for him and how Cade himself had run into the guy who posed as someone named Frank Quinn who claimed he'd been searching for his missing dog.

"I was talking to him. Let him go," Cade said, "even though initially I had a bad vibe from him."

"So you were here then, and again last night?" Dear God, had it been less than twenty-four hours since Harper and Xander had found Annessa? It seemed like a lifetime. "Watching my house?"

"Yeah."

"Did you ever think to tell me?"

"I figured you'd be pissed."

"I would have been, but wouldn't I have seen

you and thought someone was watching the place, you know, casing it or me or the kids?"

"Okay, that would have been a problem."

"To put it mildly."

"But did you? See me?"

"Well . . . no . . ."

"And wouldn't you have recognized my pickup?"

"In the dark? Probably. But I still would have ended up pissed."

He actually grinned. "One of your most endearing qualities."

"You are a bastard. You know that, don't you?"

"I think it's A-one bastard. But yeah."

God, she hated it when he was being charming, or self-deprecating or clever. And she didn't like thinking that the beard shadow on his face was actually kind of sexy. As he leaned over her shoulder to look at her computer screen, she saw the way his hair curled near the back of his ear. She'd always found that little whorl intriguing.

Stop this now!

Harper was pissed.

What were her parents thinking?

Ganging up on her?

Everything in her life was turning to shit and she hated that Xander was so far away. Her heart ached and she kept looking at her phone, hoping he'd text her, but so far, nothing but radio silence.

It occurred to her that he might just want to break up with her. There were tons of cute girls in college; he didn't need a high school girl with a lot of problems who lived like a million miles away. Sitting up in bed, she texted him again, hoping that she didn't appear desperate, which, of course, she was.

He hadn't texted since they'd left the police department early this morning and she was dying—*dying*—to hear from him.

She'd already called and left two voice messages asking him to call her back, and then there were various texts, which she scrolled through:

> The first: That was so awful and bizarre. Where are you? Are you okay? 😕
> Next: Miss U 🖤🖤💋
> An hour later: Is something wrong? Text or IM me. 🖤
> Maybe he'd lost his phone or it was out of battery or charging or whatever . . . still she was miserable.
> She'd written again: I heard that you had to move back to Eugene. That sucks!!! 💔

Still nothing. Hours later. It just wasn't like him. Had the police taken his phone? Had it been lost in the chaos of finding the dying woman at that horrible old church that had become a crime scene? She shuddered thinking of it now.

For a second she wondered if something had happened to him and her stomach soured at the thought. No, no, no! Xander was tall and smart and . . . he was fine. And probably was just over her. Her heart squeezed and she felt like breaking into a million pieces but didn't much like that approach.

No, there had to be another way. Had to be.

Then, miracle of miracles, he texted back.

And all her worries and pain disappeared.

CHAPTER 34

Cade's phone rang just as he reached for his third slice of pizza. He had actually taken time to eat dinner with the family, allowing his daughter, who was in a much better mood, to drive to get takeout. Harper had improved since the last time she'd been at the wheel but still seemed to have the same love of speed he did. They had returned home to sit familiarly around the kitchen table as they had for years, each grabbing pieces from two of their favorite pies— meat lover's versus vegetarian—Dylan devouring slice after slice.

"Gotta take this," he said, spying Voss's number on his phone, then saying into the cell, "I was just about to head back to the office; what's up?"

"We know where Hollander lives," Voss said, all business. "Got hold of his parole officer and he gave me the address, which is an apartment in Astoria. The unit is registered to Denise Aimes, who just happens to be Bruce Hollander's first cousin."

"Let's go." He was already out of his chair and heading for the back door. Rachel, who'd sat across from him at the table, was on her feet. "I'll be at the station in ten. Wait for me."

"Make it eight. I want to bust this guy."

He clicked off and Rachel, deadly serious, asked, "What?"

Glancing back at the kids, he said, "Looks like we might have a lead on Hollander." He looked like he was going to say more, something important, but instead just added, "I'll let you know. Sit tight." Both Dylan and Harper were staring at him, the dog still patrolling under the table for any scraps that may have fallen. "You two, stay in tonight."

"Like we were going anywhere," Dylan complained.

"It's like a jail here." Harper's bad mood had apparently returned.

"Hopefully not for long."

He pulled Rachel onto the back porch, yanked the door shut, and said, "Sit tight. This could be the end of it, but we don't know. I'll call you. We've got a lot to talk about."

"What?"

"I can't say right now, but when I get back . . ."

"You're leaving it like that, teasing me so I can worry?"

"Don't worry. I'm handling it." He winked at her.

Her eyes were filled with concern, but as she attempted a brave smile, he couldn't help himself. On impulse, he pulled her into his arms and kissed her. Nothing earth shattering, just a quick, light buzz against her surprised, soft lips.

"Stay safe," he said as he let her go, and she blinked, stepping backward touching her lips.

He thought she might say something about him kissing her being "not okay," or "uncool," or protest in any way she could. Instead she just stared at him as he jogged to his truck, parked in front of the garage, and roared off. "Lock up!" he yelled through the pickup's open window and then he turned his attention to the street ahead, his focus on finding Hollander. If that prick turned out to be the murderer who was hell-bent on terrifying Cade's family, it would be all Cade could do not to beat the son of a bitch up one side and down the other.

Voss was waiting outside and motioned to the police SUV they'd driven earlier.

"I'll drive!" he yelled as he collected his service weapon from its locked case, slid the pistol into his holster, and grabbed an extra clip, then stepped out of his truck. No way would he be able to stand her puttering along at two miles below the limit. Before she could argue, he was behind the wheel, so she handed him the keys, and by the time she was clicking on her seat belt, he was already driving out of the lot, bouncing over the skirt to the street and hitting the gas. "Tell me what you know," he said, connecting from the side street to the highway, turning on his lights, and deciding against the siren as he headed west. Dusk was falling, the sun having just set, traffic sparse.

"According to the parole officer, so far Hollander's kept his nose clean. Stayed out of trouble."

"Yeah, right," Cade said as he sped toward a slower-moving vehicle, a pickup with a camper attached. He nosed out, saw there was no oncoming traffic, and shot around the long vehicle, then tucked back into his lane but kept up his speed.

"Goin' to a fire?" Voss asked, holding on to the armrest.

"Worse. What about the footage at The Right Spot? And Moretti's car?"

"Still unclear. Could be that Hollander was the driver, but maybe not."

"And still no sign of Moretti." Cade's jaw clenched. He wanted to nail the ex-con, put him away forever and solve this case. It seemed likely as hell that Hollander was out and seeking revenge for the murder of his son.

Except . . .

Why hadn't he contacted Lucas, his grandson? Wouldn't that have been a normal thing to do? Lucas was his only grandchild, at least as far as Cade knew, and the only remaining link to Luke. Then again, what was normal about Hollander?

But why start killing with Violet and Annessa?

They're just the first. Could be he's just warming up.

The road curved as they approached Astoria, the lights along the riverfront twinkling.

"South end of town," Voss said, "before you get to the roundabout and the bridge over the bay, not the big one over the Columbia."

"I know that." He had to slow through the heart of the town, where taillights and stoplights greeted them. Under the overpass leading to the Astoria-Megler Bridge linking Oregon to Washington, past businesses tucked shoulder to shoulder along the highway, he drove, cars moving to the side when his lights were spotted.

"There!" She pointed to the cross street that he'd already spotted on the GPS, and he cut across traffic and up the hill for several blocks before Voss pointed to another corner where a rundown two-story apartment complex came into view. Shaped like an L around the parking lot, it was two toned at this point, in the middle of a much-needed paint job.

Cade checked the lot as he parked. No white Buick. A quick scan of the streets didn't provide one either.

He was starting to get a bad feeling about this.

"Up top. Unit 201, on the end, next to the stairs."

"Got it." Cade got out of the SUV and made his way to the stairs and up the single flight, Voss right behind. He knocked on the door, stood to one side, and waited. His fingers gripped his weapon. Voss already had her own sidearm out of its holster, thumbing off the safety.

Just in case.

Footsteps sounded from inside and a dog began to bark loudly, baying as the door swung open and a short, round woman pushing sixty peered through a slim opening held in place by a small chain. She appeared to have just awoken, her graying hair pinned up at odd angles, her eyes squinting behind wire-rimmed granny-type glasses.

"Denise Aimes?" Cade asked.

"Yeah."

"I'm Detective Cade Ryder and this is my partner, Detective Patricia Voss." She squinted as he pulled out his wallet and showed his badge and ID. "We're here looking for Bruce Hollander."

"Of course you are," she said sourly over the ruckus the dog was making. "Monty, shut up!" she yelled at the dog, who ignored her. To Cade she said, "I figured you'd show up and so did Bruce. He left early this morning. I wasn't even up yet, but I heard him tear out of here in that beater of a car of his. And guess what? He left me a present. Monty here. Lucky me."

The beagle's nose appeared in the crack of the partially open door.

"You have any idea where he may have gone?"

"None," she said.

"Mind if we come in and talk to you?"

Denise slid a glance at Voss. "Mind if you put your damned gun away? They kinda make me nervous." But she unhooked the chain. It rattled as it dropped. She opened the door and reminded the dog to stay rather than bolt onto the portico.

Dressed in a rainbow-colored kimono, she led them three steps into a small living room stuffed with mismatched furniture. "Look, I know you want to know all about Bruce, but I can't tell you much. He got out of the big house, needed a place to crash, and I said, 'Okay, but you gotta get a job, pay rent, and be out in two months; that's what I told him. Well, the only thing he did to keep his promise was to vamoose." She rolled her eyes and waved them into two overstuffed chairs and fell onto a well-worn couch. Monty kept near the door.

"Can you tell us where he's been the last few days? Give us a timeline of when you saw him?"

"Well, not hardly. You're lucky you caught me between shifts. During the day I work at Tommy's Boat Dock, running the register, and four nights a week I waitress down at Barbie's Ales and Eats in Warranto, across the bay, y'know. Here's the funny thing about it. Tommy and Barbie, they were married when I was first hired, but they split the sheets a couple of years ago and I still work for the both of 'em." She laughed at the

505

thought and reached onto the coffee table for her e-cig before lighting up and breathing out a cloud of fragrant vapor that dissipated quickly. "Anyway, most of the time, Bruce was gone, doin' whatever. He claimed to be lookin' for a job or meetin' with his parole officer or . . ." She let the sentence drop as a sudden thought hit her. "Hey, wait a minute. Why're you here? Is he in trouble? Jesus, I knew I should never have let that SOB in. Bruce has been nothin' but trouble all his life, but I figured he could use a break. Just call me stupid." Another big lungful of vapor and Cade got down to business.

"Have you ever seen him with this man?" he asked, scooting a picture of Nate Moretti across the coffee table.

"I never seen him with anyone. Like I said, we were like ships passing in the night, only my ship was sailing to work and his . . . God knows." She picked up the picture of Nate Moretti and frowned, drawing on her e-cig. "This is the guy who's missin', right? I seen it on the news."

"Yes."

"You think Bruce had something to do with that?" As the light dawned, her eyes widened. "Wait a gosh-darn minute. You're not tryin' to connect him with those murders, are ya?" She took a long drag on her e-cig. "He wouldn't do that," and before Cade could cut in she added in another cloud, "Yeah, I know he had his troubles in his past but that was because he was young and dumb and into drugs and God knows what all, but he's outgrown that." She glanced at the dog, who was still in position at the door, nose close to the panels. "I guess Bruce is just into petnapping now. I asked him where he got Monty and he said the local shelter, but that there dog?" She pointed a puffy, blue-tipped finger at the animal. "I'm bettin' he's a purebred and he belongs to someone. I used to work as a dog groomer, so I can spot one that's been loved. And that one there, someone's missin' him."

"We're in touch with the owner," Voss said.

"Then take him with you when you go." Aimes eyed the dog. "Monty doesn't like me much, nor Bruce either. Fussy little thing, that beagle."

Cade turned the conversation back to her cousin. "Do you have any idea where Bruce was last Friday night and last night?"

"Oh, geez . . . I already told ya, I can't vouch for him all that much—who knew where he went— but, let me think, Friday . . . ?" She thought for a minute, vaping as she did. "Well, hell yeah, I can. I worked an early shift at the restaurant and was home by nine, and wouldn't ya know, here he was right here on this couch, watchin' some movie, one of them Rocky movies, maybe number four or five, I think. Not that I really know. How many of them did they make—like ten? Still at it, I think. Anyway, Bruce, he never moved from the couch. I know. I wasn't feelin' well, and I went to bed around midnight and there he was, and around one-thirty or two, I got up and got me a glass of water and a couple of Tums in the kitchen and he was still there, the boob tube on. I shut it off and found him in the exact same position at seven the next mornin', when I got up to go to the bathroom." She must've read Cade's skepticism, because she added, "Hey, if ya don't believe me, check with management. They've got security tapes of the place."

"We will." He glanced out the window, noted that he could, even from his position, spy a camera tucked under the eave. "So when do you expect Bruce to return?"

"Haven't you been listenin'? He's gone. Outta here. In the wind." She flipped a wrist to indicate that he'd taken off. "Took his stuff, and maybe some of mine, and got the hell out."

"What about a cell phone? Did he have one?"

"Oh, sure. Course. Who doesn't? But it was one of those prepaid thingies. He wanted to be on my account with my cell phone company but I said, "No way, Jose! I wasn't gonna get tied up with him financially, let me tell you. He may have turned around as far as his flyin' fists is concerned, but once a deadbeat, always a deadbeat, that's what I say. That's why I laid down the law and insisted he get a job."

When asked about where he slept, she showed

them the spare bedroom, which was used mainly for storage, but had a twin bed with a TV tray next to it, all pushed into one corner. "That's where he crashed," she said, pointing with her vaping device to the bed. "Look, I'm pretty sure he won't be back. He had a backpack with a couple changes of clothes, that cell you were talking about, a shaving kit that was in the bathroom, and now everything gone."

"Can you give us his number?"

"Sure. But he won't answer. I'm not even sure the call or text goes through. Probably needs him to pay for more airtime or data or whatever. Don't really know how it all works, but I'm pretty sure that's what happened. The man's never had a pot to piss in, so my guess is the phone is dead until he buys hisself some more minutes or airtime, y'know?" Still she gave them the number, and when they asked about friends, she couldn't come up with a name. "Oh, he had some guys he talked about who served time, y'know, but no one around here."

"How about the car he's driving?" Voss asked.

"The Buick? Big boat of a thing. I don't know where he got it, just showed up in it. Had Idaho plates. He kept saying he was gonna register it, even got some paperwork from the DMV, I think, but he needed an address and I wasn't about to let him use mine."

"Did you see that paperwork?" Cade asked.

"Yeah." She scowled, thinking, flipping her e-cigarette end over end between her fingers. "Come to think of it, I might still have it . . . just a sec." She led them back to the kitchen, where cold coffee looked to be congealing in a glass pot and a pile of dirty dishes stretched from the sink and across a short counter to the stove. "Probably in here." She opened a small drawer stuffed with junk, rifled through it, then opened a second drawer overflowing with papers, envelopes, and receipts. "Let's see . . . yeah, here it is." She handed him the partially filled-out paperwork, and there in black and white was the Idaho license plate and VIN for the old Buick.

"We'd like to keep these," Cade said.

"Sure, fine. I don't need 'em." She slid her gaze to the overstuffed drawer. "Probably don't need half of what's in there, maybe all of it."

"Can you tell me if he ever brought up his son?" Cade asked. "Luke?"

She frowned, thought about it. "No. Not recently. As far as I know, he'd barely met the kid, maybe just as an infant, and Melinda, that bitch, she didn't let Luke write to his father or visit him. Never once."

"And how did he feel about that?" They were walking into the crowded living room again.

"How do you think he felt? Pissed, that's how. But he seemed to get over it. Like I said, he mellowed in the big house, came out a calmer man, not as likely to fly off the handle. Cut down on the booze, too. At least the hard stuff." She fired up her e-cigarette again. "Oh, he's a lazy ass, always was and always will be, but if you're tryin' to hang these latest murders on him? Let me tell ya, you're barkin' up the wrong damned tree."

CHAPTER 35

The last person Rachel expected to find pounding on her front door at nine-thirty at night was Lila, but there she was, big as life, Rachel's once-upon-a-time BFF and former step-mother-in-law. Lips compressed, shifting from one foot to the other, Lila, in a cream-colored sweater, matching slacks, and gold heels, looked fit to be tied. Lucas was dressed more casually in jeans and a T-shirt as he fidgeted, appearing sheepish beside her. Fortunately for the moment, there wasn't a news van camped on the street, though Rachel half expected one to return as reporters had been calling all day, wanting interviews from her and Harper. The news had spread; Mercedes was no longer the only reporter on the story of the homicides.

Rachel opened the door and before she could say a word, Lila, smelling of perfume and a recent cigarette, swept through the door, her son following.

"Hi," Rachel said. "What's—?"

"Is Dylan here?" Lila cut in, obviously upset. "He needs to be a part of this."

"A part of what?"

"Get him!" she ordered, then let out a breath

and yelled toward the bedrooms, "Dylan!" A pause. "Dylan? You get out here! Now."

Rachel had never seen her so demanding and obviously irritated.

"Geez, Mom," Lucas said, his temper flashing. "Chill out! I'll get him," Lucas said, and before his mother could stop him, took off to the hallway, the crime scene tape strapped across Dylan's door not deterring him from entering without knocking.

" 'Chill out'!" Lila repeated. "Oh, sure."

"What's going on?" Rachel asked.

"Just wait. You'll find out," Lila snapped.

Within two minutes both boys had returned to the living room, where Lila was pacing and Rachel waited near the side chair. Harper, hearing the commotion, had emerged from her own room.

"Sit!" Lila ordered, pointing to the couch. "You too." She wagged a finger at Harper, who did as she was told and took a position between the two boys.

"Mom—don't," Lucas pleaded, but beneath his worried tone there was something else, a simmering anger that, Rachel suspected, could match his mother's. Once all three kids were settled onto the couch, Lila reached into her purse and pulled out some computer wires attached to what appeared to be a recorder or something.

"Maybe you can explain this?" she said to Dylan.

Dylan swallowed hard and looked down at his hands, clasped between his knees.

"Okay, since the cat's apparently got your tongue," she said, "maybe Lucas would like to take over."

"Mom, please—" Lucas looked miserable, and if looks could kill, Lila would be six feet under at this very moment.

"No, no. I will." Dylan caught his mother's eye. "I've been selling computer equipment."

"Spy equipment, you mean," Lila clarified. "Don't whitewash this." To Rachel, she added, "Did you get that? Your son has been selling tiny cameras and microphones and recorders and God knows what else!"

Dylan let his head fall into his hands.

"And then what have they been doing?" Lila raved on, her color high, her anger visible in a vein throbbing near a neatly plucked brow. "They've been listening in. That's what! Watching. Recording. I found a damned video of the last reunion meeting! Can you believe it? Like, why? Your son had threaded a tiny camera through the vents between the floors of our house. You know what I mean? Our house has a few areas where the floor above is connected to the one below, with grates in between. So our boys thought it would be a good idea to play James Bond or whatever." She stalked dramatically across the room, past the coffee table, heels clicking on the hardwood, then handed the cords to Rachel, who recognized the devices for what they were.

"Is this true?" Rachel asked Dylan, but she could tell by his body language that Lila had hit the nail on its head and suddenly she realized where all the small cardboard boxes in the recycling pile in the basement had come from. None had shown any mailing labels, all scratched off. She hadn't really thought about it. Now she understood. "Dylan?"

"Yeah." His Adam's apple bobbed.

Oh, crap. "Why?"

He lifted a shoulder. "Just to make some money."

There it was again: the money thing. "And who do you sell this stuff to?"

Another shrug. "Whoever wants it."

"Can you believe this?" Lila demanded, her voice high. "I mean, what's it for? What high school kid wants to spy on their parents?"

"Not their parents," Rachel said quietly.

"What're you talking about? Lucas was keeping track of . . . Wait a sec," Lila said, the wheels in her head obviously spinning. "You mean, like spying on other kids? Girlfriends or boyfriends . . . or, oh my God! Like hidden little cameras for taking private, nude pictures or videos or . . ." She visibly stiffened and stared up at the ceiling as if she could personally talk to God. "This is worse than I imagined!"

"No!" Dylan's head snapped up and he shook it vigorously. "Not for that! Nuh-uh. No way."

"Then for what?" Rachel asked, and she saw that he was thinking about what to say, probably forming quick lies to cover up, or possibly that he was actually considering, for the first time, all the damage that could be wrought from the stuff he'd sold. "You know, Dylan, if your friends or clients or whatever you call them wanted this kind of stuff"—she held up the cords Lila had thrust upon her—"and they were on the up-and-up, why didn't they just buy it online?" She didn't wait for a response, just said, "Oh, Dylan, this is not good."

He nodded.

She thought about the bullies who had threatened to beat him up. Schmidt and his friend Parker.

"It's not illegal," Dylan said. "To sell the stuff."

"No, but what about ethics?" she asked. "I'm going to need a list of the people you sold to."

"Uh-uh. No, Mom. My clients deserve their privacy."

"What?" Lila said and Rachel sent her a warning look telling her silently to back off. Lila didn't. Instead she threw out, "We're not talking about client-attorney or client-doctor privileges here! These kids you sold to? Underage? Their parents need to know."

"Why? Age has nothing to do with it," Dylan

said. "Anyone can own a camera or a microphone or a recorder—just ask anyone who has a cell phone, which has all of those capabilities."

"It's different!" Lila insisted. "Those listening devices, they're for spying, invading a person's privacy."

"Then that's the owner's issue," Dylan said, thinking aloud. "Not mine."

Lila stepped closer to the couch to glare at him. "You're the supplier!"

"No, no. He's right," Harper cut in, defending her brother for once. "It's not like he's over twenty-one and selling beer to kids, right? It's not between him or you or even you"—she motioned from Lila to Rachel—"to try to police what his 'clients' are doing."

She had a point.

"The parents need to know!" Lila insisted, though her outrage had begun to evaporate a little. To Rachel, she said, "Look, I wanted you to know what was going on."

Rachel forced a smile she didn't feel. "And now I do."

"Can we go now?" Dylan asked.

"Yeah, fine." Lila made a little shooing motion with a hand and all three kids clambered off the sofa and hurried down the hallway, Reno tagging behind. They holed up in Dylan's room.

Lila, who had watched them disappear, sighed. Her slim shoulders drooped. "Oh, man, sometimes being a mother sucks. Lucas is driving me crazy with his moods. When Chuck banished Xander, you would have thought it was the end of the world." She bit her lip, her eyebrows knitting as she stared down the hall. "He's got his father's temper."

"Or maybe his mother's?" Rachel suggested. Luke had been a lot of things, but aside from a few shows of aggression on the football field hadn't been volatile. Not that she remembered.

"I guess," she acquiesced. "Were we this deceptive and secretive?" she asked, then shook her head, thinking. "Don't answer that. We were worse." And there it was again, the past, their own teenaged years and more specifically the night that had changed their lives when they'd snuck out and Luke had died. "I could be overreacting."

"Ya think?"

Lila sent her a look, then one side of her mouth lifted. "Okay, okay. I know I've been accused of *sometimes* being a bit of a drama queen and God knows I've been on edge ever since Violet was found. First her, then Annessa and now Nate . . . God, I hope he's okay." She threw up one hand. "I just can't imagine what happened to him. Where the hell is he?"

"He could turn up. Maybe he's with a girl-friend."

"Annessa was his girlfriend."

"Maybe he had another."

"Then why isn't he showing up? It's all over the news that he's missing." She rubbed her arms as if experiencing a sudden chill. "It's all so unnerving, you know? So damned scary." Another thoughtful glance down the hall. "And it's hard to believe that it's been less than a week since all this started happening. I mean, what if it continues? By the time of the reunion, half of the class could be killed."

"Don't even say it!"

"I know, but it's true! Just think what's happened since last Friday!"

Since the anniversary of Luke's death, she thought, but didn't say it, just silently agreed with Lila about how strange and eerie life in Edgewater had become.

Lila glanced at her watch. "I've got to run. I just wanted to let you know in person what Dylan has been up to." Then she walked down the hallway. "Lucas! Come on. We've got to roll!" She tapped lightly on Dylan's door and reached for the handle just as the door opened, Lucas filling the doorway.

"Yeah, I know," he said and there was something in the tone of his voice that reminded her of someone . . . Luke? No, she didn't think so, but she couldn't put her finger on it, tried and failed to make the connection. But it was nothing. Just her mind playing tricks on her.

Harper glanced at her cousin and said a quick, "Bye," then went into her bedroom and shut the door. Lila and Lucas left in Lila's new Mercedes. Rachel watched her drive away, then turned off the porch light and silently wished Cade would return. The house had always felt safer when he was around.

As she closed the door and shoved the dead bolt into place, she remembered their last kiss, so light and tenuous.

Her throat went dry for a second and she let herself recall deeper, more sensual kisses with open mouths, quick tongues, and anxious lips. Bodies hot and sweating. Hearts beating wildly, hands exploring, breath in short gasps.

"Oh, wow," she whispered, feeling a warmth course through her bloodstream and the tiniest of aches beginning to grow deep inside. An ache she hadn't experienced for a while.

It had been so long. . . .

Forget it! that nagging voice in her head insisted.

It's over.

Deal with it.

Disgusted with the turn of her thoughts, she set her jaw, double-checked that the doors were locked, and engaged the security system, such as it was. Then she told herself she was a fool for even thinking about her ex and wishing him here. He wasn't her husband any longer and there was a good reason for that. Her sexual fantasies were just memories that would never be relived.

For the time being, she and her kids were on their own.

And she and Dylan were going to have a long-overdue talk.

She sensed her son not only growing up, but slipping away from her and that couldn't happen. Not yet. He was still too damned young.

She knocked on his bedroom door and stepped inside the clutter.

He was seated at one of his computers, staring at the screen. He didn't look up, but said, "I know, I'm in trouble, probably grounded for life, and you're going to tell Dad."

"For starters."

"Great. It's not like I'm in trouble enough with what's going on in school." He glowered into the computer screen. "And you're probably pissed because Lila and Lucas are involved. Right?"

"Right."

She was standing at the foot of his bed, watching the play of emotions on his face in the light from the monitor. It seemed, for now, as if he got where she was coming from. "Okay, Dylan, that about covers it. Almost."

"But?"

"You want to tell me why you were supplying kids with spy equipment?"

"I already told you: for money, Mom. Duh."

His eyebrows slammed together as he reminded her, "You're the one who's always talking about how tight money is, and now that you're looking for a job, it's gonna be worse. Right? Harper can't get a car until she saves up what, like half of the price of it or something. Well, I'm turning sixteen next year and I figure you'll have the same deal with me. I thought I'd get a jump on it. That's all. It's not like you would ever let me get, like, a real job, not yet. Right? So this seemed like an easy way to make some cash. That's all."

"That's not all," she said. "Because, Dylan, you did it behind my back."

"Yeah. I know." He sighed through his nose. "But you wouldn't have let me."

She didn't argue, just studied him, this boy who would soon be a man. "So . . . is there anything else I need to know?" she asked and he looked up quickly. Guiltily.

She saw a lie forming in his eyes, then, second-guessing himself, he said, "Nah. Nothin'."

"You're sure about that."

"Yeah. Uh-huh." He was nodding rapidly, as if trying to convince himself.

"Okay. But if you think of something, you'll let me know."

A pause. Silence stretching between them.

"Dylan?"

"Yeah." He nodded. "Right." Then, "And you

don't have to say anything. I *know* I've got to tell Dad."

With his phone connected to his favorite hard rock playlist, Ned touched up the final coat of paint on his bathroom, making certain he didn't leave the tiniest line on the tile he'd so painstakingly laid himself, a subway-patterned backsplash that didn't look half bad.

Standing back surveying his work, he caught his reflection in the mirror, an aging man with a potbelly, once-blond hair now silver and thin, glasses perched on a nose that showed a road map of blood vessels just beneath the surface. Once a cop with a good reputation, a decent woman for his wife, and a daughter he adored, he was now doing security work, walking the mall in Astoria for the most part; divorced; and living with an ever-replaced half pack of Bud and the ghosts of his past.

A major comedown in life.

All because of a woman.

God, he'd been a fool.

He'd lied to himself and every damned person who meant anything in his life.

Over the beat of Aerosmith's "Janie's Got a Gun," he heard a faint noise.

The click of a doorknob being turned?

Odd. Frowning, he cut the playlist and peered into the darkened hallway. "Hello?" he called, feeling like a fool. He was alone. Knew it. But he looked anyway, his cop senses alert. The house was still and he told himself he'd imagined the noise. How could he have heard anything over the haunting lyrics of the song? He hit the play button on his phone and Steven Tyler was singing again, rocking out in the small bathroom.

Ned reached for his half-drunk can of Budweiser, which sat on the lid of the toilet tank next to his Glock, the one he'd gotten years before, taken and pocketed in a raid when Ned had been in his late twenties, an unregistered weapon he'd used only once.

Until tonight.

Possibly.

The cat wandered into the bathroom and actually did figure eights between his legs. "Yeah, you'd better go home if you know what's good for you."

But the skinny thing probably didn't have a home other than this place. He liked the cat. Called him or her—who could tell?—Inky. Who would take care of the scrappy cat when he was gone?

Didn't matter; the animal was a survivor.

He drained his beer in a long swallow, crushed the can, and let it fall to the floor, where he'd laid a drop cloth.

Again he eyed his work in the bathroom and rubbed his jaw. If he actually had the guts to eat a bullet, could he work it so that the blood and brain spatter wouldn't mar the job?

Oh, hell, why would that matter? Someone's gonna find your rotting body, with half your head blown off. Do you think they'll really give a rat's ass that your grout lines are perfect?

Again he looked at the grizzled man in the mirror, a guy who looked far older than his age. And a goddamned fool to boot.

Perhaps the gun was the coward's way out.

It could be that he should grow a pair of balls again. It was time to tell the truth. Long past.

He should lay his soul bare.

Deal with the fallout.

Accept the consequences—every last miserable one of them.

His daughter would hate him, and he wouldn't blame her. She'd carried the burden of thinking she'd killed her own half brother when it was he, Detective Ned Gaston, who had followed his kids to the cannery, stepped inside to the hellish darkness, and drawn his weapon. He, hidden in the shadows and the chaos, had been standing next to Rachel unseen. He'd fired his gun simultaneously with hers. Real bullets and pellets had been fired. He had made certain his gun, the Glock that was now sitting on the tank of his toilet, was never found, while Rachel's own weapon had been kicked into the chute leading to the river. It was he who had coerced Richard Moretti into signing the death certificate as DOA and letting Luke die. The kid would have given up the ghost anyway. Ned was certain of it then, even if he wasn't now. But he'd let his daughter deal with that horrendous guilt of taking her brother's life for all of her adult life. Jesus, God, maybe he should just end it.

It wasn't as if he'd really intended to kill Luke . . . or had he? Is that what a crumbling marriage had done? Guilt gnawed at his soul. It was more than that. More than a wayward teen rebelling and telling him things like "You're not my real father." No, that was an excuse, and when he'd followed the kids to the cannery that night, intent on dragging him home, he was loaded for bear. Because of what he'd discovered, because he knew that Luke . . . holy God, he should never have pulled the trigger; he should have just dressed the kid down and hauled both of them out of there. But fueled by a couple of gin and tonics and the knowledge that his whole life was crumbling, he'd lost his judgment as well as his temper. He'd been out of his mind. The fact that Luke was lying to both his parents and fucking Lila Kostas, Rachel's friend. Even now, thinking about it, Ned's hands clenched.

Being Luke Hollander's stepfather had been holy hell, but still, he should never have pulled his weapon, never fired, never, ever let his daughter take the fall for his crime, an act of passion.

Was it?

Certainly not premeditated.

No, no, no . . .

God, he'd been a fool and a coward. He rubbed the back of his neck and stopped his thoughts from creeping any deeper into that dangerous territory.

The cat meowed and he discovered it had left the bathroom while he'd been considering his options, and the playlist had moved on to a Bon Jovi song, "Wanted Dead or Alive." Perfect. He was starting to get lost in the lyrics when, with a jolt, it suddenly hit him. The cat shouldn't be inside. He hadn't left the door open.

Or had he?

He remembered the click earlier, the tiny little noise he'd dismissed.

Now, the muscles in his shoulders tight, he walked down the hallway to the kitchen and the back door.

Shut tight.

Huh.

This wasn't right.

The hairs on his nape lifted as he thought that someone might have come inside. But who? And hadn't he locked the door? No—possibly not. He remembered going outside to his truck for the drop cloth and didn't recall locking the door behind him.

So someone could be inside.

Stealthily, he made his way back to the bathroom to grab his pistol, stepped inside, and stared at the toilet tank.

No Glock on the lid of the tank.

He swept his gaze to the floor and the closed lid of the bowl, thinking it had dropped, but no and . . .

He heard a floorboard creak behind him and froze.

"Don't move," a deep voice said, directly behind him. The barrel of a gun—his, no doubt—was pressed between his shoulder blades. "Don't fuckin' breathe."

In the reflection of the mirror, he saw a shadow of a man behind his shoulder but his features were hidden.

Some freak show had walked in and gotten the drop on him!

Ned's pulse was pounding in his ears and he tried to think of what to do. If he jabbed back hard with his elbow, maybe he could knock the guy off his feet and the shot might not hit a vital organ and . . .

"Time to pay, dirty cop," the voice whispered so close that Ned could feel his assailant's hot breath against his ear.

Ned started to turn, but it was too late.

He felt the gun move, shifting from his back to be pressed to his temple. In the mirror, he caught a clearer glimpse of his assailant and his heart nearly stopped.

"Don't!" he yelled, suddenly desperately wanting to live. "Son, don't!"

His plea fell on deaf ears.

The killer pulled the trigger.

CHAPTER 36

At nine in the evening, Cade stretched in his desk chair. He was tired, the night before being short. He had a call in to Ned Gaston, but so far hadn't connected with his ex-father-in-law.

Ever since talking to Richard Moretti, Cade wanted to track down the ex-cop. There was something missing to the story about Luke Hollander's death, a piece Cade didn't understand. That mystery, the feeling that there was something just out of his reach, nagged at Cade and had, even during the interview with Denise Aimes.

He and Voss had brought the beagle down to the station. After brushing Freddy, aka Monty, and collecting some of his fur, Voss had reunited the dog with his grateful owner, who was overjoyed at having her "naughty boy" back. At least that's the way Voss had explained it with a roll of her eyes. "Like he's a real kid," she'd said. "Oh, well, to each his own. At least now the lab has something to compare to the hair found on the tape at the crime scene."

"Along with the samples from the Sperrys' dogs."

"Okay, so now the lab has more to compare," she'd said sourly.

He was about ready to pack it in for the night—go home and get a few hours of much-needed shut-eye or cruise back to Rachel's place and check on his family—when the phone on his desk rang. Yawning, he picked up and Donna Jean said she was routing a call from the Seaside police department.

"This is Ryder," he said as the call came through.

"Yeah. Deputy Max Swanson down here with the Seaside PD. We've got a visual on the '97 Buick LeSabre, Idaho plates. Same number as you're looking for." To confirm he read the numbers.

Cade was instantly alert, his sleep deprivation forgotten. "That's it."

"Well, okay then. The car is parked in front of the Luxor Apartments—they rent by the day—but we think he walked into town. One of our patrol guys spotted the vehicle, and saw the driver head toward Broadway and followed. We think he's in the Wooden Nickel, on Fourth. Near the river. I'm putting a man inside to keep an eye on him."

"We're on our way. The subject is Bruce Hollander, not long out of the pen."

"We got that."

"So, approach with caution. He could be armed." He thought about Violet Sperry's missing pistol. "Make that he's probably armed. I'll be there in half an hour, maybe a little longer." The drive was forty-five minutes, but he'd push it.

"You want us to go in after him?"

"Not till I get there, but don't lose him." Cade wanted to talk to Hollander before he dealt with any other officers and decided to lawyer up. An ex-con like Hollander knew the ropes, but he might spill a little before he clammed up. "We think if he's the guy on the tape, then he's the last person to have been seen with Nathan Moretti, who's missing, though Moretti might be a suspect himself. Hollander was in the vicinity of a violent homicide, and, believe it or not, he's a prime suspect in a dognapping, which has been solved."

"A what?"

"Don't ask. Just focus on keeping track of him." Cade was already reaching for his service weapon.

"You've got it."

"Okay. We're on our way," he said, then gave Swanson his cell number, slipped on his holster, and made certain he had his sidearm and an extra clip. "It's showtime," he told Voss. "Bruce Hollander's been spotted in Seaside. Grab your gun."

"What do you mean, it's feline?" Kayleigh demanded. She'd just gotten home and was peeling off her clothes when she'd taken the call from Akira Wu, the lab tech working on the hair found on the painter's tape. Wu had promised to get back to Kayleigh no matter what the time and she was as good as her word. "You're saying the hair on the roll of tape was from a cat?"

"That's right."

"You're sure?" Kayleigh asked and the radio silence she received said it all: Akira rarely, if ever, made mistakes. "Okay, fine, it's just that the woman who was killed lived with three dogs and one of the suspects had dog-napped a beagle and—"

"Feline." The word was clipped. "Definitely."

"Okay. Got it." And what was she going to do with it? "Thanks."

"You're welcome." And then Akira clicked off, leaving Kayleigh a little deflated and wondering about her next step.

"Forget it," she told herself; the whole cat hair thing was probably a false clue. The hair could have been picked up anywhere, the tape having a shelf life of forever. She'd run down the manufacturer, and that particular painter's tape had been produced for over ten years and was common across the country and into Canada.

So what had they gotten from it? A big, fat zero.

She dropped her clothes haphazardly into a hamper, and headed for the shower, where she intended to wash off the grit and worries of the day. And think. She was bone weary as she stepped under the hot spray and lathered both her body and hair. The case was getting to her, her thoughts swirling around the victims—two women, and now possibly a third, a man, all who knew one another, graduated together, and were working on a damned twenty-year reunion.

Unless the third victim, Nate Moretti, wasn't a victim at all, but the killer.

Did that make any sense?

And would he string his lover up in a bell tower?

How was that crime tied to Violet Sperry's homicide?

By the fricking painter's tape.

"Arrrgh." She let out the frustrated sound as she rinsed off, letting the warm water cascade over her naked body. Finally, she twisted off the taps and toweled off, and pulled on an oversized T-shirt and fresh underwear. Sleep. That was what she needed. Eight hours. Maybe nine. Or even ten. She'd take whatever she could.

She heard her phone ring as she was combing the tangles from her wet hair. Cade's number appeared on the screen. Her heart leapt but she told herself it was because of the case and had nothing to do with her emotions. Nothing.

"Hi."

"Wanted you to know," he said brusquely. All business. "We've got a visual on Bruce Hollander."

"Tell me." She put the phone on speaker and as she wound her hair into a knot on her head, snapping a band around it, then stepped into clean jeans and a sweatshirt, he relayed his conversation with the Seaside PD and also told her about his meeting with Denise Aimes, Hollander's cousin.

"So he has an alibi for the night of Violet Sperry's homicide?"

"That's right."

She let out a sigh. "Well, here's another kicker. The hair found on the painter's tape?"

"Yeah?"

"Doesn't belong to a dog. It's feline."

"A cat?"

"Bingo."

"But—"

"I know . . . all the dogs."

"Crap." He paused a second, then said, "We still need to talk to this guy. Hollander's involved. We just have to figure out how."

"Agreed," she said. "I can be there in twenty."

"Meet you there." He clicked off and she wasted no time calling Biggs, filling him in and ending with, "I'm on my way."

"Pick me up. I'm ready." In the background she heard Biggs's wife's groggy voice protesting, but then he clicked off and by the time she'd driven to his home, with its fresh coat of gray paint, he was waiting, leaning against the porch support. At the sight of her Honda pulling up to the curb, he jogged to the passenger side and slid inside.

"Explain to me again why we're interested in this dude." Biggs snapped his seat belt into place as she drove toward the highway, merging with the thin flow of traffic heading south. "What's the ex-con got to do with the Sperry homicide?"

"That's what we hope to find out." She slowed for the roundabout, then hit the gas on the far side and sped across the bridge spanning Youngs Bay, where water dark as pitch stretched out on either side of 101.

Her pulse was ticking and she felt a mix of apprehension and excitement. This could be the turning point in the case. As she squinted into the night, the wheels of her car humming along the dry pavement, she reminded herself to keep a cool head. Bruce Hollander could turn out to have nothing to do with the Sperry murder. This could all be a wild-goose chase. Cade Ryder had been wrong before.

Still, what did she have to lose?

Cade had been on the phone the entire drive to Seaside, not just alerting Kayleigh of what was going down, but also keeping in contact with the Seaside PD.

The town itself had a carnival feel to it and

had been a destination for Portlanders seeking sand and surf for over a hundred years. Its long promenade stretched along the shoreline of the Pacific Ocean, separating the heart of the town from the beach. Broadway was the main street of the town, linking the Pacific Coast highway to the business district and ending in a turnaround at the prom. As such, Broadway was lined with shops and warehouse-type malls, taverns, and amusements like putt-putt golf and bumper cars. In the summer, the sidewalks were packed with pedestrians, the streets clogged with cars, bicycles, and surreys.

Now, near midnight, at the end of May, the streets were quiet, cars parked in lots or along the street, a few people strolling the sidewalk. Smokers were hanging close to the entrances of taverns, where music and laughter rolled out of open doors, but the bumper cars, T-shirt and souvenir shops, and ice cream vendors had closed for the night.

It was the hope that Hollander would come quietly, and it was the expectation that he would not. Rather than risk a shoot-out in the brewery, where bystanders could be wounded or killed, the cops were situated around both the front and back of the building, watching the exits. Dillinger, a deputy situated inside, communicated to them through a hidden mic. They were all wired up, able to speak to one another.

"Pretty fancy for your little town," Cade had remarked when given his earpiece.

"That's what we're known for down here: fancy," Swanson had remarked, his voice deep with sarcasm.

Kayleigh and her partner had arrived. They were also linked by headsets and taking positions on the street.

Now it was only a matter of time.

So they waited.

Hidden in the recessed doorway of a closed restaurant next to the pub, Cade glanced at his watch.

Nearly 1 a.m.

The brewery would close soon.

Good.

Time ticked slowly past. A few cars rolled along the roadway only to curve around the turnabout at the west end of Broadway, then wander through the blocks. A cluster of teenagers laughing and swearing, probably high, jaywalked noisily, running between parked cars to disappear down a side street, never knowing they'd just passed several armed cops.

Suddenly there was movement in the doorway of the Wooden Nickel.

Cade braced himself, his weapon in hand.

A couple in their early twenties emerged. Their hands were all over each other, their mouths kissing hungrily as they moved as one toward a shiny Nissan four-door parked near the bridge where Kayleigh was positioned. Someone, probably Swanson, whispered into his headset, "Jesus, get a room!"

"That's the idea," another cop said. "Ooohwee."

"Shh!" someone reprimanded sharply.

The man helped his obviously inebriated date tumble into the passenger side, then hurried around to the driver's side and slid behind the wheel, only, once the door was closed, to pull the woman close. They went at it again, going so far as to start the windows steaming before the embrace was broken.

Cade had ignored them for the most part, keeping his gaze trained on the door.

With a roar, the Nissan tore away from the curb, sped down the street, the red glow of its taillights disappearing as the driver turned a corner to disappear between the buildings.

The street was once again quiet, the eerie silence interrupted only by the hum of traffic on the highway, the rumble of the sea to the west, and an occasional burst of raucous laughter from the pub.

Cade waited.

But not for long. Within minutes the word came through his headset. "He's settling his tab," Dillinger whispered. "Get ready. Wearing a Mariners cap and a camo jacket."

Cade's fingers tightened over his pistol.

Dillinger again: "He's headin' for the door."

Cade saw the movement of shadows in his peripheral vision. Other members of the team had stepped closer to the entryway. He told himself to be calm, even though every muscle in his body was tense, his nerves strung tight as bowstrings.

He set his jaw.

He saw a figure appear in the open doorway, a guy in a baseball cap and denim jacket. Hollander? The size was right, but his face was shaded beneath the brim of his cap. And didn't the man inside say he was in camo?

Cade's heart was pounding.

"Oh, shit," Dillinger said, just as the suspect stepped onto the street to stand in front of a neon sign in the window of the pub and then, as if sensing something wasn't right, cocked his head for an instant. Listening as he reached into his jacket pocket.

Was he reaching for his gun?

"Hold your fire," Dillinger whispered. "He's not the guy! He's not the guy!"

Swanson appeared from around the corner and, as the man started to cross the street between two parked cars, leveled his gun at him. "Police!"

Cade moved from the doorway of the adjacent building. Something was wrong.

Swanson yelled, "Bruce Hollander, put your hands where we can see them!"

"What?" the man in the cap said and looked up.

"Oh. Jesus." He looked like he was about to pee his pants. "Who the hell are you?"

"He's not the guy! He's not the guy!" Dillinger was repeating. "It's not Hollander. Hold your fire. It's not Hollander!"

Three cops exposed themselves, their pistols drawn.

Through his earpiece Cade heard the frantic sound of Dillinger's voice. "He's coming out now! Watch out! The other guy snuck out in front of him, but Hollander's coming out now!"

"Oh, shit," Swanson swore.

"What the fuck?" the man in the cap said.

"Get him out of here," Cade ordered Swanson, then to the man, "Sir, step aside. Now! Get down! Get down!"

"What?" the man said, his head whipping around as he noticed the other cops. "Oh, fuck!"

A second guy in full camo and a baseball cap filled the doorway.

Hollander!

"Aw, shit," Swanson said.

"I'm going for him," Dillinger announced.

Hollander, assessing the situation, quickly looked sharply around and started to back up, to retreat into the brewery.

Cade shouted, "Police! Bruce Hollander, put your hands in the air!"

Dillinger yelled, "Now! Hollander, put your hands where I can see 'em and get down."

More sounds came through the headset, sounds of patrons in the bar yelling as they tried to flee.

"We've got customers exiting out the back," another cop said.

"Keep track of 'em," Cade ordered, thinking Hollander might try to escape. "Watch for him."

But that didn't prove necessary.

As if zapped by a cattle prod, Hollander suddenly sprang forward as the man in the jean jacket hit the pavement, his cap flying off his bald head to skid along the sidewalk.

"Don't shoot!" the guy on the sidewalk pleaded.

Hollander, seeing that he was trapped, yanked a gun from his pocket. "Get back!" he yelled, frantic, his eyes wide beneath the brim of his cap. "Get the fuck back!"

"Gun! He's got a gun!" Cade warned, his own weapon trained on Hollander. Then to the suspect, "Drop your weapon! Now!"

Dillinger, weapon drawn, appeared in the doorway.

"Don't shoot! For the love of—Don't shoot!" the guy on the ground covered his bare head with his hands.

Hollander took a bead on Cade.

Blam!

The bullet hit him shoulder high, blowing him back, just as Cade squeezed the trigger. His shot went wild as he spun, his legs folding, the sidewalk rushing up at him. *Crack!* His head bounced against hard concrete. Pain jarred through his brain. His nose splintered, blood gushing in a warm rush.

"No!" he heard a woman yell. "No! No! No!"

"He's hit! Ryder's hit!" Swanson shouted.

"Get him! Get Hollander," a different man yelled, but Cade couldn't concentrate, didn't recognize the voice. The world was spinning, streetlights and stars . . . and . . . it was hard to think. His mind was swimming, the safety of unconsciousness trying to pull him under.

He heard another burst of gunfire, crackling loudly for a few seconds, and somewhere in the back of his consciousness he was aware of people running, and screaming, the world spinning.

Groaning, trying to stay awake, Cade felt someone touching him, sensed someone leaning over him. Breathing rapidly. A woman. One he knew. He blinked, thinking outrageously that it might be Rachel as he struggled to focus. She was bending over him, touching him gently.

"Rachel?" he whispered.

"No . . ." she said and her voice cracked. "It's Kayleigh. Detective O'Meara."

But he couldn't focus and was slipping further into the comfort of the darkness.

She was ordering him to respond, yelling at him, maybe crying, but he couldn't respond, didn't want to. If he could just close his eyes . . .

"Ryder! Stay with me!" she screamed. "Ryder? Cade? Do you hear me? Damn it, you stay with me! Don't you dare leave me!"

CHAPTER 37

*T*hud!

    Rachel's eyes flew open.

She was sweating, her heart racing, the dream so real and vivid.

In many respects it was the same as the others. She was twenty years younger and in the vacuous cannery with the others. She'd looked down, seen the gun in her hand, and seen Luke fall, but this time as he glanced up at her, he morphed, his image altering from one man in her life to another, from Luke to Lucas to Dylan, then her father, and finally Xander Vale. Still, she'd squeezed the trigger and the pistol had gone off in her hand and Luke was staring up at her again.

Now she was awake. Something waking her. A noise that was out of place.

A gunshot?

For a second, she listened, lying still on the bed, ears straining over the rapid-fire beat of her heart, then heard the sound of a car's engine. So probably she'd just heard the vehicle backfire, which had crept into her nightmare and jarred her awake. But that was odd, wasn't it? How many times did you hear a car backfiring these days?

And the sound had been different, muted.

And coming from inside the house.

At the foot of the bed, Reno stretched, then hopped down and padded to the door. He looked over his shoulder as if to say, "What're you waiting for?" His cue that he wanted to go outside. "It's the middle of the night," she admonished, pushing her hair out of her eyes.

He wasn't budging. Started to whine.

She was about to call him back to the bed when she heard something. A scrape against hardwood? Footsteps? Someone was up? Her heart kicked into double time even though she told herself it was probably Dylan, getting something out of the fridge. Sometimes he did that, staying up late on the computer and then being suddenly "starved" and raiding the refrigerator.

But the thump?

What was that?

Reno started to paw at the door.

"Okay, okay," she whispered. She stepped into her jeans and threw a sweater over her nightshirt.

Scraaape.

The screech of metal on metal was audible.

What was that?

Rachel didn't move a muscle. She strained to listen, hear anything out of the ordinary. And there it was, the soft scrape of metal on metal . . . like the sound of the back slider opening and closing . . . or . . . a window?

No!

Was Harper sneaking out again?

She wouldn't!

Or would she?

With the dog bounding in front, Rachel hurried down the stairs, nearly stumbling in the dark, slapped at a light switch at the foot of the staircase. She threw open the door to Harper's room, hit the switch, and stared at the empty bed with its crumpled bedding. A glance at the window indicated it was cracked. What the hell? What about the damned security system?

She flew out of Harper's room and into Dylan's. Again she hit the lights. He was asleep in the bed, one arm flung over his head, mouth agape. In a second his eyes flew open and he was blinking. "Mom? What're you doing?"

"Where's your sister?"

"What? In bed . . ." And then he came to completely. "Oh."

"Right. 'Oh.' She's not. She just snuck out, probably to meet with Xander again. Where are they?"

"I—I don't know."

"Don't you?"

"God, no!"

"But the security system?"

He groaned.

"Dylan?" Rachel said, closing the littered gap between the door and the bed.

"Okay! Okay," he said, as if she'd beat it out of him when all she'd done was drill him with her

547

gaze. "Yeah. She asked me to fix it and I did."

"You mean fix it so it wouldn't go off when she snuck out again. Like break the circuit to her window like before."

He nodded mutely.

Fury grew deep inside her. "You are so grounded," she said, trying and failing to calm down and telling herself that as long as Harper was with Xander, she was safe.

But that wasn't true.

People were being murdered, people Rachel knew, people connected to her, a classmate having disappeared. Bruce Hollander, a known felon, was on the loose, probably had been stalking her, chasing her, probably had lurked in the shadows and watched the house only to spray that horrid message on her door. Didn't Harper understand how dangerous it was?

Nowhere was truly safe.

"Stay here!" she commanded her son, who looked like he wasn't about to go anywhere but back to sleep. "Hook up the system again, and make sure it's working and stay here!"

Back up the stairs she sprang, grabbed her phone from its charger. She tapped out a message to her daughter: Call me! Come home! Now!

After sending the text, she stopped at Dylan's room again. He was falling back to sleep. "Fix it!" she ordered before speeding to the kitchen, where she snagged her purse and keys. With

Reno barking in protest in the kitchen, she locked the door behind her, pulled on the running shoes she'd left on the porch, and was inside her Explorer in less than a minute.

This was crazy, she knew, trying to find her daughter, but Rachel was desperate, her heart racing, panic threatening.

At the stop sign, she checked her phone; although she hadn't heard the ping of an incoming text she prayed her daughter had gotten back to her.

Nope.

She called Cade on the fly, hitting the gas and searching the deserted city streets of Edgewater. The call went to voice mail and she left a quick message: "It's Rachel. Harper's snuck out again, with Xander. I'm trying to track them down. Call me."

A part of her brain told her that what she was doing was nuts, that she couldn't possibly locate them, that she should just go home and wait. But that would be impossible. She knew that she'd go out of her freakin' mind.

What if Harper didn't come back until morning? What if she didn't come back at all? What if Xander had talked her into moving to Eugene or they'd decided to just keep driving and leave everything and everyone else behind? Wouldn't she have done the same with Cade if he had suggested it when she was seventeen?

So trying to find them wasn't crazy; it wasn't paranoid.

Her heart ached, her stomach cramped, and her hands were sweaty on the wheel. She had to do something. Anything. Even if it was futile. The memory of her dream and the fears that were forever a part of her propelled her to keep going. Traffic was beyond light, only the occasional car or truck driving through the night-darkened town. She swung past St. Augustine's and Charles Ryder's offices, thinking they might have returned to familiar territory, but no vehicle was in the lot or parked on the nearby streets. Charles had kicked Xander out of the apartment and presumably taken his key back or changed the locks, and she hoped they wouldn't try to break in.

But the apartment windows were completely dark; the building looked deserted.

She drove on slowly along the empty streets, peering down alleys, scouring this little town for signs of Xander's Jeep. They wouldn't go far if he intended to get her home by morning, in time for school.

But there were the hills, she thought, glancing to the south, where above the old Victorian houses such as Lila's there were thick evergreen forests, county roads and lanes winding through the hills. Would they go that far? Or into Astoria? What about Lila's home? Would Lucas have sneaked them in?

She didn't think so. Not after the blowup where Charles had in essence fired and kicked him out. Rachel doubted the kid would risk it; despite his fascination with Harper, Xander Vale had seemed like a decent enough person, and too smart to make that kind of mistake.

Except he was a horny teenaged boy. They tended to not think with their brains. "Where are you?" she asked, cruising the streets and feeling more hopeless with each passing second but bolstering herself with the thought that her daughter was safe with the college boy. She rolled into the parking lot at Abe's, where three vehicles, an SUV and two sedans, were parked. Through the large windows she saw tables and booths sparsely occupied.

No Harper.

Of course.

Idling in the lot, she took the time to text Cade: Harper's still missing. She's not picking up. I'm worried. I've searched Edgewater, but didn't see them or his Jeep. I'm at Abe's now and I'll look some more. Call me.

She slid the phone back in her purse and looked up to see the headlights of a vehicle driving along the seldom-used lane to the cannery.

Odd.

Who would be going there in the middle of the night?

Two kids who wanted to be alone?

What better place to stop and make out?

The lane was private and that's what Harper and Xander would be looking for.

Headlights cut through the darkness, and then the vehicle suddenly stopped, probably by the old gate.

The headlamps died.

Rachel rammed the car into gear, then, fingers surrounding the steering wheel in a death grip, drove out of Abe's parking lot and headed straight for the old cannery lane.

"I just don't get it," Harper said, frowning and feeling as if she'd been duped. "Why didn't Xander come himself?" She'd risked life, limb, and, worse, her mother's wrath by sneaking out of the house through the window again to meet Xander after he'd texted, but when she'd reached his car, he wasn't inside. Instead she'd found Lucas behind the wheel of Xander's Jeep.

"He's getting the place ready."

"What place?" she asked and felt a little nervous. Why the hell was Lucas here? She and Xander were supposed to be alone. That was the whole point, wasn't it? And why was Lucas driving Xander's car and not his own?

"You'll see," Lucas said with a smile that bothered her; it was as if he knew more than she did or was holding something over on her. He put the Jeep into gear and pulled away from the curb, hitting the gas, making the tires chirp.

Suddenly this seemed like a bad idea.

Hadn't her mother said, "If you want it bad enough, you'll make it happen" when she was talking about her relationship with Xander? So when Xander had finally texted, she'd jumped at the chance to meet him like before.

And then Lucas had showed up.

She probably shouldn't have gotten into the Jeep with him, she thought as he sped through town.

It just felt off.

She decided to text Xander, so she pulled her phone from her pocket and typed a quick: Where are you? I'm with Lucas in your car. Is something up?

And then she saw it. Right on the console. Xander's phone, glowing with her latest text. What? He was *never* without his phone.

The bad feeling intensified. "What's going on?" she demanded.

In the glow of the dashboard lights a tiny smile played across his lips.

She stated the obvious. "Xander's phone is here."

"He must've left it." He just kept driving.

"He wouldn't."

He lifted a shoulder. "Oops."

" 'Oops'? What does that mean?" He acted as

if they were playing some kind of weird game. What a dick! Leaning against the passenger door, arms crossed over her chest, she glared at him. "Where is he?"

"Waiting," Lucas said, toying with her.

Her eyes narrowed and she felt all of her senses go on high alert. Something was wrong here. Very wrong. "I don't like this."

No response.

"Take me home."

"No can do."

"What? Lucas, I mean it," she said with more authority than she felt. "Take me home. Now!"

"And disappoint Xander?" He shook his head, blond hair shimmering oddly in the dash lights. "Don't think so."

She glanced through the windshield and saw that they'd left town and he'd slowed in the darkness, turning onto the long, pock-marked lane leading to the old fish-packing plant. It loomed in the distance, an aging behemoth settling onto old piers over the river. "Why are we here?" she asked, her anger dissolving into fear.

"Geez, Harper. What's with all the questions? We're here to meet Xander, just like I said." Hands on the wheel, he slanted her a quick smile. Meant to be disarming.

It wasn't. Something was up with Lucas. Something terrifying.

The Jeep bounced along the lane until they reached the chain-link fence sectioning off the riverfront part of the property. A sagging metal gate, rusting in places, was hanging open, the chain that usually secured it cut and dangling over a side post where a long-handled bolt cutter had been propped.

He'd broken in. To this evil place where his father had died, at the hands of her mother.

"I don't like this." Dread was pumping through her bloodstream. Somehow Harper had to tell her mom where she was. Or her dad; that made more sense. He'd know what to do. She swallowed hard and though she was so scared she was nearly shaking she felt for her phone, sneaked a peek, and hit her father's name on her contact list. The phone was still on silent mode so, hopefully, Lucas wouldn't know what she was doing.

"But you will. Like it. Even love it. I promise."

It was a lie. She knew it.

"You broke into the cannery?" she asked, giving away their location.

"I guess if you want to get technical. Well, yeah."

"I'm not going in there, if that's the idea," she said, and pointed at the cannery. What the hell was this? She had to escape. Get away from him. Avoid that damned packing plant like the plague. This was wrong. All wrong.

But Xander? Where was he? In that menacing

old building? Her stomach curdled at the thought.

"Where's your sense of adventure?" he was asking, cutting the engine.

"Where's your sanity?" she threw back at him, then thought to use his name. "Lucas, this is nuts!"

"Don't think so." All joviality was gone. Now he was dead serious and she fought a rising sense of panic. She had to get away. Run. *Think, Harper, think. He was a football star, remember? A runningback or something? He's faster than you even though you ran long distance in track. You have to be smarter than he is.*

"Okay, let's go." As the engine ticked and cooled, he pulled the key from the ignition, and when he opened the door and the interior light flashed on she saw him withdraw a gun from the pocket of his jacket.

Oh. God. No.

"You have a gun?" she said, hoping the phone was recording her dismay.

"Think of it as insurance."

"For what?"

Cold, numbing fear crawled through her.

"To make sure you do as I say." He glared at her across the front seat, his face in shadow. She thought, for a second, of another man, one she'd known all her life, one who had no connection to him. The image—of a picture of her grandfather at a younger age—dissipated. She licked her lips.

Lucas wasn't kidding. His face was set in stone, his eyes those of a killer.

In her mind's eye she saw the woman hanging from the bell ropes last night giving up her last dying breath, and in that split second she knew she had to get away. Now.

"Move it!" he ordered, wagging the pistol across the seats. "You're going with me into that fuckin' packing plant to meet with Xander and then you'll text your mother from your phone and she'll come to save you and I'll be waiting."

"For . . . ?" A new terror seized her.

He stared at her as if she were the dimmest person on the planet. "For revenge, Harper. Haven't you been reading the papers? Don't you know that she killed my father and never paid the price? That she got off scot-free after pulling the trigger? She killed him, Harper. Your mother's a goddamned murderer and the only reason she wasn't convicted—the only damned reason—was because she was the kid of a cop and her stupid, fucking friends lied for her, came forward and lied about what they saw and heard. So they had to pay, too."

Horrified, Harper shrank away from him. If only she had a weapon. Xander didn't own a gun but there had to be something in this Jeep. He had a toolbox and camping gear in the back cargo area, behind the back seat, but she couldn't reach either. "That's not how it was," she argued.

"That's exactly how it was!" Lucas shot back. "And she has to pay."

"Why now? After all these years?"

Think, Harper, think! She glanced at the console; knew a bottle opener was inside and maybe a pen. Not good enough.

"Because I didn't really know about it, did I? Everybody including my mom whitewashed it. When I asked, I was told some fantasy story about an 'accident' with 'stupid kids' and then she warned me not to play with guns, any kind of guns. But lately, I've been hearing differently, the real story," he said, the skin over his face tightening.

The umbrella! Xander had one tucked under the passenger seat. She remembered him using it recently. Swallowing back her fear, she shifted on the seat, stared hard at Lucas, holding his eyes while her right hand moved slowly to the floor.

Caught up in his anger, Lucas continued, "I know the truth. I've been listening in, with the equipment I bought from Dylan, hearing everything. My mother has been talking to all of the fucking people on that damned reunion committee and she wanted a special shrine to my father and so there was lots of chitchat about him and how he died and I heard her talking to her friend who owns the newspaper when she was interviewed and they went off script a little. They all knew it, Harper. They all knew your mother killed him and they covered for her." His lips twisted as if he'd tasted something foul just as her fingers brushed the folded nylon of the umbrella's canopy. "They have to pay!"

She stretched, her hand sliding downward until she felt the pole. *Oh, God, help me.* Somehow, someway, she had to get away. But she had to find Xander. God, what had Lucas done to him?

Lucas was on a roll, unleashing all his pent-up rage, pointing the damned gun at her face, talking as if he'd never stop, his voice rough with fury. "Ned Gaston made sure his precious little girl didn't go to jail." His lips curled in disgust. "And all her friends came forward, swore they weren't sure how he died, but she was the one who pulled the trigger."

Oh, God, this was so sick, so twisted, but she needed to keep him talking. She had to grab the umbrella without him noticing. "So why is Xander in the cannery? What did you do to him?" She was trying to sound tough when she was freaking out inside, sweating, her heart pounding, stalling for time, stretching her fingers.

You have to make a break for it, Harper; you know you do. He's going to hurt you or worse.

But Xander? Was he really here? Was he hurt? Alive? Oh, dear God . . . "I . . . I need to see Xander."

"You will! I already told you, he's inside." Angrily he motioned through the windshield toward the building. "Now, before we go meet him, just one more thing. I want to send one more text to your mommy."

"Mom?"

"Yeah. Your cute little murderess of a mommy. Now, smile and say 'cheese.'" Before she could react, he snapped a picture, the flash momentarily blinding her. "Perfect." He turned his attention to the screen and typed quickly, sending a short message.

Now! Get out now!

She snared the umbrella, yanked it from under the seat.

He caught the movement. Realized he'd been tricked and focused on her. "What the fuck?"

Now! She dropped her phone, and with all her strength, she used the umbrella like a spear, using both hands and thrusting hard, ramming the folded umbrella with its sharp tip straight into his neck!

"Aaarrggghh!" he screamed. Blood sprayed and he flailed, the pistol still in his hand. "You bitch! You fuckin' bitch!"

She pushed harder still as he squealed in agony, writhing, trying to jerk the weapon from his neck. "Fuck! Shit!" He swung wide with one arm, barely missing her as she took one hand off the shaft and unlatched her seat belt.

Before he could get his wits about him, she found the button on the shaft of the umbrella, poked it, and, spring-loaded, it expanded with a whoosh, the canopy snapping open, the pointed ferule still jabbed deep into his throat.

She couldn't see him, but the ribs of the umbrella caught in the overhead light.

He screamed in pain trying to point the gun around the canopy, while attempting to wrench it from his neck with his free hand. In his flailing he hit the horn. Inspired, Harper hit the emergency flashers, then unlatched the door and rolled outside, her feet hitting the rough pavement.

Her phone!

Oh, crap!

She thought about retrieving it but saw the muzzle of the gun and took off, sprinting down the uneven asphalt.

Behind her, Lucas howled and raged.

The Jeep's lights blinked. The open door alarm dinged.

Harper expected to hear a shot, to feel the sharp sting of a bullet in her back.

But until that happened, she ran.

Harper Ryder ran as she'd never run before.

CHAPTER 38

The street outside of the Wooden Nickel was chaos.

Patrons from the brewery were clustered in groups, talking and smoking, being interviewed by the cops who'd shown up after the shooting or reporters who had arrived at the scene that they'd cordoned off. Pictures and video had been taken and Kayleigh had watched, distraught, as Cade had been lifted into an ambulance before it had driven off, siren screaming, lights blazing.

God, she hoped he'd survive.

As he'd lain on the sidewalk, bleeding, losing consciousness, she'd nailed that bastard Hollander, watching the gun spring from his hand as he fell, two cops from the Seaside PD all over him.

Kayleigh had run to Cade, talked to him, tried to keep him conscious, fearing his wound would be mortal.

"Stay with me!" she'd ordered. "Ryder? Cade? Do you hear me? Damn it, you stay with me! Don't you dare leave me!"

But he'd drifted away from her despite her best efforts before she could tell him that she loved him, that she'd always loved him, that he just couldn't die on her.

Before the EMTs had taken him away, she'd heard his phone bleat and she'd picked it up, reading Rachel's desperate text, then listening to the voice mail message. It didn't make sense. They'd caught the killer. Hollander was clinging to life, or had been when he'd been hauled away, under guard and by ambulance, to the hospital.

So why was Rachel panicked?

Because her daughter had snuck out to be with her boyfriend?

Yeah, that wasn't good, but not exactly abnormal. Teens did it all the time. And Rachel was a bit on the hysterical side, a woman whose fears drove her.

Still . . .

She went into the voice mail, caught the one from Rachel asking Cade to call, and then she listened to a long one . . . another message, a longer one, and her heart turned to ice. It ran for several minutes and recorded a horrifying confrontation between Harper and Lucas Ryder. Fear galvanizing her, Kayleigh started running to her car.

She didn't hesitate for a second even though she was certain her actions tonight, the shooting of Hollander, would be under review. She could be on leave. Even though when she'd blasted Hollander, the shooting had been caught on police cameras, her actions would be studied and she'd have at the minimum a few days off so that the department could verify her actions were called for.

But right now . . . while the Seaside PD was wrapping this up, she could get away. She had her own vehicle. And she needed to get to that cannery and fast.

She found Biggs standing near one of the police cruisers. "I have to leave. Now."

"Whoa. Wait."

"No time to explain. I can't deal with any red tape or even questions. Cover for me," she said under her breath.

"For what?"

"Everything."

"Uh-oh. What're you planning, O'Meara?"

"Just cover me. I'll call." She was already jogging to her car. She turned, looked over her shoulder, and added, "Oh, yeah, you'd better find a way home."

Atop his bed, Dylan stared at the screen of his laptop and frowned. Absently, as he watched his monitor, he chewed on a tough piece of jerky and ignored Reno prancing beside the bed, whining for a bite.

What the hell was his mother doing?

After cruising through the streets of Edgewater she seemed to be stalled on the west end of town. Near Harper, but not in the same spot.

He was tracking them both, as he had for the

past six months, just to keep tabs. He'd felt it was some supremely cool irony that instead of his mother tracking his phone, he was keeping hers in his sights. Just the opposite of so many kids he knew whose parents were monitoring their whereabouts.

This spy shit was amazing!

But now he was worried.

His mom was on the move again, heading toward Harper, who was at the old fish-packing plant on the edge of town. What the hell was she doing there? Yeah, he'd helped her again by shutting down the old alarm system so she could sneak out and hook up with Xander, but he didn't think they would go to the building that caused their mother a major freak-out.

What was that all about?

Nothing good.

Right?

His mom was on the move again, heading to the packing plant.

Weird, weird, weird.

Something wasn't right.

In fact, it was very bad.

He reached for the last piece of jerky from what was ridiculously labeled a "jumbo pack," then, seeing the dog out of the corner of his eye, bit off a piece and threw the rest to Reno, who caught it on the fly and swallowed it whole.

Lacing his hands behind his head, Dylan

watched the screen. He could tell that his mom had turned into the lane leading to the cannery, so she should run into Harper. Right? Harper wasn't moving . . . or at least her phone wasn't.

She wouldn't leave her cell though.

It was, like, glued to her.

But . . .

He bit his lip and pulled up his GPS for an aerial terrain view, but could see nothing more. "Come on, Harper," he said, squinting and beginning to worry, "what're you doing?"

Rachel's heart clutched as she drove down the bumpy, pock-riddled asphalt of the cannery's lane. In her headlights she saw the weed-choked ruts and her heart beat a painful drum the closer she got to the old building. Her skin crawled and she couldn't help but remember the last time she'd been here, twenty years earlier, and the tragedy that had ensued.

She crossed the bridge and her headlights caught the reflection of taillights. Xander's Jeep. Parked at the gate, which was ajar, the chain holding it closed snipped by bolt cutters that had been left in a tuft of grass.

Oh. Dear. God.

She pulled up behind the Jeep, which was all buttoned up. No one inside. The night was close, the smell of the river teasing her nostrils, a sense of foreboding in the air.

She speed dialed Cade.

And he picked up.

Thank God.

"This is Detective O'Meara," Kayleigh answered.

Rachel's heart sank. They were together? Cade and Kayleigh? She was answering his phone? In an instant Rachel imagined the two of them in bed, laughing and kissing, touching and . . . no, no, no. They were working together. That was all. And she didn't have time for anything but finding her daughter. Again she glanced at the sinister complex supported by rotting piers.

"I want to speak to Cade."

"He's . . . not available."

"And you have his phone?"

What the hell was going on?

"For the time being, yes. I know that Harper's missing and I think I might know where she is."

"She's at the damned cannery. That's what I'm trying to tell Cade. I want someone out here ASAP."

"It's more than that. She's with Lucas Ryder and I think he's the killer." Kayleigh sounded breathless, worried. And Rachel heard the sound of air rushing past, as if Kayleigh was in a car, driving. Where the hell was Cade?

"Lucas? No. She's here with Xander. His car is parked at the gate and they've broken in."

"No, you've got it wrong. I've heard Harper's

voice mail to Cade. She recorded a conversation between her and Lucas Ryder."

"Why the hell are you reading my husband's— my *ex*-husband's—texts and listening to his voice mail? Wait. Never mind. I don't care and I don't have time to talk about it. I'm going to find my daughter."

"Rachel, wait for me, or for someone from the department to get there. He's . . . he's armed. Dangerous. Unhinged. Wait for me. I'm on my way. I've called for backup, so just wait. Don't go into the cannery. I've got a deputy who will be there in three maybe four minutes and another one on the way."

"My daughter's in there. Cade's daughter. There's no waiting."

Rachel clicked off, then saw the text that had come in while she was on the phone.

From the same anonymous number that had texted before. But this time the message was different and as she read it, Rachel's heart turned to stone:

I lied. I don't forgive you. And by the way, bitch, I've got your daughter.

Along with the chilling message was a picture of a very frightened Harper.

Her knees threatened to buckle. She stared at the picture a second, then gathered her strength. As she did she spied what looked like blood. Dark splotches staining the grass and gravel, catching what little light there was, leading inward to the cannery.

To hell with Kayleigh.

To hell with Cade.

She picked up the bolt cutters.

She was going in.

CHAPTER 39

"Damn it all to hell!" Kayleigh muttered, hitting her emergency lights and driving like a bat out of hell, heading north on 101. On the way to Edgewater, she called for the deputies to converge on the old cannery.

They'd been wrong.

All wrong!

The thinking had been that Bruce Hollander, currently clinging to life at Seaside Mercy Hospital, was the killer. Not only had he stalked Rachel and tagged her house, but he'd also killed Violet Sperry and Annessa Cooper as some kind of revenge for helping Rachel avoid being convicted of Luke Hollander's murder. But there had been holes in that theory from the get-go. Kayleigh had checked. Though Hollander hadn't established an alibi for the night when he was supposed to have killed Annessa Cooper, on the night of Violet Sperry's death, he'd been at home.

But they'd been wrong. She'd heard enough of the recording on Cade's phone to know that Hollander, now near death, hadn't killed anyone . . . except possibly Nathan Moretti, as he was still missing.

"Son of a bitch," she said to the night at large.

She chewed on her lower lip.

Hollander had been armed, but his pistol had been a different caliber from the one stolen from the Sperry house.

Now, she presumed, Violet Sperry's pistol was in the deadly hands of Lucas Ryder. How had they missed the signals? Lucas had never once come up on her radar as a possible suspect.

She had to slow as she cut through Astoria, merging onto Highway 30 winding along the river's edge. There was little traffic on this stretch, and the few vehicles she came upon quickly moved aside so that she could blow past.

A deputy called, confirming that he was at the cannery and two cars were parked by the gate that had been opened.

No sign of Rachel Ryder.

Apparently she'd overcome her fears and her paranoia, when it came to saving her child.

She slid her phone into a pocket. Then, tightening her grip on the bolt cutters, the image of Harper's frightened face seared into her brain, Rachel fought her rising panic. She couldn't go there. Not now. There was time for breaking down later if she had to, but for now, she had to get past a fear that, in the past, had been paralyzing, a fear that had toyed with the edges of her sanity.

Move, Rachel. Find Harper. You can do this. She needs you!

A quarter moon had risen, stars flickering in the

night sky, the single security lamp offering weak light. The river, ever moving, stretched dark and wide with only a few lights visible on the other side of the expanse on the southern shore of Washington State.

The land around the old building was as uneven as or worse than it had been twenty years before, and the huge barn door that she'd slipped through on that fateful night was slightly agape, a sliver of an opening visible.

And the blood was visible: dark splotches on the ground.

You can do this.

She inched her way through the opening and immediately the smell of the moldering cannery hit her, that brackish scent that hinted at dead sea life, and took her back to a time when pellet guns popped, kids laughed and screamed, and death was just around the next corner.

A million memories flooded through her brain. Lila, Violet, Nate, Reva, and Luke, the ringleader, her half brother, the heartthrob to all her friends other than Mercy. It was a lifetime ago. But it felt like yesterday.

And now Harper was here.

Somewhere.

Forced to this menacing edifice by Lucas.

She hurried across the ancient floorboards, hoping that her eyes would adjust to the darkness, that she wouldn't be forced to use the light from her phone and become a visible target. She reached the midsection of the building, where some of the windows were unbroken, thin light filtering through the grimy glass. She stopped, straining to listen, squinting into the darkness.

Her throat was tight, and her hands were clammy over the handles of the bolt cutters.

Deep in the shadows, something moved, scratched across the planks, little claws scraping as a rat scurried past. She clamped her jaw tight so as not to scream. Of course there were rats and God only knew what else hiding in the corners or lurking on the crossbeams.

She swallowed back her fear.

Far in the distance—too far—she heard the faint, but shrill sound of sirens.

Hurry. Please hurry.

She took one step forward, then froze when a deep, raspy voice rumbled through the vast, nearly empty building.

"Well, look who's here," Lucas said, his voice almost a croak. "Mommy did come after all."

How could this demon, this murderer be her nephew? Luke's son? The boy she had watched grow from a baby in diapers to a tall, strapping man. Now, a monster.

"Where's Harper?"

"You tell me."

Oh, God, it was a game? "Look. I just came for my kid."

"Right on cue."

She heard a movement behind her and the hairs on the back of her arms raised. She spun, staring into the stygian umbra.

Nothing.

"This isn't funny."

"No one's laughing, Auntie."

He sounded almost disembodied, without any human emotion. Her stomach curdled. "Where's Harper?" she said again. "And Xander?" As she asked, she moved, inching sideways, coming to the ladder to the upper level, the one she'd cowered behind years ago.

No response.

She thought she heard footsteps, light and fast, and she had to swallow back her fear.

"Lucas? What's going on?" She had to keep him talking so that she could find out where he was hiding, where he was keeping Harper.

"Oh, come on, Auntie, you're smarter than this. You know what you did. You killed my father, your own brother, right here, in this very building. Right? This is the spot, Auntie, where you literally got away with murder."

"You're right. I did. But Harper had nothing to do with it."

The blood. Whose blood had she seen by the gate and leading into the cannery?

"Collateral damage."

Her heart squeezed painfully.

"Like those other two bitches who thought they would get you off. Your friends."

Oh. God. He was crowing about killing Violet and Annessa.

Where was he? Above, up the ladder, or farther back, past the chute where the fish guts had been flushed so many years ago? She closed her eyes, listening hard, her fingers clenched over the bolt cutters.

"And what about his best friend?" Lucas demanded.

She was sweating, trying to think, remembering the layout of this building all those years ago. Was he in deeper at the far end of the cannery where boats had tied up to unload their catches, where the water was the deepest?

Listen hard, Rachel. Try to pinpoint his voice.

"You know who I mean. Nate Moretti. What about that dick? Why didn't he step up and save him if they were so tight? What kind of a friend doesn't step in to save him?"

That didn't make any sense. How could Nate, could anyone, have saved Luke?

But Lucas wasn't done. "And your father. What about him, the cop who let his darling daughter get away with murder?"

Her father? Had Lucas done something to Ned? Rachel's insides turned to water but she believed it of Lucas now.

"Bunch of pansy-assed losers!" he shouted.

Her throat closed and she had to force the words out. "But not," she said, whispering before she took in a deep breath. "But not Harper. She had nothing to do with this. She wasn't even born."

"Neither was I!" he yelled, his calm veneer cracking, and she turned her head, knew where he was hiding, there by the chute.

The sirens outside were getting louder and red and blue lights strobed through the windows. "You called the cops? Jesus, are you fuckin' dumb? We'll all be killed!"

"Not if you let her go."

"Fuck!" She saw him then, in a shooter's stance, facing her. She flattened, hitting the floor just as he fired, the blast of the gun thunderous, the muzzle visible as voices shouted from outside.

"Police! Lucas Ryder, drop your weapon!"

For a second she didn't move, and then she heard a strangled cry, a tortured sound, and she couldn't wait. Nephew or not, she wouldn't let him hurt her daughter. Slithering forward like a snake, she eased toward him.

"Auntie," he called as the sound of boots echoed through the building. The old barn door creaked open.

Rachel kept moving, easing forward, dragging the bolt cutters, feeling the grit of dirt and oil and grime of dozens of years against her skin and clothing, the smell of grease and mildew and rot heavy in her nostrils.

Again the soft, agonized groan and she thought of the blood, imagined her daughter bleeding out somewhere in this malevolent structure. She heard the sound of the river flowing below her, through the opening; smelled the wet, brackish odor as she inched by the chute.

She was close now.

"Lucas Ryder!" a woman's voice yelled. *Kayleigh.* "Police! Drop your weapon! Come out with your hands over your head!"

"Fuck you!" Lucas yelled, turning his back to Rachel. In the darkness he seemed to drag a body in front of him, using it as a human shield. An anguished groan came from the body.

Harper! Oh, God, no!

She could be killed in any gunfire.

Rachel had to stop this. Do anything. She reached into her back pocket, withdrew her phone, and out of desperation hurled it at him. It hit with a soft thud against his shoulder and he jumped back, startled, and for a second stared at the phone glowing in front of him.

"What the—"

Rachel launched herself, sprang from all fours, aiming the blade of the bolt cutters at his back, to that spot between his shoulder blades. She hit hard, driving deep. With a roar he dropped the body in front of him and tried to turn. She used

577

her weight to jam the handles together, praying that she could snap enough muscle, tissue, and bone to incapacitate him, to make him lose his grip on the gun, to take him down! The short jaw-like blades snapped together, crunching bone, tearing through muscle as he screamed in agony.

This is Lucas. He's your nephew!

Still she squeezed, hanging on to the handles as he tried to shake her off. His screams ripped through the building and he staggered, firing wildly. Her hands, oily with sweat and slick with blood, slid on the grips.

"Don't shoot!" Rachel cried, bracing herself against an onslaught of bullets from the police. "Don't shoot!"

With a final thrust of his body, he wrenched the cutters from her grip and she fell backward, tripping and falling, slipping on the blood that seemed to be everywhere. She went down hard and found the floor uneven and sloped. Feet first she slithered down the hole and into the chute leading to the river below.

No, no, no! Scrambling, she caught one hand on the metal edge where the chute had been attached to the floor, but her weight dragged her down, the skin on her palm and fingers ripping as she slid down the chute and dropped into the icy river below. She nearly gasped but managed to hold her breath, dark waters of the river enveloping her. She tried to touch bottom, but the Columbia was too deep.

Swim.

Fighting the current, she pushed herself upward, her hand throbbing as it brushed against something soft and slimy. She recoiled just as a light from above, a bright beam from a high-powered flashlight, was shined through the hole in the cannery floor to illuminate the murky water of the river. She kicked again and her foot hit that same soft object. Turning, able to see through the air bubbles escaping from her lungs, she found herself staring into the bloated, tattered face of a man. His eyes were gone, gaping holes left, his mouth open, but even with the distortion and disfigurement she recognized Nate Moretti.

Oh, God. Her stomach started to wretch and she had to fight to keep her mouth closed. The corpse, tangled in vegetation and old fishing line, bobbed in the water, one hand slapping against her.

She swam away, wanting to scream, the world spinning. All the horror in her life converged in her brain as she felt the air leave her lungs.

Harper, she thought wildly, trying to concentrate. She'd left her daughter with that monster. Her heart cracked as she let out her final breath and thought, *Oh, baby, I've failed you.*

Using her flashlight, Kayleigh took one look at Lucas Ryder, Cade's nephew, a damned bolt cutter lodged in his back, his throat showing a gaping hole where blood still ran from being attacked by God knew what. He was still alive, but just barely.

She recognized the second man as Xander Vale, the person he'd used as a human shield. Vale, too, was in rough shape, suffering from a wound in his leg, possibly a gunshot. How the hell had that happened?

"Where's Rachel Ryder?" she asked just as a deputy yelled, "She went through the floor! Holy crap, did you see that?"

Kayleigh strode to the opening in the floorboards and spied a metal slide of sorts.

"Down there?"

"Yeah."

"Crap."

She pointed to the two injured men. "Take care of them. Get ambulances out here and keep each suspect under guard. Call for River Rescue. I want a boat out here ASAP. Then, for God's sake, back me up and keep that light shining down there!" Then, cursing the fates, she lowered herself into the rusting slide, let go, and slid down the damned chute after Cade Ryder's wife.

If she was lucky, she could save Rachel.

If not, they both could drown.

She dropped into the Columbia, felt its frigid pull as the current drew her westward, toward the Pacific.

She blinked, tried to see through the darkness. God damn, where the hell were Rachel and the light? Come on, where was the light? She broke the surface. "I can't see a damned thing down here!" she yelled, then took a deep breath and dove deep. A light from above illuminated the water and she nearly screamed as she spied the body of a man, floating near the bottom, his foot tethered to some rocks, the flesh of his face in tatters.

Sick!

Her skin crawled and she swam backward, then saw a woman, caught in the current.

Not on my watch!

Kayleigh kicked hard, knifing through the water, moving to the shadowy depths where the light didn't reach. She reached Rachel, whose face was milk white, her hair billowing around her in a cloud, air bubbles dancing up from her lips. *Come on,* Kayleigh thought, reaching around her and wrapping her arms under Rachel's. Freezing, her lungs tight, the pull of the current dragging, Kayleigh kicked hard, dragging Rachel upward, spying the surface where she saw light.

Come on, Rachel. Fight, damn you. You've got so much to live for. Your daughter. Your son. And Cade.

Rachel kicked, her efforts weak, and Kayleigh cursed her as she struggled, her lungs burning, her legs cramping.

Kick, kick, kick!

Up they swam, the light brighter, Kayleigh's lungs on fire.

They broke the surface and Kayleigh gasped, holding Rachel's head above the inky depths, treading water. They were downstream from the old cannery, where lights from police and emergency vehicles lit up the ghastly old complex in flashes of red and blue.

Rachel coughed and sputtered but stayed afloat, her teeth chattering as badly as Kayleigh's, but to her relief Kayleigh spied a boat approaching, its searchlight sweeping the black surface of the water, turning the dark night into day.

The crew shouted and pulled up alongside, throwing life rings before pulling them aboard. Not the rescue boat but someone out at night, a cabin cruiser that, in Kayleigh's estimation, was a yacht, with its dry towels and hot cups of coffee. Rachel looked like death warmed over, her lips blue, but, Kayleigh guessed, she would make it. They motored back to the cannery, where Rachel, like Lucas Ryder and Xander Vale before her, was driven away in an ambulance.

Shivering and half drowned, she'd refused care at first and begged Kayleigh to find her daughter and insisted on calling her son. "I will, but first I need to tell you about Cade," Kayleigh had said. If possible, Rachel had blanched whiter still until she heard from Detective Voss, at the cannery, that Cade's wounds weren't life threatening. His nose was broken, two ribs were cracked, and the muscles in his shoulders were ripped to shreds, but he would live. Then Kayleigh had given her Cade's phone and she'd connected with Dylan only to discover that Harper was home and safe, that, Rachel had reported to Kayleigh after hanging up, she'd escaped Lucas by attacking him with an umbrella.

"An umbrella and bolt cutters," Kayleigh had said aloud, thinking about it. "Beating out a pistol. Who would've thought?"

At that point Rachel, finally realizing that her kids and ex were safe, had nearly collapsed in relief. She'd agreed to go to the hospital to be checked over and have her torn hand tended to, but she'd been insistent that she be released immediately.

"I don't think you have to worry about that," Kayleigh had said as Rachel was helped into the ambulance. "These days a total knee replacement is day surgery."

With that she had stepped away from the rescue vehicle and watched as it rolled down the cannery's lane to the highway. Then, she'd decided to drive back to Seaside. When Cade was clearheaded enough, she wanted to fill him in.

And then, she swore, she'd forget she'd ever been in love with him.

CHAPTER 40

Cade opened a bleary eye. He was medicated, still groggy from the surgery. But hours had passed and it was late morning in the hospital, where he could hear soft voices and the pad of soft-soled shoes as people passed in the hallway.

A lot had happened since he'd been admitted.

Kayleigh, all business, had been by earlier and spied the splint on his nose and what was the beginning of what would be nasty black eyes from his broken nose. He didn't feel too bad, compliments of the hospital's pain medication, though his ribs would take a while to heal. Despite the pain, he remembered most of what she'd said, starting with, "Boy, you look like hell."

He'd laughed, his ribs reminding him that that was a bad idea, and he'd thanked her, hearing from Voss that Kayleigh had dived into the river and saved his ex-wife from drowning. She'd told him about Lucas and he'd felt numb inside, having known the kid since the day he'd been born. Never had he once considered his kids' cousin capable of such hatred and vengeance and violence.

He still had trouble believing it. But there had been more. Much more.

Sitting on the one chair in the room, looking like she could sleep for a week, Kayleigh had told him everything that had gone down: Bruce Hollander was still alive, in this very hospital in ICU under guard as he clung to life. In his few lucid moments he'd admitted to terrorizing Rachel for all the reasons they'd expected, but said that Lucas had been the killer who had taken the lives of Violet Sperry, Annessa Cooper, and, as it turned out, Nate Moretti. Xander Vale, whom Lucas had wounded, was in a hospital in Astoria and expected to make a full recovery, the bullet having barely missed his femoral artery, though shattering his left femur.

It seemed fair that Lucas, for all the pain and anguish he'd caused, would suffer at the hands of both Harper and Rachel, who had attacked him with an umbrella and bolt cutters, of all things. He'd smiled upon learning about it and then had heard later that Lucas hadn't survived, that he'd been DOA at a hospital in Astoria.

Kayleigh had played down her part in rescuing his ex-wife but had explained that they'd located Nate Moretti's vehicle behind one of the outbuildings at the cannery, and Nate himself, dead and rotting, had been pulled from the Columbia, a bullet lodged in his heart—or what was left of it. Cade had been spared that grisly detail.

Another shocker and hard to grasp was

that early this morning Ned Gaston's closest neighbor, a single woman by the name of Kathy Ortega, had heard a cat crying at his place. Upon inspection, she'd found his back door open and discovered his body, dead by an apparent gunshot wound to the head; possible suicide, though she'd reported seeing a Jeep pull up to Gaston's house earlier that evening, a Jeep that looked a lot like the one registered to Xander Vale, right down to the Oregon Duck license plate frame holding the plate to the Jeep's bumper.

Cade wasn't completely buying the suicide angle. Ned Gaston, despite his involvement in concealing what had really happened twenty years ago, despite his guilt, had been a fighter. The way Cade saw it, Ned, too, could very well be a victim of Lucas's wrath. Or had he realized that the truth was about to come out? That Cade had been digging into Luke's death?

Luke Hollander.

It was all about him.

Who knew the kid would go so far off the rails?

He started to slip back into slumber when the door to his room swept open. Rachel, a little worse for wear, poked her head through the doorway, deep circles showing beneath her eyes, her skin a little paler than he remembered, her expression one of concern.

She'd never looked more beautiful.

His stupid heart soared.

"Hey," she said. "You awake?"

"Does it look like it?"

She eyed his face. "What it looks like is bad."

"And here I was thinking you looked gorgeous."

"Sorry, can't say the same about you." She smiled then, some of her color returning. "But I'm glad you're still with us." She stepped into the room and his two kids joined her, Dylan in camo shorts and a T-shirt for some band he'd never heard of, and Harper, appearing sober, looking so much like her mother at that age it was scary.

The important thing was, they were safe. They were all safe.

"So . . . how are you feeling?"

"Like I've been run over by a Mack truck, and then they give me something and it's tolerable. But I'm afraid my dreams of becoming an NFL quarterback are over."

"Tom Brady will be so relieved," she said and Dylan laughed while Harper rolled her eyes. Again, like Rachel.

She smiled, that little grin that always touched his heart, and showed off her bandaged hand. "Didn't escape unscathed."

"You okay?"

"Yeah, it's nothing." But there was an unspoken message in her eyes and he knew she was thinking of those she'd lost.

"So." He looked at his two kids. "You two— stop giving your mother any trouble, okay? You're both going back to school tomorrow."

"We know," Harper said.

"And, Dylan, no more selling any spy stuff— yeah, I heard about that. Get a regular job if you want. And you, Harper, I expect you to do what Mom says, if you ever want to get a car."

Harper glanced down at the floor before meeting her father's eyes. "What about Xander?"

Rachel opened her mouth, but Cade said, "I heard about him, too. He gave a statement. He explained what happened, that Lucas, using Violet Sperry's gun, forced him to give him the keys to his Jeep and his cell phone. After he did, Lucas shot him, point blank, to make sure he wouldn't give him any trouble. I figure the only reason he kept Xander alive was as bait, for you, Harper, just as you were bait for your mother."

"I hate him," Dylan said, his face pulled into an expression of disgust. "I know it's bad to say with him dead and all, but I hate him."

"Me too," Harper said. "He was awful."

Rachel opened her mouth to protest, then shut it.

Cade, hating how the conversation had turned, said, "Hey, come on, you two, give your old man a hug." They came close to the bed and he held them for a second before the pain was too much.

"You look weird," Harper said.

"Super weird," her brother agreed, "but kinda cool, too."

"Nah." Harper shook her head. "Not cool at all."

"Speaking of 'not cool,' " Rachel said. "I got a call from Mrs. Walsh at the school today."

Dylan groaned and Harper's eyes rounded.

Rachel continued, her gaze focused on their son. "There seems to be some suspicion that you might have hacked into the school's grading system."

Dylan turned as white as the sheet on Cade's hospital bed.

"She's being lenient, I think, because of everything that's happened to us," Rachel said, "but when you go back to school she wants to talk to you."

"Oh, man," Dylan said and sent a beseeching glance at his father.

"Uh-uh. You know how I feel—'you do the crime, you do the time.' "

Dylan looked like he might be sick. Cade added, "Serious stuff, son," then shifted on the bed, his ribs and nose beginning to ache as the pain meds were wearing off.

"I told him he would be in trouble," Harper said.

"Oh, like you're so innocent."

They started bickering and he expected there was more to the story, but obviously Rachel was on it and would bring him up to speed. Right now, he didn't much care, was just grateful that they were safe, that the terror was over. "Now, give me a second with Mom, okay?"

They slid out of the room and he motioned Rachel near. She stepped closer, placing her hands on the bed rails. "I don't know if you know about Ned," he said.

"I heard. Kathy, his neighbor, called." Her eyes grew moist and she had to look away for a second.

"You okay?"

She let out a disbelieving huff as she looked at him again. "No."

"I'm sorry."

"Me too. But Lucas did it," she said, swallowing with difficulty. "You know that, right? Dad wouldn't have killed himself."

He wasn't completely certain of that but didn't let on. "We'll sort it out."

She blinked, fighting tears. "He wasn't happy. Ever since losing his job and breaking up with Mom, he was kind of lost, so maybe now . . ." Her voice cracked and she quickly brushed her tears aside.

Cade considered, then thought that she was strong enough for the truth, that she had the right to know. "There's something you should know, Rachel," he said so solemnly her head snapped up.

"What?"

"It's about your dad and Luke. They had a weird relationship and there's a chance that the gun recovered at the scene and the bullet lodged in your father was fired from the same gun as the bullet that killed your brother. Ballistics will prove it one way or the other."

"What're you saying?" she whispered and he watched her think back to that fateful night in the cannery.

"Lucas had to get the gun somewhere. And . . . hell, it's most likely . . . I mean, it looks like it might have been Ned's. Unregistered."

Rachel was shaking her head. "No."

"If it is the same gun, I think it's possible that Ned actually pulled the trigger that killed Luke. In all the ensuing years the murder weapon was never located, never turned up."

"That doesn't mean Dad had it. . . ."

"The officer who found your dad after he was called to the house? He saw a gun case left near your father's toolbox. Ned's initials were on it. That's why the first thought was suicide."

"But . . ." She paled, her forehead furrowing as she tried to grasp what had happened. "No," she whispered. "No, I don't believe it."

"Fine, but I wanted you to know," he said, and despite her denials, he noticed the doubts beginning to form in her eyes. He hated to put her through this but believed the truth was always best. No matter how much it hurt. Carefully gauging her, he said, "Also, I talked to Nate Moretti's father before all of this"—he motioned to his injuries—"before all this went down and he told me that Ned had convinced him to lie, that Luke hadn't come in DOA as we thought."

"What do you mean?"

"They let him die, Rachel. They thought he was too far gone, or at least that's the rationale. Your father said that it would be best for Melinda, that Luke could have never woken up from a coma or worse."

"So they didn't give him a chance?" she whispered, obviously stunned. She blinked back tears. "I don't think . . . I mean . . ." Words failed her. "Why?"

"When I get up and on my feet again, we'll figure it out." He felt his eyes narrow as he thought. "Someone who was there might know more."

"And you intend to dredge it up again."

"I don't have the corner on that. Mercedes—"

"Yeah, I know. Between her and half a dozen other reporters, this story will never die."

"Wouldn't you rather I looked into it?"

She paused and thought, then shrugged. "Yeah."

"I will ferret out the truth."

She held his gaze and he saw in her eyes that she'd come to terms with what he was saying; her denial was seeping away. "You think my father would really let me carry around all the guilt I've been dealing with?"

"I know it." His respect for Ned had plummeted in the last few days.

She swallowed, glanced away from him for a second, and he heard a cart rattle past in the hallway outside his door, felt the pain in his ribs begin to throb.

"I thought you should know."

She nodded. "Thank you." Then she cleared her throat, and when she caught his eye again, she looked stronger than she had in a long, long while. "Well, you just get better, Detective, okay?" she said, then after a moment's hesitation added, "And when you're released from here, you come back and live with us."

He raised an eyebrow.

"Do it. For a while."

"You're sure?"

"Positive. At least temporarily. It would be good for the kids. Something's going on with Dylan and he could use you around more. Yeah, Ryder, you do it. Come stay with us."

One side of his mouth lifted. She never failed to surprise him. "So now you're bossing me around?"

"Have I ever stopped?" she asked, and, leaning forward, brushed her lips over his, a soft little kiss that promised nothing, but hinted at so much more and made him, for the moment, forget about his pain.

Kayleigh drove home, cut the engine of her car, and rotated her neck. She was so damned tired. She swore she'd sleep for the next week solid.

And maybe the week after that.

Once all of the reports were filed and in, other officer interviews completed, body cams and audio tapes reviewed, she had no doubt that she would be cleared of the shooting of Bruce Hollander. By all accounts he would survive but had bought himself a one-way ticket back to prison. And she'd had a bit of good news. Akira Wu had called and the feline hair found on the painter's tape had been white. They were now matching it to Lucas Ryder's cat and it had just turned out that Lila Ryder had recently painted the interior of her home in colors that depicted the era of her historic home. Several rolls of blue painter's tape had been discovered in the Ryders' garage, a separate one discovered in Lucas's car. Even more damning was the pistol recovered in the cannery, the one Lucas had used to shoot his "friend" Xander Vale. It had turned out to be registered to Leonard Sperry. The enhanced footage of the tape taken from the camera located in the parking lot of The Right Spot wasn't completely clear, but the man with Nate Moretti that night, the guy in the hoody and cap who drove Moretti away from the tavern's lot, sure looked like Lucas. Kayleigh was willing to bet her badge that Lucas had befriended Nate at the bar, then followed him to meet Annessa. Once there, he got the jump on Nate, then took care of Annessa and prodded a stunned Nate back to the vehicle. But she wasn't certain they would ever know, as both Moretti and Ryder were now dead.

Yeah, the case had finally come together. And it was over. Like so many things.

She got out of her Honda, stretched, and listened to her back pop. Squinting against the sunlight of the late May afternoon, she decided she should take some serious time off. Get away from Oregon. Away from the past. At least for a while. Maybe she should go to Southern California, or Bermuda or Costa Rica . . . better yet, Australia. She smiled around a yawn. Yeah, that sounded good.

If she could afford it.

She walked into her apartment and dropped her keys onto a side table. Her stomach rumbled. It had been hours since she'd eaten but she knew her refrigerator was bare. Thankfully the local pizza place delivered. She was about to give the place a call when her cell rang.

Travis McVey's number flashed onto the screen.

She thought for a minute about answering,

let the call go to voice mail, then listened to his message: "Okay, let's get it out there. You're obviously avoiding me. A lesser man would take it that you didn't want to see him again, but I'm thinking you do; you're just afraid to admit it or of where it might lead. So, Kayleigh, I double-dog dare you to call me. Are you woman enough to take the challenge? Let me know."

She clicked off.

Erased the message and stood in the middle of her little apartment with its secondhand-store furniture and crappy view.

What the hell was she waiting for?

It was long over with Cade Ryder.

He was in love with his ex-wife and always had been. From where she stood, they were bound to get back together.

She wondered about McVey. She liked him a lot. And yet, he could piss her off like no other.

Was that a good sign? Probably not. She flipped the phone over and over in her hands as she thought, her tiny apartment bare and lifeless. She remembered the last time they'd seen each other, how easily she'd tumbled into bed with him, how good he'd made her feel.

She stopped flipping the phone and stared at the keyboard.

She considered his message. How he'd challenged her. She liked that. She liked that a lot.

So, maybe she would take him up on his dare and call him.

Then again, maybe she wouldn't.

Patient, near tears: "This is all so horrible! Horrible!"

Therapist: "Just take a deep breath. Now, go to your safe place. It's calm there."

Patient: "Yes, yes, the beach, the waterfall, the warm breeze, but . . . ."

Therapist: "Lose yourself in the beauty. In the serenity."

Patient: "But I can't feel it. It's not there."

Therapist: "Breathe in and out. Let yourself go. Feel the warm sand beneath your bare feet; listen to the birds singing in the trees."

Patient: "Yes. It's warm. It's safe. It's calm. Serene. There are fish in the water and it gets darker, deeper. I can't see the bottom."

Therapist, slightly relieved: "Just relax. Now, touch a toe into the water. . . . See the ripples?"

Patient: "Yes."

Therapist: "Soothing ripples."

Patient, suddenly frantic: "No . . . the water isn't clear. It's dark. I can't see. Oh, God, he's there in the water. And not just Ned. Rachel, too. And that other woman, the cop. They're all in the pool, no, the river. It's cold and freezing and my son . . . I've lost my son!"

Therapist, concerned: "Let's try again. You're in your safe place."

Patient: "No! It's not there. They are in the water and they know. They all know I lied. It's my fault."

Therapist, losing patience: "I think it's time to surface."

Patient: "I can't!"

Therapist, insistent: "Three. You're coming around."

Patient: "No! I should never have lied. Don't you see?"

Therapist: "Two, and you're waking . . . coming away from the water and the sand."

Patient, sobbing: "I should never have lied. I should have told the truth. Now he'll never know who his father really was and all those people who died. My friends . . ."

Therapist, agitated, but trying to keep calm: "One. And you're back."

Lila opened her eyes, felt the tears on her cheeks, remembered that both Ned and Lucas were dead. Father and son. Neither really knowing about the other. Oh, Ned had guessed and he, upon learning of her involvement with Luke, had been mad with jealousy. Hadn't she hoped he'd be? And the night that she'd gone to the cannery, to see Luke, to tell him she was pregnant, hadn't she known that Ned would be there, that there would be hell to pay?

But she hadn't expected Ned to bring a gun or to shoot his own stepson. The lie had been so easy, that she'd gotten pregnant by Luke, that he'd never gotten the chance to know his son and to let Rachel believe she'd killed her own brother. Lila had never let it slip that Lucas was really Ned's son. But Ned had suspected the truth and though he'd claimed to be looking for his own children to keep them out of trouble, he'd come to the fish plant with a gun and shot his own stepson. Or so Lila believed. She'd even accused Ned of the crime. That's when Lila and Rachel's father had really broken up. They'd fought before, of course, often, and passionately, but after the night in the cannery, it was really over.

Their affair had started innocently enough. Well, no, not really. She'd always had a thing for older guys and while Luke was still involved with Reva, and Lila had set her sights on Rachel's brother, she'd spent a lot of time with her best friend and she'd kept running into Ned. God, he'd been handsome then. Smart. Funny. And interested. He would take Rachel and Lila places, or pick them up, and Lila had turned on the charm. She'd known he was interested, had seen him checking out her butt, or her breasts or her legs, when he'd thought she wasn't looking. She loved the attention and had always been a bit of a tease, so she'd worked it. When staying over at night with her "best friend" Rachel she'd make sure she'd be only half dressed when Ned was around and loved the thrill of it as his gaze had slid over her.

He was a much older man but buff and, really, just into his forties. He'd also been a cop. And married. Making him forbidden fruit. Lila had always been a risk taker, and back then, Ned Gaston was good-looking, brooding, and sexy.

She remembered initiating the first kiss after he caught her in a bra and panties running from the bathroom to Rachel's room. In truth, she'd waited until she heard him come into the house from work in the middle of the night, while everyone else was asleep. As he'd stepped into the hallway, she'd opened the bathroom door, scampered out, and run into him. She'd gasped and pretended to be all virginal and embarrassed. But when he hadn't moved, blocking her path to Rachel's room, she'd kissed him, standing on her tiptoes, the tips of her breasts brushing his chest through the lacy bra.

That was all it had taken.

He'd grabbed her, eased her back into the

bathroom, never once breaking the kiss, then locked the door behind them and hadn't asked any questions as he'd spun her around, stripped off her panties, and entered her hard. Rough. And oh so good.

From that moment on, they'd been hot for each other, screwing whenever they could, rutting like horny animals. She loved his mature body and the fact that he knew how to make love. At that point in time he'd been able to turn her inside out. Sometimes, she remembered, he'd even toy with her with the barrel of his gun, running it over her naked body, thrilling and teasing her before he'd drop the pistol and pull her roughly atop him.

And wouldn't you know? Suddenly Luke had started getting interested in her and eventually had broken off his relationship with Reva. It was almost as if he'd smelled the sex. At first, she'd used Luke as an excuse to hang out, but Ned had gotten jealous and Luke had sensed something was up, despite the fact that she'd started sleeping with both of them.

Oh, wow, had that been a rush! The fact that Reva had been pissed as hell had only heightened the excitement.

The fly in the ointment had been Rachel's mother. Melinda had never been all that crazy about Lila being Rachel's friend in the first place, and then Melinda had started to get suspicious. Melinda claimed to Rachel that she didn't like

Lila "chasing" Luke. But that was just the tip of the iceberg as she was beginning to get the idea that her husband might be infatuated with a girl barely eighteen. It hadn't really mattered, Lila had told herself, because that marriage had already been foundering. Not really her fault. Lila had just pushed it a little faster to its inevitable conclusion. Along the way Ned had gotten jealous and weird and possessive and pissed as hell that she was still seeing Luke.

And then the night at the cannery. He'd come looking for Rachel that night—or had it been Luke, or even Lila? She'd never know now. But that night Lila had already decided it was time to end it. Despite the baby. She'd been determined to tell Luke she was pregnant and pass the baby off as his even though, in doing the math, she was pretty sure the child was Ned's.

Of course, that night everything had blown up.

And Ned had become less attractive to her.

In fact, after the death of Luke, she hadn't known what she'd seen in Ned other than the dangerous sex play and the fact that he was older and more worldly. She hadn't wanted to think that just maybe she'd come on to his father to gain Luke's attention. But after Luke's death, her interest in Ned had gone stone cold and Lila had ditched him even though she knew deep in her heart she had been the final nail in the coffin in the Gastons' marriage. And she hadn't cared.

Instead, she'd looked around for another man to care for her and her son and spied Charles Ryder, attorney at law. Poor, grieving Charles, who didn't know what hit him when she first showed empathy, then interest, and finally enticed sexual awakening to a broken man who'd thought his life was over with the passing of his wife.

But he'd been so, so wrong.

And, not only had Lila not had to deal with an ex-wife, because he was a grieving widower, but also there was that very interesting fact that he was wealthy as well, at least by Edgewater standards.

Even though he had three nearly grown sons, he'd not only married Lila but taken Lucas on as his own boy.

And now, despite the horror of Lucas's involvement in the murders, Lila and Charles were still married. He hadn't wavered in his commitment to her, nor had she to him.

They would be together until the day he died.

She'd make certain of it.

And, for her part, she'd take her secrets to the grave. At that thought she crossed her fingers, because Edgewater was a small town, people gossiped, and she already knew that Cade, her own detective of a stepson, was looking into the past. And then there was DNA these days. Lucas's DNA would link him to Ned Gaston if the cops ever dug that deep. And then her lies would be exposed.

That would be a problem.

Already the gossip was sizzling through the town.

Hopefully it would die down.

She blinked, realizing she'd been daydreaming in the hypnotist's serene little office. She found him watching her and wondered what he'd seen, what he'd gleaned, even what she'd said when she was under. It might be an issue as she suspected the thin, somber man, with his pencil nose and thin, hip glasses, of being a bit of a charlatan. There was just something to suggest that a few drops of snake oil might run through his blood.

"Are you all right?" he asked with that worried little smile she found irritating.

"Never better," she lied, picking up her purse and leaving the check as always on the small table near the smoldering incense. Lemongrass, she thought idly as she walked out the door and slid on a pair of sunglasses to protect her eyes and hide the fact that she'd been crying. She saw a news van driving down the street, maybe looking for her, the mother of the killer. When once she would have welcomed the attention, had even gladly interviewed with that nosy gossip Mercedes, now she'd rather hide, couldn't manage the false front she'd cultivated for years.

Inside, she was broken.

Lucas had been her life.

And he'd died, pronounced DOA at the hospital.

Just like Luke, the man he'd thought was his father.

Lila's whole world, once filled with color, now seemed black and white and the town was changing again, Clint Cooper pulling out of all his real estate deals, wanting nothing to do with Edgewater, a reminder of his wife. So all the plans for that ugly old cannery would be scrapped and it would sit, hulking and rotting on the shores of the Columbia, filled with new horrors, new secrets, the gossip around it forever swirling.

She sighed and looked through her shaded lenses at the town where she'd grown up, where she'd resided all her life.

It really was true what they said, she thought, as she slid behind the wheel of her new Mercedes: *What goes around comes around.*

Just ask Rachel.

Now, for the first time, she really was a killer.

Lila's heart turned to ice as she reached for an emergency cigarette.

The bitch had better watch her back.

AUTHOR' NOTE

I wrote *Paranoid* about the same time my sister, Nancy Bush, wrote *Bad Things*, her latest thriller. We were discussing the fact that the books were scheduled to be published around the same time and thought it would be a unique idea to change the structure of each novel to include scenes with a therapist. So we did it! And we loved it! I hope you see why. So, check out *Bad Things* by Nancy Bush for a book that will keep you up way too late at night!

Center Point Large Print
600 Brooks Road / PO Box 1
Thorndike, ME 04986-0001 USA

(207) 568-3717

US & Canada:
1 800 929-9108
www.centerpointlargeprint.com